Lovers

OTHER BOOKS BY NORMA KLEIN

Love and Other Euphemisms *(stories)* · Give Me One Good Reason
Coming to Life · Girls Turn Wives
It's Okay if You Don't Love Me · Love Is One of the Choices
Sunshine · Domestic Arrangements · Wives and Other Women
Beginners' Love · Sextet in A Minor *(stories)* · The Swap

BOOKS FOR YOUNG READERS

Mom, the Wolf Man and Me · Confessions of an Only Child
It's Not What You Expect · Taking Sides · What It's All About
Hiding · Tomboy · A Honey of a Chimp · Breaking Up
Robbie and the Leap Year Blues · The Queen of the What Ifs
Bizou · Angel Face · Snapshots

PICTURE BOOKS

Girls Can Be Anything · Dinosaur's Housewarming Party
Blue Trees, Red Sky · Naomi in the Middle · Visiting Pamela
A Train for Jane · If I Had My Way

NORMA KLEIN

Lovers

VIKING

VIKING
Viking Penguin Inc., 40 West 23rd Street,
New York, New York 10010, U.S.A.
Penguin Books Ltd, Harmondsworth,
Middlesex, England
Penguin Books Australia Ltd, Ringwood,
Victoria, Australia
Penguin Books Canada Limited, 2801 John Street,
Markham, Ontario, Canada L3R 1B4
Penguin Books (N.Z.) Ltd, 182–190 Wairau Road,
Auckland 10, New Zealand

First published in 1984 by Viking Penguin Inc.
Published simultaneously in Canada

LIBRARY OF CONGRESS CATALOGING IN PUBLICATION DATA
Klein, Norma, 1938–
Lovers.
I. Title.
PS3561.L35L6   1984   813'.54   83-40651
ISBN 0-670-44319-0

Grateful acknowledgment is made to Chappell/Intersong Music
Group–U.S.A. for permission to reprint lyrics from "If This Isn't
Love," by E. Y. Harburg and Burton Lane. Copyright © 1946
by Players Music Corp. Copyright renewed, assigned to
Chappel & Co., Inc. International copyright secured. All rights
reserved.

Printed in the United States of America
by R.R. Donnelley & Sons Company,
Harrisonburg, Virginia
Set in Caledonia

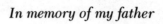

In memory of my father

PART ONE

♦

1966

Moses Supposes

"Call me the minute you get there, okay?"

I wish so much Marilyn hadn't broken that damn Polaroid I got her for her birthday! If she hadn't, I'd take a picture of her the way she looks right now, saying that. She's just wearing her bathrobe, a pink, lightweight thing—the breeze is blowing it to one side, showing her legs; she's barefoot. She has a sensational figure, but that's not what I'd want to catch in the picture—not her blond hair loose down her back (it's not real, comes from a bottle, Spring Honey, number twenty-seven, she's dyed it since she was sixteen). It's her expression. That anxious, concerned, abandoned-wifeish expression, like she won't rest for a *second*, not have *one* peaceful moment till my plane lands in Boston and she knows for sure she's not a widow. Christ.

All she means by "Call me the minute you get there" is: so I can relax and plan an overnight or whatever with what's-his-name. You'll forgive me for not having his name on the tip of my tongue. It's a name like a dog in a comedy series on TV or the movies. Benjy, that's it. Benjamin, probably, but his wife and everyone around here call him Benjy. Actually, Marilyn "wears" that expression often. It's a real part of her personality, that uncertain, timorous, little-girl look. Oh sure, she knows it works with men. What woman doesn't learn what works by the time she's six? But it's also genuine. She really does have some sense that we stout-hearted men are marching out daily into the strange, mysterious, complex world, doing battle with it, while she and her female friends stay at home with the kids, babbling, watching TV, shopping, whatever they do once we vanish down the driveway in our Fords, Chevies, Plymouths. We have two kids, by the way: Aaron's eight, Linus is seven. A mixture of problems and pleasure. I won't go into that now.

I'm lucky in a way. I don't have high blood pressure and no one in my family has ever had an ulcer. My father died last year, at the age of sixty-five, hit by a school bus, but he probably would have lived forever otherwise. Listen, my *grandparents* are still alive, *both* of them, almost ninety, but still "active." So I can handle this physiologically. In fact, I can handle it every way. But it's thrown me, I have to admit that. It was three months ago, June, that what's-his-name's wife gave that idiotic fucking surprise birthday party for him. Surprise parties are dumb enough—I'd kill anyone who gave one for me—but, to top it off, one of life's little coincidences, it was Marilyn's birthday too. She and Benjy have the same birthday! Cute, huh? They were both thirty on June seventh. So right away they had something in common. Maybe that started it off. I don't know. Frankly, I didn't notice anything at the time. Marilyn talked with him a little while he was burning the steaks, but, hell, that could have happened at any suburban party around here. Marilyn likes to flirt and I always thought—still do, in principle—why not? I mean, she married me when she was twenty, she never had any serious boyfriends, she's sexy. Why shouldn't she flirt? Flirting's free, it's an outlet. Especially if she does it when I'm right there. It's like saying: I'm having fun, but that's all, just a little smiling and eye contact, nothing to get hot and bothered about.

I wish you could see this guy. Okay, so probably no husband can comprehend the appeal of a guy his wife prefers to him, but I don't think I have any especially inflated view of myself, of my looks. Though in point of fact—I'm not pleading my case, I just want to be accurate—I'm good-looking for a guy of forty. This Benjy Fetterman—that's his full name—looks like a kid! Yet at the same time his hair's almost white! At *thirty!* Okay, not white, but he's grayer at thirty than my father was at sixty. He has all his hair, but it's a lot more gray than black or whatever it was to begin with. We've only had the pleasure of his and his wife's acquaintance since last year.

They have two kids, girls, who're in school with Aaron and Linus. But it's not just the hair. He's short, five nine at most, probably more like five eight (I'm six two). He looks—I don't know how to describe it—kind of dazed. Like, when I smelled the steaks burning, I didn't think about it—I don't mind them burned—but he looks like the type to burn steaks, to forget things. In fact, I remember his wife saying something to him when he finally staggered up with the platter of meat, like "Benjy, didn't you remember to raise the grill?" She sounded exasperated, as wives usually do at moments like that. He just stood there, almost with his mouth hanging open, like some guy in a comic strip. "Oh yeah, right, I forgot." Oh look, I've forgotten things too, millions of things, but it's the way he *looked:* abashed, cringing, pussy-whipped. He looked like a schnook, like a nonentity! Maybe women like that. I don't know. Tell me. What *do* they like? I wish I knew.

I'm trying to look at it from Marilyn's point of view. Not to be "sympathetic," just to understand. Things happen for a reason, right? So, first, like I said, she was pretty young when we married, no sexual experience till I came charging up and wouldn't take no for an answer. You could—I tried!—attribute Marilyn's "succumbing" to my ineffable charm or technique. Face it, I was ten years older than her, I'd seen a fair bit of action. I must have made it with thirty, forty women, maybe more. I was fooling around. I gave myself till I was thirty to get it out of my system, and I did, more or less. No one really gets it out of his system. How can you, unless you're dead? But I played the field. Some of them were serious, some of them wanted to marry me, some were just fooling around like I was. What made it easy was I reached my present height when I was sixteen. So lots of ladies took me for older than I was and I played into it. Never lied, but let them think whatever they wanted that would make them happy. Plus I was an amateur actor. Nothing major, but I did a lot of summer stock in college and for a couple of years afterward. Actresses are easy to convince about sex. They're like guys, if they're serious about their acting. They don't want to be "tied down." So I didn't, with most of them, have to try all that hard. I told a lie or two, sure, exaggerated, I had my stock of mournful expressions when rejected, all that shit. But I was basically a good guy. My conscience is clear. One girl—I met her eight years later, she was married with kids—actually thanked me! Said if it hadn't been for me she wouldn't have been able to clarify what she was looking for in a man, I "helped" her. I guess you could take that both ways, but she certainly looked grateful, beaming. Introduced me to her husband, in fact.

When I met Marilyn, she was in college. I can't say it was love at first sight, that I took one look and went *boing!* this is the kid I want to marry. Let's just put it that I was ready by then, and we got along, and she didn't pressure me, which is the one thing that might've made me turn tail and run. Because *she* wasn't ready to settle down. She was living in a dorm—she was at NYU—and she was ready for four years of college, dating, being independent. I think she saw me as kind of threatening, settled down compared to her college friends anyway, earning a good living, my own apartment. It was tantalizing, no doubt, but for a while I think she wasn't interested in getting serious. I was just "a date." I took her places, good restaurants, dancing, orchestra seats at the theater. What could she lose? I'm not even sure why she finally broke down and had sex with me that first time. For four months we kind of horsed around, but she was pretty strict or anyway, pretty typical for a girl of the fifties. Touch here, not there. Don't want to get carried away. The usual. Nothing I hadn't heard many times before. It wasn't, as I recall, "I'll only do it if you marry me." More "I only want to do it with someone I'm sure I really love." A variation on a theme. So why *did* she do it? Curiosity? Lust? I doubt it.

You know what I think it was? It was because she cut her hair. You'd have to see Marilyn's hair. It's gorgeous. I don't care if it comes from a bottle. Lots of women pour stuff on their heads from bottles. But this is a light, soft blond color (she claims the real color is sandy brown) and, when I first met her, it came down to her waist. She used to wear it piled up in a big upsweep, but when she wore it loose, pinned back on the sides, it was beautiful. She could sit on it! Said she hadn't cut it since eighth grade. So one night I'm about to pick her up to take her to a play, and she opens the door and there she stands with her hair shorn up to her ears! You remember that kind of gamin short hairdo they wore then with bangs? Audrey Hepburn? That was it. She looked cute, it wasn't that she'd wrecked her appearance, but I was horrified. I just stood there. I didn't even walk in the door. I couldn't *say* anything I was so shocked. "Don't you like it?" she said, looking hurt. I tried to say, sure, I love it, but I guess my voice and expression gave me away. "It's just—you had such beautiful hair," I said. "I know!" she said, and burst into tears.

Then I felt like a jerk. I mean, it's hair, it'll grow. So I took her in my arms and kissed her and said she looked adorable with it short. "Just as adorable as before?" she wanted to know. "Sure," I lied. Though it wasn't *totally* a lie. She looked more adorable, but less beautiful, if you get what I mean. So we went out to the play and then went back to my apartment. I figured it would be an evening like many others, necking, a little struggling, then I'd take her home. I went into the kitchen to get some brandy, and when I came back, there was Marilyn, sitting on the couch, naked as a jaybird! I'd like to have a photo of that moment too. I do have one, in my mind, but I'd like to have a real one. It was her expression, sitting there, that beautiful body, girlishly pointed breasts, soft nipples, and that pleased, slightly nervous look, like: aren't I pretty? aren't you lucky? aren't I going to make you happy? I was so stunned, so startled—no one had ever done that before. I mean, I'd had one-night stands, but no girl of Marilyn's type had ever just, without a word, stripped naked and said, in effect: here I am, fuck me, do whatever you want with me. I finally came to my senses, set down the brandy glasses, and went over to the couch. I put my hand on her hair. Her skin looked so luminous, so soft I was almost scared to touch it. "I'm really sorry about cutting my hair," she whispered.

So that was it! She had to make it up to me for cutting her hair! And it was great, the way it usually isn't the first time, especially when the girl's a virgin. I know they all differ a lot, but Marilyn just seemed to take to it. I don't think she came, not while we were fucking, but she didn't yell and scream or start shrieking, "Stop!" right in the middle. Some guys may find that a turn-on, but I never have. I mean, if someone actually yells "Stop!" like they mean it, I stop.

After that, we got engaged. Not that very night, but within the next month or so. I figured: why look further? Here's a girl who's gorgeous, who's fun to fuck, who seems to like kids, who's malleable up to a point, but with a certain amount of character, charm, fire. I'm an impatient person. I couldn't marry a lump, a housewife type. I don't want a career woman, someone who's never there, but I wanted someone who'd keep my interest. Not a dummy. Marilyn isn't a dummy, even if she did drop out of college and never go back. And she's a pretty good mother, too. A little scattered, but nothing serious. No drowning the baby in the bathtub.

So I figure maybe this thing with Fetterman is a phase. In fact, obviously it's a phase, and you know what I think the main problem is? The problem *and* the solution? The problem is that since the kids are in school all day—this year—she's got too much time on her hands! She doesn't have hobbies, she's not really athletic. She hasn't made a whole lot of friends since we moved here four years ago. So what's she going to do all day? Call her friend, Jeanette, long distance in San Diego? Visit her parents in Sloatsburg? See, I have this theory. It's that women ought to work, they ought to be drafted even, they ought to do *everything* we have to do. Why? So they'll know what it's like! So they won't sit at home envying us for going off to this exciting wonderful world which is really, for most of us, a lot of pure shit. Marilyn's *got* to go back to college and get a job. The kids'll be fine. I don't want her hovering over them. My mother, who made nine million mistakes raising me and my sister, didn't hover. Oh, maybe she was around a lot when we were really little. But by the time I was ten, maybe younger, she was helping my father out in the business. They set off together every morning of his life and came home together. Not that I'd want that as a husband. It would drive me bonkers in one second. But what I mean is, my mother wasn't sitting on her duff playing Mah-Jongg or bridge or getting sloshed by four in the afternoon.

I think that's it. I think that's the solution, and when I get home, I'm going to lay it on the line. Not that I found out about the two of them. Just that it's time she got a job. There's this woman in my office. She's my age, Josie, in her forties, just turned forty, whatever. Anyway, we were once chewing the fat about another woman who works in the branch office in Washington. She's Josie's age, married, three kids, and she's making it with the manager of the branch office in Boston. "Where does she get the *time?*" Josie wanted to know. "I wish she'd tell me. Not just the time, but the energy!" That's the point. Once Marilyn's working, she won't have time, energy, *or* interest. Now it probably gives her a high point to her week or month or however often they do it.

I have to make a small confession. Like I say, basically, I'm a good guy and I think that's proven by the fact that I have no intention of showing my hand on this. But it's also a fact that in the ten years we've been married, I haven't been exactly . . . Well, there haven't been that many. Just occasional overnight things. There's a woman I see in Boston sometimes when I go there. The point is, these are harmless minor things. Marilyn may suspect about some of them. I made one foolish mistake about two years ago. There was this very sexy lady who lived next door. She was a swimmer. She taught swimming at the local high school. A little muscular but in great shape. Divorced. She just moved into the house next door, by herself, which is unusual for where we live. Usually when women get divorced, they move out. But this woman, Liana, had money and two kids so she bought the house next to us. She used to work out all the time, jogging, exercises. I'd see her on the lawn, knee-bends, push-ups. She was always lathered in a fine sweat, glowing. She must have been nearer my age than Marilyn's, but maybe from all that exercise, her body was young. She was very casual, used to drop over to borrow things, a lawn mower—she did all that herself since she wasn't married. One day Marilyn mentioned that she and I sometimes jogged in the morning. "Listen, why don't you drop over when you're done?" Liana said, smiling. "I can give you mouth-to-mouth resuscitation." Marilyn was horrified at her even saying that, but I kept wondering what she'd meant. I've always had a fantasy of making it with Marilyn and another woman. I've done it with two women, but both of them were women I didn't know. Anyway—I *realize* this was dumb, don't tell me—after Liana went home, I said something like, "Maybe we ought to take her up on it."

Whew! Marilyn started screaming her head off, said that was the sickest thing she'd ever heard of, she would no more do a thing like that than set herself on fire, that I had a diseased mind even to *contemplate* such a thing. "You can do what you want when I'm not around, but don't expect me to get involved!" she yelled. I think those were her words. Anyway, it was the first time she'd indicated she knew I did *anything* when she wasn't around. At the time I was almost relieved. I thought she was saying: I understand you may have needs that exclude me and I accept that as long as I don't have to hear about it or take part in it. *Was* that what she was saying?

Our sex life is okay. I hear enough to know what's bad, and ours is good. It's pretty frequent, I've always gotten the feeling she was enjoying it. Sometimes—more in the beginning, the first couple of years, than now—if I wanted to do it more than once a day or night she'd sigh and say, "Not again?" but in a playful, almost pleased way, like she took it as a tribute to how sexy she was. Never: I have a headache. I mean, look, she has moods. She's locked me out of the bedroom, she's had fits about this and that. In the bad ones she always takes off her wedding ring and plunks it down on the night table. It's like a gesture in a movie. Plunk! Nose in the air, disdainful. Then a day or two later I notice she's wearing it again. Once she actually flew out and spent a week with Jeanette in San Diego. But came back fine. Marilyn has a temper, but it blows over. She's emotional, but not crazy. The point I'm trying to make is, I don't think she has anything to complain about in the sex department. Of course, *she* may not realize that. She's never been married to anyone but me. But that's the fact. If she were out in the world more, she'd hear enough hair-raising stories to make her delighted to be married to me.

Listen, she *is* delighted! I don't mean that ironically. I mean that on our tenth wedding anniversary last year we left the kids with a baby-sitter and went on a two-day trip to Las Vegas—I like to gamble just a little, not a problem, just for fun—and we had the best time, in and out of bed, we've had in years. I always stay at The Riviera. It's gaudy, but everything there is, and they usually have a pretty good floor show. Marilyn squints at the topless dancers and looks over at me to see how I'm reacting. She says it's disgusting and they must all lead empty, hideous lives, but for whatever reason she always seems turned on afterward. The only thing that ever bothers me is driving outside the Strip—the Southern-style poverty you see, the shanty-type homes. It's probably no more of a contrast than going from one part of Manhattan to another, but it seems more shocking because I always forget that part of it.

We were getting ready to go out for dinner, she was wearing a red dress I bought her a couple of years ago which still fits her perfectly, and she said, "You know, we're really lucky! I mean, like, we still like each other, we have fun together . . . Don't you think we are?" "Sure, I do," I said. I went over and put my arm around her and we just stood there a couple of minutes. It was one of those good moments, the kind you remember at odd moments during the day when all the everyday shit of coping with things threatens to do you in. If I was a movie director, I would have said "Cut" right there.

Actually, that whole weekend was pretty good, too. I love taking Marilyn with me when I go gambling. She's so nervous, it's really a turn-on. The fact is, I almost always win. I have a system that isn't infallible—what is?—but which works most of the time. Marilyn can't believe that. "If there's a system, why doesn't everyone use it? Why doesn't *everyone* win?" That's a rhetorical question, by the way, coming from Marilyn. I've tried answering it maybe a hundred times, but she never listens. So when she gets all dressed up, looking gorgeous—I can see guys eyeing her—and sits next to me, watching anxiously, practically trembling with fear that I'm going to do something insane and wipe out all our savings, I get a kick out of it. It's interesting, though. When I really get into gambling, I get half hooked, hooked enough to see how guys go over the edge. You should see the expressions on some of their faces; it's scary. That whole self-destructive thing, the greed. Sometimes I feel it deep down inside me, but I'd never let it devour me like that. Then you're lost. I won a couple of hundred and took Marilyn back to the hotel and fucked her a few times: that's enough. She was still confused about how I won, still a little scared—look how close we were to danger!—but kind of admiring in a way I don't see every day. "I guess you really do know what you're doing, huh? I really shouldn't worry?" "Depend on me, kid."

Listen, I never really introduced myself. My name's Moses Greene, Mo, for short. I run my parents' business, Find-a-Job, a career counseling service. I go to Boston pretty often, once every two weeks or so on the average. That's where I grew up, where my mother still lives, my sister and her husband. It's where my parents started the business. Really, my father started it with two of his five brothers. One of them, Jake, switched to the food catering business in thirty-five and Willie moved to Switzerland in the thirties to work for IBM, so from the time I was a kid my father had the whole thing on his shoulders. Luckily for him, it was kind of a fail-safe business. There weren't too many career counseling firms then—they got in early—and even though my father had no head for business, it survived, even prospered in a low-key kind of way.

How can I describe my father? It's not that I'm overwhelmed with nostalgia or reverence now that he's no longer around. I didn't hate him, but we were never all that close. Maybe fathers and sons never are. Mine are still too young to tell how it's going to turn out. He wasn't exactly a dynamic, hardheaded business man, but he wasn't a schlemiel either. Maybe something in between. A dreamer, my mother used to call him, in a tone halfway between admiration and derision. I don't know. I don't buy that. In fact, he wasn't *enough* of a dreamer. He was a fairly conservative, literal-minded guy, scared of taking chances, terrified of change. My mother didn't know a thing about business, but after the two brothers pulled out, she supplied the moral support he needed to keep the thing going. What she did there every day, who knows. But without her, he would have been in big trouble. Till I came along.

Nobody wants to buy into their parents' business. Nobody with sense. *I* didn't. First of all, I didn't especially want to go into business. Like I said, I spent a couple of years pursuing the acting thing. I don't think I ever really fooled myself into thinking I could make it as an actor, but it was fun. I enjoyed the life, the people, I got a couple of small parts. But by the time I was twenty-five, it was clear I couldn't earn anything resembling a living out of it. Real actors don't care. Or they care, but they keep going on sheer love of what they're doing. I didn't have that kind of dedication, so I went back to business school. I never got a degree, but I took a bunch of courses that I thought would help, and I landed my first job through some contacts. It was one of those amazing things, that job. I'm convinced this can only happen when you're in your twenties. I walked into this place and they were on the verge of bankruptcy. That's why they hired me probably. They were like my father, but worse, two of them: Mort and Manny. Conservative, but crazy at the same time, or both alternately. So I walk in and in a year, in *less* than a year, I turned the place around. They were in the black, profits quadrupled, they made me vice-president! I was twenty-six! The fact is, I couldn't do it now. Now I'd realize the odds against anything working and I wouldn't want to take the chance. But then I had this brash, I-can-do-anything cockiness. Boy, I wish they could bottle that! I could use some now, actually.

So, there I was a vice-president, my own office, a secretary, moved into a bigger apartment. A very heady year. Except very soon after that it got dull. The business was dull. Once it was on its feet, that was it. And the guys, the twins (M and M, I used to call them) were still crazy. They listened to me, but they didn't understand *anything* I said! They knew they had to listen, but mentally they were still where they were before I came. I just couldn't take it. Like I said, I'm impatient. Either I catch onto things quickly or never; I can't stand working with dummies. And my father was sick by then. He developed tic douloureux, a horrendous illness. It's not psychological and not curable. Either you have an operation where they slash your nerves and your whole face just kind of hangs there or you have splitting, horrible pain that's only controlled by a heavy drug that really puts you under. Frankly, though I don't think his being hit by a bus was anything like suicide, I think he was totally numbed by that drug. He looked terrible, though he didn't talk about it much. "I just don't know how I'm going to cope," he kept mumbling over and over. So finally I got the message. Superboy to the rescue!

My parents were ecstatic when I told them I was quitting my job to help them run Find-a-Job. "He's a *vice*-president!" (emphasis on vice, who knows why), my mother told everyone, "and he's going to use his expertise, everything he's learned for *us!*" In fact, Find-a-Job wasn't doing badly. Basically, it was being run exactly the same way it had been thirty years ago when they started it. It wasn't a matter of performing miracles like with my first job, it was just modernizing the way they handled things, expanding once they got off the ground. They were lucky, like I said. *I* was lucky. It was a growth business, and the competition was scattered and weak. When I came in, they had just one office, the one in Boston where we lived. Now there's the one in New York, where I work, and eight others all over the country. My parents would never have done that. Can you believe this? My father, to the day he *died*, never saw any of the other offices. Not through fear of flying, I think just the *idea* made him too nervous. Expansion, success, made him nervous. Maybe it was based on some feeling that it had to fail, he'd have to "pay" in some way. He was more comfortable, if not with failure, then with moderate success, nothing flashy, nothing extreme. Not me. I like extremes. Under every category you can think of I'm a success. Money, career, marriage, family. I'm not kidding. I'm not saying that to be defensive or as a sick joke. What I like to do is figure out the problem and find a solution. I did that with Find-a-Job and I'll do it with Marilyn. Don't tell me women aren't the same as running a business. I *know* that. I'm not dumb, remember? Marilyn thinks because I'm earning a lot of money I must not be "sensitive." It's something she learned from her sister, Blanche, who's a psychiatric social worker. Look, don't get me started on my sister-in-law. Not after a day like today. There's one good thing about Blanche; she lives in Detroit. Her favorite pastime is "analyzing people's motivations." You'd think since she does that all day long, she'd take a break when she gets home. Nope, absolutely not. A person cannot walk into the *room* without her starting in. "Did you notice the way he . . . ?" If the waiter brings the wrong wine or comes back with the steak rare instead of medium, do you think you can just send the food back and enjoy it? Never! You've got to hear *why* he does that, what his parents were probably like. I know I'm obsessive on this topic and I don't even know why I'm going on about it, but my personal opinion is that all shrinks and lady shrinks are crazier than coots. I'll solve my own problems, thanks.

When I got off the plane, I passed a bunch of phones. I called home. My eight-year-old son Aaron answered.

"Is Mom there?"

"Uh uh." He's completely laconic on the phone.

"Do you know where she is?"

"Uh uh."

"Well, just tell her I'm in Boston, that my plane arrived safely, okay?"

"Okay."

He'd make a good undercover agent, Aaron.

Maybe she was too eager even to wait for my call. Shit.

My mother still lives in the same house in Newton Highlands where I grew up. It's a big two-story turn-of-the-century house, nothing fancy, a small yard. My parents could have earned three million dollars a year and they still would never have moved, never would have bought new furniture. No, wait—let's be precise—I think five years ago they got a new couch. They discussed it for about a decade and naturally they didn't throw the old one out—it's in the basement. I'll just give you one example since this kind of thing can get tedious. Everyone's parents are crazy. Why give examples? But the last time I visited, my mother, at sixty-one, was down on her hands and knees repainting the flowers on the linoleum! That linoleum was put in fifty *years* ago at least! The business is highly successful. The *best* linoleum might cost four hundred dollars— that's an upper estimate. So my mother, who has a bad back, is down on her knees with a little tube of green poster paint and a number four sable brush painting in the leaves. I never knew they *were* leaves! "I think it's almost as good as new!" she said when she was done. "What'd you think, Mo? Tell me honestly."

From a mixture of socialist convictions and her self-styled image as "not just a housewife," my mother never paid a lot of attention to housekeeping. She grew up poor and maybe because of that, the upstairs of the house, where all our bedrooms were, was barely heated in winter. Downstairs was the living room, dining room, and kitchen, with some of the hallways blocked off by heavy old rugs hanging from the ceiling. She had the idea this would make the house warmer! I remember huddling downstairs as long as possible every night till I was ordered up to bed, then making a headlong dash for my room. Even now I think of the house as being essentially those three downstairs rooms with their shabby, serviceable furniture. Since little has changed or been replaced in the last thirty years, it's like a literal return to childhood to come home for a visit.

My mother looks good for sixty-one. She's petite—five feet tall and weighs one hundred and ten pounds. She's made of stainless steel—you could run a train over her and she'd get up unharmed—but my father had this idea that she was extremely delicate, "a little slip of a thing" as he always put it. He was always bundling her up in blankets, buying her heavy sweaters. "Joe, what's wrong with you?" my mother would say. "I'm like an ox! I'm strong. You can be little and strong." Well, it was his illusion, and evidently he's not the only one. According to her, two men have proposed to her since he died, both widowers, one a guy who lives around the corner, another she picked up at the movies. My mother's very friendly with strangers. She'll talk to anyone, any color, any age. Once she was so busy talking after a movie, she walked right into the men's room. My sister was with her at the time. Evidently all the men started yelling, but my mother stayed calm. "Boys, take it easy," she said airily. "You've got nothing to show me I haven't already seen." My sister, who's very shy, almost died of mortification, but my mother thought it was hilarious. She loves to tell that story.

My sister was already there when I arrived, but without her husband. "He had to work late," she explained to me. She kissed me and then put her head to one side. "You look tired . . . doesn't he, Mom?"

My mother gave me a hasty glance. "A little maybe. . . . Want a drink? We're having mai tais."

I never drink mai tais except when I'm visiting my mother. They're vilely sweet and I don't especially like rum. But what the hell. I smiled at my sister "Everything okay?"

She made a face. "I want to talk to you later," she said in a low voice. My mother was in the kitchen. "Okay? If you're not too tired?"

My sister is very sensitive to my moods. She always was. Usually I like it, but at times, like now, when there's something I don't want to discuss, it can be unnerving. She's four years older than me, Harriet, married twenty years to a kind of dull guy, a professor of anthropology at Tufts. Three kids, two in high school, the youngest around ten. She's a teacher, a drama teacher at a private school in the city. I love my sister. She's the kind of woman—I hate admitting this, even *thinking* it—that I'd never look at twice if I wasn't related to her. It's not just her looks. She looks like me, actually. She's tall—five nine—with a long face, a big nose, not great skin which she covers with makeup, brown hair to her shoulders. It's not so much that she's bad-looking. She's not a knockout, but she's not ugly. She's just a nice, solid, sincere, *worried* person. Always was. Since she was ten. My mother never worried much about the things mothers are supposed to worry about—whether I ate enough, whether I wore the right clothes to school. "I'm a blithe spirit," she'd say. So my sister had a built-in role: family worrier. She worried about my father, about the business, but especially about me. All through my adolescence, for instance, she gave me "tips" on how to get girls. She worried that I liked the "wrong" girls, worried that I'd never get married, worried that Marilyn wasn't the right person for me, that our kids would have problems. I feel like if I come to Boston without something for Harriet to worry about, it's like coming without a gift. Only this particular worry I'm going to spare her—and myself.

My mother appeared with the mai tais. "I was about to play Harriet your tape," she said. She kissed me again. "What a present! I couldn't believe it. I opened it—out pops this little thing. I thought: what *is* this? Music? What? So I put it on, and I'm telling you, Mo, for half the tape, I didn't know it was you. I thought it was Gielgud! Bertha called and I said to her on the phone, 'Mo sent me a tape of Gielgud reading Shakespeare's sonnets for my birthday,' and she said, 'I'm coming right over.' She's a Shakespeare freak, like me. She runs over, I start the tape again, and she says, '*That's* not Gielgud. That's Mo!'" My mother turned to my sister with delight. "'It *sounds* just like Gielgud,' Bertha said, 'but it's not.'"

This is embarrassing. But you have to understand, my mother is a very hard person to get presents for. You cannot get her anything that costs over twenty dollars or she'll return it to the store. She likes handmade things. Which is fine when you're five or ten, but when you're forty? So here's what I did. She loves Shakespeare's sonnets. More than the plays even. So I recorded all her favorite ones plus one of the big soliloquies from *Hamlet* and mailed it to her last week when she had her sixty-second birthday.

I was Hamlet once in Maine. If you weren't there, don't worry about it. You didn't miss anything. We had two weeks to rehearse, the director's wife had just left him, Ophelia came down with mono and they had to substitute her roommate who couldn't raise her voice above a whisper. You get the picture. Actually, the highlight of the performance—we only did it four times—was when a dog roamed on stage just as I had started "Oh, that this too too solid flesh would melt." It was a local dog that used to hang around during rehearsals—a medium-sized, shaggy mutt with a tail that swept the ground. I couldn't decide whether to ignore him or what. At first I thought he might exit on the other side, but he just stood there for about two minutes, staring out at the audience, panting. Maybe he knew someone; maybe he was hoping to be "discovered." Anyway, finally I picked him up and said, "Begone, pernicious hound," carried him offstage, and went back to carry on where I'd left off.

My mother put on the tape. I could search the world over and not find a more sympathetic audience than my mother and sister, but still I felt like an idiot. I have a special voice for Shakespeare, kind of a phony English accent, a little thick and fruity.

> "Let me confess that we two must be twain,
> Although our undivided loves are one:
> So shall those blots that do with me remain
> Without thy help by me be borne alone."

Because I couldn't stand listening to myself, I looked over at my sister. Her eyes were half closed, she had a dreamy, beatific smile on her face, one shoe slipped off her foot. She looked different somehow, but I couldn't put my finger on it. Maybe a new hairdo?

Once that one side was over, I begged them to listen to the other when I wasn't around.

"He's so modest!" my mother exclaimed. "You're good! Never be modest when you're good. Wasn't it wonderful?" she asked my sister.

"It was beautiful," my sister said softly. "Mo, you have *such* a beautiful voice!" After a second, "Those sonnets are wonderful."

"Listen—" my mother was bringing in the chicken— "there is

nothing like those sonnets. Nothing! I don't care what you say."

"He knew so much about love," my sister said wistfully, sitting down.

"He knew everything," my mother said. "What he didn't know doesn't exist. . . . Mo, I tell you, that record should be recorded by a real record company. Why should it just be for us?"

"I think the sonnets are already recorded," I said dryly, "by Gielgud, Olivier, Ralph Richardson."

"I don't care," she said, loading my plate. "This is *better* than Gielgud!"

I laughed.

"Don't laugh! I know what I'm talking about. I've seen him. I saw him in *Romeo and Juliet,* I've seen all of them. I'm not just talking."

"Maybe Gielgud's mother wouldn't think so," I said.

"Gielgud's mother would agree with me," my mother insisted. "Bring her here, and I bet you anything she'll agree with me. I'm not talking about your Hamlet. There maybe, okay, Olivier had a few tricks you never learned, but for the sonnets, you're way out front."

"I'm not sure his mother is alive, actually," I said, helping myself to bread. My mother's not a bad cook if she sticks to the basics— roast chicken, pot roast—but one thing she always does that drives me crazy is store bread in the refrigerator; it's always cold as a stone.

"Whose? Olivier's? Gielgud's?"

"Either." I have a vision of the three elderly ladies sitting there in my mother's living room listening to the tape. My mother's the only Jewish mother of the three, so when the tape is done, she says, "What can I say? Your sons are talented, but mine's the best," and they just nod politely, as though to agree.

I was beginning to feel not so hot. I'd eaten too much, had too much to drink. I turned down the pound cake with frozen raspberries and asked for a cup of tea.

"So, it was a wonderful birthday," my mother said, setting the tea down in front of me, pouring coffee for herself and my sister, "and guess what, I got a proposal!"

"Another one?" My sister looked puzzled. My sister got one proposal in her life and I think she said yes practically before Ward got the words out, she was so relieved and delighted. "Who was it?"

"Emil." She looked smug.

"I thought he proposed already," I said.

"No, just hinted around, which I pretended not to get. So my birthday comes. We're supposed to go out to eat. First, a huge and I mean *huge* bouquet of yellow roses arrives—my favorite kind. Then he shows up all dressed up with a big package, a silk blouse, pure silk, and before I know it he's talking about how he's made reservations for the two of us to go to San Francisco next month for two weeks on our honeymoon! He's made reservations and he hasn't even asked me yet!"

"What did you say?" my sister asked.

"What am I supposed to say? He's a sweet guy, I like seeing him, but marriage? We've never even been to bed! . . . I said, 'Look, Emil, you're a sweetie and all that, but slow down. I'm an old-fashioned girl. I don't go at this modern pace. Let's get to be good friends, maybe lovers. Let's savor it.'"

My sister looked at me. She looked embarrassed. "Mom, how could you? What'd *he* say?"

"He turned bright red and said he hadn't been sure if I was interested in sex. I said, 'So, why'd you propose? Do you want to be married to someone who isn't interested?'"

I laughed. "Mom, you can't . . ."

"Look, like I say, I'm an old-fashioned girl. I say what I feel. Now he knows. I don't need to marry for money. I've *got* money. I don't need to marry for companionship. I've *got* friends. So, what's left? Romance! But that takes time, doesn't it?"

Neither my sister nor I said anything.

"Okay, maybe in the circles you two move in everything is wham-bang, straight into bed, but that's not my style, I'm sorry. I've led a sheltered life." She grinned impishly.

"Mom, you're going to scare these men off," my sister said wryly. "You ought to be flattered. Two proposals at your age, from nice men! There aren't that many nice men around."

"There aren't?" My mother looked surprised. "What do you

mean? Joe was nice, Mo's nice. I know *lots* of nice men."

My sister raised her eyebrows. "Well, you've led a sheltered life, like you say."

My mother accepted this tribute or accusation calmly. "Maybe it's kept me young. That's what Emil says. He says I have more pep than any of his daughters, and they're all in their forties."

After dinner I said I had to get to the hotel. I was just too beat to stay on my feet any longer.

"I thought we'd listen to the other side of the tape," my mother said, disappointed.

"I'll come over and we can listen to it another time," Harriet said.

"You know the one I like best?" my mother said. She thought a minute. "How does it go? 'Let me not to the marriage of true minds admit impediments. . . .'"

I struck a pose and declaimed:

> "Let me not to the marriage of true minds
> Admit impediments. Love is not love
> Which alters when it alteration finds,
> Or bends with the remover to remove:
> O, no! it is an ever-fixed mark
> That looks on tempests and is never shaken;
> It is the star to every wandering bark,
> Whose worth's unknown, although his height be taken.
> Love's not Time's fool, though rosy lips and cheeks
> Within his bending sickle's compass come;
> Love alters not with his brief hours and weeks,
> But bears it out even to the edge of doom.
>   If this be error, and upon me proved,
>   I never writ, nor no man ever loved."

My mother and sister stared at me, transfixed. When I was done, my mother sighed. "Wouldn't you think he'd studied for years at the Royal Shakespeare Academy? That voice! That diction! I'm telling you, Mo, the American theater lost something very very special when you went into the business with us. Not that I'm not grateful, but it was our country's loss."

"Listen, it was a great meal," I said, hugging her. "I'll call you tomorrow."

My sister's car was parked about four blocks away. "I'll drive you back to the hotel," she said, and started the motor. I was praying she'd forgotten about whatever it was she was going to tell me. I had a ferocious headache. She stared straight ahead and then glanced at me quickly. "It's a terrible thing," she said.

"What is?"

"Only, listen to the whole thing, okay? Promise?"

"I promise."

She took a deep breath. "Well, the thing is, Timmy got in trouble at school." Timmy's her youngest—he's ten. "He was stealing books from the school library. It's funny because I would have bought them for him if I'd known he wanted them, but evidently he thought Ward would mind. Anyway, the principal said he wanted to see us together, me and Timmy, to discuss the whole thing. So we went in and had a conference. He's only been the principal about a year. His name's Kevin McDonnell."

"A good Jewish name," I said, joking, but she instantly looked stricken.

"Anyway, it went fine. I mean, Timmy talked about why he'd done it and Kevin, Mr. McDonnell, was *so* nice about it! He didn't yell at him or say he'd punish him in any way. He said he'd loved books too when he was Timmy's age and had even stolen some himself because his parents didn't have any money. He said he was delighted a boy Timmy's age cared that much about reading. He was lovely! And then we went home."

There was a pause. One thing with my sister—never ask her to tell a joke. Because you'll never know when the punch line comes. Harriet tells everything the same way, the same earnest, flat inflection. "That's not so terrible," I said finally.

"That's not the terrible *part*," she said darkly. "Wait! So I go home and about a week later Mr. McDonnell calls and says he'd like to meet me to discuss how things are going, how Timmy seems to be taking it all. He said I should meet him after school for a drink, and I said fine, I could. When I got there, he said how impressed he'd been by the way I was with Timmy. So many of the mothers that come in get all hysterical when their kids have problems, but I seemed so calm and concerned and loving. See, he doesn't have children himself. He's married, but his wife couldn't have children and didn't want to adopt. That's why he's a principal partly, the vicarious thing." She cleared her throat. "Okay, I'm getting to the bad part. I just want to warn you."

"I stand warned," I said, hoping this wouldn't take all night.

"Suddenly he looks at me, Kevin, Mr. McDonnell, and he says, 'Are you always this animated?' I said, 'No!' Because I'm not! I'm *never* animated! At least, no one ever said so. And then—you may not even believe this, Mo, but it's true, every *word* of it—he said he was madly in love with me! That ever since I'd come in for that conference, he couldn't think of *anything* except me, that I was the most fascinating, scintillating woman he ever met! Scintillating!"

Now I really felt sick, on top of the headache. I was afraid I knew the ending of the story, but I hoped I was wrong.

"I went home," Harriet went on, "and from then on the funny thing was *I* couldn't think of anything but *him!* Every *second!* How nice he'd been with Timmy, the nice way he listened, everything. So when he called again and said would I—see, his wife just isn't interested in sex. She's a lovely person, evidently, she's something high up on the Massachusetts Board of Education, but she just isn't. It's not her fault, he doesn't blame her." She took another deep breath. "So—okay, here it goes—we went to bed together!"

"How was it?" I guess I was being half ironical, but suddenly Harriet turned around and looked me straight in the eye.

"It was wonderful! Mo, it was so, *so* wonderful I can't tell you. It was the most wonderful thing that ever happened to me. And he's the most wonderful person. I wish you could meet him. He's the most wonderful, kind, sweet, caring person. . . . Do you hate me? Do you think it's terrible? Tell me honestly."

What I was thinking was that my sister was going to get horribly hurt by this bastard and that I'd go out and strangle him if I had the energy. You should have seen my sister's face. She has this gentle, vulnerable, funny face, a little like a tapir, and it was radiant. She looked absolutely beautiful, and I knew she was going to get shafted.

"I hope it works out," was all I could manage.

She was looking straight ahead again. "I don't know . . . I know in some ways this makes me a bad, evil person, but, see, there's one thing. I never mentioned this because, well, it's sort of intimate, but it's partly why I said yes. . . . Ward and I haven't slept together for ten years, not since Timmy was conceived."

I stared at her. At first I thought I'd heard wrong. "Ten . . . *years?*"

"Well, I think that's not so uncommon," Harriet rushed on, flustered. "That's what I read somewhere. That when the woman has kids, her husband sees her as a mother, not as a . . . and he stops being interested in sex. He just loses interest! There's no other woman. Ward just doesn't—"

"You hadn't had sex with anyone for ten *years?*"

Harriet giggled nervously. "It *was* a long time. I *did* kind of miss it. . . . But I also thought: maybe *all* marriages are like that, lots of them, and maybe, well, I thought I had the kids and Ward is a good person and I have my job, I thought maybe it just wouldn't matter. I didn't go crazy or anything. Well, maybe sometimes a little crazy, but inside mostly. . . . But now it's like it's all I think about! It's awful! I think about sex every single *second* of the day! When I'm doing the grocery shopping, while I'm teaching, even—this is terrible—even while I was listening to you recite the sonnets!"

"Listen, it's okay. After ten years, you're entitled."

"Am I?" she asked eagerly. "Is that what you really think? You're not just trying to make me feel good?"

"It's what I really think."

She sat there, smiling, bemused, looking happier than I'd ever seen her: not like a forty-four-year-old drama teacher who'd been celibate for a decade, but like a rosy, turned-on lady. Suddenly she smiled mischievously. "He thinks Jewish women are so sexy! Isn't that great? He thinks we're so exotic and earthy and strong-minded. All that stuff you grow up thinking is bad, he *likes!* He says he wants to be reborn as a Jew!"

"He'll have to change his name."

Then she drove me back to the hotel, and for the first time since I was in my teens, I threw up everything I'd eaten for the last twenty-four hours.

I woke up feeling terrific. Like I've said, I have a good constitution. And I think I have a good approach to things too. If there's a solution, find it and act on it. If there isn't, forget it. Don't let it eat at you. But my sister! Jesus. Ten years! And that oily Irishman who wants to be reborn as a Jew. Saints preserve us!

I spent all day at the office and that was good. When I'm working, I forget everything else. I only come to Boston twice a month, so there's always enough to catch up on, enough to be attended to. The day passed quickly, like a thousand other days. I called Noorbibi during lunch, just to see if she was free that night. She said sure. At first she sounded hesitant, but finally said eight would be fine, that she was writing a paper and needed till then to work.

Okay, where do I begin on this? About five years ago, precisely five years ago, in fact, I was in L.A. setting up the office there. I have a friend from college, Arnold, not a good friend, but I see him whenever I'm out there. He's divorced and has a lot of dough—he owns two restaurants that're doing extremely well. Anyway, he started in on how he'd been going to this Oriental call girl and she was dynamite and she had a friend and I should call her friend.

It wasn't the call girl part that bothered me. I've been to a few before and sure, you don't always get your money's worth, but you don't when you go to the movies either. What's the difference? It's just a little more expensive. No, it's that—I know this is a prejudice—but I don't like Oriental girls. That whole obsequious, docile thing: a little is okay, but the few I've known carry it over the edge. They're like little dolls. I don't know. Maybe it's because my mother is so little and perky, but I've always liked fairly tall, statuesque women. They can be light or dark—that part I don't care about. So I said no thanks and explained why. Then Arnold said his friend had a woman who was Indian, Hindu, and maybe I'd like to try *her*. He got her picture and I really liked the way she looked. Very thick long black hair, big black eyes. I'd never made it with an Indian woman before. Once with a girl whose grandmother was some kind of American Indian, but never with an *Indian* Indian. So I said sure, why not.

Right away we hit it off; it was great. She has a wonderful body. Kind of old-fashioned (Marilyn would say she should lose ten pounds): full breasts, a very small waist, and wide hips, short legs and a long torso. But when I asked if I could see her again, she looked funny. Then she told me she was about to give up being a call girl, that she'd just gotten accepted at BU and was planning on getting her doctorate in sociology! She explained how she felt she knew so much about American men through her work and she wanted to use that knowledge in a way that would make her financially independent once her looks were gone. She seemed pretty young— twenty-two—to be thinking that far ahead, but why not? Why wait till you're desperate the way some of them get when they hit thirty or thirty-five? That made sense to me. She's a sensible girl, very. She's shown me her fiancé's photo. Ravi. He's back in India getting his degree in electrical engineering. Once Bibi gets her doctorate, he'll come over here and they'll start a family. He looks a lot like her, actually. Tall, dark, big black eyes, a turban.

I'm not precisely sure what she does about men now. If I had to guess, I'd say she does it now and then just to get some extra money. I still pay her and she doesn't make a fuss about that. I think we both like the fact of me paying—she because it separates me from her fiancé and me because it makes her not a girlfriend.

When she let me in her apartment, she was wearing a sari. She has dozens of them, all beautiful. I love the way she looks in them and the way she takes them off, unwinding the yards of material. I've seen the clothes in her closet—she has lots of Westernized clothes, for everyday—but she knows I like the saris and whenever I come over, she's wearing one. To tell the truth, I wouldn't want to see her in Western dress, though she probably looks good that way too.

"Finish your paper?" I asked affectionately.

"Almost . . . This teacher is so strict! First she said we didn't need source materials, didn't need to list them, then she said we did. I think she's a very ambivalent person."

I have a slight horror, I admit, at the idea of Noorbibi—I call her Bibi, usually—getting her doctorate and starting to sound like my sister-in-law. Ambivalent, conflicted, neurosis . . . And at times I've wondered: am I described in her dissertation? Am I one of the "case studies" of Erotic Deviations in Upper Middle Class American Men? Am I a deviation?

"You look bushed," she said, taking my coat. In a funny way—the analogy is very distant—Noorbibi reminds me of my sister. Not in looks, but in being very sensitive to whatever mood I happen to be in. With Marilyn, I could come home with my head on a platter and she'd rush out with, "Aaron got an A on his spelling test! Linus had another asthma attack!" and maybe an hour or two later, "Gee, Mo, did something happen to your head?" I'm exaggerating a little, but not much. But it's funny—at times it bothers me, Marilyn's self-absorption, but at other times I like it. It gives me a kind of mental space at home which I like. Living with someone who could see right through you to what was inside could get pretty uncomfortable.

I lay down on the couch with my head in Noorbibi's lap. She began stroking my forehead. She has wonderful hands, long delicate fingers. Yet strangely, I didn't feel all that sexy. I don't know why. Mainly I felt really zonked, even though I'd slept well and it hadn't been that bad a day. Maybe it was that she keeps her apartment somewhat warm and the lights are always dim. "Is something bothering you?" she asked, leaning over, her hair grazing my ear. I like her voice too, very soft. Sometimes I even have trouble understanding what she says.

"No, nothing special." Then I told her about my sister. She knows about her in a general way. You know, it's funny, my sister-in-law—*why* am I thinking about her again?—and I once had a big argument about prostitutes, call girls, etc. She claimed that men who go to them do it because they want to humiliate women, that paying proves that. I just don't get that. If someone does a good job at anything, you pay them. How is that humiliating? Do people drive buses cross-country or wait on tables or do anything just for the sheer fun of it? It's the opposite of humiliating—you're telling someone you think they're good at something. Christ, I wish someone would say that to *me* more often! Okay, so part of it's acting. But part of *everything* is acting! I'm acting when I'm on the job, when I'm with my kids. What I mean is, I'm playing a role, to some extent. Tell me who isn't. And the fact is, that my relationship with Noorbibi is one of the better deals I've ever had with a woman just because it's *not* based on sentiment or whatever. Like, I don't call her every time I come to Boston and sometimes, when I do, she's busy. But if I don't call, she doesn't get all antsy and hysterical the next time, like "Where were you? You promised this, you promised that . . ." And if she's busy, I don't get rampant with jealousy and wonder if she's with some other guy. If she is, fine. She has to pay the rent like anyone else.

At the end of telling her about my sister, I said, "I guess I'm afraid she's really going to get shafted by this guy."

"Not necessarily," Bibi said. "Your sister sounds like she can take care of herself."

Maybe it's some kind of oedipal thing. Weirdly, it's almost easier for me to imagine my mother having sex with someone than my sister. "That whole number about his loving Jews, wanting to be reborn as a Jew!"

"That's not so unusual. My fiancé feels the same way."

That startled me. Do they *have* Jews in India?

"He studied in London once," she went on, "and he became very attached to a Jewish girl."

"What happened?"

There was a pause. "I'm not sure."

Actually, Jews and Indians don't look that unalike—maybe he felt he'd met a kindred spirit. I yawned. God, I was so sleepy! I hoped she wouldn't feel offended. You come over to fuck someone and you fall asleep!

"Just rest a little," she said softly. She got up, slipped a pillow under my head, and came back with a blanket which she draped over me. By the time she did it, I was asleep.

I slept heavily, no dreams, like falling down a well. Usually when I sleep like that, waking up is hard, almost painful. But this time I woke up slowly, looking around the room, getting my bearings. All the lights were off except the desk light where Bibi was sitting, writing. She was wearing a green sari, with threads of gold in it that caught the light. There was something cosy and comforting about being there, the quiet, attentive way she was bent over whatever she was doing.

Then I thought: Jesus, practically every woman I know is cheating on her husband! Marilyn, Harriet, Bibi. Even my mother! Okay, she's a widow, but still, my father's only been dead a year and already she's getting bouquets of yellow roses and some guy is making plans to spirit her off to San Francisco! I don't know what Bibi's fiancé knows about her. Maybe it's some kind of formal agreement, that while they're apart, they'll "satisfy their needs" but keep it at a purely physical level. But still, these are all "good" women. Marilyn would claim Bibi isn't because she takes money, but to me that's a prejudice. What does she know? She takes my money too, maybe not as directly, but it amounts to the same thing.

Bibi turned around and saw that I was awake. "Slept well?" she said, smiling.

I nodded, then sat up. Are women ever what they seem to be? I suddenly got this suspicion—was Bibi really getting her doctorate in sociology? Was that guy in the turban—I could see his photo, gold-framed, on the desk in front of her—really her fiancé? I went over and looked down at the paper. "What're you doing?"

"Footnotes."

I glanced down and sure enough, it was all there, all the right jargon. I let my hand rest on her hair. "Let's go inside, okay?"

We moved into her bedroom, kissing, groping. After a moment she stood up, unwound her sari, and let it fall to the ground. Watching her come toward me, I wondered who she thinks of when she's with me, while we're doing it. Sometimes I have the feeling she's not quite there mentally, but then I have that feeling with Marilyn too. Once we're fucking, it's not all that different. (A footnote: Sure, I know some guys go to call girls to get them to do things they'd never ask their wives to do. Not me. Marilyn's pretty versatile, and I don't have any hairy fantasies that can't be satisfied the regular way. It's just—from time to time you need to fuck someone you're not married to. Only with most women it gets involved, no matter what they say at the beginning. If the sex is good for them, they want more. You end up paying more than I pay Bibi, a lot more.)

But I have to admit I like it when I feel she's enjoying it. I don't want her to be thinking of me just as a client, just a source of money. Vanity maybe. Unlike Marilyn, she always keeps her eyes open and I like that, seeing her pupils suddenly dilate and blur, the whites almost blue. She has a funny, musky smell, like incense or furniture polish. Sometimes I wonder how often she bathes. She doesn't shave under her arms either—big tufts of black hair, like the hair between her legs. But it was lousy. As soon as I was inside her, I felt panicky, scared. I fucked her as quickly as possible, not giving a damn if she came or not. Usually I try to bring her along with me. So she's getting paid—she might as well enjoy it. But this time I just wanted to get it over with. Afterward, I rolled over to one side of the bed and closed my eyes a second. Maybe Bibi thought I was going to settle in for the night because she gave me a poke.

"Listen, uh, Mo, I have a really early class tomorrow. I have to get up at eight."

"So?"

"So, maybe it'd be better if you don't stay over."

Sometimes I stay the night, sometimes not, depending on my mood, whatever. "Look, I'll leave. Can't I lie here five minutes?"

My voice came out harsher and more angry than I'd intended. "Of course you can," she snapped. "I just meant—"

For this I'm paying three hundred dollars? I can go home and have Marilyn scream at me. I turned around. Bibi was lying naked, staring off into space. "Does *he* know about all this?" I said.

"Who?"

"Your boyfriend, Ravi. . . . about me and all the others?"

"He's my fiancé, and there are no others. I don't do that anymore. I told you that."

"So, why do you see me?"

She hesitated. "I think of you as a friend."

"How come you take my money, then?"

"I thought it made you more comfortable."

"Oh come on! That it made *me* more comfortable?"

"Doesn't it?"

I grabbed her arm. "Wait a sec. This doesn't make any sense. . . . You're doing this just for fun? You just like fucking me?"

"Sometimes I like it."

"But not today?"

"Today you seemed in a funny mood."

I sat up and started to get dressed. "Yeah, well, I am, I *am* in a funny mood." I finished dressing in silence.

"Because of your sister?" Bibi leaned forward, her arms folded under her breasts.

"What?"

"Is your mood because of her?"

"I don't know. Look, forget it." I took three hundred-dollar bills out of my pocket and threw them on the bed. "Here."

"Keep it."

"No, I took up your time. Take it."

Bibi looked at me for a long time, then took the money and folded it up on her night table. Then she got into a robe and walked with me to the door. "It'll get better," she said as I put my coat on. "Don't worry."

"What will?"

"Whatever's bothering you."

"Look, Bibi, leave me alone, okay? Nothing's bothering me. And we're not 'friends.' Please! That's hypocritical shit."

She just stood looking at me with a concerned, mournful expression. I felt a pang of remorse. I sighed. "Listen, I'll call you when I'm here again," I said, squeezing her shoulder. "Finish your footnotes."

Back at the hotel I felt worse than before. I shouldn't have seen her. If I had, I should have fucked her, left, and that's it. Why tell her about my sister? Why make things complicated? We've had a lot of good times together and now I have the feeling that's over. Friends! What women mean when they say "We're friends" even Einstein couldn't figure out.

I wonder what she'd have said if I'd told her about Marilyn.

It's only half an hour from LaGuardia to our house in Westchester. I always feel a kind of satisfaction coming from my parents' house to the one we bought five years ago. It was a real bargain financially. A newly built California-style house, five bedrooms, glossy bathrooms—everything new, modern, functional. No crumbling walls, rusty water dribbling out of the drains, mysterious creaks in the night from ancient plumbing. The reason we got such a good deal was they were planning to build a new sewage plant a few miles down the road. A lot of people panicked, expecting they'd have to breathe that industrial New Jersey–type smell all day. But the community banded together and got them to build the plant somewhere else. We only have an acre and a half of land, true, but right behind us is a thirty-acre plot that our neighbor has been unsuccessfully trying to sell for a decade. I figure I'll gradually acquire a couple more acres, maybe put in a pool, a tennis court—even though I'm not much of a tennis player. It's not that I'm the last of the big spenders, but my parents were so tight-fisted, I like the idea of enjoying it while you have it.

When I got home, around dinner time, everything was perfect. Marilyn in the kitchen, fixing supper. Pork chops, sweet potatoes, green beans—one of my favorite meals. She was wearing jeans and a light blue T-shirt and her hair was in a pony tail, swinging back and forth. She looked beautiful. I thought of that incriminatory snatch of conversation I overheard on the phone a few weeks ago. My fault—I forgot my umbrella and drove back to the house fifteen minutes after I left. Marilyn was on the kitchen phone and I opened the door so quietly, she didn't even hear me. Nor did she hear me leave. I just got out fast, as though I'd been an unwilling witness to a hit-and-run accident.

"We can eat in a sec," Marilyn said. "Call the kids, okay?"

They were lying in front of the TV, Linus kneeling about four inches away from it, Aaron stretched out on the couch, his legs crossed. "I can't *see* if he sits that close," Aaron whined. "Tell him to move, will you?"

No "Hi Daddy, how great you're home." Do they even know I've been away? "It's time for dinner. Go wash up."

Linus didn't even hear me. He's seven years old and either he's a genius or we'll have to put him away in some special home. He just tunes everything out, everything! For a while we thought he was deaf, but his hearing's been tested, it's fine. I'm not even talking about the asthma. God, one summer the four of us rented a house in New Hampshire and every single night he had asthma attacks that would kill a man my size. No one slept more than two hours a night. I think we were all lying there thinking of ways to kill him. And yet, it's crazy, but I love him insanely. He is the weirdest kid you could find. He doesn't even look like a boy! Not like a girl, but more like some androgynous elf. Big hazel eyes like Marilyn's, sandy hair falling in his face, pale pale skin, under-sized. Another thing: from the age of three to five he just stopped talking. At two and a half he was perfectly normal, had a regular vocabulary. Then just stopped. Altogether, not just with us, but at school, with Aaron. We kept thinking maybe he'd talk to Aaron, but Aaron said no. We tried everything —special doctors, consultations—it was hideous. A shameful, horrible time. And then suddenly he started talking again, just like a normal five-year-old. No explanation, nothing.

I picked him up and carried him into the kitchen. If I tried that with Aaron, even when he was six, he would've screamed bloody murder, but Linus lets me and even smiles. "Did you have a good trip?"

"Yeah, it was pretty good. I saw Grandma Leah and Aunt Harriet."

"How about Uncle Ward?"

"Uncle Ward wasn't there."

"Where was he?"

"I don't know."

Aaron came in and saw Linus already sitting there. "*He* didn't wash up," he said accusingly. He's chunky and handsome, black hair, dark eyes—a better-looking version of me as a kid.

"I did so."

"You did not!"

"Kids, shut up, will you?" Marilyn said. "Daddy's tired. He's been away two days, working hard."

They both looked at me, almost in surprise. Behind Aaron, I see his note to Marilyn Scotch-taped to the refrigerator: "Mom, Daddy called. He arrived safely." Very neat, perfect handwriting. Even the time. "4:07." An uptight little kid.

"You know, I was thinking on the way home," I said to Marilyn after we'd finished the main course. "Maybe now would be a good time for you to go back and get your degree, finish your B.A., what do you think?"

"Is that college?" Aaron said.

"Yeah," Marilyn said.

"You never finished college?" he pursued.

She smiled at him dotingly. She adores him. "I dropped out to marry Daddy."

"Why?"

Marilyn laughed. "You don't think that was a good reason?"

"Why couldn't you marry him *and* finish college?"

"Yeah, why?" Linus echoed, not really interested.

Marilyn had a slightly mocking smile. "I wanted to be a good wife and mother."

Aaron looked up at her. "You are, Mom. You *are* a good wife and mother."

Marilyn struck a pose like a beauty queen. "See, it was all worth it."

"How about it?" I said impatiently. "You could commute into the city, it's only thirty-five minutes, or you could transfer your credits to a place out here."

"What's the point, though?" Marilyn said, setting down bowls of chocolate pudding. "What for?"

"Well, the kids are in school. Eventually, you're going to get bored just staying home."

"I'm not bored," she said defensively.

"You'll feel better, being independent."

"How do *you* know?" She sounded hostile.

"Okay, forget it. Spend twenty more years yacking to your friends on the phone, watching the soaps on TV—"

Don't tell me. I know that was dumb. Marilyn looked as if steam was coming out of her ears. "I have never in my entire *life* watched a soap on TV! And I never will! And what friends? What friends do I *have* around here? No one!" A plaintive wail.

I made my voice as soothing as possible. "That's what I mean. It would be different if you had a lot of friends to do things with."

She sighed. "Yeah, I know, I wish I did. . . . Maybe you're right. I'll look into it."

"What're you going to be, Mom, once you get your degree?" Aaron asked. "An astrophysicist?"

That struck him and Linus as so funny, they both started choking with laughter. I had to clap Linus on the back a few times.

"Maybe I'll be the first woman astronaut," Marilyn said. "How about that?"

Suddenly, Linus looked extremely anxious. "But you might not come down!"

Marilyn ruffled his hair. "Honey, I can't even work a vacuum cleaner. I'll never make it as an astronaut . . . Maybe I'll do something with design."

"You mean like drawing pictures?" Linus said.

"Yeah, some kind of commercial art."

"You could take one of those tests," Linus said, "where you draw a face and they tell if you're a good artist."

"Those are fakes," Aaron said contemptuously. "They tell everyone they're good just to get money. They're quacks."

I pushed the pudding to one side. "If you apply now, you could start in January."

"January!" Marilyn yelped. "That's in three months!"

"So? You'll be done that much faster. You could have your degree in two years, at the end of 'sixty-nine."

"What's the hurry?" Marilyn said. "People start in the fall."

"What else do you have to do?"

She reddened. "That's not the point. . . . Look, I'll send away. But I don't even think you can get in so fast. You need recommendations, transcripts. It's a whole big deal."

"You could be a model," Linus said thoughtfully, his mouth coated with chocolate pudding. "For clothes. For fur coats."

Marilyn smiled. "You don't need a college degree for that. . . . Anyway, I did that once."

I hadn't known that. "When?"

"In high school. My friend's father had this place. It was awful! We had to wear these fur coats in July. It was about ninety-five outside and a hundred and ten inside. It was murder! Never again."

"You could be on the covers of magazines," Aaron suggested. "That wouldn't be so bad."

Marilyn touched her nose. "Not with this."

"What's wrong with your nose?"

"There's nothing wrong with it. It's a Jewish nose, that's all."

"It is?" The two of them stared at her.

I like Marilyn's nose. She claims she was the only Jewish girl in the class of 'fifty-four not to have a nose job when she graduated from high school. It's not very curved, just slightly, and it's not big. It makes her face more interesting, Slavic slightly.

"I like your nose," Linus said.

"Anyway, why can't people with Jewish noses be on the covers of magazines?" Aaron wanted to know.

"It's not considered sexy. You're supposed to have a little upturned thing," she said. "Men can have Jewish noses, not women."

"That's crazy," Aaron said.

"Yeah, that's crazy," Linus repeated. He looked at me. "Your nose is a lot better than *his*."

"I agree," I said.

They went off to play and we were left alone in the kitchen. Marilyn was leaning against the sink, looking pensive. "So, did you have a good trip?"

"Yeah, nothing special." Suddenly I decided to tell her about Harriet, just to see her reaction. I told her the story.

"She hasn't been laid in ten years?" Marilyn said. "God!"

"She says he's just not interested in sex anymore."

She snorted. "Sure."

Marilyn doesn't like Ward, partly because he regards her as a dumb blond and talks to her in a very condescending, almost sneering way. "Sure, what?"

"He's probably been fucking every co-ed he can lay his hands on, and he doesn't have time for her."

Actually, I assume something like that is true, but I said, "He may just have lost interest."

"Men never lose interest."

After a moment I said, "I guess what I'm afraid of is Hari's going to get really hurt."

"In what way?"

"Well, women, if the sex is good, tend to get kind of carried away—"

"So? Men don't get carried away?"

"Not in the same way. They put it in perspective. Women go crazy, they—"

Marilyn looked furious. "And that's supposed to be so wonderful about men? That they don't feel anything? Well, it's *not!* It's horrible! . . . Plus, it's not even *true!* Men get carried away, *they* fall madly in love too! *Lots* of them!"

A very tense silence.

"Men tell women what they think they want to hear," I said, watching her.

She began picking at her nail polish. She has long dark red nails. "Some do. . . . Some say what they really feel. Not everyone is so cynical." Her voice was shaking.

"It's more cynical to lie and then, when the thing cools, to walk off, the way he'll do with Harriet?"

Marilyn's lips were tight. "He may, just possibly, love her. Did you ever think of that? Maybe his wife really *isn't* interested in sex. Maybe he's a lonely, unhappy man and Harriet's the first person who's made him feel good about himself, really *happy* in years, in his whole *life!*"

Oh shit. I can't believe, I don't want to believe anyone has been heaving that kind of garbage at Marilyn *or* at Harriet. I stood up and started to go inside. Suddenly Marilyn came after me. "I think the idea about college is good," she said quickly, softly, touching me. "It's nice of you to think about it."

I squeezed her ass. The kids were sprawled out on the floor in the living room watching TV again. "Let's go upstairs," I whispered.

Marilyn looked conflicted. "They'll be asleep in an hour or two."

"Let's go up now."

She followed me reluctantly, but even after the door was locked, she looked worried. "I'm afraid they'll know what we're doing."

"So?"

In the bedroom I pulled her T-shirt over her head and undid her bra, put my hands over her breasts. "Mo, that hurts. Don't be so rough, okay?"

"Come on, get undressed then." I knew she wouldn't say no, no matter what mood she was in, out of guilt.

"I think I might be getting my period," she said, taking her jeans off. I was naked already, lying on the bed. "There was some blood this morning."

"That's okay."

It was a kind of turn-on, her being at the same time so nervous and eager to please and so inwardly conflicted and resentful. Usually I spend a long time trying to get Marilyn worked up, especially if she's not quite in the mood to start with, but this time I just entered her after a couple of minutes. She closed her eyes right away, but wrapped her legs obediently around me. Where was she? If she ever says his name while we're doing it, I'll kill her. She came right away, much faster than usual, gasping inarticulately. I thrust into her again and again, angrily, wanting to hurt her. When I was finished, I stayed inside her, looking down at her face. Her eyes opened slowly.

"I guess you get horny when you go away," she said, slightly ironically.

"Sometimes."

"I feel sore. It must be my period."

That was my moment. I could have said, "Or maybe it's . . ." But I didn't want to. You have to do things for a purpose. Let the thing run its course. Let all that shit about "true love" play itself out, and she'll come home with her tail between her legs. What am I losing, really? He's giving her something she needs. Romance!

Oh, and his wife just had twins. I forgot about that, I don't know why. A few months ago we were at a party at their house and she looked as though she was about to give birth to two baby elephants. No wonder. "Benjy, you forgot to raise the grill." "Benjy, you forgot to take your galoshes. . . . Benjy, you said you'd bring home a quart of milk. . . ." Maybe that's why he's so gray and cringing at thirty.

And they're loaded. Did I mention that? I think he's a lawyer, but there's got to be family money somewhere with that house. It's old, Victorian style, but every room has a thirty-foot ceiling, fireplaces everywhere, two huge porches, about ten acres of land. Frankly, I wouldn't live in a house like that if you paid me, but some people like it. And two daughters who passed things around: a chubby dark-haired one and a sexy little one with pigtails, wearing a bikini. The little one brought me a beer and poured it carefully, then looked at me a long time with a grave, beckoning look. "Is there anything else you need?" At least I don't have daughters.

I showered while Marilyn went downstairs to get the laundry out of the dryer. Look, there are a lot of guys, married as long as I've been, who can't even get it up with their wives! The main thing is, if I walk out and Marilyn remarries, which she's bound to do, I'd lose the kids. That once-a-week thing is murder. They don't know who you are. They start getting to like the stepfather because he's around all the time. There are a lot of worse things than this, a lot.

I gave the kids a bath and read them a story. They share a room, but we're fixing up the study so Aaron doesn't have to be kept awake with Linus's coughing.

For Aaron's sake I started off with a book with chapters, something about a little boy with magic powers who can fly when he wants to, but his parents never catch on. Linus listened, staring off into space, but all he wants is for me to read *Goodnight Moon* for the thousandth time. Whenever I start *Goodnight Moon,* Aaron gets a very superior, exhausted look, and even chimes in with the words. "Goodnight nobody. . . . Goodnight mush." "God, is that a dumb book!" he said. "I can't believe anyone wrote that! It's not even a *book!*"

"I like the pictures," Linus said. He was sitting next to me, sucking his thumb. He doesn't wet his bed anymore, but he always smells a little like he does.

"Why do they call it an old lady when it's a rabbit?" Aaron said, pointing to the "old lady" sitting in the rocking chair.

"She can be a lady *and* a rabbit," Linus said.

"No, she can't," Aaron said. "You're either a lady *or* a rabbit! You can't be both."

He had a point, but then I pointed out that two different people worked on the book, one wrote the story, another did the pictures.

"That's dumb," Aaron said, getting into bed. "They should get one person. I bet the person who wrote the book meant 'lady' but the person who did the pictures didn't know how to draw people, so he put in rabbits!"

He'd better be a lawyer some day. Why does Marilyn love him so much? I can see Linus getting on her nerves—he gets on everyone's nerves—but Aaron gets on my nerves in another way, that precise, slightly hostile accuracy about everything. Maybe it reminds me of myself. I know he'll do all right in the world. He's a handsome little kid, smart. But he irritates me. I tried to get Linus to go to the bathroom, but he was too sleepy and almost fell asleep standing there. Maybe he'll be a great artist or something. That's the only thing that'll save him. I don't know how he's going to make it otherwise. Then I thought of Harriet's Timmy, who gave them problems, used to cut school a lot, but who's now okay.

When I bent down to kiss Linus, he grabbed me and hugged me, giving me a long passionate kiss. "When you go away next time, can I come?" he asked.

"Sure, if you don't have school."

"He'll have school," Aaron said. "He always has school."

"I don't like it when you go away," Linus said.

"Why not?" I asked.

"I just don't. . . . I don't like the way Mommy reads the story."

"She reads it the same way," Aaron said, exasperated.

"She skips. . . . Sometimes she says she's sick of that book."

"Who isn't?" Aaron said.

"Next time I'll take you with me," I promised, and tucked Linus in. Sometimes he falls out of bed, but even when he does, he goes right on sleeping. A crazy kid, no doubt of it.

Winter Is Summer

*S*ometimes I think Mo is crazy. No, not crazy, but obsessed.
He gets an idea in his head and he won't stop talking about it. Probably that's good at his job, that's why he's so successful, but not everyone's like that! I'm not. I need time to think things over. Suddenly,
since his last trip to Boston, he's gotten this bee in his bonnet about
me going back to finish college. What's ironical is two, three years
ago, when I was at home with the kids and Linus was acting so weird
and we were lugging him from doctor to doctor, most of whom
thought we were crazy and wanted both of *us* to go into analysis—
then, sure I would've loved to go back to school. I would've loved to
do anything! But now, even apart from Benjy, I feel like I've kind of
adjusted to things, though the house is still basically a mess, and I
miss Jeanette horribly. I think you need women friends, someone to
talk to, whether you're married or not. Jeanette says it's the same for
her. She works, but her field—market research—is mostly men,
and she says she goes crazy, just wanting to talk to someone. We call
long distance twice a month—she pays for one time, me the other—
but it's not the same. You want someone to be actually sitting there
so you can see her expressions. Oh, I know it's all trivia and most of
it's stuff that'll pass within a week or a month or a year, but still.

It's funny, though. I haven't told Jeanette about Benjy yet. Here
we've been friends since seventh grade and she knows everything, I
mean *everything* about me, things I'd never tell Mo in a million
years—but about this I feel funny. It's not that she has a perfect

marriage or that she's a censorious person, not at all. That's what I
like about her. You tell her anything and, even if it's that you've
robbed a bank or killed someone practically, she'll listen and figure
out a way that shows you're really a nice, good person. That's why—
if she *didn't* do that about this—I'd feel so awful. I will tell her
eventually. But the last time we spoke, I didn't. I talked about all
the other things, like Mo wanting me to go back to school.

"I think it's a good idea personally," she said. "Really, Val, you
should."

This doesn't make any sense, but when we were twelve we made
up these imaginary names for each other—I was Valerie and she was
Amanda—and we still call each other that sometimes. That's what I
mean by crazy things that I'd never do with anyone else.

"Linus is just seven, though. . . . And he's still kind of strange."

"You said the teacher said how well he was doing, how he has all
these friends."

"True."

It *is* strange how all of a sudden, like overnight! Linus has become
practically normal. I mean, not normal, but no weirder than any of
the other regular kids in his class. He has friends, he does all right
with his work. One reason Jeanette is probably on Mo's side in this is
that she did finish college and has a job, has had one since her kids
were in nursery school. She just says right out that she would have
murdered them if she'd stayed home. That's not true—she's a terrific mother and her kids are great—but the point is, she just did it
and her husband, Rich, said fine. He's a playwright and not that
many of his plays get put on, so I guess he was glad to have a second,
stable income.

The thing with Mo, the reason he feels the way he does about me
working, is his mother. Blanche, my sister, says everything, especially with Jewish men, goes back to their mothers. She says I'm
lucky, that most Jewish men of his generation had these mothers
that doted on them nonstop for twenty years and they turned out to
be spoiled, self-absorbed egomaniacs. Mo's self-absorbed sometimes, but he's not spoiled and he's not an egomaniac. But the thing
is, it was different with Mo's mother, Leah. It was a family business.
She didn't have to go back and get any special degree. She just did

it. It was more like with my mother. My parents run this pet store in
Sloatsburg. They don't sell puppies or kittens. They tried that, but
they (the puppies and kittens) were always getting sick. They sell
fish and pet supplies; dog collars, turtle food, little rock castles to put
in aquariums. I'm not comparing it to Mo's parents' business. They
make a living, but just barely. But they always did it together. Usually Daddy sits in the back, reading, and Mom stands up front and
handles most of the customers. That's one thing Mo and I have in
common. It was our mothers who ran things basically. Our fathers
were both sort of quiet people who liked to just sit back and not be
bothered.

I think that was one of the things that attracted me to Mo, actually, how different he was from Daddy. I love my father, but I
think it was hard for Mom a lot, his hardly ever talking and being so
antisocial. Mo seemed, when I met him, so exuberant and self-
confident. Of course, now I know that was somewhat of a pose, but
some of it is real. He really does love his work, for instance. And so
maybe he's really thinking of me when he says I'd be happier working. He shows he has confidence in me and thinks I'm smart.

What would I be, though? It's true I used to like to draw, but
that's not enough to get a job in commercial art. You need a lot more
technical training. I thought—well, I like clothes and fashion.
Maybe I could design clothes. I don't know. Every day I sit there,
mulling it over, and think of some new profession and Mo says,
"Great," and the next day I think of nine million reasons why I won't
be good at it. "Did you send away for the catalogues yet?" he asked
last night.

"Some of them," I lied.

"Which ones?"

I mentioned a few he'd thought were a good idea. Basically, I
don't feel like schlepping into the city. I'd rather go to a community
college out here where maybe the students won't be so bright and I
won't feel so intimidated.

"I'll pick them up on my way to work," he said. "I pass by there."

Now that I have the catalogues, he keeps asking, "Did you fill
them out yet? Did you write away for the recommendations?"

Who am I going to ask? It's over ten years ago that I was in college. The teachers I had are dead or not even teaching! I know I could call or look them up in the NYU catalogue. I'm scared, basically. That is a bad part of my character. A lot of things, especially new things, make me extremely nervous. I'm scared the other students will think of me as some old bag, going back at thirty, while they're just in their teens. Mo says lots of women my age go back and I won't be the only one, but still, I'll probably be older than the *teachers*, some of them!

And what about Benjy? When will I see him?

I want to tell about this chronologically. Whenever I did a report in school, the teacher always said, "You're wandering, Marilyn!" So I'm going to do this chronologically. Which means starting with Benjy's wife, Becky, because if I hadn't gotten friendly with her, I'd never have met *him*. She has two daughters in the same school Aaron and Linus go to—Chelsea and Dawn. Chelsea is about nine, a class ahead of Aaron, and Dawn is seven. Plus she's gigantically pregnant—Becky, I mean. They just moved here last year and even last winter she was big. I wasn't like that when I was pregnant. I was really strict with myself. I only gained twelve pounds with Aaron and fifteen with Linus and I got back to what Mo calls my fighting weight within a month. Becky's the kind of person who'll probably put on five pounds with each kid and never lose it.

Oh, I don't want to be mean about Becky. I want to be objective, but it's so hard! But otherwise you won't get a real picture of what she's like. Okay, her good points. One: her hair. She has really pretty auburn hair. She wears it the way kids do in grade school, just loose down her back, pinned back with barrettes, and you know she'll never change it. What I mean is, she's one of those women who don't seem to care that much about their looks. I admire that, in a way. I spend so damn much time getting my hair just right, putting on my eye makeup, making sure my stockings don't have runs. What for? For men? I guess. But anyway, even if I didn't do any of that I'd still be prettier than Becky. Two, besides her hair, she's a nice person. She has a round, friendly face and a really nice smile. She's shorter than me, just around five three or four, I think, and wears clothes like corduroy jumpers and white blouses with round collars and tweed skirts. Knee socks even! But, like, one day when I'd dropped the kids off at school, my car died on me and I didn't know how I'd get home. Becky had just dropped their kids off too. She drove me to the car repair place and stayed with me all morning while I waited for them to fix it. That's what I mean about nice: thoughtful. Benjy says that about her. It drives me *crazy* when he talks about what's nice about her, but I have to admit she is some of those things.

Maybe Becky and I would even have gotten to be good friends if this hadn't started with Benjy. I don't know. I could tell she needed a friend and I did too, but it was like I wasn't quite *her* type and she wasn't quite *my* type. Like, she went to a really classy all-girls prep school and she's not Jewish. Plus, she's rich, from a rich family, I mean. I think maybe I seem sort of beyond the pale to her, lower class or not that intellectual or something. She was a government major in college and for two years afterward she worked on a magazine, *Human Rights,* which had to do with various injustices around the world. To me she seems sort of earnest and plodding, plus fanatically absorbed in her kids. I mean, I'm absorbed in *my* kids too, but that's *all* she talks about practically! Either boasting about how wonderful they are or worrying about some little tiny problem anyone could tell her would go away.

I asked her once if she wasn't overwhelmed at the idea of having four kids, and she said oh no, when she was little she used to imagine having twelve! If I was Benjy, I would sew a diaphragm into her because if he's not careful, he's going to end up with a million kids. I'm not kidding. It's her money, by the way. I mean, the reason they live in that big house which cost a fortune is because her father gives them a lot of stuff. He paid the mortgage, almost the whole down payment, and he's set up trust funds for all the kids. Benjy's just a lawyer. They couldn't live like that on his income.

Anyway, this is how it happened. One day in May, Becky came up to me and said she was giving a surprise party for her husband who was going to be thirty on June seventh. Which was really a funny coincidence because *I* was going to be thirty on June seventh. Mo thinks horoscope things are a lot of garbage, and maybe they are, but I do think I'm like a Gemini: I am mercurial and I *do* like to flirt and I *can* be frivolous a lot (I don't think I really am, but that's how I appear to some people). What's funny is in all the horoscope things they say how Geminis together never work because they're too much alike, but I don't think that's true of Benjy and me. I think we get along because we are alike in some ways. Anyway, when Becky asked me, I said we probably could but I'd have to ask Mo.

Mo is funny about social things. He's definitely not like my father, who despises going out for any reason, to *anything*. But sometimes he acts kind of supercilious about the people out here, like they're "beneath" him, philistine, not smart enough. But when I mentioned the Fettermans' party, he just said, "Sure, why not?"

It was starting at four and since it was my birthday, I wanted to look especially nice. Mostly people don't get too dressed up out here. I decided to wear this white piqué sheath, which fits me perfectly, and my white sandals and put my hair up. I think I look more elegant that way. It takes a long time for me to put my hair up the way I like it, but when it was done, it did look really pretty. And I took this bright pink Mexican shawl Blanche once brought back from San Miguel for me.

Right away Mo got into some conversation with a man named Nelson Westerling about chess. Mr. Westerling is an editor of a chess magazine, and Mo used to like playing chess a lot, so instantly they got into this really technical discussion. I can't even play checkers! It's terrible and I don't know what it is, but I can't concentrate on games, even simple ones like Monopoly. The kids beat me already, and they're just seven and eight. So I wandered off to where Benjy was standing grilling the steaks. He was doing a terrible job. They were practically on top of the flame, all charred and smoking, but he didn't even seem to notice. He was just standing there, staring off into space with this kind of moody, depressed expression.

"Maybe you ought to raise the grill," I said.

He looked over at me. "Oh, yeah, I guess. . . . How do you do that?"

I never met a man who didn't know how to raise a grill! I showed him and he smiled and said thanks. Then we looked at each other and smiled and introduced ourselves. *Now* I think Benjy's the handsomest man that ever lived practically, but I have to admit when I first met him, that wasn't what I thought. Usually I like tall men and he's not tall. Plus, his hair is really gray for someone of thirty—he says it's hereditary, his father's is too. But he has a youthful face, especially when he smiles. He has a wonderful smile, and also wonderful eyes. Big, brown, sort of melancholy eyes that look at you like he understands everything you're thinking and saying.

You know how sometimes you meet someone at a party and *boing*, before you can even stop yourself, you're imagining nine million lurid things you might do with him? Well, with Benjy it *wasn't* like that. We talked, but even if they'd broadcast my thoughts on a loudspeaker, Mo could've heard and not been worried at all. Benjy says it was different for him, but he certainly didn't show it. Some men right off look you over and just look at you in a way that you know what they're thinking, but he just acted friendly, like he thought I was a nice person and he enjoyed talking to me.

"It's my birthday too," I said. "I'm thirty today."

"You look a lot younger."

I shrugged. I didn't know what to say, like, "You look a lot older?" I just said, "You're Gemini too."

"Right."

"Do you think it suits you? I mean, do you want two things at once a lot, contradictory things, impossible things?"

He smiled. "Of course. . . . Doesn't everyone want impossible things?"

"I think Becky said you were a lawyer?"

He made a funny expression. "Well, yeah . . . I was. I am, actually, but I'm thinking of changing." He told me his father was a big lawyer in a big New York law firm and he'd felt he had to go into law to please his father, but he hated it. "I think I'm basically an anarchist," he said.

I wasn't sure what that was. I thought they were Russians. "So, what're you going to do?" I asked.

"I'd like to do something with design." He said he wasn't sure if he should get an architectural degree or just take some design courses.

Then I told him how I never even finished college, though I completed two years, and how I used to be interested in design too. "I dropped out to marry Mo," I said apologetically.

"Who's Mo?"

"My husband." I pointed to where he was still sitting talking to Nelson Westerling.

I saw Benjy take a long look at him. It's funny. I know women always size each other up, but I never knew men did it too. He said later he was hoping Mo would be a fat, cigar-chomping businessman type and was really disappointed he wasn't.

"Will your father mind," I asked, "about your switching?"

"Sure, he'll definitely mind. . . . But, hell, I'm thirty! Am I supposed to live my whole life according to what my father wants?"

"No," I said. "I don't think you should."

"If only my older brother, Stef, had gone into law," he said. "It would've been perfect."

"What does he do?"

"Well, it's a long story. First he decided to be a rabbi and he entered Union Theological Seminary. Then, after about a year, he decided he didn't believe in God and he wanted to be a doctor so he got into medical school. But after two years of that he decided he wanted to be a rabbi, after all. So he went to Israel for a year and came back, again deciding he didn't believe in God and maybe didn't like Jews all that much either. He went back to medical school and now he's training to be a psychiatrist."

I had been thinking how nice his eyes were, but also half listening. "He sounds like an indecisive person," I said finally.

"Terminal. Worse than me. It runs in the family. . . . My sister has dropped out of college four times already and she's just twenty-three."

"To get married?"

"I forget. Once to get married, only she didn't. Once because she needed 'space.' I don't remember the other two times."

"It must be hard for your parents."

"Probably." He didn't sound that concerned about it. "What do *your* parents do?"

I hesitated. "They run a pet store in Sloatsburg." Try to imagine what it would be like if every time anyone asked you, "What do your parents do?" you had to say, "They run a pet store in Sloatsburg." I mean, everyone else's parents are lawyers or doctors or engineers or businessmen. In college—I know this is terrible—I used to lie about it sometimes. I'd just make up what they did or I'd steal other people's parents. Like, Jeanette's father is a radiologist and her mother's a registered nurse; I used them a lot of times. It's everything, not just the pet store but even the name: Sloatsburg! It must be the ugliest name of a place for someone to come from in the world.

But Benjy didn't look that disgusted. He just said, "Do they have tropical fish? I'm thinking of getting some for the girls. Why don't you give me their address?"

The thing is, they do have tropical fish, but there are hundreds of better places if he wanted really fancy ones. But I didn't want to do my parents out of business, so I gave him the address. Even if you have the address, you could walk right past the store without even noticing it. About the only interesting thing is this big goldfish in a tank in the window. He's really big, about six inches long and swims around there all by himself. When I was really little I used to have this game where I talked to him and he talked back. I called him Marvin—I don't remember why. Then one day, when I was around eight, I noticed that he had some black spots on his stomach that he hadn't had the last time. I told my mother and she told me it wasn't the same fish, that they had to change the fish every six months or so because they died. I was so shocked! Even though I'd known it was imaginary, I still thought it was at least the same fish.

At around that point in the conversation Benjy finally took the steaks off the grill and we all had dinner outside. After dinner I went into the house to go to the bathroom. It's a gigantic gray stone Victorian house with turrets, bay windows, a huge porch sweeping around one whole side. All the land around it is beautifully planted with willow trees, a flower garden, the kind of gracious living that seems effortless, but you know it took tons of money, time, and years of knowing how to do that kind of thing. The inside of the house was the same—delicate flowered wallpaper, antique-looking desks, a harpsichord even! I felt so ambivalent about it, guilty to even be thinking such critical thoughts. Really, I like modern things myself that don't take much fuss and bother. I'd go crazy in a house like that, even with a million servants. But it all seemed to imply some kind of qualities and virtues I don't have: neatness, decorousness, serenity. I don't mean I'm a total slob and I think our house is really nice, but as I looked around the bathroom with matching towels that looked fresh out of the laundry, my heart sank.

Going back, I passed their daughters' room. It was around the size of our living room, but fixed up in an old-fashioned way with a rocking chair and lots of stuffed animals on a wicker bench and a huge dollhouse with a gabled roof. Their daughters were kneeling in front of the dollhouse, playing with it.

"Do you want to see it?" Chelsea, the older one, asked. She looks like Becky, round and friendly, with thick brown hair. Dawn, the little one, is shy but with Benjy's big brown eyes.

I went into the room and right away they both started telling me all about the dollhouse, who lived in it, why there was a rubber giraffe on the chimney and a large white china snail in the front parlor. It was really two bookcases back to back, on wheels so they could play on both sides of it, and on top of that a real dollhouse. Some of the rooms were fixed up in a regular way, but some were really strange. One had just a plastic board with holes in it with a reclining chair in the middle holding a grungy-looking Barbie doll. "That's the Green Goddess Beauty Salon," Chelsea explained. "They go there to get fixed up."

I always wanted a dollhouse when I was little, but I never even imagined one like this. It had a real piano that played music, real tiny newspapers and magazines, a fireplace with pokers, even a chess set! While I was in there, Becky looked in. "Oh, did you find the bathroom?" she asked.

I nodded and stood up. I felt like I could have spent all afternoon there, playing with the dollhouse. "It's such a beautiful dollhouse!" I said.

Becky looked pleased. "Isn't it? I love it too. At first I got upset that they move everything around, but that's the point really, for them to play with it the way they want. My mother was always so scared I'd break things, and by the time she really let me play with it, I was too old."

"Grandma's grouchy," Dawn explained.

"I never had one," I said. Then I was afraid that sounded plaintive and envious. I guess that was basically how I was feeling. Not about Becky's being married to Benjy. More just the big beautiful house and her having two daughters who seemed so sweet and quiet and cute. I looked at her pregnant stomach. "I guess you want boys this time?" I asked.

"No, I'm hoping for two more girls," Becky said. "I just love having daughters. And I've always had this fantasy of four daughters like in *Little Women*."

"We're moving out if she has boys," Chelsea said.

"Boys can be nice," Becky said quickly, as though afraid I'd be hurt since I had boys.

"No, they can't," Dawn said. "They can *only* be disgusting and mean!"

"Daddy isn't disgusting and mean," Becky said.

"He's not a boy," Chelsea said. "He's a man. That's different."

Becky and I went downstairs together. She was puffing from climbing the stairs. I'd never let myself gain that much, even for twins! When we came outside, Benjy came over and asked Becky if it was time for him to make the coffee yet. I noticed him look from her to me, but it was such a quick glance that it was more later that I remembered it. Then I just thought that he seemed a very considerate husband, remembering about the coffee.

And that's all, as far as the party goes. Except that driving home I felt in such a wonderful mood. It's true that if you have a June birthday it *is* lucky, because it's almost always a beautiful day. Blanche's birthday is the worst time of all! December twenty-fourth. I always felt guilty about that. I asked Mo if he'd had a good time and he said yes. He'd just spent the entire party talking to Mr. Westerling! Mo is like that. Mostly at parties he talks to men. I guess because he wants to talk about chess or politics or things like that. I don't think he'd ever talk to a woman unless he wanted to flirt with her.

"Did you think they were nice?" I asked.

"Who?"

"The Fettermans."

He shrugged. "All I saw was her stomach. . . . And the steak was tough as nails."

"I think he cooked it a little too long," I said.

That was June seventh.

Okay! So June twenty-second I was doing the food shopping for the week. I do it once a week and if we run out, Mo picks things up on the way home. I'm fairly organized about that. I was wheeling my cart along the meat section, when I saw Benjy. He had two carts. One he was pushing, the other pulling. You should have seen how much food he had! I've never bought that much in my life. Even if you added together what I get every week for four weeks, it wouldn't be that much. He had three whole prime ribs of beef, millions of lamb chops, chickens, frozen vegetables.

"Hi," I said, wheeling my cart next to him.

"Oh hi." He turned around, looking pleased to see me.

"What are you doing here?" I asked. "I mean, how come you're doing the shopping?"

He smiled. "Because I'm a good and dutiful husband."

I laughed. "I guess I must be a good and dutiful wife too, huh?"

"Sure."

Then we wheeled our carts around together. He just took things off the shelf. I don't think *once* he stopped to look at the prices of anything! Once he took four cans of spaghetti sauce for forty-nine cents each when about a foot away was a big sign: Spaghetti Sauce— thirty cents each! I guess if you're rich, you just don't care. "I just do this once a month," he said apologetically while the checker was ringing everything up.

It was another beautiful day, maybe even more beautiful than the day of the party, warmer anyway. "Can I drive you home?" he asked.

How did he think I got there? "I have my car," I said.

"Oh." He sighed, looking around. "Let me help you load every-thing." He did that and then said dreamily, "What a gorgeous day!"

"Yes." Usually I talk a lot, but I couldn't think of anything to say. It was awful. "It's a good day for a picnic," I said.

His face lit up. "It is, isn't it? Why don't we?"

"What?"

"Let's go on a picnic!"

"You mean right now? Right this *second?*"

"Sure." He glanced at his watch. "It's twelve-thirty, time for lunch. I have enough stuff for fifty picnics!"

"What if everything thaws?"

"No, it'll keep. . . . Where should we go? Are there any parks around here?"

It was like suddenly we were going on this picnic, even though I couldn't remember saying I would. I told him about Stewart Park, where I used to take the kids. It's on a lake and so big, it's quiet, even on weekends. "You lead the way," he said. "I'll follow."

In the car I suddenly felt good, though I was still worried about the food. I had about twenty frozen things: fruit, pancakes, vegetables. And some meat too. But he had even more stuff and he didn't seem at all worried, so I decided not to worry either.

We sat down on the grass near the lake and Benjy rummaged around in his fifteen bags for something to eat. He came back with rye bread, sliced tongue, strawberries, a box of chocolate fudge cookies, beer. It was just like a real picnic.

I stuffed a slice of tongue in a piece of bread and folded it over. Benjy made a regular sandwich for himself and opened two cans of beer, one of which he handed to me. I can get high pretty fast, even from one can of beer, so I sipped it slowly.

"I'm vaguely on a diet," I said. I decided to eat just my half a sandwich and some strawberries and maybe one cookie.

That time he really did look me over. I was wearing just jeans and a T-shirt. "You don't look like you need to be."

I turned red. "I just don't want to get fat," I said, and then thought maybe that was tactless, considering the way his wife looks.

"I'm five nine and I used to weigh two hundred pounds," he said, biting into his sandwich.

"Really? How did you *get* so fat?"

He laughed. "It was easy. Just ate nonstop till I was fifteen."

"And then what happened?"

"Then I got this job as a lifeguard and my uncle, who got me the job, said I had till the end of July to lose or else he'd fire me. He said I was a disgrace. He shamed me into it. I lost almost a hundred pounds that summer."

"That's a lot," I said. It was hard to imagine him so fat. He didn't seem like the fat type.

Then we just lay there on the grass, looking out at the lake, talking a little, drinking beer and getting gradually drunk. Not horribly, just enough so I totally forgot about the frozen food and didn't especially care if I ever got home.

"What does your husband do?" he said.

"He's a businessman. He runs a career counseling firm." It was right then, for some reason, that I started feeling attracted to him. I don't know why then. Maybe just from feeling relaxed. Also I could tell he was feeling the same thing. We kept having these awkward exchanges, like we couldn't keep a conversation going about *anything!*

"Becky's due in six weeks," he said.

"I know," I said.

Then suddenly I leaned over and kissed him. I just did it, like that, not planning it or anything. I don't do things like that usually. I mean I have sometimes, but not often. He looked pleased, but embarrassed. "So what now?" he said wryly.

I shrugged.

"Did I tell you I was happily married?"

"I forget. I think so." All I wanted to do was kiss him again. I wasn't thinking so much beyond that.

He sat up. "I believe in monogamy," he said. "My wife is a good and terrific person and I love her. She's a wonderful mother. I believe in the importance and sanctity of the family."

"I'll vote for you," I said. "What are you running for?"

Then he lay down and kissed me again. "I just wanted to make myself perfectly clear." That kiss lasted a longer time and when it was finished, we were both somewhat disheveled. "Where should we go?" he asked. He looked a little dazed.

I thought of the Fairmont. When I used to take Linus to this doctor about his not speaking, I always turned off Route Six Eighty-four and passed a place that said Fairmont Motel. It always had a Vacancies sign outside and I wondered if anyone ever went there.

It was like the picnic. I drove and he followed in their station wagon. I think the fact that Mo was away in L.A. and wouldn't be back for two days definitely made the whole thing easier. Also that feeling you get when you're high that whatever is happening isn't really happening. I mean, you know it is, but it's all a little blurry.

"What do I do?" he said nervously after we'd parked the cars. "Do I make up a name? I never did this before."

"Me neither." I waited, and after about five minutes he came out with a key.

I'm trying to think how to describe what it was like. In the beginning it was extremely awkward, and then suddenly it wasn't. What I like with Benjy is how careful and loving he is when we make love, even that first time when we hardly knew each other. Mo is a million times more experienced, but sometimes he just pounces on me, like he's horny and I'm there, and I hate that! We kissed for a long, long time and he kept stroking my body with this sort of awed expression, like I was some precious vase. It seems like with some people you just fit together in every way, emotionally and physically. You don't even have to try! That's what it was like.

Afterward, we lay there, not speaking, till finally Benjy said dreamily, "You know, it's strange, I don't regret this at all. I wonder if that makes me a moral degenerate."

That sounded so awful: moral degenerate! "I don't either," I said.

"It's probably like radioactive fallout," he said. "Twelve hours from now I'll probably be radiating guilt and anxiety from every pore, but right now I feel terrific."

We were still touching all the length of our bodies, and my hair was hanging over his shoulder. "How many people have you done it with?" I asked. "Altogether?"

"You mean before I was married?"

I nodded.

"About half a dozen."

"Just that many?"

"Yeah, why?"

"I thought men always did it with millions of people!"

"I got married at twenty. . . . How many have you done it with, besides me and your husband?"

I hesitated. "No one besides you," I lied.

Blanche says you have to lie to men about that, that no matter what they say, they go berserk if they know you've done it with anyone but them. I never told Mo about the other two people either, and I never will. One, the first one, was my cousin, Andrew. I was sixteen. See, my mother and Andrew's mother, my Aunt Marsha, are sisters and are extremely close. They talk to each other every day on the telephone. They're closer to each other than to their husbands, I think. Almost every summer Blanche and me and Andrew (who was Blanche's age, two years older than me) and Andrew's sister, Suzie (who was two years older than him), went to Atlantic City together. When we were little, all of us shared a room. In fact, I never thought of Andrew as a boy. I saw him naked millions of times, taking baths, on the beach. Then this one summer Suzie and Blanche were both away. Blanche was on a bicycle trip, a youth hostel thing, and Suzie had a job in New York, as a receptionist at a place that sold fur coats. (That's how I got that job there the next summer.) Andrew was working too—it was the summer before he entered college and he had a job as a part-time taxi driver. He used to come back really late, at two or three in the morning. Normally I wouldn't have even heard him. I would've just slept through it, but I was sleeping really badly that summer. Either I wouldn't fall asleep till late or I'd wake up and toss and turn. I don't know what it was. I'd broken up with my high school boyfriend that spring. I didn't have anyone else. Maybe it was just horniness or anxiety because the next year I'd have to apply to college and wasn't sure who would take me (my SATs in math especially weren't that great).

One night, hearing Andrew come back, I went downstairs. I was in my nightgown with a cotton robe over it, but they were both short, just reaching to my knees. Like I said, I thought of Andrew more as in between a brother and a boy who's been in your class since you were three, someone I knew so well that I never would have thought of him romantically, even if there hadn't been the fact of our being cousins. Plus, he was engaged to marry someone, a girl from California he'd met the summer before. Both my mother and my aunt were mildly hysterical about that. (In fact, he didn't marry her in the end, but not because of them.) When I came downstairs, the two of us sat a while in the kitchen, talking, and then he asked if I wanted to take a walk on the beach. I said sure.

I've talked to Andrew about this since (he's happily married to a really nice girl, Ann-Marie, and they have two kids) and he says he felt about me pretty much the way I felt about him, that when he said, "Let's take a walk," he really had in mind just that, not that anything would happen. He was a virgin too—that girl he was engaged to didn't let him get very far evidently. But it was a beautiful summer evening, and, without even thinking about it, we started holding hands and then he put his arm around me and pretty soon we were lying down on my robe making out and all of a sudden we were doing it. It happened so fast that we were sort of shell-shocked afterward. We didn't say a word, just raced back to the house. Without talking about it, I think we both realized that our mothers would kill us if they knew. Maybe Andrew even more than me. I don't even mean that metaphorically: I mean they might have actually *killed* us! So needless to say, we weren't planning on doing it again. Except a few nights later I heard him come in at around two-thirty—both my mother and his mother slept on the upper story and slept like logs—and went down to the kitchen again, we took a walk on the beach again, and guess what?

All in all we did it maybe six or eight times. After about the third time we confessed how hysterically nervous we both were about Mom and Aunt Marsha, but when we started imagining them knowing, we laughed so hard we couldn't stop. And Andrew told me right off that he'd been a virgin and he didn't know anything about sex, except from his fantasies, and since it was the same with me, it was comfortable. We horsed around a lot and imagined what our future spouses would say if they ever knew, but agreed we'd never *ever* tell them. Andrew's never told Ann-Marie either, and I'm glad because I like her a lot.

So, that was how I lost my virginity officially and I guess, as ways to do it go, it wasn't bad. Maybe the almost-incest taboo made it exciting.

But when I went to college, I decided to be what Jeanette calls a born-again virgin. No one ever asked me point-blank are you, but if they had, I'd have lied. I really decided then to wait till I'd met someone I was crazy about and was engaged to. Only one day I had to interview this guy, Harvey Stempler, for the college newspaper.

He was on the basketball team and even though the NYU team never did especially well, with him they were doing better. I went over to interview him and there was this total hunk. I know that's a stereotype and maybe lots of basketball players are really sensitive, bright people underneath, but I'm sorry, this guy was a hunk and nothing but. He was six feet five and had a perfect body. I mean *totally* perfect—very broad shoulders, a tiny waist, just enough muscles, but not like those bulgy awful men in muscle-building ads. I interviewed him or tried to while he just sat there, chewing gum, and looking at me like he wanted to fuck me. I'm sure that was one of his two and a half expressions. Can you imagine someone who doesn't even stop chewing gum for an interview? You'd think it would lose its taste! I'd ask him to describe how it felt to make a winning shot and he'd say, "It felt good," and I'd say, "Good in what way?" and he'd say, "Just good. . . . You know, like the way you feel when something good happens. You just feel good." I knew I'd have to go home and translate it into normal English or they might kick him out of school.

But it was strange. I was totally transfixed by this guy's physical presence. Not just his body but his physical self-confidence and seemingly total lack of dividedness over who he was. It was like he was all body and no head! After the interview he said, "Hey, you want to come over to my place for a beer?" With some guys you might not have known what that entailed. They might have literally wanted to just sit around and have a beer and talk, but with Harvey Stempler it was clear. Women were to fuck, period. He had obviously made it with nine million girls—I'm sure he'd lost track years earlier—and probably no one ever turned him down or, if they did, you could tell he didn't lose any sleep over it. You might think, given that, why did I bother, but I'd never done anything like that and there was something so wonderfully clear-cut about it. It wasn't as hard as it might have been with someone you really hoped would want to see you again. We went back to his place and fucked: that was it. I got what I came for. He wasn't such a terrific lover—I have the feeling guys that look like that never are. They don't have to be. But it was still a sexy experience, just stroking his body, being with someone with none of the usual hang-ups about women. We even parted in a friendly way. Just "See you around," no promises about other dates. In fact, ironically, he called me after I was engaged to Mo and asked if I was busy that Saturday (it was a Thursday). I said, "I'm getting married." I didn't mean that *very* Saturday, but he said, "Oh . . . well, have a good wedding." He didn't sound too devastated.

When I lied and said I hadn't had sex with anyone but him and Mo, Benjy just accepted it as normal, though he did say, "A lot of guys must've tried, I imagine."

"The normal quota," I said. Then I leaned over and began kissing him again. I wasn't necessarily thinking of making love again. He just looked so nice lying there, but he pulled away with an alarmed expression.

"Listen," he said. "I've really enjoyed this. I don't have any regrets at all, but this is it. I can't. . . . My wife is having twins in six weeks!"

"I know!" So she was having triplets or sextuplets? Would he not even be here, then? I felt awful, like even kissing him was forbidden.

I must have looked hurt because he pulled me over to him and said in a gentle, kind voice, "It's me. I'm just not the type for what you're looking for."

That got me so mad. "What do you mean? I'm not looking for anything! I was just wheeling my cart around the Grand Union. I didn't know you'd be there."

He looked abashed. "I just meant, I'm not even the right person for a fling, much less anything else. I'm a combination of terrible traits. I take everything much too seriously, *and* if I get carried away, I'm a complete maniac."

"In what way?" I was worried. I wasn't sure what he meant. Did he have a jail record or something?

"I just meant, you need a cool, sophisticated guy who—"

I socked him. "Stop that! I don't need *anyone!* I love my husband and I have two kids."

"Good," he said. "No, seriously, that's perfect. Because I love my wife and I have two kids, well, almost four, which makes it even worse."

"Why does that make it even worse?"

He cleared his throat. "What I'm trying to say is you're gorgeous and extremely sexy, but I would go insane if. . . . I don't even know what profession I'm in and I'm thirty years old! We're living on my wife's money. And it's like Kipp said—he's my best friend—about affairs. He said, 'If it's bad, why bother? And if it's good, it wrecks your marriage.'"

"What does he know?" I said. I knew I was sounding belligerent, but I couldn't help it. "I mean, has he ever done it?"

"He tried, but it didn't work. It started getting good and he started going crazy. Well, I'm like that but *worse!* You'd be getting a basket case. I'd probably be impotent, God knows what."

What was ironical was he was lying there with an erection, but I decided not to mention that. "Look, who says I'm looking for *anything?*" I said. "I don't happen to think you're right, but stop putting words in my mouth, okay?"

"Okay."

Then we both lay back, disgruntled. There was a long pause.

"Christ," Benjy said, "what kind of a schmuck am I? After all this, I still want you." I guess he'd noticed he had an erection also.

I couldn't help smiling. "Well, we're here. . . . Is twice so much worse than once?"

He started kissing me. "I don't know. Let's find out."

It was better the second time, despite or maybe because of our argument. It was like we both knew (or thought) it would be the last time and we were more playful. For some reason, I didn't come, I don't know why. You'd think it would be easier the second time. Usually it is. Jeanette says she has a foolproof way to come. She just imagines one of the pornographic stories we used to write in high school about Amanda and Valerie and, bingo, it happens. I tried that once but it didn't work.

But it was still extremely nice, and when it was done, we lay there together calmly, peacefully. "I think if I don't get out of here extremely rapidly," Benjy said, "I could be in *very* big trouble."

"Why?"

"I'm teetering on the verge of being madly in love with you."

That made me feel wonderful! I think I already *was* in love with him, but I didn't know it. "You can teeter back," I suggested.

We started getting dressed. "My brother always said to stay away from blonds," Benjy said, but affectionately.

"I'm not a natural blond," I said, fastening my bra. "You can relax. . . . It's just light brown."

I think maybe it's true: men *are* more ill at ease with blonds. Jeanette says they feel ill at ease with any woman they're attracted to, no matter what their hair color, but I think being blond makes it worse. But I don't even know if I'd recognize myself anymore with light brown hair! The reason we did it—Jeanette changed her hair style the same weekend when we were both in tenth grade—was because of this book we were reading, *Betsy in Spite of Herself* by someone named Maud Hart Lovelace. In the book, Betsy and her best friend, Tib, decide (they were in tenth grade too) to completely change their looks and personalities. Betsy, who's a friendly girl with brown hair, decides to act exotic and mysterious, use a lot of Jockey Club perfume, wear mainly green (her eyes are green), and throw a lot of foreign expressions into her conversation like *"Nicht wahr?"*; and Tib, who's small and blond but very practical and can make sauerbraten and dumplings and fix furnaces, decides to laugh provocatively and act helpless and silly. It doesn't work with Betsy, but Tib does it for the rest of her life, almost.

What Jeanette and I decided was I should be an all-American girl. Even with my Jewish nose. I should be blond and neat and become good at some sport, like golf or tennis. In fact, I was and am a hopeless klutz, but we decided I should pick some easy sport and just get good enough to look good. I was supposed to act jaunty and lighthearted, and toss my hair back, making fresh, but not mean, comments to guys. Jeanette decided to leave her hair the same color—black—but to get a perm so she went from her hair totally straight to this big curly mass. We decided she would be the bohemian, "interesting" type with dangling earrings and vibrant color combinations like purple and orange at the same time.

In the end, I gave up on sports, and Jeanette, though her hair is still puffy and curly, gave up orange and purple together when she went into market research, but for a while, for the last years of high school, if we went to a dance and met two boys we didn't know, they always said, "You two are so different! How come you're friends?" Whereas in fact we're a lot alike.

I left the motel first. I'd left the kids with Alice, our baby-sitter, and I suddenly felt a little guilty about that because it was five and I'd said I'd be home by three. I've been late other times, but never *that* late. When I got there, she looked all worried and said she'd been afraid I was in an accident. I made up some story about the car breaking down, paid her extra, and checked on the boys, who seemed fine.

When I unloaded the groceries I realized the true wages of sin. The meats looked all pinkish gray and the frozen stuff was totally melted. I decided to take a chance with the frozen stuff, but I had to pitch the meat. What if I poisoned the kids by mistake? I wondered what Benjy would say when he got home. Three prime ribs of beef! If I was his wife, I'd kill him, but she seems like a calmer, nicer person. And, like I said, they have money so maybe it won't matter so much.

Just as I was about to throw the meat away, the phone rang. I thought it might be Mo because he usually calls the evening he goes away. But it was Benjy.

"Is your food okay?" I asked. "Did everything melt?"

"I don't know. . . . I haven't unloaded it yet."

"Where are you?"

"In a drugstore. . . . Listen, I know this is both an insane *and* totally irresponsible thing to say, much less think, but I think I am madly in love with you."

"Me too," I said, so excited I could hardly speak. "Totally."

"Okay," he said. "I've got to go. Remember, everything I said before is still true. This is *not* a policy change."

"I'll remember."

I hung up feeling so excited and happy I told the boys we would go out for pizza and that I'd take them to any movie they wanted to see. Blanche says that one thing it's hard for her patients to realize is that no matter how well they've been analyzed, no matter how well adjusted they become, they're still not going to be happy all the time. In fact, maybe no more than they were when they were crazy. She says everyone is just allotted a certain number of happy days. I think that's true. If you were religious, you could think of God sitting there with a big book, checking off, "Okay, she's had four happy days this year. That's it," or ten or however many he'd decided was the right number. I do think there are some people who don't even *like* being happy, who, if they're happy, are miserable. But I'm not like that. I *like* being happy! Only I'm not, in the way I felt that night, all that often. It was like some scene out of a musical comedy where suddenly everyone starts to sing and dance and leap all over the stage.

The kids took it in their stride. I didn't even get mad when Aaron started snorting up his Coca-Cola and it came out of his nose, or when Linus spilled his chocolate milk shake all over the table and then just sat there while it soaked into his jacket and slacks. I took them to some unbelievably idiotic movie and let them have buttered popcorn and giant candy bars that'll probably ruin their teeth forever. When we got home, Linus was already asleep, but Aaron said, "This was really a great day! This was one of the best days of my *life* practically."

I felt the same way.

There's a song from *Finian's Rainbow* Benjy had to learn when he was in high school. He went to this small, strange, very left-wing school where the principal was called up before the House Un-American Activities Committee. He said in nineteen-forty-eight, when they had a class election, Henry Wallace got almost all the votes. I never even heard of him! The song he sang was "If This Isn't Love." It's kind of dopey, but the trouble is, I can't get it out of my head.

> If this isn't love, the whole world is crazy
> If this isn't love, I'm daft as a daisy
>
> If this isn't love, then winter is summer
> If this isn't love, my heart needs a plumber.

Oh, and there's a part which Benjy always horses around while he's singing:

With this I cannot grapple, because, because
You're so adorabelle!

The other line he likes is:

I'm getting tired of waiting and sticking to the rules
This feeling calls for mating
Like birds and bees
And other animules.

Benjy says that's the story of his life: sticking to the rules. But isn't
it the story of everybody's, more or less? Like with Blanche and me,
she was more conforming and did better at school, but occasionally
she'd do wacky things like break off her engagement to Dwight, her
husband, two weeks before the wedding and then, four years later,
get engaged to him again and actually marry him. Blanche has this
theory that Jews should never intermarry. She says all Jewish husbands are unfaithful, that if they meet bright women, they're threatened, and if they meet dumb women, they're bored so they boing
back and forth from being threatened to being bored all their lives.
Her husband is an ear, nose, and throat doctor, and, if you ask me,
he's supremely boring, but they seem to be happy.

With Benjy he says it was being the middle child—that his older
brother was always a problem, going from being a rabbi to being a
doctor and back again, and his younger sister, who's really pretty,
sleeps with lots of guys which horrifies his mother. So the only role
left for him was to be "good." Only he hates it. He only became a
lawyer because his father is this very big-deal lawyer who started his
own firm and who wanted at least one of his children to carry on the
family trade. "Ginger would've made a terrific lawyer," Benjy says
(that's his sister), "but she can't sit still long enough to even finish
college."

What's strange is that I've been seeing Benjy for three months
now and it doesn't (so far) seem to have affected my sex life with Mo,
knock on wood. It's true I almost always think of Benjy when we're
doing it, but how is that so much worse or different than thinking of
Gregory Peck or some handsome guy you've seen on the street that
day? Probably Mo's doing the same thing.

I wonder why Benjy seems to me to be so much better a lover than Mo when Mo has had so much more experience. Maybe that's why, partly. I feel like since Benjy hasn't done it with so many people, each one is important. And also I always feel with Mo sex is a kind of abstraction. Like once he told me about the time he did it with two women at once. "I just wanted to see what that was like," he said, as an explanation. Or once he was walking down the street and some very tall elegant black woman winked at him and he took her home and they spent the weekend together. "I'd never done it with a black woman before," he said. But, like I say, it's almost abstract, wanting to see what it's like in this situation or that situation. Whereas Benjy, I think, is more like me. It's more being in love with the person that counts.

I know Mo's been unfaithful since we've been married. At parties he used to come on to women much more, even with me right there, until I started screaming at him about it, but probably he just does it when I'm not around. When he travels, for instance. He says he'll call whenever he has to be out of town and he does, but I always feel he makes the call and then breathes a sigh of relief: whew, now I can go out and do whatever I want. I used to be much more jealous than I am now. Because I could never buy all that shit about men being naturally unmonogamous and women being naturally monogamous. We'd probably do it a lot more too if we weren't scared of getting pregnant or of not being able to support ourselves and all that. Well, maybe not a lot more, but somewhat.

I knew Jeanette was going to call on Thursday afternoon—she always does, every other month. But I wasn't sure how to bring the topic up. We talked about various other things—our kids, her job— till finally I asked, "Do you believe in crime and punishment?"

"You mean, like in Dostoevsky?"

"I mean, like in life."

"Explain."

I cleared my throat. "Well, I mean, say you do something bad, not so much bad, but something you shouldn't have done—do you think necessarily you have to pay for it some time, either immediately or in the future?"

There was a long pause.

"Who is he?" she asked.

I told her.

"I had one of those once," Jeanette said with a sigh.

"One of who?" I hated her putting Benjy down like that.

"Tied to his wife's apron strings. You end up spending more time talking about their guilt than fucking. It's not worth it. Cut your losses, kid."

"But I'm in love with him!" I wailed.

"Seriously?"

"Of course seriously." I hesitated. "And he is with me. He says he's never . . . with his wife it just—"

"I know, I know. I can finish the sentence for you."

"Don't be sarcastic, please. It hurts my feelings. You're the only person I've told."

Her voice softened. "I'm sorry, hon. . . . Well, let it play itself out, take its course, whatever. You can't predict what will happen."

"Don't you ever—I mean, you must meet men all the time on your job," I said. "You don't ever feel like. . . ."

"Not really," Jeanette said. "Maybe I got it out of my system. Remember I married at twenty-eight. Six years of screwing around wears you out."

"How many people did you do it with altogether?" I'd never asked her that, point-blank.

There was a pause.

"You don't have to tell me if you don't want."

"No, I'm just thinking. . . . Oh, say two dozen, as a rough estimate."

"Two dozen!" I was impressed, surprised. "And, well, were you basically glad about all of them?"

"Maybe not all. I might scratch a couple, but I don't regret the fact of it. I mean, now I won't ever be like you. I won't ever sit there wondering what it's like with a Catholic or with a brain surgeon or with a married man or with an ex-priest or with a—"

"An ex-*priest?*"

"Yeah, that one was fun, actually. He was married to an ex-nun who was pregnant, so—talk about guilt! And my being Jewish made it something forbidden beyond his wildest dreams. I felt like Marlene Dietrich in *The Blue Angel*. I wonder what happened to him. I should look him up if I'm ever in Boston."

"So, what do you think I should do?"

"I think if you go back to college, which I think is a super idea, and get a job, you won't need him. He's a stop-gap. You're lonely, you're bored, so of course fucking twice a week gives you some kind of routine, something to look forward to. I used to feel that way the summer I was fired and all I had to do was go for electrolysis twice a week. Horribly painful, but it gave me something to do."

Imagine comparing making love with Benjy to electrolysis! How awful!

"It's *not* just that! We *love* each other! The sex is wonderful! It's not just being lonely and bored!"

"So, relax and enjoy."

There was a pause. "Okay," I said weakly. "I'll try."

"How old did you say his two youngest are?"

"Six weeks. . . . They're twins, Robin and Roper."

"Roper? What kind of name is that?"

"It's a family name. . . . In his wife's family, if you have four kids you name one of them Roper, whether it's a boy or a girl. She's a girl."

Jeanette sighed. "I don't know, I mean Jews are crazy, lord knows, but would we ever name a kid Roper?"

"They call her Bear for short."

"Don't tell me any more. I think this is all I can handle for one day."

Actually, I think Jeanette's right. Roper! Especially for a girl. When you think of all the pretty names there are. Blanche didn't even name her daughter for two months because she couldn't decide between Francesca, Susanna, or Marianne. (She chose Marianne in the end.)

By the way, I know how Becky's family got their money. They're Quakers and evidently her great-grandfather invented something basic like the sewing machine. They weren't people who were especially acquisitive—but they felt it was their duty to the country to build factories to help people sew better and before they knew it they were insanely rich. Benjy says Becky's father's favorite saying is, "Never spend the capital. Live on the interest." I guess that's good advice if you *have* capital. He says Becky isn't at all money-minded, doesn't spend much on clothes or fixing up the house. She sounds like such a horribly virtuous person sometimes, the way he describes it. I hope she has some awful vice he's not telling me about or doesn't know about. Well, she's dull. And she doesn't like sex that much. I guess those aren't vices, though.

Last week I had a bad moment. I was in this sporting goods store, shopping for a baseball mitt for Aaron, when Becky came in. She was wheeling the twins in a big carriage—people had to sweep aside to make room for her. When she saw me, she waved gaily and I immediately felt really sick with guilt and fear. But I went over and peered in at the babies and said how cute they were. Actually, you could hardly see them because they were sleeping, turned to the side.

"So, you got what you wanted," I said.

"In what way?"

I swallowed. "You said you wanted two more girls."

She beamed. "Yes, I'm so happy. They were tiny at first, but now they seem fine."

I wonder if she's the kind who breast-feeds in public. I always hate those women who sit there so smugly, like: look what a maternal person I am, look at my big boobs which I'm not showing to be an exhibitionist but just because my poor babies are starving. I think those women must be awful mothers, the kind who slap their kids if they whine at the movies.

She was there to buy a tennis racket. "I really *have* to get into shape," she said. "I gained twenty-seven pounds. Of course, with twins you have to. . . . But now nothing fits! And I'm afraid if I get a whole new set of clothes, I'll never have the impetus." She tried waving around the racket that the salesman had brought her. "Do you play?"

"Sort of. . . . Not very well."

"Oh great! Let's play some time then. . . . I'm awful too."

I can't, I just can't play with Becky! "Actually I'm almost not a beginner, even," I lied. "I can't serve and my backhand hardly exists."

"Me too! . . . Oh, I'm so glad. All the women around here seem so terrifyingly good and energetic. I get winded after half an hour. Are Thursdays all right?"

Well, I usually fuck your husband on Thursday, but any other day. . . . "Um, it's also—I have a bad back and recently the doctor said it would be better if I took it easy. Maybe if it gets better. . . ."

"Super! I should take lessons anyway. Benjy isn't that good, but I know it drives him crazy to play with me. Either I can't get it over the net or I wallop it like a home run."

She finally bought a racket and left. I stood there, in a catatonic state, forgetting why I was there, who I was, and everything else. The salesman said, "Is that what you're looking for?"

I jumped. I looked down and saw I was still holding the mitt I'd picked up before Becky came into the store. "Is this okay for someone who plays . . ." But I couldn't remember which position Aaron plays. I looked in my purse: I'd written it down on a slip of paper. "An outfielder."

"Perfect," he said, and before I knew it, he was wrapping it up. While I was paying, I watched as Becky's car pulled out of the parking area. And before I could stop myself, I began imagining the car going over a cliff! No more Becky. How can I—with the twins in the car? I whisked the twins home. But even so—say she *was* killed? Is that what I'd really want? To be a stepmother to two baby twins and two little girls who would hate me? What would we do for money? Becky's father wouldn't subsidize our life, would he? And I'd have Aaron and Linus too. Six kids! The fantasy dribbled away.

This is so inconsistent and terrible, but I hate the thought that Benjy still makes love to her. I don't care if he thinks about me every second while he does it, or if she just lies there like a lump and counts sheep, or if they do it only once a month. I don't want them to do it *ever!* Which, as Benjy points out, would be the most suspicious thing of all. But the thing is, I can't believe he's just doing it out of duty. He must enjoy it in some way, he loves her. . . .

Does he love her? Sometimes I think: well, if he does, really, why does he talk about it so much? Doesn't that show a guilty conscience? I don't tell *him* every second how much I love Mo. I keep hoping we'll get through one time without his mentioning Becky. Last time we almost did. Only just as we were lying there, entwined, he said, "Oh God, I forgot to pick up Becky's birthday present. I wonder if the stores are still open."

And then, just as I was thinking what a perfect, wonderful afternoon it'd been, he started in on Becky's parents, whom they visit on special occasions. They live in some big mansion on the tip of Long Island with a special couple, the Marshalls, who've worked for them for a million years. Mrs. Marshall cooks and Mr. Marshall—Buffie—does the gardening. Benjy said how terrific it all was, how Becky's parents have the Marshalls eat with them. They don't think of them as servants, but as friends. And they eat only organically grown vegetables and healthy things like fish. Becky's mother has MS, but Benjy says her father is terribly attentive and kind to her and reads her poetry at night. They both know most of Emily Dickinson by heart. "They're just extraordinary people," he finished up as I was ready to howl in despair.

What if he meets my parents? He'll never want to make love with me again! "Maybe it's all a front," I said spitefully. "Maybe once you're gone, her father acts mean and surly and they go out and nosh on Hostess cupcakes and make the Marshalls crawl around on the floor, bringing things in their teeth."

Benjy hugged me. "Don't be jealous."

"I can't not be! I'm a jealous person! It's a basic part of my character."

"I love you. . . . Can't I also like my in-laws?"

"No!"

One more thing: Becky's an only child so evidently everything she's ever done they boast about nonstop. They've framed every picture she ever made, all her little poems from high school. "Only children are supposed to be extremely maladjusted," I said. "They don't know how to relate to other people."

Benjy laughed. He started rubbing my belly button. "Maybe that's why Becky and I get along so well. *I* don't know how to relate to other people either."

"You do so! Stop it!"

He stopped rubbing my belly button.

"I didn't mean stop that. I meant stop running yourself down. . . . You relate to *me*."

"Well . . ."

"Well, what?"

"Relating to you the way we are now isn't the most complex task in the world."

I felt like he'd chopped me in two. "You mean, it's just fucking and anyone can do that?"

"No, of course not." Benjy put his arms around me.

"That's what you meant," I accused him.

"It isn't. . . . What I meant was, you accept me as I am. You aren't that demanding, so far, and so—"

"So far?" What an awful conversation!

"Sweetie, please. . . . Why're you so explosive today? Wasn't it good? You seemed to be really happy before."

"Maybe we should just fuck and never talk about things," I said, turning away. "If we hadn't started talking about Becky's parents . . ."

"I *want* to talk about things," he said, pulling me close to him again. "I don't talk to anyone else."

That made me feel good again. Benjy says he has some men friends from college and work, like that awful Kipp who has all those terrible theories about affairs just based on doing it around twice with some person he hardly knew. But he says they don't talk about such intimate things. Or, if they do, they kind of skim around the topics. And he says with Becky—well, I know this from being married—they spend so much time talking about things like the house and the kids that that's about it.

Now that the twins are born, I can see Benjy is trying to search around in his mind for an excuse to keep seeing me. Before, I think it was that she was so pregnant they couldn't have sex. Why do men always have to have excuses? We're doing it because we're doing it! I mean, I feel guilty too, but not to the extent that I have to make up reasons which aren't even true.

"It's just," he said, "she's such a good person—such a terrific mother—"

"So?" I said, starting to get all upset again. "So am I! I'm a terrific mother too!" I'm not so sure of that, but I don't think I'm terrible. "Go ask my kids."

"I didn't mean you weren't," he said quickly. "I just meant, what justification is there for my being here?"

"You want to be. Look, you said how you hate being the kind of person who always sticks to the rules. So now you're not sticking to them. You ought to feel good."

He sighed. "See, that's the problem. I don't feel good if I do, but I can't seem to totally enjoy violating them either."

"No one totally does."

"*You* don't seem to have any problem with it." He sounded halfway between admiring and accusing.

"Sure I do. . . . I just don't talk about it every second!"

"Women are just more . . . direct," he mused. "Like the way you leaned over that day and kissed me. You knew what you wanted, you set the thing going—"

"I *didn't* know what I wanted! . . . Anyhow, *you* set it going by saying, 'Let's have a picnic.'"

"But you came up to me in the supermarket with that sexy smile."

"You smiled *back!*"

"Even at the party. You helped me raise the grill, you stood there talking to me for about half an hour instead of mingling with the other guests the way you're supposed to."

How can someone I passionately love get me furious so often? "Look, we're both guilty, okay? You're trying to make it sound like I'm the criminal and you're just the whatever-they-call-it to the crime."

"Accessory," he said glumly.

If I can get Benjy past that, he's fine. He's wonderful. But it's like each time we get past it and then—wham—the next time it starts all over. But, nothing's perfect, right?

When I got the letter from NYU saying I was accepted and could start again in January, I was so excited. By now I've decided Mo was right, it is a good idea. But I was also thinking how Benjy works in the city and how now we can meet there, maybe have dinner, everything. I got the catalogue and began circling courses that sounded interesting. I started having fantasies of getting all these wonderful jobs, earning lots of money. I know Mo wants me to find out how shitty and awful the working world is so I can appreciate his troubles more, but who says I'll be like him? Maybe I'll find something I'm really good at which I also like which also pays well. Some people must.

At Thanksgiving, Blanche and Dwight came over. They were staying with Mom and Daddy, but Mom had a terrible cold and had to stay home and Daddy never goes anywhere without her. Even though Blanche is older than me, she got a later start on a family, partly because of that thing of breaking off her engagement to Dwight and then marrying him four years later and then having trouble getting pregnant.

We sat around in the living room, having drinks. Linus and Aaron were being pretty good. Aaron came in about every five minutes asking when we were going to eat, but that was all.

"I can't get over the change in Linus," Blanche said. "He seems so well-adjusted now. After not speaking for, what was it, two full years?"

Blanche always does that, remembers every bad thing that you'd like her to forget. "It was more like eighteen months," I said.

"He's a terrific kid," Mo said. He and Blanche don't get along, though so far, this visit, they haven't had any major quarrels. He thinks she's pig-headed and bossy, and she thinks he acts condescending to me, as though he were a million times smarter.

"Now, actually, would be the perfect time to get therapy for him," Blanche said.

"Why now, when he's okay?" I asked.

"Because it's all underground now, waiting to come gushing out when he's a teenager."

I started feeling awful. "Why does it have to be underground? Maybe it just went away."

Blanche downed her whiskey sour. "It never goes away," she said firmly. "How can it? Where would it go? The person, the child, just learns to deal with it, but ultimately it trips them up again. . . . Aren't there any good doctors around here? There must be."

"It's just, I'm going to be so busy," I explained. I'd already told her about going back to school.

"Well it's your child," Blanche said. "I'm just telling you what *I'd* do."

"We believe in letting things fester," Mo said. "Hey, Dwight, want to go for a walk? Do we have time, hon?"

"Sure," I said. Here I have time to go twice a week to motels with Benjy and I can't take my own child to a therapist even when it might make all the difference in his later life. I thought of all those murder cases you read about where the neighbors all say what a quiet, pleasant boy he seemed to be. . . . I went into the kitchen to see how things were going.

"It's good you're going back to school," Blanche said, following me. "I'm surprised Mo's going along with it."

"It was his idea. He thinks all women should work, like his mother."

"Wait till you start earning more than him and he'll scream bloody murder."

At least that's one thing I don't have to worry about. I'll never earn more than Mo! I looked at Blanche. She was leafing through the NYU catalogue which I had out on the counter.

"Dwight seems sort of quiet," I said tentatively. "Is he okay?"

Actually Dwight almost never talks much. He's a tall, thin guy with glasses and a sort of glazed, impenetrable expression. "*I* don't know," Blanche said, wearily. "You tell *me*."

"What do you mean?"

"He's sick," she exploded. "He's just a sick, awful person. I hate him—not just for the way he is with me, but with the kids."

I felt shocked. Blanche's never said much about her marriage, and I'd assumed it was pretty much okay. Maybe, just as I wouldn't tell her very personal things about myself, she feels the same about me. "I thought—"

"I'll give you an example. Over the summer I had to work. I'd set up a mother's helper at our country place and commuted there every day, but still, the deal was he was supposed to be out there for the three weeks, just to be there. He didn't come out once! Not *once!*

Not even on Marianne's birthday. Didn't even call. He just stayed in our city apartment. Can you imagine? His own kid and he couldn't pick up the phone to call her on her birthday."

"Why is he like that?" I asked.

She sighed. "I don't *know*. He's a cruel person, but in such a passive way. I didn't notice it so much at first. Or maybe till it started showing itself with the kids, I didn't care." She lit a cigarette. "The other day I came home late, he was napping on the sofa and both kids were watching a horrible, scary Hitchcock movie. They're sitting there, tears streaming down their faces! Evidently they went in to him and said how scared they were and he told them to go back and watch the rest of it."

Mo has nine million faults, but he is basically good with the kids. I think I would kill him if he ever did something like that. "Maybe you should leave him," I suggested.

"I know. . . . I want to. I think about it every second, but they're so young, and I'm earning so little." Blanche is just working part time since the kids were born.

"Wouldn't he have to pay you alimony?"

She shook her head. "He'd just move to another state. They can't track down men like that, and how can I afford to spend the rest of my life in court? You know how many men pay alimony? About ten percent. . . . Yet I'm like a single parent now, as it is."

"Still, maybe it would be worth it, just for peace of mind." I was afraid I was sounding saccharine.

"Oh, peace of mind! Tell me about it." She shook her head. "And when I broke up with him before the wedding that time, I remember I felt so relieved."

"So, why did you marry him?" It did seem strange, doing it twice almost.

"I admired him in a way. The thing of his coming from this dirt-poor, crazy family in Kentucky where none of them went to college and getting out of that, becoming a doctor."

"A self-made man?"

"Right."

There was a long pause.

"You know what the worst thing is?" Blanche said. "The other night he was late coming home, like almost always, and I thought maybe he's been in an accident, and I realized I would feel happy if I learned he was dead. That's such an ugly feeling! I hate thinking of myself as someone who wants someone dead."

"I would leave him." I opened the oven to look at the turkey, feeling shaken by her intensity.

"You're such a baby, Marilyn," Blanche said bitterly. "Everything's always been so easy for you. You just don't know what it's like."

I reddened. "No, it hasn't. We've had lots of problems. . . . Mo sees other women sometimes," I said, just to throw something at her, "when he travels."

"So? They all do. That's all so minor, who fucks who."

My mouth felt dry. "Do you ever? I mean . . . is there anyone you like?"

"You're talking about men?"

I nodded.

"Not really. I mean, face it, I'm not that gorgeous, I don't have a 'winning way with men.'" She looked like she was going to cry. "I don't even want a sex life. I can live without that. I just want my kids to grow up happy, reasonably happy. I want to be able to have friends over." Her voice broke.

I hugged her. I felt terrible about everything she'd told me. "You will," I said. "I promise."

"Will I?" It's so rare for Blanche to act so vulnerable, turning to me for comfort.

"Definitely," I said, trying to sound cheerful and confident.

All during dinner I kept staring at Dwight. I never liked him, but I always thought it was me, that he thought I was dumb and not worth talking to. To be mean to your own kids is the worst. If I was Blanche, *I'd* want him dead for that too. . . . And I thought of how maybe in some ways she's right. I haven't had major problems in the sense she was talking about. I *have* led a sheltered life. "That's all so minor, who fucks who." I wonder if she'd think that if I told her about Benjy. I wonder what she'd say. That I was a spoiled brat who had a decent husband and couldn't resist fooling around just out of boredom? I won't tell her because I think she'd hate me even more if she knew. No, that's not true, she doesn't hate me, but she does think I've always gotten the best of things. I remember how after she had her nose done and I said I wasn't ever going to, she suddenly turned on me and said, "You don't have to! You don't even look Jewish! You have a *perfect* nose." That's not true. I don't have a perfect nose, but she said it like she would've yanked it off my face.

And when we were out once one summer and two guys picked us up and one of them said, "You're sisters?" in this incredulous way. You could tell he meant that I was pretty and Blanche wasn't. "Yeah, I'm the dog and she's the princess," Blanche said. "I carry her slippers around in my mouth." I think it's not so much the difference in our features—Blanche just has a longer, thinner face and lighter eyebrows. It's more her expression, which is always tense and worried, like either something had just gone wrong or was about to. She's really small, just over five feet, and built pretty much like a boy, which I guess never helped as far as men went.

I started thinking about how Thanksgiving must be going at Benjy's house, or rather at his in-laws'. Hannah, Buffie's wife, is probably bringing out a beautiful golden brown turkey, not a tough, overdone one like mine, and they're all sitting at this long rosewood table and Becky's mother is reciting Emily Dickinson, and the little girls probably have perfect manners, not spilling and snorting and saying "Ugh, what's *this?*" about everything they don't like. They don't even have TV! They sit around reading fairy tales in front of the fire after dinner and roast chestnuts. No wonder Benjy married a shiksa. He claims he isn't like that, that his other girlfriends in college were partly Jewish—that is, some were, some weren't—but then he admitted that when he met me at the party, he thought I wasn't. "I thought you were Scandinavian," he said. "Finnish. Like you probably skiied wonderfully." He should see me try to ski. I hardly make it up the tow.

"Why is turkey always so tough?" Aaron asked.

"Just dump a lot of gravy over it," Linus suggested. "Then you don't taste it so much."

"How come you didn't put marshmallows on the sweet potatoes?" Aaron asked.

"They're not good for your teeth," I said.

"Nothing that's good is good for you," he observed sagely. "What's for dessert?"

"We haven't finished eating the main course," Mo said. "Slow down."

"*I'm* finished," Aaron said. "Do I have to just sit here?"

"Go," Mo said. "Give us some peace and quiet."

Today is Thursday. I'll see Benjy on Tuesday. Four, almost five days. If I could have one wish, it would be to call him and speak to him right now. He gave me the number there "in case of emergency," but what could I say, even if I disguised my voice? Pretend to be someone from his office? I went in to clear. The phone rang.

"Hi," Benjy said softly. "Happy Thanksgiving!"

The kitchen door had swung shut. I lowered my voice. "Where are you?"

"In the bedroom, resting."

"Alone?"

"No, the whole family's right here. . . . How're things? Can you talk?"

"No," I whispered, "but I'm so glad you called."

Just then the door swung open. It was Blanche, bringing in the basket of rolls.

"I miss you," he said.

"Me too." I changed my voice. "Well, thanks for reminding me, and I'll send it in as soon as I can."

"Someone just came in?"

"Right, and, listen, have a happy Thanksgiving also." I hung up. My hand was shaking but I felt so happy.

"Who was that?" Blanche said.

"Um, Georgia. She works at the kids' school. She wants me to help out there next week."

"You won't have time for all that once you start classes, will you?"

"I guess not." I took the apple pie out of the oven.

"I like that, being so busy I don't even have time to think," Blanche said. She lowered her voice. "Listen, Mar, don't say anything to Mom or Daddy, okay? They know nothing and I don't want them to."

"Of course," I said.

"They want to think we're as happy as they've been." She stared out the window. "God, it's gotten dark. How bleak it looks! Want to play Scrabble after the pie?"

"Sure," I said. "I'd love to."

First Loves

I did a peculiar thing a few weeks ago. I went all the way to Sloatsburg to Marilyn's parents' pet store to buy some fish for the kids. I could've gone to the place five minutes from our house or the one I always pass on the way to work. But I had a sudden desire to see what it was like, an impulse. Marilyn says she's a "practical person with a streak of impulsiveness." Actually, I think that describes me better than her. She's more an impulsive person with a streak of practicality. Anyway, it was like she said: I could hardly find it, even though she'd written the address down clearly. Evidently they've had the place thirty years! It looked it, looked like they have the windows washed once a year, at best, and haven't basically changed the window display since they moved in. "Marvin" was in the window, swimming idly back and forth. Marvin, the Jewish goldfish with one hundred and one lives.

It's interesting how differently Marilyn and I grew up, so relatively close geographically. When *I* was a kid in Manhattan, almost everyone in my grammar and high school was Jewish. I thought that was the world and was surprised at Amherst to find so many non-Jews. Whereas Marilyn says her grammar school was almost entirely not Jewish, that she was even chased home from school one day by kids saying she'd killed Christ! I've never had any experience with things like that, except from books. In high school, she said, it was better but there was still a division and a carefully restricted social life, with non-Jewish sororities and fraternities. So when she went to college, *she* was surprised there were so many Jews! Her parents were odd about that too—kosher, but they went to Chinese restaurants and took food out: their favorite dish was lobster with shrimp sauce. For mine, the synagogue was a social thing, cultural rather than religious. I doubt either of them believe in God in any but the most mythical, vague way, if that.

In the end I didn't go in. I drove to a fish store closer to our house, and bought six guppies, four angelfish, and a small eel. Yet I felt guilty in some peculiar way and would to some extent have liked to meet Marilyn's parents, even though I haven't the slightest desire to have her meet mine. I want to keep that part of my life separate. My father's disappointed enough in me, as it is, now that I'm trying to break away from the law practice. I can almost imagine his expression: scornful, though in a totally under-the-surface way, like all his expressions. "And her parents run a fish store in Sloatsburg?" "Not a fish store, a *pet* store." "In Sloatsburg?" Not that they adore Becky's parents, but I think, deep down, they're impressed by their graciousness and tasteful manners.

At home I put the fish in the tank while the girls watched. Since the babies were born, they've been irritable and cranky. Even with the fish they seemed only half pleased.

"You should have gotten more of *those*," Chelsea said, pointing to the angelfish.

"We can," I said. "We have to see how they work out."

"Are they the kind that eat their babies?" Dawn asked. "Judy has a fish that did that. She ate all of them right after they came out."

"Well, fish get nervous, sometimes, just like we would if we lived in a tank," I explained. "But if we see one of them getting pregnant, we'll put her in a separate bowl so the others can't harass her."

"How can you tell when they're pregnant?" Chelsea asked, her nose almost against the glass.

"The booklet will explain," I said, giving them the little pamphlet I'd bought along with the fish.

"You should have had us come with you," Dawn said. "*We* should have picked. It's *our* tank."

"Next time," I promised.

Becky was pleased with my selection. "Where did you go to get them?"

"A place I heard about."

She was carrying one of the twins and was too preoccupied to inquire further. Becky is so happy now, with the twins flourishing. I wish there were a way to keep her always looking and acting so delighted with herself, the world, us as a couple. Maybe if I went to her and said, "Hey, I'm having an affair," she'd just say, "Fine! *I'm* so happy with the babies. *You* deserve something too." Sure. . . . No, more likely, she'd just stand there, looking anxious, bewildered, horrified, as Kipp said Ariel did when he made such a confession. There are times when I think Becky idealizes me to the point where if my true self, whatever that is, and her image of me stood side by side there'd be two totally different human beings, bearing only a passing resemblance to each other. At other times I feel she knows everything, but has a maternally accepting attitude: to love is to forgive. But I don't want to test it.

How I met Becky.

But before that comes that horrible, but triumphant summer as a lifeguard. Being fat all through school, and especially high school, fat and two grades ahead of myself, was like being trapped in some ghastly disguise. Maybe that was the point, but why? I don't think I'm a masochist, but there must have been something self-punishing in continuing it so long. But it's curious. Now that I've been relatively thin for as long as I was fat, I realize it's not that hard to continue *anything!* Once you get into a pattern, you adapt to it, without even realizing it. I got used to being ridiculed, an outcast. Though deep down I think I never stopped thinking to myself: some day I'll show them. Who? The kids in my class who couldn't have cared less? Actually they liked me, a lot of them. I was cuddly, innocuous, the class clown. Some of the girls thought I was "cute," meaning harmless; they'd never have to worry about me. I think to them my fatness meant I was devoid of sexual thoughts and intentions, whereas, if anything, like all the feelings you never expressed, it only fed on itself. I was probably one of the hornier guys in the school. A lot of the girls confided in me "as though I were a girl." Christ, there's a pattern too. I've always wormed my way into the confidence of girls and women through the guise of "a friend." Becky, definitely.

I didn't know Uncle Herman well. He was Mom's oldest brother and was the safety director at Jones Beach over the summer. At any rate, I don't remember seeing him as I was growing up. I think Mom didn't like the woman he married, who knows. Anyway, the summer I was sixteen, about to enter college, he said—all this conducted via phone—that he'd hire me as a lifeguard since I had all the proper qualifications. I excelled at swimming—in the water you're weightless! I showed up June twenty-fourth and walked hesitantly into his office. He was a tall, deeply tanned, baldish man. He looked up, irritated.

"I'm Benjy, Sophie's son?"

He looked me over with a glance so deeply scornful and disgusted it's a wonder I didn't dissolve on the spot. "What's the matter? What's wrong with you?" he said.

"Nothing," I stammered.

"You want me to hire you as a lifeguard?"

Since words had deserted me, I simply handed him my papers. He glanced through them, and then stood up. "Come with me."

I followed him, frozen with anxiety. I'd been counting on the job, the extra money, even had had fantasies that simply being a lifeguard would change my status with girls, just sitting there in that high chair. And saving people's lives! He hauled me over to a floor-length mirror in the front. "Look at yourself!" he commanded.

Would that it had been a fun-house mirror. That's the reason that short schlumpy little guy has a belly that makes him look eight months' pregnant, no legs, no neck. "You have some kind of glandular problem or what?"

I shook my head. For years, my parents had prayed that was the case. It seemed so much simpler than out-and-out hopeless gluttony.

He sighed. "You ought to be ashamed." he said. "Have you got psychological problems? What's your excuse?"

Shame and rage were battling back and forth inside me. "No excuse. . . . Listen, I'll get another job." Where? With who?

"Who's going to hire you? . . . Okay, Benjy, I'm going to do you a favor for which you'll thank me for the rest of your life. It's June twenty-fourth, right? So you report to duty July second, five pounds lighter, and every week after that you lose five pounds. So in four weeks you're twenty pounds lighter and by the end of the summer, you're a mensch. You know that word?"

I nodded. I knew that word.

"I don't care how you lose it. I don't want to talk about it *or* hear about it. But each week I'll weigh you, right here, on this scale, and if you haven't lost five more pounds, you look for another job. Okay, step on the scale!"

Even now, fifteen years later, I don't have the courage to say what I weighed. Use your imagination. It was bad. Uncle Herman wrote down my weight on a slip of paper and put it in his pocket.

You could ask why did that work when nothing else had: no special diets, no tears or coaxing from my mother, no lectures from the family doctor, no heckling from my brother Stef or my sister, Ginger. Maybe I was just ready. It was a turning point in my life, about to enter college. I don't really know. All I know is I lost fifty pounds by the end of the summer. Lost so much my mother got alarmed. "What if he's sick? You don't just lose *fifty* pounds!" Every day when I came home she questioned me: had I had any lunch? Did I ever suffer dizzy spells? I shared my post with Ernie, the other lifeguard, a short, perfectly compact, muscular guy who looked the way life-guards are supposed to, straight from central casting. Ironically, he was married, at eighteen, and his pregnant teenage wife sat docilely on a towel, not far from his lifeguard chair, knitting, seemingly un-perturbed by the luscious girls who pranced around him, flirting, joshing, asking the time. Usually Uncle Herman would have placed us farther apart, but I think for the first month he regarded me as an ornament, there just because he loved my mother or felt he owed her something. When he weighed me and my weight kept dropping, according to schedule, he showed little emotion. What was it to him anyway? "Good work," he once said, slapping me on the shoulder.

Then there was my first drowning, a girl hysterically waving her arms and yelling, Ernie off duty. I was three weeks into the job and sprinted down to the water, then dove in and swam toward her. Once in the water I felt, as always, safe, powerful, like some sleek fish cleaving the waves. She was pretty far out, but I got there and started pulling her into position. Her hair was plastered on her face, water dripping into her eyes, but she took an angry look at me. "Not you!" she said. "I wanted the other one!"

I couldn't believe it. She'd actually staged a drowning, literally taking her life in her hands, just for the sake of having sexy Ernie lug her back to shore and, possibly, perform mouth-to-mouth resuscitation? "Okay, great, you want to drown," I said furiously. "Go right ahead."

"Oh okay." In fact, she only let me take her halfway back, then swam the rest herself.

There were other, smaller humiliations, but nothing to take away from the pride and excitement of seeing that I actually had a body beneath all that blubber. At the very end of the summer a woman came over and said she wanted to introduce her mother to the lifeguard who had saved her little boy in early July. "That was me," I said. I remembered her. He hadn't been in much danger. He was just four or five and got swept out a little.

"Are you sure it was *you?*" she said. "The man who saved my little boy was . . ." She stopped, then said almost shyly, "He had a weight problem."

"That was me. I've lost forty pounds."

"Goodness! You must have fantastic willpower." She called her mother over and the two of them oohed and ahed for a long time about how great I looked and what a wonderful thing I had done. "Your mother must be very proud of you," the older woman said.

When I went to college, nothing fit me anymore, but I didn't, for some odd reason, want to throw my old clothes away. Partly I wanted them as mementos of the past. I'd try them on and look at the elephantine waistlines with pleasure. But also I had a fear, deep down, that it could return. Maybe this new thin self wasn't "the real me." Maybe the other was and would reclaim me, like some Indian spirit repossessing a lost soul.

It was as the new me that I met Becky. Yet all that first year, even now to some extent, but especially my first year of college, I felt I was posing as someone I wasn't. Maybe all kids that age feel that and my thinness was only a symbol of it. Not that I looked *that* fantastic.

I still looked very young for my age, which was two years younger than most of the class: a big mop of black hair, big brown eyes, pale, kind of rumpled and schnooky looking. Stef, though not much better looking than me, is at least tall, almost six feet, which enabled him to look down on me literally, as well as figuratively, all through high school. I know if Marilyn had seen me then, she would have given me one glance and walked away. She says no, if only we'd met when we were teenagers, in high school even. I've told her about how fat I was, but I know she doesn't really understand what that was like, how it made me feel. "Being fat isn't so terrible," she'll say. Becky was three years older than me, one year ahead in college, a sophomore. We met at a mixer, both of us huddling somewhere at the fringes of the room. I had just gone to get myself a drink and, as I was returning to where I'd been standing, I saw Becky and, without thinking, offered the drink to her. She took it without asking what it was and smiled. Becky has a wonderful smile. Then, since I was lonely and ill at ease, it seemed even more wonderful: friendly, kind, sweet. She was a little plump, but more just healthy looking: bright pink cheeks, beautiful auburn hair braided down her back. She was wearing the kind of dress she still wears: little flowers, a full skirt, a white lace collar, maybe even knee socks and flat ballet-dancer-type shoes. Usually there's a classic division between the popular girls who are surrounded by hundreds of guys and the total losers who cling to the fringes. Becky was neither. She explained in a cheerful, down-to-earth way that she'd had to drop out at the end of her freshman year due to mono, that she was at the mixer because her boyfriend, the ultimately infamous Ellis Stein, had to go home that weekend to see his parents. (Probably, in retrospect, a lie on his part.)

But those facts, her being older, her already having a boyfriend made her perfect. Right away she seemed to like me, maybe not in a sexual way, but in such a warm, accepting, big-sister way that I felt terrific. I found myself telling her everything: my weight loss, my mixed feelings about going to law school, and she listened with what seemed true fascination. I wasn't her first Jew: Ellis had that distinction, but she did share with so many non-Jewish girls the feeling that Jews who'd grown up in Manhattan were some special breed, highly cultured, intense, brilliant. While with her I felt, to some extent, I *was* those things. "I've got to fix you up with someone wonderful!" she exclaimed, eyes shining, at the end of the evening when I'd confessed my abysmally bereft social life. "There's a girl in my dorm I think you'd like. What's your type? Is there any special type you like or don't like?"

Her assumption that I could afford to be that choosy, that I deserved "someone wonderful," her fears that this one might not be bright enough, that one not quite pretty enough, made me feel almost as good as I had after losing fifty pounds. "I have catholic tastes," I said blithely. Thus followed two years of double dates with Becky, Ellis, and whatever girl Becky found for me. Later she confessed that she was always, deep down, delighted when, the morning after, I'd call her and ridicule whoever it had been, pointing out scarcely existing flaws. "Oh Benjy, don't!" Becky would gasp. "That's mean. That's not fair! She isn't *really* like that, but I know what you mean." She loved it. Meanwhile, though, Becky made it ultra clear that Ellis was her boyfriend and that meant nothing with other boys, no even momentary slips from grace. She was (is) a one-man woman. A fact I appreciate now, but which exasperated and disgusted me then. I don't think it was just out of a growing fondness for Becky that I couldn't stand Ellis Stein. He was a tall, good-looking Jewish guy from Scarsdale, a hooked nose, glossy black hair, blue eyes, so full of himself that if his whole dorm had burned to the ground and two hundred students had been killed, he would have gasped, "My God, my history term paper was in there!" Absolutely no sense of humor. If I'd met him apart from Becky, I would have dismissed him as a pompous jerk, but what really riled me was the way he acted with her, as though she should be totally awed and delighted that he, the great Ellis, had deigned to choose her, from all the many gorgeous girls begging for his favors. Becky told me stories of his many high school girlfriends who were, as he told it, distraught to the point of suicide when they learned he was engaged to her. "They were hoping he'd wait for them." I'm sure it was Becky's money that entranced him. He didn't come from a well-to-do family. Not that she acted or even seemed aware of being rich, but that was one of her charms, that slightly innocent, protected quality. In any case, he blew it, much to my delight. One summer vacation Becky's father caught him fucking one of Becky's girlfriends in the garden house. Exit Ellis.

That was the summer between my sophomore and junior year. In the two years till then, I managed finally to shed my burdensome virginity and even make it with another girl. In short, two altogether. Not six, as I told Marilyn. I wonder why I lied about that. Maybe suspecting she was used to men who'd had more experience? But why six? If I was going to lie, I should have said a dozen, a baker's dozen, even. Two dozen would have been pushing it. I'm convinced no one would believe I could have scored with two dozen girls or women. But six is so close to reality and yet so meagerly pretentious. Oddly, though, Marilyn never seems especially curious about who those six were, which is a relief. I'd have to invent, put together girls from bits and parts of women I've known.

The woman I lost my virginity with was Karen Osterling, a twenty-six-year-old divorcée who conducted one of the sections of my Renaissance History class. She was tall, skinny, intense, a chain smoker with a fascinating raspy voice. Small glinting green eyes which would sweep the class with a scornful glance. "So, once we get past all that bullshit, what do you think he's *really* trying to say?" I'd had no experience with women that self-confident intellectually, who used dirty words with such flair. Everyone knew she was screwing the professor who taught the main part of the class. We all overheard their screaming arguments, even when they were behind closed doors. Once Karen stormed into class and just said, "God, men are fuckers! Sorry, boys, maybe you're exceptions, but Jesus!" I felt Karen liked me, respected my mind; she wrote in her dashing handwriting, "Marvelous comparison!" on the papers I handed in. I watched her from afar, hopelessly fascinated, bewitched, but unable to make any move even when rumor had it that she and the professor had finally definitively broken up.

One New Year's Eve I got totally smashed and appeared at her door, bleary eyed, reeling, and stammered, "I love you!" She was in jeans and a long white shirt, knotted at the waist, holding a glass of champagne. She smiled at me affectionately. "Come back tomorrow, Benjy," she said, "at eleven." When I appeared, chagrined, ashamed, she started unbuttoning her blouse, while saying, "I basically don't really believe in fucking undergraduates, but what the hell. Happy New Year!" I believe that in the three months we were together, till she grew bored and found a replacement for me, someone nearer her own age, I fucked her more ardently and assiduously than I've ever done since. She loved sex, knew about birth control. All those endless arguments one normally had with girls one's own age, all the fears weren't there. And she liked me, though in a slightly indulgent way. "I wish I could meet you in ten or twenty years," she said at the end. "You're going to be a super person. Some lucky woman will benefit from all I've taught you."

Only no lucky woman came along. After Karen there were long months of nothing but double dates with Becky and Ellis. Until the also brief interlude involving Cleo Glassgold. Cleo was a version of me, Manhattan born and raised, her father also with a prominent law firm, law school bound. She'd gone to the same kind of schools, had the same friends. With the exception of a more active social life and the absence of blubber, we might have lived the same life, as different sexes. Maybe that was the trouble. There was no sense of discovery, no amazed delight. It was more a matter of arguing (which we both enjoyed), analyzing our sex life, discussing our dreams (she'd already been analyzed, was a psychology minor, was in love with Freud). She and Becky didn't get along at all. We tried some double dates with Becky and Ellis and they rapidly disintegrated into shouting matches between Ellis and Cleo. "She must be truly desperate," Cleo would say. "He is the most pig-headed person I've ever met! And he's wrong about *everything!*" She was convinced only a shiksa like Becky would tolerate anyone of Ellis's "profound conceit and total dumbness," something with which I was glad to concur. I only demurred when she went on to say how she didn't understand either, my friendship with Becky. "She's so bland. She agrees with anything he or you says! Doesn't she have *any* opinions of her own?" Clearly beneath the vehemence, at least toward Ellis, there must have been some sexual attraction since it was Cleo who was caught, bare-assed, by Becky's father that balmy August afternoon while Becky was out shopping with her mother.

The start of Becky's senior year, my junior year, was a set piece.

She in tears, betrayed, but forlorn, passive, gentle. "Maybe I did something to make it happen"—she'd never had sex with him, thought he, like her, was enjoying the ritual of waiting till they were married. But deeply, deeply wounded. What a delicious role for me to play! It was so easy to denounce Ellis and comfort Becky at the same time. "I never told you this, but I always thought he was a total schmuck." "Really? But he was so smart." "He was a jerk." She snuggled against me while I patted her, kissed her affectionately, murmured that some day she would find someone truly worthy of her. . . . And so the inevitable day when we looked at each other and realized we were no longer "just friends."

That first time I went home to meet Becky's parents, as her new fiancé, I came as her savior, the person who had single-handedly gotten her through senior year, showed her that men were to be trusted, possibly brought her back from a nervous breakdown and despair. To say her parents welcomed me with open arms would be a total understatement. They adored me. I would spend long afternoons sitting with Becky's mother, Jane, in the gazebo while she recited Emily Dickinson or Christina Rossetti and I, dazzled, sipped iced tea, reclining in a hammock. Becky's father and I took long walks during which, as I recall, nothing much was said, but Becky declared he had told her privately he was "very proud" to have me as a potential son-in-law, that he, too, had felt Ellis was not worthy of his precious daughter but had hesitated to say anything at the time. . . . He believed in noninterference.

This year, in late September, we went to Becky's parents' house for her birthday. Maybe it was guilt, but I suddenly felt, standing beside Becky's father, that maybe in some way I was fused in his mind with Ellis Stein, the two on-the-make Jewish men who had screwed his daughter, betrayed her in their different ways, been after her money or at any rate not indifferent to it. I'm attached, deeply, to my daughters, but I don't think my love for them equals Rolf Gibson's for Becky. He's a tall man, over six feet, lanky, with a bemused smile always playing around his lips. He looks like someone who's just won the Nobel Peace Prize or invented something that will benefit mankind for centuries to come, yet who'll give all the money from the prize to a favorite cause. Standing beside him, I remembered what he said that first weekend, describing his feelings when he "discovered" Ellis and Cleo humping in the garden house. "You know, I'm a pacifist, Benjamin. I even went to jail for my beliefs once, but if it hadn't been for Becky, I'd have gone over and broken that young man's neck, flung him out to sea, and not felt one second of remorse."

Standing there, my mind wandering with hideous precision over two days ago in bed with Marilyn, I felt a version of guilt so profound it seemed to imbue every cell in my body. My own father, if he knew, might be disgusted, disdainful; Becky's father would literally kill me! Now, glancing out at the pond—they have their own pond for swimming—he said, "I feel like I'm a lucky man, extraordinarily lucky. Of course, Jane's illness has taken a toll on both of us, but when I think of you and Becky and the girls, the wonderful family you've created, my great good fortune in having all of you so near by. . . . What else can a man ask for?"

At that moment, sparing me from having to answer, Buffie strode by. Buffie is barely younger than Becky's father. I can best describe him by saying he's a cross between a gardener in a comic Italian opera and one of those laconic brothers in an early O'Neill play. He's always dressed in overalls and a red flannel shirt with a ragged straw hat perched on his head, stout walking boots caked with mud. "Looks like the rain won't come till tomorrow," he said.

"We could use some," Becky's father said.

"It'll come by nightfall."

These conversations about the weather have, to me, an urban Jew, a wonderfully stylized quality. The world will have two minutes till its end and Buffie and Rolf will still be standing here, peering at the horizon, discussing if the wind is going to damage the rhododendron bushes or the snow be so heavy, the early cherry blossoms may frost at an untimely moment. Maybe it's also that, although Rolf has a detachment like my father's, it's different. My father's always seems convoluted, ironical, whereas Rolf's detachment is Olympian, genial, like some kindly god deciding whether to invent a new form of apple. "How do you like having four daughters?" he asked, smiling. "Must keep the two of you pretty busy."

In fact, what with Becky's possessiveness about the babies and our

full-time baby-sitter, Mrs. Morgan, I've scarcely developed any relationship with them so far. When I take Chelsea and Dawn out, it's as
though the three of us are bonded in some mutual disgruntlement at
the new arrivals. I am forced to agree with them (I actually do) that
little girls of nine and seven are infinitely more charming than little
wrinkly "blobs" that can't even walk or talk. I've always felt some
slight uneasiness when visiting Becky's parents. I'm not even sure
I'm right, that, when I'm not around, Jane says to her friends, "Our
son-in-law, Benjamin—he's Jewish, you know. . . . " But this particular visit the uneasiness is heavily compounded by knowledge of
my unfaithfulness. Am I just a repeat of Ellis, a more benign version? As though to exacerbate it, Becky's mother, at dinner, began
talking about one of her neighbors whose husband first fucked, then
married a woman he knew from work.

"Rosalie read me the letter he wrote her the day he was marrying
that woman," she said. "All this nonsense about how much their
marriage meant, how you never forget first love, how he's going to
keep his insurance policies in her name. How can that *ever* make up
for what he's done?" She stared indignantly first at her husband,
then at Becky, then at me. This sequence was due merely to our
positions at the table. I felt relieved not to be the first person she
turned to for an answer.

"I think it's true, you don't forget first love," Becky said thoughtfully. "I still sometimes wonder about Ellis, whether he and Cleo
are happy together."

Becky wants to believe Ellis and Cleo are married, that only love
of a deep and permanent nature could have justified what they both
did. I would bet my life that if he heard her name, he wouldn't
remember who she was and vice versa.

"That young man is leading, unless I miss my guess, a miserable
and thoroughly dissolute life," Becky's father said.

"Sometimes people change," Jane remarked hopefully.

"Not him," Rolf said.

"I agree," I put in, just to not seem too guiltily silent.

"As for Rosalie," Rolf went on, "she'll find a better man and be
glad she lost him. I have no worries about her."

"It may be hard for her, at fifty-nine," Jane said, "don't you think?

With her son causing all those problems, and then, though I love Rosalie, she has that terrible problem with her skin. It's a nervous condition, but . . ."

"She'll find someone," Rolf repeated with total assurance. Then he beamed at his wife and at Becky and me. "We are all very lucky. We married our first loves. Not many people can say as much."

Becky knows about Karen and Cleo, but Jane said, "Why darling, you're forgetting Zane Stockdale! I was madly in love with him from second through seventh grade, and it broke my heart when he sent Julie O'Conner a valentine instead of me when I'd worked for two solid weeks on mine for him."

Becky smiled at me and touched my hand under the table.

After dinner Becky and her mother played anagrams. Jane is a fanatic, perhaps more so now that she's ailing and unable to get around much. Her eyes dart over the letters, stealing words, re-arranging them in amazing, inventive ways. I sat in an armchair, letting Dawn play with my shoe, tying and untying the laces. I felt the sense of unease melt. Fucking Marilyn seemed something I might have done once, ten or more years ago. Marilyn who?

Among my many fears, at this moment of my life, is that my obsession with Marilyn, or with sex with Marilyn—I can't tell which is which—is a version of my obsession with eating, returned in another form. Those drives that plunge underground seem to have vanished, and then gush at horribly inappropriate moments to the surface. Why can't I do things in a more restrained way? Am I an "addict personality"? My father has admitted he will never give up smoking, no matter how many tests are conducted to prove how injurious it is to his health. I've never smoked, alcohol isn't a problem for me, but food and sex! Or am I just inventing connections? And, if there is a connection, doesn't it prove that, as with food, I can finally, at some point, control it, simply say, "Enough is enough"?

But at some point? When?

And, alas, this isn't just sex. I'm in love with Marilyn and she, certainly, is with me. Maybe it's that I just don't have a strong enough ego to resist the fact of a beautiful woman adoring me that much. The way her voice softens when she hears mine, her expression when she sees me. The way her eyes open after sex with that radiant helpless smile. Christ. I saw her husband the other day, parked at a gas station—I recognized the car—and felt a certain pang. But what the heck. I'm not going to get into worrying about him. He's fucked fifty women, he's unfaithful. It's not like with Becky, true to the tips of her toes, to the hem of her flowered flannel nightgown.

The structure of my life has changed this fall. Since I'm taking two design courses, as well as doing some free-lance work for Lapidus Brothers, a furniture company, my father, as head honcho of the law firm, has decreed that I can have three afternoons off a week. Actually my father, at sixty-four, is semiretired. Not that he's any less active than before. On the contrary. Apart from still keeping an eye on what goes on in the firm, he's now thoroughly involved in lecturing on Jewish history at the synagogue he and my mother attend. I should let my mother tell this story, and, indeed, I've heard it so many times I get somewhat ill hearing it again whenever a new acquaintance drops by. The essence of it is that one evening the rabbi of the synagogue, a friend of my parents, called up hysterically because the man who was to lecture on some aspect of Jewish history, a "world authority," was very ill. Yet the posters had gone up, attendance of several hundred was expected. Could my father, whom the rabbi knew read extensively in the field, possibly fill in? So my father, with about thirty-six hours to prepare, whisked into his study, prepared a lecture, and gave a presentation so profound, so witty, so "effortlessly erudite" that everyone in the audience secretly admitted they were *glad* the world's authority had been taken ill. Then, in the weeks that followed, there was a ground swell of letters, calls, appeals to the rabbi and my father that he should give a series of lectures every year. He did. They were, in my mother's words, "Successful beyond anyone's wildest dreams," and now he's asked to lecture all around the country. I wish I could tell this story straight. Why all the bitter irony? It's just that this is, literally, the story of my father's life. Success, my mother's ecstatic pleasure in his success, his own modest delight in sharing with the world all he knows. Am I jealous at some deep subterranean level? Of course! Need you ask?

Why, given my terribly ambivalent relationship to my father, am I working in his firm? Partly because I failed the bar exam twice, because I would never, on my own steam, have gotten a job with a firm so prestigious, so firmly rooted. Now I know it was a mistake, that the annoyance with which I'm regarded both by the senior partners and the men my age who feel, rightly, I shouldn't be there, isn't worth it. If I cared about the law, I'd do the sensible thing and simply switch to another firm. But somehow I could never do that. My sister Ginger ridicules my father for doing corporation law and says if she ever goes into the field (if she ever graduates from college!) she will "do good": help the Indians, poor blacks, battered wives. I'm all on her side, but I don't have her reckless courage in locking horns with my father. I watch the two of them, entranced and delighted by her audacity, but I never take sides (except in my head). Maybe it's easier for her as a girl. My father finds her feistiness charming, but not quite to be taken seriously. Someday, he is confident, she'll "give up all that nonsense."

What worries me is that I'm not altogether sure I have any more talent at designing furniture than I do at legal matters. I have some talent, some flair. Jake Lapidus loved my ideas, got all excited, and said possibly within the year, he could offer me a full-time job. I know I'm good enough to get that job or, if not that one, another one, but I fear that I'll never rise much above mediocrity, that I'm relying on the knowledge of Becky's father's money to indulge what my father would call "a fancy." The best designers, I think, are European, have architectural degrees, know how to design everything from coffeepots to houses. I know that, due to a certain facility at picking things up, I'll learn enough to semi-bluff my way through, but I'll never have, I don't think, that confident passion for the field that I've seen and admire. Yet I still believe, even if I'm never a more successful furniture designer than I am a lawyer, I will get some pleasure in striking out on my own. And, at any rate I'll have the satisfaction of knowing I'm having my mid-life crisis at thirty, instead of forty-five. Or at forty-five will I want to run off and join the circus? Probably.

I had hoped that this fall Marilyn and I might go our separate ways, what with my trying to balance studying design and still being at the office part-time, and her going back to college. I was hoping (also, of course, hoping the opposite) that she would go to a community college so arrangements to meet would be too complicated to contemplate. Instead, God seems determined to toss the ball back at me. He is depriving me of perfect ways to sever the relationship, in fact seems bent on making it as easy as possible for it to continue. To wit: the apartment.

Marilyn went over to the apartment of a fellow student, Ramsey Krosneck, to borrow a book. He's gay and works from nine to five at a bookstore in midtown. She was hardly in the door when he began telling her how hard it was for him to pay his rent, how little he earned. Marilyn, after quickly glancing around the apartment, piped up, "Ramsey, I'd love to help you with your rent, if you'll let me." Thus the arrangement. She (with my help) pays him fifty dollars a month for the privilege or opportunity of "using" his apartment any weekday from one to five. If he's sick, he's to leave a note on the door: "I'm home." So far he hasn't been sick. Easy as pie! No scurrying up to hotels. No worrying about running into anyone. His apartment is up near Columbia so it's comfortably far away from the law firm, Lapidus Brothers, anyone I might know.

Sometimes I wonder: say I had six months (better a year) to go off with Marilyn somewhere where we could fuck our brains out for that entire time. Would I then return home, pick up the reins of my former life, and live happy as a clam with Becky and the girls? Or would I instead be like one of those businessmen who takes off for the South Sea islands and never returns? Since I only see Marilyn a few times a week, it's so much harder to feel satiated. I would so much love to wake up one morning and think, wearily, "Oh God, today I have to fuck Marilyn." Maybe that day will come and when it does, I'll regard this present madness with nostalgia.

I think part of the problem was that I went too quickly from fat boy to Becky's husband, too few years, girls, in between. And then the fact that in my relationship with Becky, our sex life was imbued from the start with her big sister sweetness. Becky is aghast when my sister says, "God, I was so horny I was crawling the walls!" or "I'd have fucked Abraham Lincoln in the mood I was in!" "Does she really *mean* that?" Becky asked me anxiously. She had assumed talking that way was something only girls from "emotionally deprived backgrounds" did, not upper middle class Jewish girls who were planning to spend their lives defending the rights of Indians and battered wives. To Becky, sex is an expression of love. "Is that terrible?" she'll say. "Does that mean I'm horribly old-fashioned? Ellis thought I was." There are questions to which there is only one answer. No, Becky, it's not terrible. And in fact do I really want Becky to come dancing out in a black lace nightie saying, "Wanna fuck?" I chose her for her sweetness, her stability, her gentle calm. I would miss those qualities grievously were they to vanish.

"We're so much alike," Marilyn said one afternoon as we were returning from our mutually induced spaced-out delirium.

"In what way?" I asked cautiously.

"Well, we both married too young, didn't really know much about sex. . . . So now we're doing what we should have done earlier. I never even *liked* sex that much till now." She laughed delightedly. "I really didn't. I didn't hate it, but I didn't get what all the fuss was about. Like you know all those crimes of passion you read about? I never understood that, why someone would kill out of love. Sure, I used to get furious when Mo flirted with women at parties, but now, if I found you making love with someone, I'd just kill both of you without even thinking about it!" After a second she added, "And myself too, of course."

I believe the first part, but I wonder if Marilyn *would* actually kill herself too. I have the feeling she'd dispose of the bodies, mail them C.O.D. to Jeanette in San Diego, and sit down and have a whiskey sour on the rocks. Within half an hour she'd be flirting with the guy who came to fix the dishwasher and wondering if life wasn't worth living after all. Marilyn is a true democrat when it comes to men, well, people in general. If someone comes to fix the dishwasher, she'll start asking him about himself and three hours later, he's still tinkering around, sipping a beer and telling her the entire story of his life from the time he left Peoria, Illinois, to the day his business with his best friend, Joe, went bankrupt. "He had such a sad life!" she'll exclaim. Or "The time just flew by. It was like going to a movie."

"I don't think I'd kill you, under similar circumstances," I said. "Maybe that shows we *are* different."

She looked hurt and disappointed. "Wouldn't you even *want* to? Wouldn't you be jealous, even?"

"I'd be horribly jealous, but . . ."

Her color is starting to rise. "But what? But you'd figure I can just walk around the corner and get someone just as good in three seconds?"

"No. . . . I'd just try to accept the fact that there was someone you loved more or had better sex with than me." My nobility sounded a bit unconvincing, even to me.

She began nibbling on my ear. "There is no one in the whole world I'll *ever* have better sex with than you! . . . Now or ever! You're *so* good. I never even have to tell you anything, where to touch me or anything. You just know. I wonder why that is."

I grinned. "Natural talent."

Marilyn remained solemn. "It is. . . . You should give a course. Most men just pounce. Jeanette says Rich does, and he's a writer. They're supposed to understand women, and she says he doesn't understand *anything!*"

Wednesdays I have my class at four, but Thursdays, like today, I'm free, unless I have an appointment. We've decided to go to a movie playing on the upper West Side, *Devil in the Flesh*, appropriately enough. It's Kipp's favorite movie, but somehow I've never gotten around to seeing it. We showered together, playful but not letting anything go beyond that. If we miss the four-thirty show, that'll be it, and anyway, I felt pleasantly exhausted.

I watched Marilyn get dressed in her leopard-patterned dress. It's a simple style, slightly too form-fitting. She slipped on her high-heeled sandals and, observing me watching her, stood up straight, self-consciously. "I know I should lose two pounds," she said. "But I just love this dress. Don't you? I bought it on sale and I knew, right from seeing it in the window, that it would look great."

It does, yet sometimes I wish Marilyn and Becky would get together and swap half their wardrobes with each other. Becky could give eight pairs of knee socks to Marilyn and Marilyn could give Becky some of these dresses that look—well, they look fine, but a little cheap, flashy. I try not to even think things like that because Marilyn often picks up on my expression. This time she didn't.

We got to the movie ten minutes before it was due to start. I bought the tickets and then sat down in the lounge while Marilyn excused herself to go the ladies' room. I went over to get a drink of water from the fountain and, turning around when I was done, saw my father who, at that same moment, saw me. Oh my God. "Hi," I said, going over to him. "What brings you here?"

"It's one of my favorites," he said. "Have you ever seen it?"

"No." Crazy schemes rush through my head. I'll excuse myself, stay in the men's room for half an hour. Then, once the movie has started, I'll come out and look for Marilyn. Maybe if I'm not there, she'll assume. . . . Forget it. There she is, walking toward us.

"This is my father," I said, trying to keep my voice steady. "Dad, this is Marilyn Greene. She, uh, works for the firm I've mentioned to you, Lapidus Brothers."

"I'm so glad to meet you," Marilyn said, poised, cool, extending her hand. "We're really delighted with Benjamin's designs. He's very talented."

My father smiled back. "Yes, he is, isn't he? . . . And what aspect of the business are you involved in, Miss Greene?" Fucking clients?

"I'm in shipping," Marilyn said, licking her lips quickly, the only sign of nervousness so far. Things about her I normally don't notice now seem to glare out, her long dark red nails, the leopard dress. My father likes "quiet elegance" in women and my mother, whose main aim in life is to please him, has about eight hundred understated black dresses. She would no more wear a leopard print than Becky would.

At that moment the usher began beckoning people into the theater. We're going to have to sit through the whole movie with my father! Marilyn went first, then my father, then me. He sat in between the two of us throughout the movie, a perfect chaperon position. I decided to try and concentrate just on the dialogue and not read the subtitles, just to do something to prevent myself from breaking down and howling. In the middle of the movie, my father asked Marilyn if she minded if he smoked. "Not at all," she replied gaily. If only I'd thought of that, should have said Marilyn was allergic to cigarette smoke and we had to sit in the no smoking section.

Don't ask me about the movie. I don't remember one word of what was said. All I could do was indulge in fantasies of either my father or Marilyn quietly and painlessly going up in smoke during the performance. When it was over, we walked out together.

"How did you like it?" my father asked Marilyn.

"Oh, I liked it a lot! I don't know French that well, but Gerard Philippe was really adorable. Is he French? I guess he must be."

"He died of cancer some years ago," my father said. "A great loss. He acted on the stage too."

"I guess the French have a thing about that," Marilyn said. "I mean, the older woman, younger man thing. I don't know. I'm about her age, thirty, and I don't know how I'd feel about a guy who was just sixteen. They seemed like such babies when I was that age."

Where is a sock I can stuff in Marilyn's mouth? But my father is watching her with interest. "I think the French are more understanding about all kinds of relationships," he said. "They aren't burdened, as we are, by the Puritan heritage."

A pause.

Who me? Burdened by the Puritan heritage? Never!

"I think I'll excuse myself a moment," Marilyn said, and went off to the ladies' room again, her ass twitching in the clinging skirt. Is my father watching her ass?

"A very charming young woman," he said.

I cannot, with all the words of the English language at my disposal, find a single one with which to reply.

My father smiled at me, gently. "I did something like that once," he said.

What did he say? Did he say "I had something like that once? *Did* something like that?" I just stammer, "Marilyn is a very intelligent person."

"I could tell that," my father said gravely.

All three of us were on the street again. "Well," my father said. "I'm afraid I have to rush off, but I'm delighted to have had the opportunity of meeting you, Miss Greene. Make sure Benjamin does his job properly!"

Marilyn flushed slightly. "I will."

After he had vanished from sight, she turned to me anxiously. "Did he like me? What do you think? Did he say anything?"

I moaned. "Oh God . . . this is terrible. This is the worst thing that's ever happened to me."

She looked startled. "Why? What's wrong?"

"He knew everything."

"How could he?"

"He just did. . . . Why would we be going to a movie together in the middle of the afternoon?"

"Benjy, don't be silly. Lots of people do."

"It's not just that. . . . While you were in the ladies' room, he said, '*I* did something like that once.'"

"Something like what?"

"Something like what we're doing!"

She looked anxious, mainly I think because of my mood. "You mean, he had a girlfriend?"

I nodded. I still hadn't digested that fact, it flew by so rapidly. My father? Who? When?

"Well, that's good," Marilyn said. "Then he'll be understanding. If he was in love with someone he wasn't married to."

"My father's never loved anyone but himself," I said contemptuously.

She looked puzzled. "I thought you said he and your mother were so happy together."

"They are, that's different."

"Then what did he mean, 'I did something like that once'?"

"That he screwed around, that—"

"But with who?"

"Marilyn, Christ! How do *I* know with who? With whoever would let him! With some secretary in his office! . . . But, believe me, it wasn't love. It was sex!"

Suddenly Marilyn frowned. "That's terrible!"

"What?"

"That means he must think that's all it is with us—just sex."

I shrugged.

Marilyn grabbed me by the sleeve. "You've got to call him up tomorrow and tell him we love each other, that it's not what he thinks."

"Darling."

It was a brisk, chilly February day. The tip of Marilyn's nose was pink. "If you don't call him up, I will!" she threatened. "I mean it. I'll call him at work. I know the number."

I exploded. "You'll call him up and say, 'Hey, Mr. Fetterman, I just wanted you to know Benjy and I are fucking, but it's not what it seems. It's 'true love.' . . . Is *that* what you're going to say?"

Suddenly Marilyn burst into tears. "It *is* true love!" she wailed. "It is for me. . . . Isn't it for you? You said it was!"

I felt rotten. I drew her close to me, as close as was possible with her bulky winter coat. "Of course it is," I said.

We staggered into a nearby coffee shop, Marilyn still snuffling and sobbing quietly. "He probably envied us," she said, "if all he ever did was fuck his secretary. He probably wishes *he'd* known someone like me."

I was holding her hand. "I'm sure he does."

She pulled some Kleenex out of her purse and blotted her cheeks. "Was I all right? Do you think I made a good impression on him?"

"Very good."

Then she looked down at her leopard dress, as though discovering, for the first time that day, what she was wearing. "I hope this dress wasn't too flashy. What do you think? *I* love it, but—"

"It's a beautiful dress."

"Oh, and that dumb remark I made about the movie!"

"Which one?"

Marilyn laughed and blew her nose. "Did I make more than one?"

"No, I just meant—"

"The one where I said I didn't understand why women my age liked teenage boys. Of course I do! They have gorgeous bodies, they can fuck six times in one night. . . . But I didn't want him to think I was some kind of sex maniac."

I felt slightly appalled at Marilyn's vehemence about the attractions of teenage boys. "But you wouldn't actually do it with one, would you?" I asked anxiously.

"Do what? With who?"

"You wouldn't actually be tempted by a teenage boy?"

She laughed again. "No one's asked me. . . . Actually, there's a cute checker at Grand Union, but I think he's taken. He's always flirting with the girl at the next register."

"Teenage boys are spaced-out idiots," I said. "I should know. I used to be one."

"Oh sure," Marilyn agreed easily. "I mean, I know you wouldn't have profound discussions about life or anything. It would be just like it would be if you screwed a teenage girl. She'd have a lovely body, terrific skin, perky breasts."

"It doesn't interest me."

"Good! . . . So why are you still looking so worried? Are you scared your father will say something to your mother?"

I sighed. "It's the whole thing, that he actually *did* it." That part of it is dawning on me now, slowly. My father, who is so hypocritically "devoted" to my mother was off—once? many times?—putting it to some . . . some who?

"Who do you think it was?" Marilyn asked, dumping sugar and two containers of cream into her coffee. "You really think it was a secretary?"

"My entire knowledge of the subject is summed up by the sentence, 'I did something like that once.'"

"What do you think, though, based on your knowledge of your father's character?"

For some reason it's a topic with which my mind refuses to engage itself. "Anything could be true."

"Maybe they were deeply and passionately in love," Marilyn invented, with a dreamy expression on her face. "Maybe he thought he would leave your mother and run off with her, but at the last minute lost his nerve."

"Maybe."

"You're so uncurious! . . . And, you know, it's funny, you've always said what a prick your father was, and I thought he was darling, really courtly and charming and sweet."

"I never said prick. Prig maybe."

"Same difference. . . . I can imagine he might be terrific in bed, just like you, very thoughtful and caring—"

I raised my hand. "I don't want to talk about my father's sex life, okay?"

"How come? It's such an interesting topic!"

"Because it involves my mother, it—"

"You mean you feel disillusioned, because you thought they were so perfectly happy?"

"I never thought that." What *did* I think? I think I thought my mother doted on him and he was extremely fond of her, that they were as happy as any couple their age I knew, far happier than the parents of many of my friends. But about their sex life, as with most people in regard to their parents, I drew and still draw some kind of mental curtain.

"My father's never *looked* at anyone but my mother," Marilyn observed, "but they're different. It's like they're welded at the hip. I don't even think it's healthy, especially."

I wanted, more than anything, to stop talking about it.

"I hope he thought I was prettier than Becky," Marilyn concluded wistfully. "I hope deep down, deep *deep* down he thought: I don't blame him."

Throughout the next week every sentence that passed from my father's lips on that afternoon echoed through my mind. I turned them over and over, like fragments from the Dead Sea Scrolls. "They aren't burdened by the Puritan heritage." "I'm sure she is." "Make sure Benjamin does his job properly." When I spoke to him on the phone, about two weeks later—we were planning to have dinner at their house for his sixty-fifth birthday—he didn't refer to it. I wasn't sure what that meant.

We left the twins at home, but brought Chelsea and Dawn. They are both fond of my father, Dawn especially, and he of them. I think he relives with them the nicer memories of raising a daughter, before the rebelliousness set in. My parents have a full-time maid who also cooks. She is not the cook my mother wishes she was, but with time she has learned to prepare a variety of—to me—very delicious meals, based in part on my father's need for low-salt food. We sat down at their long beautiful rosewood table to roast duck which Mildred had carved in the kitchen and was passing around.

"Gilbert says he ran into you at the movies a few weeks ago," my mother said just as the duck reached me.

I brought the piece slowly to my plate, waiting for her to finish the sentence, "with a perfectly charming young woman from the shipping department." But evidently my mother *had* finished—"ago" was the end of her sentence. My father hadn't told her! "Uh, yes, it was wonderful," I stammered. *"Devil in the Flesh."*

"Was that the movie it was?" my mother said. "Gilbert is always so mysterious about what he's seen. Yes, I loved that. It stood up, then, did it?"

"I thought so," my father said.

"I don't think I've ever heard of it," Becky said. It would be perfectly possible for Becky to feel as ill at ease while at my parents' house as I feel at hers—"the shiksa our younger son married"—but evidently it has never occurred to her that my parents do not love her and accept her totally. And maybe they do. Certainly, when I announced my intention to marry her, there were no ugly scenes, no comments, even, about the fact that she wasn't Jewish. The only person who commented, in fact, was Ginger, who clasped her head and said, "Oh great, typical! Benjy's marrying a shiksa! Does she have great legs and play a terrific game of golf?" I wrestled her to the ground and she shut up. Actually, Becky's legs are not one of her strong points and she's almost as inept at sports as I am.

While eating, I glanced down the table at my mother. It's all but impossible to judge one's parents objectively, but I'd say my mother is considered, justly, by everyone to be "a very handsome woman." Impeccable posture—she once studied ballet—and a ballet dancer's hair style, black (dyed now) and parted in the middle, swept up in back in a chignon, delicate diamond and pearl earrings, a steady, thoughtful gaze. She has never seemed to have any regrets about not pursuing a dancing career. "I was too short," she has said. "Just five two. I never would have made it." There are photos from my

mother's girlhood of her, leaping about the stage in a leotard, looking intense and graceful, the same reflective gaze she now fixes on
my father.

And the "I did something like that once"? One of their friends? A
quickie while he traveled? True love, as Marilyn hopes? I'm sorry,
maybe it's oedipal, maybe it's envy, but I cannot imagine my father
feeling "true love," even in the confused hyper mixture of sex and
love I feel for Marilyn, for anyone.

After dinner, Dawn and Chelsea put on a magic show. Chelsea
stood at the front of the room with Dawn close by to give her the
hints needed for her to guess the right cards. I used to be my
brother's accomplice in similar shows. Chelsea, slightly too plump in
a velvet dress, was charming as she flubbed some of the tricks. Dawn
watched her like a hawk, occasionally crying out, "No! That's not it!"

When they were done, they presented my father with the gifts
they had made and bought for him. The bought gift was a bag of
freshly ground coffee, his favorite kind. They had wrapped it in pink
and white spotted paper and tied it with a ribbon. "Isn't the paper
nice?" Dawn said, hanging over him.

"My favorite kind."

"It isn't what you think," Chelsea said excitedly as he tore off the
wrapping. "It isn't what it seems."

My father smiled. "Nothing ever is." Opening the package, he
took a deep sniff. "Ah! Wonderful! A perfect present."

They kissed him, delighted. "We knew you'd like it."

I tried to envision myself years ahead. Will I effortlessly grow into
that role, or was my father that way at my age too? Becky was staring
at me and I smiled across the room at her. Later, as we passed in the
hall, she gave me a hug and said, "I love the way you look in that
shirt! You look so handsome." The shirt is one she gave me for
Christmas.

I reached up and touched her hair, let my hand slide down her
back. "I love you."

"I love *you*."

Will I ever say those words to her again without a twinge of guilt?
They emerged unrehearsed, a genuine expression of what I felt, but

the instant they were out of my mouth, I felt ashamed.

At the end of the evening my father went into his study to get me a book about which he said he was interested in my opinion. I followed him and, impulsively, closed the door behind him. As he was searching for it, I said, "Thanks for not saying anything about . . ."

He looked up with the barest glaze of a smile. "It never happened."

"I'm glad you understand."

"Man's dearest possession is his right to a private life."

It wasn't as though I expected or even wanted a clarification or expansion of "I did something like that once," but that dry aphorism, so like my father, shut the door with total firmness on any personal disclosures. He handed me the book. I took it and went to join the others.

Yet I felt—maybe angry is too strong—but annoyed. I had wanted just one added word, something along the lines of "She was very lovely." Why? Why the fuck does it matter what my father thought or felt about Marilyn? Yet curiously, in a different way from her, I want to elevate my relationship with her. I don't want him to think I'm just screwing around. Maybe it's that I feel he has such disdain for my professional life so far, that I want him at least to respect my private life. Not that he has much more respect for Stef, who's two years older than me, but Stef has wisely put many miles between himself and my parents, whereas I still live within forty minutes of them.

At home that night I made love to Becky with more ardor and genuine feeling than I've been able to muster of late. Not that I think she senses any difference, but I felt relieved that I could. I've accepted the fact that fantasies of Marilyn will intrude or stimulate, but the nightmare of impotence seems still a fear, rather than a reality. Whew.

My sister, Ginger, asked if she could stay with us for a few days in March. She was home to celebrate her twenty-second birthday but didn't want to stay with my parents, with whom she still has a stormy relationship. "Do you mind?" I asked Becky.

"No, why should I mind?"

I don't think Becky is crazy about Ginger, but because I am fond of her, she tolerates her existence. Ginger strode in, mini-skirted, a short leather coat, boots, Was there an Irishman somewhere in one of my parents' pasts? Ginger has gorgeous legs, light reddish-brown curls, freckles even and a nose which, if not up-turned, is still as far from Jewish as Debbie Reynolds'. "Look at all of you!" she exclaimed at dinner. "I can't get over it."

"Can't get over what?" Becky asked.

"Here all my friends, who're ten years younger than you guys, are getting divorced or breaking up, and you're still—just like Mom and Dad! The nuclear family. It's really impressive."

There was clearly more than a shade of irony in this observation. But Becky took it straight. "It's funny how with us, it's the opposite. We don't know anyone who's divorced. Or even thinking of it." She laughed contentedly. "I guess the people we know are just dull old fogeys."

Ginger gave me an affectionate glance. "I can't think of Benjy as a dull old fogey . . . *or* as a father of four! My God!" She glanced in the direction of the twins, who were in a portable crib in the corner of the room. "You're lucky they're not identical."

"I know," Becky said. "Though we never would have dressed them alike."

"Still," said Ginger, "they all seem so warped for life, twins, with their own parents not even knowing who they are. Identical ones I mean. It's like they have this permanent identity crisis from the second they're born!"

Like me, I thought. "So, how's Schuyler?" I asked. The latest of her boyfriends, an agriculture major from Indiana.

Ginger sighed. "Gone the way of all flesh."

"What does that mean?" Dawn asked.

"I pitched him."

"You mean you broke up with him?" Chelsea asked.

"Yeah. . . . Aren't I vicious? I really am. I'm terrible. Here's this sweet, darling, perfect guy and his whole aim in life is to plant good things to eat, to raise horses, I mean literally the salt of the earth . . . but God he was boring! My friend Nancy said, 'Ginger, Schuyler is one of the nicest guys I've ever met in my whole life. But nice can be dull.'" Ginger raised her glass. "I'll drink to that."

The girls are fascinated by her. "What was dull about him?" Dawn wanted to know.

"Our sex life was just—we might as well have been married—listen, no offense to you guys, but, God, every Saturday, he'd, like, climb on top of me and—"

Becky was looking more and more ill at ease. "Ginger, maybe . . ." she stammered. "The girls are so young."

Ginger looked puzzled. "Oh you mean, to talk about sex?"

Becky nodded.

Dawn stuffed a large bite of chocolate cake into her mouth. "We know about all that garbage," she said.

Becky stiffened. "It's *not* garbage."

"Yeah, Mom, seriously," Chelsea said. "Relax. We know!"

"Listen, I didn't mean just about sex," Ginger said quickly. "All I meant, with Schuyler everything about our life was so organized, so. . . . I mean, like he'd follow me around: did you take your vitamins? Did you take your birth control pill?"

"Was that so you wouldn't have a baby?" Dawn wanted to know.

"Yeah," Ginger said. "Oh, I want to have one eventually, but look at me! I'm just a baby myself! I wouldn't know what to do with it."

"I'll help you," Dawn offered. "I can come and live with you and help you take care of it."

Ginger beamed at her. "What a terrific offer! Well, someday I may take you up on it, but not for a while."

I looked from Becky, who was still looking concerned, to Dawn, who was clearly mentally packing and ready to leave with Ginger on the next bus.

"I'll only come if you have a girl," Dawn amended.

"Great. . . . You know, it's funny, poor Schuyler just adored babies and all his girlfriends have been like me. Really scattered careerish types who wouldn't know a diaper from a roast beef bone."

The girls doubled over with laughter at this image.

After dinner Becky drew me aside and asked, "Benjy, please speak to her. . . . They're so young! And it's not just that. All her attitudes! She's so . . ." She stopped, evidently not wanting to offend me by attaching too strongly derogatory an adjective to Ginger. "And say something to the girls too."

"What should I say to them?"

"Just that . . . well, that, even though she's your sister, you don't necessarily condone or share her feelings about sex or love, that you feel it's something really special, that you hope they'll wait for someone they truly love. . . ." She looked so anguished and pleading that I said quickly,

"Okay, sure. I'll speak to them."

When I went into the girls' room, Dawn was already in bed, staring dreamily at the ceiling. Chelsea was brushing her teeth. "I love Aunt Ginger," Dawn said earnestly, before I'd even broached the topic. "I want to be just like her when I grow up."

"If you do, Mom'll have a cow," Chelsea called from the bathroom.

"I want to have lots of boyfriends who really love me," Dawn embroidered, "from the bottom of their heart."

"Hearts." Chelsea came into the room and, seeing me, hugged me. "I just want one, someone as nice as Daddy."

Dawn gave me an appraising look. "You want to marry someone like Daddy?" she said, surprised.

"Yes," Chelsea said stoutly, "because he's so nice."

I patted her. "Thanks, sweets."

Dawn was continuing to gaze at me with her steady, almost detachedly wide-eyed stare. "I haven't decided yet," she concluded.

I sat down on the edge of Chelsea's bed, feeling awkward. "There are a lot of ways to lead your lives," I said. "The main thing, both of us feel—"

"Both of who?" Dawn said.

"Mommy and me. . . . We both want you to find someone you really love." I stopped, uncertain how to go on.

"Well, sure," Chelsea said. "We're not going to find someone we really *hate!*"

"Mommy had a boyfriend in college before she met you," Dawn said. "And you had ones before you met her."

"True."

"So, why can't we have a lot, if we want?"

"You can." I sighed. "You can have as many as you want."

"I wonder what's the most boyfriends anyone ever had," Dawn said. "A thousand?"

"Missy Braun has a thousand already," Chelsea said bitterly. "They all fight over who should sit next to her."

"They don't love her, though," Dawn said.

"They do so! You should *see* all the valentines she got! She had to bring a special shopping bag to school!"

"Big deal."

I kissed them both and wandered out, wondering if I'd said what Becky had wanted me to. Dealing with Ginger would be more tricky. When I came into the bedroom later that evening, Becky was reading. She looked up.

"I *like* Ginger," she said. "It's not that. . . ."

"I know." I started getting undressed.

"All I want, really, is for the girls to have what I've had, someone worthy of their total loyalty. I don't want them to waste it."

Help! With my halo slipping down around my knees or ankles maybe, I crawled into bed. "I don't think I am worthy," I admitted.

"You are," Becky insisted. "I don't know why you still have such an inferiority complex, sweetie. Of course you're worthy."

I smiled uneasily.

"Mother had so many friends who were so bitter about their husbands," Becky said, putting down her book. "I grew up, wanting so *much* not to be like them." She snuggled into my arms. "If I hadn't found you, after what happened with Ellis . . . maybe I would've gotten like that."

"Never," I said, kissing her, hating myself. "Not a chance."

In the morning the girls raced off to school, Becky took the car in for a checkup, and I was left at the breakfast table with Ginger, who was still in her nightgown. Mrs. Morgan was busy with the twins. I glanced surreptitiously at Ginger. Her nightgown was almost see-through. At least even without twenty-twenty vision one could clearly see the contours of her slender, lovely body. Thank God Ginger was just eight when I left for college! What a torment adolescence could have been had we been two or three years apart instead

of eight, her frolicking around the apartment in all her nubile care-
less splendor, me, grossly overweight, burdened by rumbling in-
cestuous longings, wolfing down Mounds bars in the bathroom. Now
I can appreciate her loveliness, but it doesn't cause any dire sexual
torment.

"Becky wanted me to speak to you," I said.

"Oh God, I'm sorry," Ginger said. "You mean, with the girls?
About sex and all? I never will again, talk about it to them, I mean.
It's just—they're so mature! They're so terrific! I just *love* Dawn. I
feel like kidnapping her."

"She loves you."

"What a heartbreaker she's going to be one day! . . . She looks just
like you, Benjy, your eyes." She looked solemn. "Does Becky think
I'm a bad influence, slutting around like I do?"

"Not really," I retreated. "She's just had such a different background."

"I know!" Ginger bit into a frosted doughnut. "I think it's genera-
tional, a little, don't you, though? I mean, I just have the vague
feeling women didn't in her day, or if they did, they felt all overwhelmed with guilt if it wasn't true love, quote unquote."

"Men too, to some extent," I said, watching with fascination as she
licked the frosting off the tip of her nose.

"I thought men just went out and did it," Ginger said.

I sighed. "Not all, alas."

She gazed at me fondly. "You're lucky, you and Becky. Maybe I'm
the black sheep of the family. But it's strange, Benjy, really, coming
from a family like ours, with Mom and Daddy so hopelessly screwed
up, that *you* emerged unscathed. I don't know how you did it."

I burst out laughing. "Definitely scathed. . . . Anyhow, do you
really think they're hopelessly screwed up? I thought they were
pretty happy."

"Happy?" She looked amazed. "Well, but it's all so . . . Mom
sucking up to Daddy, that hideous, seething idolatrous thing, and
underneath wanting to kill him."

"I don't think she wants to actually kill him, do you?"

"Of course she does!" Ginger smiled. "I remember once she was
giving me this lecture on how important it was for a wife to 'mother'

her husband, take care of him, but instead of 'mother,' she said 'murder.' I thought: aha!"

"Well, maybe deep down."

"Not just deep down! . . . And that whole thing with Vivien Velthaus!"

"What whole thing?" Vivien Velthaus is Czech, a violist who plays in small baroque chamber orchestras. She and her husband, Hans, are friends of my parents. I remember her as small, like my mother, with large luminous dark eyes and short fluffy white curls.

"*You* know! The way Daddy fawns over her and goes to all her concerts, rain or shine. They had this monster fight one night because it was ten below and Mom wanted to stay home and Daddy insisted on going and Mom tried to bar his way and said it was disgraceful and disgusting."

I wonder if Vivien was the "I did something like that once." "I still think they're happy together," I said, wondering why I was clinging to that.

"Maybe," Ginger said. "It seems like death to me. . . . But Daddy always had that conflict with women, wanting to be married to someone who'd wait on him hand and foot, but deep down lusting after women with more of their own thing. . . . That's what he likes with Vivien, I think, how she teases him, not putting him on a pedestal the way Mom did."

What does Ginger really think of Becky and me? And are we just repeating that same pattern? I don't think so. I think Becky loves me, but I don't think she regards every word that issues from my lips as sacred . . . thank God. "What do you think about Stef?" I said, realizing I'd never talked about any of this with anyone. "Do you think he's made a good marriage?"

Ginger made a face. "I'm such a bad person to ask," she said. "Lois always seems so uptight. Everything has to be so perfect and neat and tidy. God, I'm a feminist to my fingertips, but seriously, sometimes I think what she really needs is to go off and fuck some brainless oaf ten times a day for a year."

"Maybe she is."

"I wouldn't bet on it."

"How about Stef?"

"He's just dull. . . . To me he's like Mom and Daddy, another generation. I mean, he's twelve years older than me and he talks to me like I'm still in junior high! He's always asking if my 'social life' is good. . . . But who am I to talk? My life is pure chaos." She grinned. "At least it's fun, some of the time, anyway."

"That's all that counts."

She kissed me. "Thanks. . . . Listen, drive me into the city, okay? I'm having my hair cut before I brave the lion's den." Meaning our parents' apartment.

I waited for her. Usually, on Tuesdays, I meet Marilyn at the turn-off onto the highway. We come into the city in our separate cars, but we drive side by side or one in back of the other and pause when we stop at the bridge to exchange a few words. I glanced at my watch. Nine-forty. Probably she's in the city already. We're meeting at the apartment at three-thirty.

As I was driving along, Ginger in the seat beside me, I saw Marilyn's car in my rear-view mirror.

"I think that woman's trying to pass you," Ginger said.

"She can, if she wants," I said. I caught Marilyn's eye, but made no change in my expression.

Ginger turned around. "What's wrong with her? Is she trying to pass or not?"

"Don't worry about it."

A few minutes later, Marilyn did pass me on the right. As she did, she smiled just slightly and winked.

"Hey, get that!" Ginger said. "I think that lady just winked at you."

"What?" I said, pretending to be self-absorbed.

"That blond. . . . What do you know! Does that happen a lot, women trying to put the make on you?"

"Not really."

"Maybe you ought to . . . No, I didn't mean that. You've got something good. Why mess around?"

I didn't say anything.

"Did you ever try celibacy?" Ginger asked.

"For sixteen years."

"No, I mean, once you'd started, did you ever stop, just to, like, get your bearings? Clear your head, all that?"

"Never."

"I tried it for two months last spring because I have this girlfriend, Eliza, who said it really made her see things in perspective. She said she missed it the first month and then she stopped and felt tons more energy for her work. But that never happened with me. I just kept missing it. Finally, one night I just went out and picked someone up at a bar. It was like bolting down junk food, but I was just going *crazy*. . . . So, are you really switching fields? You think you'll make it as a designer?"

"I don't know. . . . My life is a total mess, Ginge," I suddenly heard myself say. "I don't know what the hell I'm doing."

Ginger looked alarmed. "What do you mean?"

"Oh, nothing really," I retreated. "Just I know Dad feels I'm letting him down and—"

"So? That's ridiculous, wrecking your whole life just to please him!"

"I don't know if I have any more talent at design than I do at law."

"Don't be silly. You're good at *both*." Ginger said. "You're lucky. You have *lots* of things you could do. . . . Look at all these guys that plod along, hating every second of their lives."

"I feel Becky married me as a good, solid guy who knew what he wanted, and——"

"You *are* a good, solid guy," Ginger said. She touched my shoulder. "You *are*, Benjy."

I hesitated. I wanted very much to tell Ginger about Marilyn. I knew she wouldn't mind, wouldn't scream in horror, but I somehow just couldn't get the words out. "I pretend to be good," I said morosely. "My whole life is just pretending to be whatever people want me to be—Dad, Becky."

She looked at me solemnly. "It's funny, I always envied you. I always thought you were good *naturally*. It seemed like I couldn't turn around without driving them crazy and there you were, doing 'the right thing' without even trying."

"At a terrible cost."

"Really? I'm sorry. Then stop! Seriously, just stop doing it."
I laughed. "Yeah."

"No, I know, it's hard. Giving up the rewards. . . ."

That's it. I don't want to give up the rewards. I want, though I hate myself for it, to keep playing the game, keep having Becky love and respect me, keep having my parents think of me as the nonrebel, a little confused maybe, but still on the right track.

"Maybe I'm lucky," Ginger said, stretching. "Not caring about all that. I never thought of it that way."

"You are."

She smiled. "The question is: can I do great things, get my act together? 'Cause I don't want to just fuck around till I'm forty. I want what *you* have: kids, a good job. Remember Mom's friend Fiona? The 'rebel without a cause,' blaming society, men, anything she could lay her hands on. I don't want to *be* like that."

"Not a chance."

I dropped her at the beauty shop and watched as she sprinted into the store. For some reason I felt as though, having come so close to being genuinely revealing, I'd escaped from a danger that might have caused me great harm. Driving away, I felt absolutely light-hearted, almost buoyant. Or was it just the knowledge that, at three-thirty, Marilyn would be lying naked in my arms?

PART TWO

✦

1976

Call Girl

"So, he takes out this gun, and points it right at me, and says, 'Gimme the money or you're a dead duck!'" Aaron laughed delightedly. "Just like in the movies!"

Marilyn was looking very pale. "What did you do?"

"I gave it to him. Listen, I wouldn't be here if I hadn't."

I leaned over, pointing my finger in his face. "You're quitting that job tomorrow, do you hear me?"

Aaron sighed heavily. At eighteen, his attitude to me is usually sarcastic, dismissive. "Dad, come *on*, nothing happened. . . . What're you getting into such a sweat about?"

"Because you've been working there a month and there've been two holdups already! Lots of those guys just shoot, they don't give you time to get the money. It's not worth it."

"He's right," Marilyn echoed. "Please quit, sweetie. I go crazy with worry all day thinking of you there."

Aaron looked sullen. "But it's a great job. I like the people. I need the money."

He's starting college in the fall, the University of Vermont. His grades were good, but his SATs weren't fantastic. I don't care. What the hell. I went to CCNY and I've done all right. "Look, I'll pay you, okay? I'll double whatever you're getting there."

"For what?" He looked suspicious.

"For not going there! Do whatever you want! Take a course in something."

"I want a real job. I'm sick of studying."

"Come into my office. I'll find something for you to do."

"That's not real work. They'll all know I'm just there because of you. They'll look down on me."

"He's got a point, Mo," Marilyn said. "I can see that."

Marilyn still adores Aaron, only now she has competition. At first, it was just a bunch of anonymous girls, calling at all hours. Then, last year, Valeska appeared on the scene and we hardly saw him for nine months. She's a sweet girl, really, a little plump, shy, black hair, a Ukrainian Catholic. Her father's a union organizer, rabidly right wing, a big, beefy guy who came up to me at a school meeting and said he thought Aaron was a very bright, responsible boy and I should give myself credit, not like some of these bums who just want to prey on pretty, innocent girls.

Thank God I don't have a daughter! Can you imagine what that would be like, having to eye every boy that walked in the door, knowing they're probably all on the make and total schmucks but she "loves" them. Even with the boys I worry, but it's different. With Linus I worry that he's practically seventeen and looks like twelve and knows as much about sex as I did at six. That is, he knows everything but I'd take an oath he's never even kissed a girl. He's not gay. I have no fears about that, but his idea of a perfect Saturday night is to stay home and read Dostoevsky or some science fiction trilogy. With Aaron, what I worried about was whether this shy little cutie Valeska was going to sink her claws in him and get him to marry her. The shy ones can be worse than the others that way. The way she'd hold his arm with that possessive, clinging look in her big brown eyes. Well, he's "deeply in love," but it doesn't seem to have prevented him from having a crush on a girl at work named Aimee. I'm sure that's ninety percent of the reason he doesn't want to quit the job.

"Look, I'll call some people tomorrow," I said. "Will you at least consider something else? Is it worth getting killed just because you like the people there?"

Aaron sighed wearily. "Dad, no one's getting killed! Why don't you go down and talk to the owner? How come *he's* not scared? He's had the store five years and so he's gotten ripped off a few times. It's not, like, a major problem."

"What *is* a major problem then, if getting shot for a job where you're earning eighty dollars a week isn't?"

Just then the phone rang. Aaron sprang to answer it. If it's for him, especially if it's a girl, he has extrasensory perception. He got it on the second ring. "Oh hi," he said, sounding really casual. "Yeah, I was just telling mine about it too. Right, same here. They're into this big trip about how dangerous it is and how I'm going to get my head blown off. . . . Well, thanks. I didn't *feel* cool, but I'm glad I *seemed* that way. . . ."

His voice trailed off as he carried the phone into his room.

I smiled at Marilyn. "Aimee?"

"It must be."

Marilyn was jealous of the thing with Valeska, especially the habit Aaron had gotten into of sleeping at her house all week, just stopping off at home to pick up fresh clothes and drop off dirty ones. But now that Valeska's spending the summer at her uncle's farm in Ohio, Marilyn's gotten worried that Aaron may be "straying." "Has he said anything about her? I don't even know where she comes from or goes to school."

"Nothing." Aaron is pretty closed about his "private life." He's not too tall, but has a compact, well-built body, dark hair, a brooding intense expression which I can see appealing to girls.

"I think she's in college."

"Older than him?"

"I imagine."

When Aaron got off the phone, Marilyn asked, "Does she have a friend?"

"Who?"

"This—Aimee . . . I just thought maybe you and Linus might double date sometime, if she knew someone."

Aaron rolled his eyes. "Give me a break, Mom. Linus?"

Marilyn reddened. "Why not? He's a little shy, but lots of girls like that. Not everyone wants some macho hulk."

"Look, fix him up yourself, will you? Any girl *I* know would take one look at him and head for the hills. He's just a loser, in that particular respect."

"I think that's cruel and untrue." Marilyn looked at me. "Don't you? Don't you think lots of girls would like Linus once they got to know him?"

"Definitely." But it worries me too. Linus is almost through high school, has never been on a date. He still has the same hair style he did at six, sandy hair falling straight into his face. And those big moony hazel eyes. An elf. I used to worry about his being kidnapped by one of these sex perverts. He has that dreamy androgynous look that could get some sicko really turned on. Aaron's constant teasing doesn't help, though Linus seems to tune a lot of it out. But I've seen his face get a stricken, anxious look at some of Aaron's jibes. Well, I have a plan. Marilyn would kill me if she found out, but she's not going to. First I have to see if Linus is interested.

That night, as we were getting ready for bed, Marilyn said, "I found out Aimee's three years older than Aaron. But girls are so much older to begin with. What does she want with him?"

I grinned. "Guess."

"I always liked boys that were older when I was that age. . . . Oh dear, poor Valeska."

"Look, if he quits the job, he may never see her again."

"I pray he does." She touched my arm. "You were so good, Mo. I hate the thought of his being there. Today it was all I could think about at work!"

Marilyn's working now, has been for six years. She's a buyer for a moderate-sized department store out here, Taylor's. It's her first job, and basically she seems to like it, except for her boss. I've told her no one likes his boss, but she insists Lauren Taylor is the prime bitch of all time. Marilyn's invented a new version of S and M: analyzing Lauren's character at two in the morning. I've told her: a bitch is a bitch. They come in all sizes and colors and can be found anywhere. Who cares what "made them the way they are"?

"I'm afraid she's going to fire me," Marilyn said frowning. "She's just looking for a chance. Why? I've done such a terrific job. Everyone there loves me but her! Sometimes I think that's it! *She* hates me because they all love me."

"So, you'll get another job."

"Mo! It's not that easy!" Her face was flushed with anger and fear. "I might not get *anything!* They fired Anne four months ago and today I met her downtown and she told me it's impossible. There's nothing out there."

"You'll get something. Will you believe me?"

"No! What do you know about it?"

"I know something about business."

"This is different. . . . Lauren's a powerful woman. She can blackball me everywhere if she wants."

I sighed. "Look, it may not even happen. Why go through all this every day?"

Marilyn lay back. "Yeah, you're right. . . . But it seems like every day she finds something to go at me about. I swear, I think she lies in bed at night thinking of things. Like, just for an example, she ordered all these terribly expensive party dresses for the preteen department. A hundred dollars a dress! Velvet, with lace collars. Kids don't dress like that anymore. They wear jeans. I tried to tell her that, but no, she orders a whole pile of them. So now they're all hanging there, reduced to a quarter of what they cost originally and *still* no one wants them. . . . So she says to me, we're not displaying them prominently enough, we're not encouraging customers to buy them! People wouldn't take them *free!* They don't *want* them. It's her mistake, so she blames me."

"That's what business is all about." I reached for her and kissed her shoulder. "Forget it, okay?"

Have you ever fucked a woman while she's mentally figuring out how to get back at her boss for ordering two hundred velvet dresses that won't move off the racks? Sometimes I have the energy to try and get Marilyn to relax and forget Better Dresses and Lauren Taylor and really space out the way she used to, but tonight I didn't have whatever it takes. Look, at forty she still has a terrific body. I'd say eighty, ninety percent of the time she gets as much satisfaction as I do. What more can you expect after twenty years?

Saturday I saw Linus, practically for the first time all week. He's taking two physics courses at Columbia Summer School and spends most of his free time at the library. We were alone in the house, but even so I closed the door to his room behind me. He was lying on his bed, reading. He's always reading.

"So, your birthday's in two weeks," I started off.

"Yeah, right."

"Have you given it any thought?"

"What?"

"Hey, put down your book a sec, okay? Have you thought at all about what you might like for your birthday?"

He shrugged. "I guess cash is the easiest. There're some books I might get. One of them is pretty expensive."

I stood there. I didn't know how to begin. "I had an idea," I said.

He just looked at me calmly, expectantly. He's not a sarcastic kid, like Aaron, though he's a lot smarter in some ways.

"About your birthday . . . I was wondering. You know sometimes men, at my age, your age, any age really, find it hard to find what they're looking for in a woman and so some of them go to women who are really beautiful and experienced, who—"

"You mean prostitutes?" His look of disgust was so palpable, I froze.

"No, nothing like that. . . . Just—call girls."

"It's the same thing, isn't it?"

"No, not at all. Prostitutes are dead-end characters, hard-bitten, sleazy. . . . These girls are a whole other thing, very bright, charming, maybe temporarily in need of extra cash."

"Dad, could you be a little more specific? What do you have in mind?"

"Well, I don't know how much sexual experience you've had, but . . ."

"Give a guess."

I looked at the L.L. Bean panda poster over his bed. "So, I thought maybe for your birthday we could drive to Boston and, if you wanted, I could arrange for you to. . . ."

Linus smiled. "You're afraid I'm never going to get laid, huh?"

"No, not at all. I just—"

"You may be right, but—" He sighed. "I don't know. It just seems kind of . . . Would she really be pretty?"

"Gorgeous. . . . You just tell me what you want and I'll set it up. Any hair color, size, personality."

Linus looked thoughtful. "I guess—this is if I decide to do it. I haven't, so it's hypothetical—well, not too tall, not over five four, and, well, she wouldn't have to have a fantastic figure . . . just so long as she wasn't totally flat-chested."

"They rarely are."

He was silent, gazing intently into space. "The thing is, I thought these women were kind of . . . you know, like, basically they hate men. That's why they're into it."

"No! . . . Maybe some do, but so do some regular women."

"Did *you* ever do it? I mean, go to one of them?"

I hesitated. "Once, many years ago."

"How was it?"

"Fine. I can't remember it too well, but it was good, no problems."

"You didn't pick up any virulent diseases that turned your brains to mush?"

"Not that I've noticed."

"What kind of background did she come from?"

"She was getting her doctorate in sociology, actually."

"No kidding?"

About fifteen minutes later, as I was having a sandwich in the kitchen, Linus came downstairs. "Uh . . . about what we were talking about before?"

"Yeah?"

"Well, this is still hypothetical. I haven't decided one way or the other."

"I understand."

"Okay, so let's just imagine that, even though this woman, or girl, or whatever, is a pretty, sexy, nice person and all that, for some reason I just don't feel like doing it. I'm not in the mood or whatever. Or for some reason the whole situation turns me off. . . . What I'm getting at is, do you think she'd be angry or maybe hurt?"

"Of course not!" I took a swig of beer. "Listen, the point of this is: *you* call the shots, okay? Whatever you want to do or don't is up to you. You can read her *Remembrance of Things Past* in French if you feel like it."

He took a pickle off my plate and bit into it. "You don't think she'd take it personally? Like, assume I didn't find her attractive? Because I don't want to hurt anyone's feelings, someone I don't even know."

"You won't hurt her feelings." I looked at him. Six feet two, a half inch taller than me, if it weren't for his lousy posture. He weighs a hundred and forty-five pounds. Skin and bones. Why do I love this kid so much? It doesn't make sense, even to me. I love, am fond of, like, other people—Marilyn, my mother, my sister, Aaron. But if someone tried to hurt Linus, I'd give up my life to save him without even thinking about it for a second. And I consider myself to be a fairly self-absorbed kind of guy. He's as different from me as anyone I've ever met. It doesn't make sense, but there it is.

I've decided to stage this happening, if it ever occurs, in Boston. I figure telling Marilyn I'm taking Linus there for the weekend for his birthday sounds better than just taking him into New York for the day. And that way, no matter how it works out, we'll have the whole weekend together. I asked Bibi last time I was in if she knew anyone, but she said she's totally lost contact with all that, what she considers her "past life." She's married now. Ravi finally came over about five years ago and they moved to Newton Center, not far from my mother, actually. She has two kids, a boy and a girl, real cuties, she's shown me photos. The little girl looks just like her, her dark eyes, dusky skin, long black hair. She teaches at Tufts and doesn't ever dress Indian-style anymore. She says her husband doesn't like it. When he first came over, he wore a turban, but now he just wants to blend in with the crowd.

When she sees me, she wears a sari sometimes, just for old times' sake. We don't go to bed together anymore. She told me, once she got married, she wanted to be straight; I sympathize with that. So we just meet and talk, a couple of times a year. I like her. She's a nice, warm person, really interested in me, in my life, in my kids. I know Marilyn wouldn't believe that, but it's true. Once or twice I have to admit, we did end up doing it. But it was basically a friendly, almost nostalgic kind of thing. My sex drive is still alive and well, but I'm not ravenous anymore. I look, I appreciate, but I don't seem to meet anyone where I instantly go into a frenzy.

I've never regretted not calling Marilyn on that escapade of hers ten years ago. She did it, she got it out of her system. What's the big deal? I mean, sure, I could have divorced her, remarried, but, like I thought then, I would have lost the kids, and from where I sit, at fifty, marriages are all pretty much the same. Sure, some are horrendous, but the good ones are like mine: days that are terrific when you think you're the luckiest man on earth and days when you want to walk away and forget the whole thing. I'm not sorry I encouraged Marilyn to go back and get her degree and work. True, sometimes now she's exhausted, not there, but I do think it makes her appreciate what I go through, even if she doesn't always admit it.

It was funny, the other evening at a party some woman was bitching about her husband not being "supportive" enough and suddenly Marilyn launched into this speech about how terrific I'd been, how encouraging, how if it wasn't for me she might just be another bored, anxious housewife. Not only that, she claimed I'd given her lots of helpful advice in her career, that she was glad I knew the business world so well. Needless to say, at home she's never said anything like that! By the end of her speech, all the husbands were staring at me resentfully, like, who is this paragon, kill him! And the women were all murmuring about how ahead of my time I'd been. Marilyn ended up, "Seriously, Mo could've written *The Feminine Mystique.* He really could. He had lots of those ideas before Betty Friedan did." Is there any glory sweeter than undeserved praise? But maybe I do deserve it, who knows.

I called Rich Kushner in Boston and told him the situation with Linus and what I was looking for.

I know Kushner from work. He's in our Boston office. He's a bit of a weirdo, but he knows these girls, goes to them fairly often. Two days later a photo arrived. It was a five-by-seven, a svelte, lovely creature with hair curving over her shoulders, lying on one side, her hand almost touching her pubic hair, an inviting but "sensitive" expression. Perfect. I went to Linus's room and showed it to him.

He studied it carefully. "Can I keep the photo or do you want it back?"

"You can keep it."

I hope he keeps it out of sight. Once, about three years ago, I met a young woman on an airplane who told me she'd been in *Playboy*. They ran an issue on college girls. You definitely wouldn't have suspected from her manner or even her way of dressing. I happened to have the issue and she signed her photo. I gave it to Aaron who'd just gotten a subscription to *Playboy* for his bar mitzvah, a present Marilyn thought was "in the worst possible taste." Anyway, he loved the photo. He put it up over his bed and I think his applying to the University of Vermont was definitely in part because he expects a younger version of Cindy to turn up in his dorm.

Marilyn said it was fine if I took Linus to Boston that weekend. Aaron was busy with Aimee. She quit her job at Foot Rest also. I asked him what his plans were for the rest of the summer and he said he thought he'd "play it by ear." I think she's enrolled him in a modern dance class she takes. The rest of the time I imagine they've got pretty well taken care of.

Aimee slept over the night before Linus and I went to Boston. In the morning she was in the kitchen scrambling some eggs. I felt a kind of pang. Poor Valeska. One morning a few months ago, to surprise us, Valeska got up at dawn and baked some special Polish sweet rolls. They were fantastic. She could open a bakery any day. Marilyn said Valeska asked her for an apron and she had to confess she's never worn one. At nine Valeska sat there, beaming, as we all tucked into the sweet rolls. She looked a little like a sweet roll herself, soft, white, floury skin, a fragrant, honey-like sweet smell.

Aimee, the government major and future mayoral candidate, is a different kettle of fish. Skinny in tight jeans, she cast me a foxy, appraising look. "Hi, Dad," she said. (We'd just met the night before for the first time.) "Want some eggs?"

"No thanks."

Aaron was watching her in a dazed, fascinated way. Maybe Valeska was too sweet, too adoring. This one is going to give him a time. "Maybe you could find Aimee a job," Aaron said. "She's graduating in January and she thinks she'd like something in the Boston area."

"I've got a super résumé." She grinned. "A lot of it's even true."

"Send it to me. I'll see what I can do."

"I put it on your desk."

I guess she doesn't waste time. I sat down, poured myself some coffee. "So, how're you kids going to spend the weekend?" Or need I have asked?

"Aimee has to go to the doctor," Aaron said. "He's in New York. I thought I'd drive her."

"Nothing serious, I hope?"

She flipped the eggs on a plate and set it down in front of Aaron, taking another plate for herself. "No, it's just this idiotic thing. For the second time in nine months my IUD fell out! The first time it just kind of vanished so the doctor thought maybe it was wandering all over my body and might come out through my nose or something. That evidently happens. But this time it just fell out, plop." She reached in her pocket. "This is what it looks like. Isn't it weird? I mean, men have worked for *centuries* to protect women from pregnancy and all they can come up with is something like this. It looks like an amulet the Egyptians might have worn to ward off evil spirits! Maybe I should just hang it around my neck and pray to Osiris."

Aaron was industriously eating his eggs. I wish the kid the best of luck.

Marilyn came back from shopping just as Linus and I were ready to set off. I'd decided to drive. Linus drives now and we can take turns. I figured it might be more relaxed that way. Marilyn hugged him. "Have a wonderful time, hon."

He smiled his usual shy smile. "I will, Mom."

I got a big hug too. "See you Sunday."

"Will you see Leah?"

"I think so."

I'd thought we might eat together, just the two of us, then stop over at my mother's for coffee later. She's married again, to Emil. It was a slow courtship. They became lovers, lived together for two years, then went through a big fuss about whose house they should live in. Both of them were deeply attached to their respective houses, which are only about half a mile apart. Finally, they decided Emil would keep his house, but rent it out to boarders. He left himself a room there where, as he puts it, he can "retreat" if he feels like it. I saw the room once. Books from floor to ceiling—you could hardly see out the window. He ran a building contracting firm, but once confessed to me he hated every second of it and was glad when someone offered to buy it from him. He seems to adore my mother, who runs his life with the same peppy zest with which she ran my father's. And, like my father, he thinks of her as very delicate and fragile. Last year she had pneumonia, admittedly serious for a woman in her early seventies. But for six months afterward, every time she coughed, even lightly, he'd rush over with blankets, sweaters. At night, precisely at nine, he makes her drink something he calls an "Adenauer cocktail," some mixture of brandy and eggs and hot milk. When he's out of the room preparing it, my mother says, clearly pleased at the attention, "He wants to fatten me up. He likes zaftig women. So, if he likes them, he should have married one, right?"

I'm glad she remarried. It makes it easier, less guilt if I don't have time to call or write. And my mother's of the generation of women who, whether they worked or not, had to be married, had to have someone to fuss over, boss, be concerned about. "He's not the lover Joe was," she confided once, "but he's a good man. He's kind, thoughtful. I never was one of these women who were looking for Prince Charming. I want someone I can live with, who'll laugh at my jokes, who likes my back rubs, who forgives my cooking. That's enough."

I let Linus drive till we got to the Mass Turnpike at Hartford. He got his license recently and is an excellent driver, except for those moments when I get the feeling he's in some other world, solving the problems of modern physics. It was a beautiful summer day. I felt good about the two of us being together. I never feel Linus is critical of me the way Aaron is. He seems to accept me in his shy, bemused way, or, to the extent he doesn't, he keeps it to himself.

At Hartford we stopped for gas and I took over. Linus glanced at me. "Dad, did you have a lot of girlfriends before you got married?"

I hesitated. "Quite a few. . . . It wasn't like now. There wasn't any, with nice girls, sex before marriage, living together, none of that. And I knew I didn't want to marry till I was thirty, so I had to . . . It limited the kind of women I could see. I didn't want some father after me with a shotgun."

"Did you know right away, when you met Mom, that you wanted to marry her?"

"Not instantly, but fairly soon. . . . I was ready then. I'd fooled around enough."

"Did you, like, do it with her before you got married?" He paused. "Maybe that's an overly personal question."

"No, no. . . . Well, actually, we did do it a few times. It's a good idea. To see if you're sexually compatible. Not everyone is."

"Yeah," Linus suddenly looked gloomy. "I guess one reason I'm doing this is, I figure most girls I'm going to meet, if I ever *do* meet someone who'll want to do it with me—I realize that may never happen—"

"It'll happen."

" . . . well, most girls today have quite a bit of experience and I don't want to *totally* make a mess of it, be just *completely* inept so she figures, 'Oh my God, who *is* this jerk?'"

I smiled. "Don't worry. . . . It'll happen. And it'll be great. You're worrying about it too much."

"Yeah, probably. . . . Well, with Samantha—it seems weird to be talking about her when I haven't even met her!—but I decided I'll tell her I've never done it, just so she won't. . . . I mean, I don't want her to expect this great lover or something."

"She knows already."

He looked at me. "How?"

"Well, I think Rich, the guy who—I think he told her."

"Oh." He was silent a minute. "She isn't, like, someone who specializes in weird cases, is she? Like guys who've never done it before?"

"No, he just thought . . . Also, you're not that weird, Li."

"I am. . . . I hate to break it to you, Dad, but I *am* extremely weird."

"Everyone is."

"Maybe. . . . But look at Aaron! He's already had around six girlfriends."

"So?"

"I'm not trying to make a federal case out of it. I'm just saying by most standards he would be considered an average, normal guy, and I wouldn't."

"You're going to do okay, believe me. Everyone feels that way before they get started."

"Did you?"

Did I? God, it seems so long ago I can hardly remember. "Sure," I said, more to make him feel good than because I remembered it as true. "I felt the same way."

We had dinner at the hotel and then stopped over at my mother's. She's never fixed up a guest room and assumes we'll stay at a hotel, which is fine with me. Certainly, in this particular case, it's a lot easier. When she opened the door, she looked up at Linus. "Look at him!" she cried. "My baby! You're growing a mile a minute. How tall are you now?"

"Six two," Linus mumbled.

"Six two!" She called over to Emil, who was reading the paper. "He's six two already. I can't believe it." After putting our coats away, she brought out coffee and cake. Beaming at Linus, she said, "So, you must have a million girlfriends?"

Linus shrugged. "Not exactly."

"He's bashful." She smiled at me. "I bet you have to lock the door at night to keep them out."

I just smiled back.

"No, it's good," she said, as though we had agreed with her. "The more you have, the bigger choice." To Linus she said, "You pick a nice girl."

"Maybe he doesn't want a nice girl," Emil suggested. "Maybe he wants someone sexy."

"So? Nice and sexy don't go together?"

"Not always."

"She should be nice, sexy, intelligent—"

". . . and Jewish," Emil finished.

"No!" my mother exclaimed. "Who cares about all that? That's old-fashioned. As long as she's not religious, I don't care what religion she is."

Linus laughed. "I don't have a girlfriend, Grandma," he said. "Not yet."

"He's just fifteen," Emil said. "What do you expect?"

"I thought he was seventeen," my mother said surprised. "How old is he?"

"He'll be seventeen tomorrow," I said.

"Seventeen isn't so young," my mother said. "But you probably study all the time, right? That's okay. Your father was like that."

"He was?" Linus looked at me in surprise.

It's true, my mother never knew much about my sex life. Maybe nothing. I made a noncommittal gesture.

"He never got serious about anyone till he was out of college. Lots of girls were serious about *him,* but he didn't reciprocate. You broke a lot of hearts, Mo."

I smiled sheepishly. "What can I say?"

"That poor little red-haired girl, you know the one. She played the violin."

I couldn't think who she meant.

"You remember! She was always getting free tickets to concerts. She lived with her father. . . . "

"Oh, Dee Donnelly." I did remember. Timorous, sweet, an "everything but" girl as far as sex went.

"The way she looked at you!" my mother reminisced. "True love!"

"But no sex," I added.

"Listen, you can't always have both."

"Nowadays it's different," Emil put in. "Nowadays they have both. . . . Right, Linus?"

Linus smiled shyly. "I guess. . . . So they say."

My mother laughed. "So they say!" To me she said, "You keep an eye on him."

"I will," I promised.

On the way back to the hotel Linus said, "I wonder what Grandma would say if she knew—"

"Bite your tongue."

"People her age think everything is so easy now. It's not! I wish they'd stop saying that."

"It's never easy," I agreed.

Back at the hotel, he got into his pajamas. As I was getting into bed, he smiled. "So, my last night as one of the uninitiated."

"Sleep well, kid."

The next day I dropped him at the library. He said he needed to do some research for a report. I thought of calling Harriet, but decided against it. Her thing with Saints Preserve Us is still going, though not on a sexual basis. According to her, they decided "the guilt was too great" so now they meet and take forlorn drives in the country and have melancholy conversations about life. She said once, one beautiful autumn day, they broke down and did it in the back seat of the car and then felt so terrible, neither of them could drive the car back to the city. "Terrible because it was terrible, or because it was wonderful?" I asked. "Because it was wonderful, because our lives are terrible, because we belong together!" She practically started crying, talking about it. Oh, and he converted to Judaism, and now goes to temple regularly. I wonder how he explains that to his wife. He felt, according to my sister, that he was a Jew at heart and that by becoming one, he was blending with my sister spiritually. So now Kevin McDonnell has the distinction of being the only red-haired, freckled school superintendent in Boston who celebrates Yom Kippur.

When I dropped Linus off at Samantha's apartment, he waved and smiled and I sat in the car, feeling horrible. I suddenly felt afraid I had done a really foolish, maybe criminally foolish thing. Maybe he just has a low sex drive. Maybe he'd have been perfectly happy being a virgin till he was thirty or forty or even forever. There are guys like that who sublimate it all into their work. And what if she isn't right, makes fun of him, whatever. If she does, I'm going to kill Rich Kushner! But what good will that do? He'll say he tried his best.

I decided to see a movie, just to pass the time. I ducked into some double feature, but I felt too restless and left halfway through the second feature. By then it was eleven, so I figured I might as well go back to the hotel. I'd told Linus he should take a cab when he was through. Maybe he'll be waiting for me when I get there. The deal was he could stay all night if he felt like it, but he could leave any time also. I told him to forget the money, if he wanted to leave at nine, he could.

I opened the door to our hotel room and dashed frantically over to the beds. Empty. I glanced at my watch, and then tried to give myself a pep talk. It's not even midnight. Relax. If it was terrible, he'd be back early, humiliated, miserable. He's probably having a great time. She's a pro, she's taking it slow, making him feel good about himself, about the situation. Finally, after popping two Valium, I got into bed and gave a small prayer: *please* let it have been okay. Eventually I fell asleep, but I slept fitfully, waking up every hour or so to check the time.

At three-twenty the door opened. "Li?"

"Hi. . . . You still up?"

"Basically. How'd it go?" I could see him in the dark, sitting down on the edge of his bed and starting to take off his shoes.

"Well, let's put it this way, I doubt—I could be wrong, but I very much doubt—she will ever get her doctorate in sociology." He sounded a little crocked. His voice was slow and wobbly.

"How'd you like her, though? Was it okay?"

"It was. . . . Let's see. Well, first, just to set your mind at rest, we actually did it. Twice, in fact. On a scale of one to ten, the first time was two and the second was . . . eight." He stood there, wobbling, considering it. "Maybe even eight and a half. . . . No, eight."

"What was wrong with the first time?" I asked anxiously.

"I was too nervous. . . . Oh, listen, we didn't just jump into bed the second I got there. It was interesting. I thought she'd come out in a transparent nightgown or something really sexy and instead she opened the door just in jeans and a T-shirt. Maybe because she knew I was a student. She didn't look like what she is, is what I'm trying to say."

"So, if you didn't go to bed, what'd you do?"

"Just sat and talked. She asked me about school, all that. I mean, it was basically like she was acting this part of trying to be really interested in everything I said. Like I said I was taking this advanced physics course? And she said, 'Oh, *I* almost took physics in high school, but I was afraid it would be too hard.' I felt like if I'd said, "My hobby is dissecting live dogs,' she'd have said—" he mimicked her voice—"'Oh, *I* used to do that, it's so much fun!' She was trying really hard, is what I'm saying."

"And then?" I was halfway on the road to feeling okay again.

"Well, I guess she saw I was sort of nervous. Actually, I was about a million times more nervous than I acted, but I must have seemed a little nervous to her, so she started plying me with all these drinks. She had about a hundred kinds of brandy and stuff like that. I told her I didn't drink, but she kept saying it would make me feel good and she always had a 'little something' at night. . . . So I finally figured what the hell. Otherwise maybe we'd still be sitting there. I just kind of bolted it down. Man, it was strong! Some kind of pear brandy or something."

"Having a drink isn't a bad idea."

"No, it was good. You get this kind of weird, euphoric feeling. . . . Well, then she began sort of coming on to me, but she was good. I mean, obviously for five hundred bucks she ought to be, but she didn't, like, just rip off her clothes and suddenly appear naked in the doorway. We just kind of ended up in bed. I don't exactly remember how it happened."

"Yeah?"

"The trouble was, I was so scared I wouldn't do it that I kind of pounced on her and it only took around two seconds." He laughed. "I doubt it was one of the great erotic experiences of her life. God, she had a *perfect* body! I kept thinking how weird that must be, to go around all day knowing that any man in the world, if they saw you naked, would go crazy. But to her it's probably just like a body. She probably doesn't even think about it most of the time." Still seeming stunned, he ambled into the bathroom to brush his teeth. I was wide awake by now and feeling a hundred percent better, even mildly euphoric myself. What had I been so worried about? The kid was fine!

Linus came back and sat down again. "I guess the second time was better just because I figured we weren't going to do it again, and she seemed more relaxed, like she wasn't trying so hard. She began telling me about her family—she's from a farm in Idaho—and how I reminded her of her younger brother and she was sure I'd be a big hit with girls. I mean, obviously, she *has* to say that, but still. . . ." After a pause he said, "She didn't know I was Jewish."

"Why should she?"

"I don't know, I just thought she would. Anyway, she said she was surprised, that Jewish men weren't usually so—I forget the word. I think she meant shy or something." He got under the covers. "Wow, that pear brandy was really powerful! I can still feel it. I think I might still be a little drunk, actually. So, Dad, thanks, seriously. It was an interesting and maybe even potentially useful present. Only time will tell, to coin a phrase."

I laughed. "I was a nervous wreck all evening. I saw one and a half horror movies and then came back."

"Were they any good?"

"I don't know."

Linus laughed. "If I was Thorpe Emery, I'd come to school Monday with a T-shirt saying, 'I got laid in Boston.'"

"Who's Thorpe Emery?"

"He's this guy in my class. Anything that happens to him, he has it printed on a T-shirt. I think his uncle runs one of those stores that do it. Once he came to school with a T-shirt saying, 'I failed the Botany final.' Another time, 'My Aunt Rosie is a yenta,' but the best one was, 'I fucked Clover Reedy on the Ferris wheel at Jones Beach.' On the other side, it said, 'Twice.'"

"Who's Clover Reedy?"

"No one knew. . . . Maybe just a figment of his imagination." He yawned. "So, sleep well."

"You too."

We both slept till almost noon and woke up slightly hung over, me from the Valium, Linus from the pear brandy. Then I remembered I had told Bibi I would meet her at one. I'd told her I was coming in with Linus, but I hadn't been sure I would bring him along. I still wasn't.

"Do you need to go to the library again?" I asked.

He shook his head. "I got most of it done yesterday."

I considered. "Well, maybe you'd like to come along and meet a friend of mine. Her name is Bibi Dahr. She teaches at Tufts."

"Sure, why not? I don't have anything better to do."

He seemed totally incurious about who she was, which was a relief. Bibi was waiting downstairs when we came down. Whenever I know I'm coming to town and want to see her, I write her care of a friend of hers, Sasha Weinberg, and tell her the time and place. I tried to look at her through Linus's eyes, but it seemed to me he would just see a tall, attractive dark-haired woman in a blue dress, just like someone we might have over for dinner. "Bibi, this is my son, Linus. It's his birthday today. He's seventeen."

She shook his hand. "Happy birthday, Linus."

We sat down and the waiter asked if we wanted anything to drink. Linus shook his head. "I still feel sort of . . . I had some pear brandy last night," he explained. "It was really strong."

"I never have after-dinner drinks," Bibi said. "I don't have the head for it."

"Dad said you're, like, a teacher?" Linus said. "What do you teach?"

"Sociology."

He laughed. Bibi looked puzzled. "No, I'm sorry," Linus said. "It's just something . . . Maybe I'm still drunk from last night. Can you be drunk eight hours later?"

"I don't think so," I said.

"Your father mentioned you're interested in physics," Bibi said.

"Yeah, I haven't basically decided yet. I don't think I want to teach. Most people are so dumb. . . . Maybe that sounds sort of snobbish."

"No, it's a problem," Bibi said. "There aren't very many bright students. I'm not even sure I'll get tenure. I'm up for it next year, and it's so much harder for a woman."

"Yeah?" Linus said. "Is it?"

"Much."

"You could go into some other field."

"I like the field I'm in." She glanced at me. "You don't look alike, I don't think, do you?"

"Everyone says I look more like Mom."

"You're both tall, of course, but—"

Before she had finished speaking, Linus suddenly sucked in his breath. "Oh God."

"What?" Bibi and I both said together.

"I did something really stupid." He seemed very flustered. "I forgot my watch." He glanced back at me. "I left it—you know, where I was last night."

"We'll get it back," I said soothingly.

"Some girl I know," Linus said to Bibi. "I left my watch at her apartment."

Bibi smiled. "I'm sure she'll keep it for you."

"The thing is, I don't know her that well. . . . Maybe I should call her up, only I don't know her number." He looked at me appealingly.

"Li, relax. . . . We'll get the watch."

"This is typical of me," Linus said to Bibi. "I'm always doing things like this." To me he said, "Dad, I'm sorry but I'm really worried about the watch. Would you give me her number and I'll call her?"

I took the slip of paper out of my pocket and gave it to him. He disappeared, sprinting down the hall.

A few minutes later he returned. "She found it," he said happily. "I'll just run over there and pick it up, okay?"

"Take a cab. We ought to get started not too late."

After he left, Bibi smiled at me. "He's darling."

I told her about Samantha. "I was manic last night, that it might've been a really stupid thing to do."

"He seems fine."

"He's . . . The thing with the watch is typical. He can figure out the intricacies of modern physics, but you ask him to buy a quart of milk and he comes back with orange juice."

She smiled affectionately and reached out, touching my hand. "You're like a Jewish mother, so concerned about him."

"Yeah, well, it's true. How can you help it?" Looking at her, feeling her warm hand on mine, I began wishing it was the old days, that we could go upstairs and be together for the rest of the afternoon. Maybe it was as much nostalgia as horniness or some combination of the two, but I felt a pang of longing which must have transmitted itself to Bibi because she said softly, "Maybe we could . . ."

God, I was tempted! I looked at my watch. "The trouble is, he'll probably be back any minute." I couldn't face the possibility of that.

Li coming into the room, watching us together. It may seem foolish, but I want his respect, whether I deserve it or not.

"Some other time, then," she said, taking her hand back. But she looked a little hurt or cool.

"I would've liked to," I said as we embraced when she got up to leave. "It's just—"

"I understand."

After she left, I went up to the hotel room and packed our stuff. I felt edgy, irritated, even though there really hadn't been any possibility of its working out other than the way it had. I glanced at my watch. Almost three. I decided to go down to the lobby again and check out. Linus had said he'd be right back, and that was almost an hour ago.

I checked out and sat down to wait for him. Three twenty-five. Damn. Where was he? I was getting more than irritated. Bibi and I could've . . . But what if something's happened to him? An accident? Three-forty. Still no Linus. I imagine him mugged, in an alley, trying to explain to Marilyn. Finally at ten of four he came sprinting into the lobby. "Oh hi, Dad." He was out of breath.

"Where the hell were you?" I felt furious.

"What do you mean? I told you . . . I went to get my watch."

"It took you two hours! What'd you—get lost in traffic or something?"

He turned red. "It just took longer than I expected. Should I go up and pack?"

"I did all that. . . . Let's get going."

In the car he said, "I didn't know. . . . I figured you'd be talking to that lady, and, well, okay, we did. . . . She just acted so nice and friendly. She said she'd noticed I'd forgotten it right after I left but she didn't know how to get in touch with me and she was worried I'd think I'd lost it. She's a really nice person."

I didn't say anything.

"So, what was I supposed to do? Say, 'Sorry, I'm so busy I can't possibly find time to go to bed with you?' Give me a break!"

Christ. "What was *this* time, a nine and a half?"

"Why're you so sarcastic all of a sudden?" He looked hurt. "It was excellent."

"Good."

"Who *was* that lady, anyway?" Linus said.

I don't know if he was trying to turn the fire on me. "What lady?"

"The one we met."

"I told you. . . . She's a friend, from a job I once had a long time ago."

"How come she has that Indian name?

"She's Indian."

"*She* was Indian?"

"Yeah, what of it?"

"She sure didn't look it."

"Well, she used to dress in a more traditional style, but her husband wants them to try and blend in with American customs."

"I don't think she's Indian, Dad, I really don't."

I felt like killing him. "Well, she is, I'm sorry."

"So how come she's teaching sociology?"

"Indians can't teach sociology?"

"It just seems . . . There's something funny about it. What is she, some old girlfriend of yours or something?"

"Something."

"I figured. I just had that feeling. . . . Listen, I don't mean she wasn't attractive. Did you, I mean, was this someone you. . . . Did you just date or what?"

"Or what." I smiled wryly. "Can we not talk about it?"

"Sure." He leaned back. "I feel sort of sleepy. Do you mind if I sleep a little?"

"Go right ahead."

Linus slept, I drove. My irritation vanished as I glanced over at him, breathing heavily. He's still a baby. My mother's right. And it was nice of Samantha to throw in a freebie.

The business is doing well. In fact a guy offered me six million for it a few months ago. I was half tempted. I suddenly thought, now that the kids are in college or almost, maybe Marilyn and I could take a year's trip around the world, stop off at all kinds of exotic islands, maybe live on one of them for a couple of months. First, Marilyn got semihysterical. "How can I leave my job?"

"I thought you said you were going to be fired."

"I said I *might* be. . . . But even if I am, I want to look for another one. Look, Mo, you've been working for thirty years. I just got started. I don't want to throw it all up now, just when I'm getting going! Go around the world without me, if it means that much to you. But count me out, okay?"

For a while I even thought of that, just take off, a year by myself, doing whatever. But at fifty, I don't know. It's hard to get up the momentum. It's funny, at thirty or even forty maybe, I would've leaped at the chance, but no one was offering me the chance then. Now I have it, but it doesn't seem quite so enticing. Even if I did it, what happens when I get back? I don't have hobbies, there's nothing special I've been hankering to do all these years that I haven't had time for. I'm not saying I love every minute at work, but I don't think I could function without it. The long and the short of it is, I told the guy no thanks and here I am, still.

About two months after I took Linus to Boston, I was getting ready to leave for the day. It was four-thirty Friday afternoon when my secretary buzzed that a Mrs. Fetterman wanted to see me. For a second I couldn't think who that was. Then I remembered, Mrs. Benjy. I've seen her, seen both of them at parties over the years, but I can't remember ever talking to her. "Put her on."

"She's here, in the office. She'd like to speak to you for a few minutes."

I hesitated. If I leave after four-thirty, the traffic is murder. "Okay, show her in."

Mrs. Fetterman edged hesitantly into the office. She has a round, sweet face, a little heavy, a housewife look, hair going gray. "Um . . . Mr. Greene?"

"Mo. . . . Have a seat."

She sat down tentatively. "It's really nice of you to take the time. I know I should have called first or written. I hope I'm not interrupting you."

"No, not at all."

She licked her lips nervously. "Well, this . . . I feel funny even bothering you about something like this, something so . . . I don't even know!"

I waited.

She took a deep breath. "The other day I was looking for something, our will, actually, we're redoing it slightly, and I found this photo among my husband's papers and I thought—well I'm not sure—I thought it might be a photo of your wife?" She reached into her purse and handed me the photo.

Oh Christ. Marilyn. A snapshot. Naked as a jaybird, lying belly down on a bed, gazing wistfully at whoever—guess!—was taking the photo.

"Do you think it *is* your wife?"

I nodded.

"Do you have any idea, I just wondered, I could have asked Benjy of course, what it was doing there? I realize I shouldn't have been looking through his papers, but I really needed the will and, well, there it was, in an envelope, actually."

By then I had time to collect my wits. I smiled. "Well, I'm afraid I really am the culprit in this situation, Mrs. Fetterman."

"Becky," she urged.

"You see—you'll understand none of this should be repeated—"

"Of course!"

"When Marilyn was in college, she was asked, a group of girls in her class were asked, to pose for *Playboy*, and, well, she was young. Just for a lark, she accepted."

"Goodness." Becky was looking at me with big, slightly frightened eyes.

"I have the shots at home—they only used one—and I'm afraid one night, many years ago, I got a bit high, well, more than a bit, I got fairly smashed actually and—it was at a party, I don't remember who gave it. I showed a bunch of those photos to some of the men that were there. I guess feeling proud, Marilyn having such a good figure. It was adolescent, no excuse for it, Marilyn would have killed me."

"I can imagine," Becky said earnestly. "She never found out?"

"No, but when I got home, I realized I didn't have the photos. I must have left them around and probably some of the men took copies of them."

"I see." She digested this information. "It's just, Benjy doesn't seem like the kind of person who . . ."

"I think all of us, under certain circumstances, do things we might not normally. He may well have just pocketed the photo, being a bit smashed himself, tucked it away in a drawer, and completely forgotten it was there."

"Yes, that's true." She looked relieved. "Benjy *is* very forgetful. I don't think he'd have kept it, if he'd known. . . . So, you don't think I should mention it to him?"

"I wouldn't. I mean, it was a decade ago, easily. . . . He'd only be embarrassed. And I'd hate for Marilyn to find out."

"How awkward for her!" Becky said. "Your sons don't know, do they?"

"I don't think so."

About halfway through the conversation I began feeling like my head was about to split apart. I must have leaned forward because she said anxiously. "Are you all right?"

"Fine, I just . . . I get these headaches occasionally."

"Are they migraines? My mother gets them."

I nodded. Suddenly, at the word *migraine* the headache became one. The power of suggestion! "I'll be fine."

She had risen and was standing near my chair. "Are you sure? I know how awful they can be. Do you have any pills?"

I shook my head.

"Please let me drive you home," she said. "I'd feel terrible if you drove, feeling that way."

I considered. It was true, I didn't feel like driving, but I could take the train. These headaches don't scare me except the fear that they're connected to the disease my father got, tic douloureux. I know I should get a checkup, find out what's going on, but I haven't so far.

"Do let me drive you," she said in her quiet, insistent voice. "I'm so afraid I've upset you by bringing this up."

"No, it's just . . . I have these headaches. I had it before you came."

"As you said, what happened ten years ago, well you can hardly blame yourself for what *you* did, especially if you'd been drinking. That's what my father says, why he never *ever* drinks. It makes you do things you might regret later."

"Right." I followed her out the door and told Shirley I'd see her in the morning.

In the car, on the way home, I allowed myself the luxury of closing my eyes and not speaking. With migraines even a soft word sounds like a scream. Becky Fetterman was good, she didn't say a word, no jolly attempts at conversation. By the time we were near our house, I was feeling a lot better. "Listen, could you let me out at the corner?" I said. "It just might seem odd if *you* drop me off."

"Oh, of course." She looked at me, frowning. "I feel so guilty that I may have . . . Really, it's *my* fault. Benjy has said so many times that I shouldn't fiddle with his things, try to rearrange them, all that. I'll just put the photo back right where it was and forget all about it!" She smiled brightly.

"Good girl."

I gave myself an A-plus for Improvisation. There's only one problem. That photo wasn't taken ten years ago. Marilyn started wearing her hair that way two, three years ago, at most. I walked in the door, wanting simply to go upstairs, put a cold pack on my head, and lie down. Marilyn came rushing out, waving something in her hand. "How could you?" she shrieked. "How *could* you?"

I staggered backward. "How could I what? What are you talking about?"

"This!" Triumphantly she handed me the photo of Samantha that Rich Kushner had mailed for Linus. On it in a wavy girlish hand, "To Linus, a real sweetheart, much love, Samantha." "Don't try to get out of it," Marilyn said. "He's told me all about it."

"Marilyn, listen, I have a terrible headache. We'll talk about it later." Fuck Linus. Can't he lie for once?

"We will *not* talk about it later!" she said. "We'll talk about it right this second! He's a baby!"

"He's not a baby. Not anymore. He's seventeen years old."

"He's a baby for seventeen. You've said so yourself. These women are hard, cruel, vicious people! If it was someone his own age—"

"She's eighteen."

"They're depraved, selling their bodies—"

I grabbed her by the shoulders. "What the fuck do you know about it?"

She looked startled. "I—"

"This was a nice, sweet girl, recommended by someone I know."

"A nice, sweet girl who sells her body to men?"

"They're just like any other women. They're just more honest."

Marilyn stared at me. Gotcha! "They're not the same," she said weakly.

"Look, will you shut up for a second? One, I'm not talking about this any further now because I feel sick. Two, all that hypocritical shit about morality strikes me as slightly ironical coming from you, or from any middle class woman who—"

"I—I don't know what you mean," she stammered.

"Think about it, okay?"

I climbed the stairs, feeling a cold, bitter, wonderful kind of triumph. A few minutes later Marilyn looked in the room. "Is it a migraine?"

"Yeah."

"Well, I—I brought you some ice water." She came over to the bed and placed the bowl with water and a tray of ice cubes in it on the floor. Then she squeezed out the washcloth and put it on my forehead. "Does that feel better?"

I couldn't help smiling. What a quick transformation! Doting, concerned wife. "It feels great."

"How did you drive home?"

"I took the train."

Ten minutes later, Linus poked his head in the door. "Dad, listen, I'm really sorry. Mom found the photo and—"

"It's okay."

"I guess I should have lied, but I couldn't think of anything. You know how your mind goes blank?"

"Sure."

He stood there. "I didn't mean to get you into any kind of trouble."

"It's okay. Don't worry about it."

He left the room quietly, closing the door behind him. A couple of times the cloth on my forehead heated up and I dipped it in the ice water again. I could feel some water trickle down my neck, but it felt good. Marilyn peeked in sometime later.

"Can I get you something to eat?" she whispered. "I saved the chicken."

"I'm not hungry."

After that I must have fallen asleep. When I came to, the clock on the bedside table said three-twenty and my headache was gone. That moment after a migraine headache goes away is magical. You wake up, a little groggy, and suddenly: no more pain! And just the fact of that, of that horrible, drumming insistent pain not being there makes you feel so lighthearted and light-headed you're ready to forgive everyone in the world anything they've ever done or said or thought. It's like a mystical experience. Needless to say, it never lasts more than an hour or two.

Marilyn was sleeping next to me, breathing quietly, innocently. Is there any other way to breathe? Can you breathe guiltily? I guess it's that in sleep people look so vulnerable it's hard to feel or maintain the intense fury of waking life. I thought of Becky Fetterman, her eagerness to believe anything I would tell her. If she'd found a photo of her husband and another woman fucking, I could have explained that away with little trouble. Tell me what I want to hear, said her big worried eyes. Make me feel secure again. So I did. It's fun, maybe disquieting, how easy it is to be a magician. Improvisation. It reminded me of those acting classes long ago. Imagine you are a businessman whose wife may have been unfaithful many years ago. Imagine that one day a woman enters your office, the wife of your wife's former or maybe present lover. She hands you a photo. . . .

When the photo was in front of me, though it was slightly out of focus, I felt certain that the hairdo was a giveaway that it had been taken in the last few years. Now, lying in the dark, that certainty, knowledge retreated. How does Marilyn wear her hair? It's always been the same color, basically the same length, slightly below her shoulders. It just seems to me that at some point she began letting a piece of hair fall forward over her forehead. What does it matter? Do *I* want to know?

Becky Fetterman needs to believe in her husband's "innocence" for herself, so she can put him on a pedestal, so he can fit into her image of the world, of marriage, of men. I don't think I have that need. I've never put Marilyn on a pedestal. I don't think I've done it with any woman, come to think of it. "You're not a romantic," Marilyn once hurled at me in an argument about something. True. I feel proud of it, actually. What does romantic mean? Seeing the world not as it is, but through rose-colored glasses. And then, at some point, the misty pink fuzzy stuff fades away and—kaboom! Unless you want to spend a lifetime maintaining it, even against every evidence to the contrary.

Benjy Fetterman. Let's just say, for the purpose of argument, that he and Marilyn are still making it together. He must be forty, forty-five. He has a pile of kids, four, five at least. I get the feeling he's not that successful at what he does, something with furniture, I think. In short, all the usual tsimis of everyday life. Yet for ten years this guy has been risking his marriage, his mental and physical health for the sake of banging my wife once a week, once a month, however often they do it? If so, you've got to hand it to him. Maybe he has some secrets he could share with the rest of us.

What do I want? To run out, at fifty, and find "the perfect woman," to go through all that courting shit again? I don't think I could, frankly. Or no, I guess I could, but Christ, do I want to? No. And it's funny, knowing and not letting on that I know, just having Marilyn anxious, is like having a nuclear bomb. You don't have to use it. Just having the other side know you have it is enough. Maybe I'm a perverse son of a bitch to savor that kind of power, but I do. I get a kick out of it.

Night thoughts.

At eleven in the morning, the sun streamed in the window. Marilyn was already up. I dressed and went down to the kitchen. I felt ravenous, not having eaten since lunch the day before. It was Saturday. In the kitchen were Aimee, Aaron, and Linus, gathered around the kitchen table.

"Hi Dad," Aaron said, looking up guiltily.

"Where's your mother?"

"Having her hair done or something. She said she'd be back at eleven."

I poured myself some orange juice and went to find the cereal. When I sat down, I saw that they were looking at the two photos, the one of Cindy, the *Playmate*, that I'd obtained for Aaron, and Samantha's "personally inscribed" photo to Linus.

"I'm sorry," Aimee said, "but I don't think either of them are that gorgeous. They're, like, malformed! Who wants breasts like sacks of wheat? *I* wouldn't. Even if God himself appeared and said, 'Here, pick a pair, any pair,' I'd stick to what I have."

"You're not posing for *Playboy*," Aaron pointed out.

"So? I'm supposed to cry my eyes out because a million horny teenage boys aren't jerking off looking at my wonderful body? No thanks. . . . What do you think, Mr. Greene?"

"Mo," I said, sprinkling sugar on my cereal.

"Which one do you like better, Dad?" Linus said. "Be objective."

"How can he be objective?" Aaron said. "There's no such *thing* as objective. Everything is a matter of opinion."

They placed the two photos side by side. Maybe it was because I had a slightly fond feeling for Samantha, for having broken in Linus, but I finally said, "It's a tough choice, but I've always liked brunettes."

"So, how come you married Mom?" Linus said. "She's a blond."

"He's talking about sex," Aaron corrected him, "not marriage."

"Anyway, she's not a natural blond," I said.

"No, but Mr. Greene," Aimee said, "I mean, Mo, seriously, would you like a girl with such gigantic tits? Don't you think they're kind of gross? I mean, look at them!"

I laughed.

Suddenly Aimee pulled her T-shirt over her head. She stood there with nothing on top except her two small pointy breasts. "Now look," she said, grinning. "Perfectly proportioned!"

"You're crazy," Aaron said, shaking his head.

She was looking at me. "What'd you think?"

"Lovely," I said.

"See!" She stuck her tongue out at Aaron. "He thinks I'm perfect."

"He didn't say 'perfect.' He said 'lovely.'"

"Same difference." She put her shirt on again. "So has your mother calmed down?" she asked Linus, who'd been standing there staring at her in a semi-daze.

"Basically," Linus said. "I think she was afraid I might have been traumatized for life."

"That's all such a prejudice," Aimee said hotly. "I bet most of those girls are just like anyone."

"Only better," Aaron said grinning.

"Not better," she snapped. "They just need a little dough."

"Would *you* do it?" he asked.

She looked uncertain. "I don't know. . . . Maybe not, but I'm still not prejudiced against it."

"But how *was* it?" Aaron asked Linus. "Was she really terrific?"

"How's he supposed to *know?*" Aimee said. "He never did it with anyone else."

Linus cleared his throat. "Actually, she was a very nice, intelligent person."

Aaron laughed. "Yeah? What'd you do, spend all night talking about black holes?"

Aimee put her hand over his mouth. "You're a pig."

"That's from physics," Aaron sputtered.

"You're still a pig." She looked at me. "Anyway, I think it was a super idea. . . . Maybe my mother should have done that for me at sixteen, found a gorgeous, perfectly built guy, and—"

"Girls can get laid without any trouble," Aaron said. "What's the point?"

"Not by guys who're the male equivalent of these critters."

Aaron took his photo. "She's not a critter," he said, pretending to be hurt. "You've wounded me to the core."

"Yeah, Dad said he knew one once who had a doctorate in sociology," Linus said.

They all looked at me.

"That was *after* she'd been a call girl," I said. "Not during."

"Huh." Aimee looked at me with that inquisitive foxy expression. "So, you've been to them too? What do you know? How come? Weren't you getting enough at home?"

Aaron socked her. "He's my father. . . . Stop embarrassing him!"

I smiled. "It's okay. No, this was before. . . . I didn't marry till I was thirty."

"Thirty!" She whistled. "Wow. . . . I bet you had lots of girl-friends, huh?"

"What's wrong with you?" Aaron said. "It's none of your business."

"I had a fair number," I admitted.

"How many were Jewish?" she persisted. "What percent?"

I laughed. "God, let me think. . . . Maybe twenty percent?"

She made a look of mock despair. "Only twenty? How come? I thought we were so sexy, so lush and intense. . . . "

"Jewish girls are terrific," I said. "Only in my day they didn't . . . They wanted to get married before having sex."

Aimee mulled this over. "God, can you imagine how weird that would be? You'd marry this guy, never even having seen his *body!* Like, he could not even know how to screw, and there your parents had spent all that dough on the wedding."

"Everyone knows how," Aaron said.

"They do *not!* A woman's body is like a fine Stradivarius. It needs a delicate touch, fine artistry, all that junk. . . . Right, Mo?" She looked at me again.

"Right," I said. God, she was sexy, and I had the feeling she was definitely attracted to me, not just flirting. A first: making it or even thinking of making it with one of Aaron's girls. I wouldn't, not in a million years, but it felt good to have her come on that strongly. Suddenly I said, "I think I'm going to go around the world."

"I thought you said you didn't want to," Linus said. "I thought you turned down that guy's offer."

"It'd still be good."

"Around the *world?*" Aimee said, eyes widening.

I explained, adding, "Marilyn doesn't want to go. She says she's just getting started in her work, but I figure when will I ever have the chance again?"

"I'll go," she said, excited. "Take me!"

"You?" Aaron looked horrified. "Why should he take *you?*"

She grinned. "I'm great company, wonderfully sensual, witty. . . . "

He really looked upset. "He's married!"

"So? Boy, do you have bourgeois values!"

"I don't think Mom would like it," Linus said seriously.

"What wouldn't Mom like?" Marilyn said, walking into the kitchen. She was carrying a bag of groceries.

Everyone looked embarrassed.

"Your husband was telling us how he might go around the world," Aimee said.

"Oh?" Marilyn looked at me. "I thought you decided against that."

"I've been thinking about it again." I met her glance. "You'll have a free year to fuck whoever you want, and so will I."

"Well, go if you want. You're entitled." But her mouth was set.

"You know where I'd like to go," Aimee said, "one of those South Sea islands like Micronesia, where they don't wear clothes and they just, like, totally blend in with nature."

"Sounds infinitely boring," Aaron said in a condescending voice. "She wants to go with Dad," he added to Marilyn, "but I told her you'd mind.

"Listen, I was just kidding," Aimee said quickly.

In my mind I went around the world with Aimee. Tropical beaches, fucking all day, no meetings, no traffic. "Well, I don't know. . . . "

"I can manage by myself," Marilyn said. "Go if you want."

"I don't really want to."

Her expression softened. "I'm glad. . . . It would be horribly lonely without you." She put her hand on my shoulder, caressingly, then slid into my lap. The three kids were watching us with a mixture of conflicted expressions.

"How cute," Aimee said. "My parents don't do that."

Marilyn is still slim. I put my arm around her. As I did, she looked down at the photo of Samantha. "She *is* pretty," she said softly.

"Mom, seriously," Linus said, "it was okay. She was just, like a regular girl."

"What would her parents think?" Marilyn said, still studying the photo. "How upset they'd be if they knew!"

"They don't know," Linus said. "They live on some farm in Idaho, only I think her father's dead or something."

"But he's looking down from heaven," Aaron said, "thinking, 'My poor little girl.'"

Linus, looking offended, took the photo back.

"Well," Marilyn said to me, rubbing her nose against mine, "I forgive you."

"Thanks," I said ironically.

The kids wandered out of the room.

"I guess I flew off the handle," Marilyn said, getting up. "I've been so tense lately, the job thing, everything. . . . "

Everything what?

She smiled at me wryly. "You'd better watch it with that girl of Aaron's. I think she has her eye on you."

"Sacred. Wouldn't go near her in a million years."

"Because of him or because of me?"

I shrugged. Let her guess.

She looked hesitant. "I'd miss you if you went. A week, okay, a month, but a year! I never understand those women who say they want 'space.' What for?"

"Don't ask me, sweets." I looked at her hairdo, freshly done, trying to reinvoke the photo in my mind. "Did you always have that piece in front?"

"What?"

"Your hair. I like the way it goes forward. I just can't remember when you started wearing it that way."

"Oh, I go back and forth. I never can decide. It's more classic the other way, straight back, but I think maybe this way is softer. Which do you like best?" She seemed pleased at my interest and touched her hair with her palms, smoothing it.

"This way, I think."

So? Erase the slate. The photo doesn't exist, is ten years old, is six months old, is . . .

In the afternoon we made love, snoozed. A good peaceful day. At three Marilyn went out again. Aimee was standing alone in the hall as I came down the stairs. "Give me a rain check?" she said smiling.

"On what?"

"Going around the world. . . . If you ever change your mind."

"I'll do that."

We stood for a moment, looking at each other.

"I guess I've always liked older men," she said wistfully. "My father, something. . . . "

I kissed her and went out the door, feeling her eyes on me as I skipped lightly down the front steps.

The Man in the Cake

"*I*f it's what you want, sure, I'll do it." He smiled and touched his mustache. "When would it be?"

"A week from Saturday," I said. "I'll let you know the details." I gave him a hug. "Thanks. You're a sweetie."

He blushed.

It's true, he's a darling! He must be Aaron's or Linus's age, but more of a street kid, stocky, well built. Angel Caruso. He oversees the parking lot at Taylor's where I work and always saves me a parking space, even when I get there late. Recently he grew a mustache, a big handlebar-style one, and it looks funny, like he's pretending to be a brigand or a Mexican guerrilla. "My girlfriend thinks I should shave my mustache off," he said. "What do *you* think?"

"I like it. . . . It makes you look macho."

"That's what she doesn't like. She says she woke up at night and saw me lying there and got scared." He laughed with pleasure at the idea.

"Well, don't shave it off for two weeks, okay?"

He followed me across the parking lot. "What should I wear?"

"Just, you know, underpants or whatever men call them. . . . Do you have any sexy-looking ones? Even a bathing suit would be okay."

"I have these silver ones Josie bought me for a joke. I hardly ever wear them." He looked uncomfortable. I guess men feel ambivalent about being seen as sex objects, even in jest.

"Perfect."

Angel was staring at me, puzzled. "You're sure Miss Tretler will like this?"

"Why not? I don't think she gets that much fun out of life."

"No, it's just that she reminds me of one of my aunts in a way and if anyone ever gave a party like that for my aunt, she'd scream bloody murder."

"Don't worry about it, hon. It'll be fine."

But hurrying into the building, I wondered just a little. It wasn't just my idea. It was Ila's. She's my best friend at work. She runs the housewares department and she's only been working at Taylor's for about a year and a half. She's divorced and this is her first job, but she worked before she got married so it wasn't so hard for her to find something. She's one of these superefficient people whom I might hate if I didn't like her so much. Benjy and I go to her house once a week because it's closer to Manhattan. We can both get there from work in less than half an hour. It's a small two-bedroom house, comfortable, neat. I feel it was generous of her to let us use it. I felt awkward even asking, but she just hugged me, gave me a copy of the key, and said to call first in case her boyfriend or a relative was staying over. Here's what our idea is. Griselda Tretler is retiring. She's been with the store practically since it opened—thirty years or more. Angel is right. She's like everybody's aunt—kind of chunky and good natured and always worrying about something. If you sneeze and she hears you, she runs out to get you lemon drops and keeps asking if you're better for the next week. She's never been married. She used to live with her mother in a retirement community, but her mother died. Yet she still lives there! It sounds morbid to me, living surrounded by such elderly people when she's just in her sixties. She said she moved there because her mother needed constant medical attention, and now she kind of likes it. She has her own apartment and all, but still.

Anyhow, Ila and I want to give her a party when she stops working and we thought we'd have a dinner at Ila's house, do all the cooking, order a big cake. But just for fun, at the end, we thought we'd make a big hollow cake out of paper. Angel will be huddled up inside, we'll wheel it in, and he'll jump out yelling "Happy Birthday" and kiss her. Then he can go get dressed and join us for cake and coffee. Ila says she thinks Griselda has a crush on Angel in an auntish kind of way. She's always saying what a thoughtful young man he is. Just because you're sixty doesn't mean you don't enjoy some fun occasionally. I bet I will at that age. And you can't judge just because Griselda isn't married and lives in a retirement community. Ila and I discussed once if she might be gay, but we decided she wasn't. More that maybe she was shy and heavy-set and it just never worked out. Or maybe she even has some lover on the side that nobody knows about.

What I hate these days—I've felt it for the last year actually—is how tense I feel when I go to work. The best time was when Lauren had pneumonia and was out for two whole wonderful months. It was like a holiday! I'd walk in, do my thing, no bother, no hysterical scenes. Mo says everyone has bosses like that at some time in their work life, male or female. Maybe. But what makes it so awful is she can't be fired because her grandfather started the store. So she not only works for it, she *owns* it partly. It's a bad feeling, going around all day waiting for someone to pounce on you, knowing if you do good things, she'll just ignore them, but if you do *one* bad thing or not even bad, if you just make some tiny error, she'll catch it in a second and will keep harping on it for the next *month*. Ila said maybe I should just quit. She's sure I could get another job.

I don't know. Maybe I could. But this is so convenient, it's five or ten minutes from where we live, and I like Taylor's. I like that it's not so gigantic. You really feel, after you've worked here a few years, like you know everyone. It's like a family business almost, and maybe because my parents had one, on a much smaller scale, that suits me. If only Lauren weren't part of the family! If only she were a man! I want to think—I do think, despite this—that women should be better at running things than men, kinder, more concerned with human values. But not Lauren. She's just a spoiled bitch. I'm sorry. I hate saying that, but it's true. I even feel bad that she's Jewish. Ila, who isn't, says that's silly. There's no reason Jews should be better any more than women should be, she says. But when Lauren has one of her fits and starts screaming at someone who isn't Jewish, I'm just

afraid they're thinking: a typical Jew. Especially if they don't know
that many. Lauren alone has probably done more to promote anti-
Semitism in Westchester than any other single person since Hitler!
Ila says, "There are just wackos in the world and she's one of them.
I've met dozens of men just as bad and dozens of non-Jews. You take
it too personally."

It's true, I do. Because basically I *like* working. Okay, so I'm not
doing something important in the great scheme of things. I'm not
earning vast sums of money, but I truly think I'm good at what I do.
It was funny the way I got started. I certainly didn't expect, when I
graduated from NYU in the beginning of 1970, that I'd work for a
department store. I'd taken some business courses—Mo said that
would be a good idea—and I took some courses in fashion merchan-
dising, but mostly I just took basic, nonuseful courses like Ancient
History and Modern Poetry. I figured I'd never learn about those
things again, so this was my chance. Then, when I graduated, it was
June and there just didn't seem to be *anything*. I'd go on interviews
and nobody would call me back. Mo said, after I'd been looking for
six months and was feeling totally demoralized, that I could work at
his office, but I just couldn't face that. It seemed such a comedown. I
could've done that without having a degree! So as a last resort I took
a job over Christmas at Taylor's because they needed extra people in
the wrapping department.

I never told Mo how much I hated it because I didn't want to
sound like a quitter just when I was getting started, but, boy, that
job was the absolute pits. I was on my feet all day long, wrapping,
wrapping every second. I didn't even have time to look up and take a
breath before someone would shove another package in my face.
One day, Christmas Eve, it was nine in the evening and I'd finally
come to the end of the line when an old lady staggered up with—I
swear!—twelve packages in some kind of shopping cart. The rules of
the store are that if someone appears after closing hours you don't
have to wait on them. But she looked about as tired as I felt, maybe
worse. You know that look old people get, all wrinkled and sunken
and pale? And she had such a sweet, soft voice. "Would you mind,
dear? I'd be glad to pay you extra. I know I shouldn't have saved it for

the last minute." We're not allowed to take money, so I just said, "That's okay," and started wrapping her packages. I was so tired, I almost felt like I was going to cry. My hands were shaking as I made the bows and tied the ribbons. When I was done, she smiled at me and asked my name. I told her.

Well, it turned out she was the sister of Oscar Taylor who started the store—he's dead now—and she called them up and said how helpful and gracious I'd been and bingo, that Monday they transferred me to the preteen department as a salesgirl. In a way, though I'm earning more now and wanted the extra responsibility, I liked working in the preteen department the best of anything I've done so far. Maybe it's because I never had daughters and it was kind of a vicarious thing. I'd see them troop in, sometimes alone, sometimes with their mothers, and the mothers would be trying to force them to buy something they hated and they'd be looking disgruntled and angry, and I'd come over and gently suggest the mother might take something that was in between, more of a compromise. Girls that age are so hopeless looking, most of them. Some are real little beauties, but most are skinny as rails with knobby knees and scraggly hair or chubby, somber little things with big eyes. So when you'd find something that made them look halfway decent, they'd look so happy and their mothers would be so relieved, it was a real thrill. Or waiting on the ones that came in alone, shyly, cruising around, with birthday money or bat mitzvah money, tempted by something you knew would fall apart the second they got it home. I'd find them something that was on sale, almost like what they wanted but costing half as much. That was one of the times Lauren screamed at me. Why was I pushing old, marked-down stuff when we had a new shipment of dresses hanging right there? She grew *up* with money! She doesn't know what it's like to not have that much, but to still need something pretty for a party. Fuck her!

On slow days I'd just stand there, watching them, imagining sometimes that one of them was my daughter. Maybe someday I'll have a granddaughter. If you have boys, you go to the boys' department, get them what they need. There's no fun in picking out something special. What do they care, as long as it's something roughly

like what their friends are wearing? Linus looks like he gets dressed
in his sleep most of the time, anyway. One day Benjy's middle
daughter, Dawn, came in. She doesn't know me, not to recognize. I
stood there, watching her. She was in her early teens then, slim,
sandy-haired. Her hair is the color mine was before I started dyeing
it. She's a terrific athlete, Benjy says, great at gymnastics, full of
energy. She looked so lovely, drifting around, looking at things with
a kind of wistful, uncertain expression. I went over to her and asked
what she was looking for. "Oh, nothing special." She looked up at
me and it was like a shock going through me, how much her eyes
were like Benjy's, as though he were standing there, staring at me,
and suddenly it all came back, how I used to fantasize about Becky
dying and my suddenly being the mother of all those little girls, how
scared I would be at first, but would do such a super job they would
adore me. Sure. Even as a fantasy, it never lasted long.

After she left, I couldn't stop thinking about it for the rest of the
day. I guess everyone does that, how things could have been different, how life would have gone if you'd done this rather than that.
Jeanette thinks I'm crazy. "Most women have enough on their hands
with kids, a job, and *one* guy who bitches about his life, and all that.
. . . You had to go out and get *two!*" But it wasn't *like* that! I certainly
didn't set out thinking I'd get two, wanting that. That time I met
Benjy in the supermarket the first time, even when we ended up in
bed, I never thought it was something that was going to last. I didn't
think, period. I guess sex does that to you. It must fizzle through
your brain so all those decisions which normally you could make in
one second, you just can't make at all. Or maybe you just don't want
to. It was like I kept expecting it would end, that some event would
take place that would end it without my having to make any decision. Once about five years ago Benjy got a really good job offer in
Michigan and I remember, because he was really serious about taking it, how mixed I felt, partly scared out of my wits—how could I
live without him?—and partly almost relieved because that would
end it. But he didn't take it in the end. I can't even remember
why now.

A fling. That's a funny word when you come to think about it.

Fling, flang, flung. It reminds me of something you hurl into the air and it hurtles upward and then just as rapidly swoops to the ground. Crash landing. But what we're doing is more like something you fling up and, for some reason, it *never* comes to the ground! It sails along, getting caught in air currents, getting tangled in the tops of trees, but somehow still airborne. Why *is* it still going? Sex? The trouble is, when you're involved in something you can't tell. It's always so many things. It's true, sex with Benjy is still the way I think sex should be at its best. Even now, ten years later—not always because we're human and often tired or disgruntled or whatever—but it's still something special, wondrous, something that I think of during the week which makes me smile even when everything else seems rotten or a mess.

Last month a funny thing happened. We were in the city together to see a comedy, *Same Time, Next Year.* Jeanette saw it and called me right away. "This is for you," she said. "It's *about* you." So I sent away for tickets and I was standing there in the lobby, waiting for Benjy, when all of a sudden I saw his father entering the theater, handing his ticket to the man at the door. Benjy didn't show up for ten more minutes, and while I was waiting, I wondered if I should tell him, even. I remembered how once, years ago, when we ran into his father at the movies, he was such a basket case. But when he finally came racing up (he never wears a watch, says he wants to be "free of the constraints of time"!), I said, "Your father's here."

He stepped backward, horrified. "What?"

"He went in around ten minutes ago."

"Then we can't go!"

"Benjy, of course we're going. We have the tickets. They're expensive orchestra seats."

"*He* always sits in the orchestra."

"So? What's wrong with you. Why are you so afraid of your father?"

"I'm *not* afraid of him! It's not that. I just won't be able to enjoy the play with him sitting there."

I was furious. Here I'd sent away weeks ahead for tickets, concocted dozens of excuses to have the day off in the city. "Well, *I'm* going!" Then, just as I was about to wheel off, I turned. "Listen, how about this? I'll go in, see where he's sitting, and if it's as close as ten rows in any direction to our seats, I'll come out and tell you. But if it's in another part of the theater, will you go?"

He still looked reluctant. "Okay."

As the usher was taking me down the aisle, I looked all around the theater. It's good my parents never go to the theater or the movies. I never even thought to be grateful for that. Just as I was getting into my seat, I saw Benjy's father. Our seats were in the second row, far to the left, almost on the aisle; he was way back, row R or S on the right. I took off my coat and went back out again. I beckoned to Benjy who was standing off to one side with that brooding, unhappy look he gets. "It's okay," I said. "He's nowhere near us." I explained the seating.

Benjy still looked like he didn't want to go, but finally handed his ticket to the usher. "Why are we seeing this anyway?" he said.

"Because Jeanette liked it." I hesitated. "She said it was our story, quote unquote."

He made a face. "We're paying money to—"

I put my hand over his mouth. "Hush."

The curtain rose the second we sat down. I kind of enjoyed the first act, despite all of Benjy's fuss. I think Jeanette is wrong. The two people in the play, this couple who meet once a year to sleep together even though they're married to other people, well, *he* wasn't like Benjy and *I* wasn't like her, and the people they were married to, their lives, everything sounded different. But in a way that was good. I could just enjoy it. It was funny. I laughed.

When the intermission came, Benjy slouched way down in his seat so his head was just level with the back of his seat. "Where is he? Did he go out to smoke?"

Benjy's father wasn't in his seat. "Yes. . . . Sweetie, come on. Sit *up!*"

He inched up a hair. "Tell Jeanette she has lousy taste. It's like some idiot comedy on TV. *How* is it like us?"

"Just the situation, I guess."

He laughed. "Once a year?"

"She meant in a general way. . . . I think it's funny, don't you?"

"Not especially. It's a farce. . . . Are our lives a farce?"

"No." I wish he wouldn't take everything so seriously. Jeanette never said it was a great play. She just said it was funny.

When the lights went down, Benjy straightened up again and sat in a regular way. But somehow I just couldn't enjoy the second half of the play. I don't know if it was the play or me, but I got more and more angry as it went on. I kept having this imaginary dialogue in my mind with the man who wrote it. Who can do it just once a year if they meet someone they like and love and the sex is wonderful? I don't believe that! It's a fantasy! It's like he took a real situation and then set it up in this perfect, neat way. Even their fights seemed like petty squabbles. I was surprised when Benjy began clapping really hard when it was over, even though he was scrunched down in his seat again.

"I thought you didn't like it," I said.

"No, it kind of grew on me. . . . I think it was quite moving, actually." He glanced nervously around. "Listen, tell me when he's left the theater. I don't want to leave till ten minutes after he's out of here."

This is a forty-year-old man! Gradually everyone left the theater while we sat there, Benjy still halfway visible. I must have looked like a woman married to a paraplegic or a dwarf. "I just think that guy who wrote it made the whole thing up," I said indignantly. "No one could do it just once a year if it was good. What does he know?"

"He's a writer. They always make things up."

"Why? Why don't they write about what they know?"

Benjy shrugged. "Look, take my friend, Joe. He writes these really scary horror books where people are always taking their lives in their hands and confronting all the terrors of the supernatural world. . . . Well, this is a guy who once, when a German shepherd crossed his lawn and took a lamb chop off the grill, actually fainted! I don't mean, looked faint. I mean, fell in a dead faint on the grass."

"I feel like writing him a letter," I said. Suddenly I looked down at Benjy. "Would you want to marry me if Becky died?" That was how the play ended. The man's wife died, after twenty-five years, and he proposed to his mistress. She turned him down because she said it wouldn't be fair to her husband.

Maybe it was a funny time to ask such a weighted question. "I don't know," Benjy said slowly. "I can't imagine Becky not being alive. Maybe I don't *want* to imagine it."

I felt like he'd struck me. "And what if *I* died? That would just be—big deal, no more Marilyn?"

He was still looking distracted and strange. "Listen, tell me—is he gone yet?"

I grabbed Benjy by the shoulders. "He's gone! What's wrong with you? Why are you so ashamed of being seen with me? You should be proud!"

Benjy looked chagrined. "I am proud . . . but not with my father! God, Marilyn, use your fucking head for a change."

"If I met *my* parents and I were with *you*, I'd take you over and introduce you right away."

"We're different, okay? Maybe you're more honest. Maybe it's just—"

"Maybe it's just you never grew up!" I yelled. "Maybe you still act like ten years old when your father is around. Maybe—"

The usher came down the aisle. There was no one left in the theater. "Have you lost something?" she asked gently.

"We're okay," Benjy said wearily, straightening up.

As we walked down the aisle, he said, "Maybe I'm just a little nervous, that's all."

"About what?" Those words kept echoing in my mind: "I can't imagine Becky not being alive. Maybe I don't want to imagine it."

"My operation. . . . It's next week."

I'd forgotten. This just seems so ironical but now, at forty, with four kids, Benjy's decided to have a vasectomy. Great timing! What made him think of it was when Becky got pregnant last year. She was forty-two, but despite that, she decided she wanted the baby. "Look, she's a wonderful mother, she loves kids. . . . Should I drag her by the hair to an abortion clinic?" So she had amniocentesis—it was going to be another girl, and then, in the sixth month, had a miscarriage. Or maybe it was a premature birth, something halfway in between. The baby was only a few pounds, too small to live. But they had a funeral for it, she goes around telling people she had five children, but one died. That strikes me as so insincere, even crazy! I know I'm not objective about Becky. I *know* that! But still, it's not like she had a real child that died. Anyhow, Benjy had a talk with the doctor and he said it really wouldn't be good for Becky to have more kids at this age, but Becky absolutely refused to have her tubes tied so Benjy offered to have a vasectomy. "It'll give me an excuse if I'm impotent with her," he said wryly at the time. Or was it "when I'm. . . ."

Good! I hope he's impotent with her *all* the time! But I guess it can't be all the time or how did she get pregnant? Benjy never wants to talk about his sex life with Becky. Maybe he feels it's betraying her to admit there are any problems. Well, why would we still be together if it was that wonderful? I don't claim my sex life with Mo is that wonderful. It's not terrible, but I don't feel I have to lie or not talk about it.

When we were on the street, I suddenly gasped. "There he is! He's with your mother!"

Benjy's eyes widened. He looked terrified. "Where? Where?"

"Nowhere," I said. "I made it up."

He just looked at me, his head to one side. "You have a strange sense of humor, kiddo."

"At least I *have* one."

We just stood there, staring at each other. "I'll marry you if Becky dies," he said gently, giving me an Eskimo kiss. "Is that what you wanted me to say?"

I hesitated. My nose felt warm where he'd rubbed it with his. "I don't want you to say anything you don't feel."

"Do you really think we'd be happy, day in, day out?"

"Yes."

He just looked off in the distance. "Maybe we would. I don't know."

"Well, relax. She'll live to be a hundred and ten."

"It's true." He smiled. "Women live forever, like sea tortoises. . . . Will you take another lover if I die?"

"Instantly. . . . I'll pick someone up on my way home from the funeral. Only he has to be married and have at least eight kids. I don't want another of these relaxed, easy relationships. It's not challenging enough."

On the way home in the car Benjy said, "It's interesting the guy's wife knew. . . . At least for the last ten years."

He meant that the wife of the man in the play found out, somehow, that he'd been unfaithful, but never said anything about it. Benjy has said that at times he feels Becky knows. I think it's just his guilty conscience, that she looks at him with some kind of mournful expression and he's sure she knows everything. One thing I know for sure: Mo doesn't know. Because if he did, he'd have such a fit. I'd never hear the end of it. He has *such* a double standard! Like, supposedly he can go off with whomever he goes off with on business trips and I'm supposed to sit meekly at home, waiting for him to call. I don't know who they are and I don't care. But I'm glad Mo doesn't know. I couldn't live with that, that open marriage way or whatever they call it. Maybe this is more old-fashioned, but it suits me better.

"Maybe wives always know," Benjy said. "Deep down."

I shrugged. "Because of our much vaunted female intuition?"

"Yeah, something like that."

"What if you found Becky had someone? What would you do?"

For a moment he didn't answer. "It's so hard to imagine. It would be a violation of her whole personality."

I felt myself starting to tense up again. "Pure, devoted, selfless. . . ?"

"Sweetie, let's not talk about Becky, okay?"

"You started the thing about wives."

"What about Mo? What if he knew?"

"He'd be out the door in one second flat."

"What does that mean?"

"He'd probably divorce me and remarry in one second. Or fuck a hundred women for revenge. He's not like you."

Benjy glanced at me. "What do you mean—he's not like me?"

What *did* I mean? "I mean, he thinks of me as a virgin. He thinks he married a virgin, that I'm this typical unspoiled American girl, wife, etcetera."

"I thought he *did* marry a virgin."

It's funny. Here I've told Benjy so many intimate things, but about that I still said, "Well, that was a long time ago."

I wonder if things have been tense because we hadn't been to bed together in almost a month. First one thing came up, then another. Maybe instead of going to the play, we should've just . . . And Benjy's nervous about his job, too, as much as I am with mine. He says he doesn't regret at all not being a lawyer anymore, but there's some office politics thing going on where he works. It's strange with Benjy. He seems so insecure about his work that sometimes I've assumed he's just a total failure, and then he'll tell me about some tribute he got, some mention in a big magazine. When I went down to his office a month ago, I saw it was twice the size of the one he used to have. When I commented on it, he mentioned off-handedly that he'd been made a vice-president and had been given a big salary increase. I wonder if he even would have told me if I hadn't brought it up. He says it's that he doesn't see himself as a boss type and that his successes seem to him flukes, as though he was some kind of impostor. Mo is just the opposite. With him everything at work is always terrific. The business could fold and I'd only know about it the day it happened.

We'd driven to the city in my car. I let Benjy off at the train station where he said he'd get a cab home.

At the end of work on Tuesday, Lauren called me into her office. "I hear you and Ila are giving a farewell party for Miss Tretler?"

I nodded.

She smiled. "I've been hoping for an invitation. Or is it just a small, select group?"

I managed to force a smile. "We'd love for you to come." Lauren is a past master or mistress of the art of saying one thing and meaning another. "It's going to be at Ila's house in two weeks. Just dinner, really."

"That sounds lovely. . . . You're having it catered?"

"No, Ila's fixing fried chicken. It's her mother's recipe."

"Marvelous. . . . I'll look forward to it."

I hope this isn't true, but I feel Lauren knows exactly how I feel about her, how I hate her, how I'm afraid of her. Also—this is ironical, I guess, in a way—but for the past few years she's been screwing this married guy, Weber Whitfield, who came to Taylor's from Bonwit's where he'd been a vice-president. He's just her height, about five seven, with big flashy teeth, someone who'd lie about the color socks he had on just out of habit. Ila used to call them the Bobbsey Twins. I know I should have felt sorry for her because he was such a bum, but every time I'd see them together, she staring at him with this entranced, obsequious expression, I got a perverse kick out of it. I don't know what's happening now. I haven't seen them together so often. Ila says he realized it wouldn't help his career—Lauren wouldn't promote someone if he gave her multiple orgasms ten times a day—so he's moved on to greener pastures.

I took a Valium at lunch. I only take them three times a week, during the day anyway. I'm not addicted, but when I have one of those run-ins with Lauren, I can't stop thinking about it for the rest of the day. Sometimes I wonder what I'd be like if I had her power, if I'd grown up rich, the way she did. I want to think I'd be benign and gracious, but maybe it gets to you. Maybe you can't help using it, needling people, getting a secret thrill out of watching them cringe. I told Ila about our new guest.

Ila winked. "She'll love Angel. Now that Double W is out of the picture."

"You don't think she'll . . ."

"Listen, it's our party, right? She forced herself in. What does she give a shit about Griselda, anyway? If she had, she could've let her stay on."

"Did Griselda want to stay on?"

"Sure. . . . She's still healthy. She was just doing desk work. She knows the store upside down."

The night of the party I went home to change. It'd just be ten of us, all women except for Angel, so I decided to wear just my orange dress, the one with the ruffled collar. As I was getting dressed, Aimee looked in. "That's beautiful," she said.

I'm getting a little irritated with Aimee. She lives here now, basically. Maybe it's partly I feel sorry for poor Valeska, who still writes to Aaron almost every day. I saw a letter of hers open on the table. "I've devoted today to thinking only of you. . . . " And Aimee always scantily dressed, playing up to Mo, whether because she thinks he can get her a job or because she's just a hard-core flirt, I don't know. But I try to be friendly because Aaron's certainly smitten with her. I told her about the party and about Angel jumping out of the cake.

"Wow, what a great idea!" she said. "I'd love it if someone did that for me. . . . Is he cute?"

"Very."

She raised her eyebrows. "Does he have a girlfriend?"

I nodded.

She sighed. "Yeah, those sexy ones always do."

Is she already looking beyond Aaron? Probably. "Tell Mo I'll be back at around ten," I said as I was leaving. I'd told him that morning, but sometimes he forgets.

"Sure thing."

When I got to Ila's, no one had arrived yet, but there was a mouthwatering smell of fried chicken permeating the whole house. We'd told Angel to arrive early since we had to set him up before the other guests were there. Ila had just a little house, one level. She lives alone, most of the time, except for when her boyfriend, Sloan, comes out and stays with her. He's divorced too, and they've been, as she puts it, "semi going together" for seven years. The "semi" is because every six months or so they break up, violently, rush around looking for new people, and then end up together again. "It's the weirdest thing," she once said. "With Frank, I couldn't have been more insanely in love, and sex with him was the most boring, agonizing thing on earth, like some Chinese water torture. And with Sloan, who doesn't get along with *any* of my friends, who's impossible at parties, we're still totally going around the moon. . . . Well, you know what I mean, I guess. Maybe we all need two men, do you think that's the answer?"

I think I know what she means, but you never know. Maybe I could have sex with Frank and love it. Ila says she can't handle more than one steady relationship with a man at a time, but to "solve" it, at least a little, she has men friends. Some from college, some from other jobs, some she just meets at parties. She'll just meet a man at a

party and ask him to lunch, whether he's married or not, not wanting to sleep with him, just to get to know him. I've never done that;
I've never had men friends. Ila says she likes it, even though she
doesn't talk with any of them about really intimate things the way
she does with me.

I helped her fix the salad and get the table ready. We'd made the
paper cake a few weeks earlier. It's really just a roll of pink card-
board, about four feet high and five feet around, taped together in a
circle with no bottom. On top we covered it with pink tissue paper
and put up paper candles and a sign saying "Happy Birthday." Ila's
idea is we'll put Angel inside and wheel him into the room on a
serving cart she has. "I wonder what he weighs," she said, pressing
down on the cart with the palm of her hand. "Does it look strong
enough?"

"I think so," I said. I felt nervous, mainly because Lauren was
coming. It's enough dealing with her at work, but I hate having to
face her during off hours as well.

Angel showed up in slacks and a T-shirt. It was a warm day, in the
eighties. "So, how're we going to set this up?" he asked.

We took him in the bedroom and showed him the "cake." "You
don't need to squat in there all through dinner," Ila said. "We'll
come in at the end and give you the cue. Want to try it for size?"

Unself-consciously he stripped down to his silver briefs and
crawled into the cake. He had to squash his head down a little so it
wouldn't rip through the paper. "Terrific!" Ila said. "You can get
dressed for now, if you like. . . . God, Angel, how do you keep such a
great shape? Do you work out?"

He smiled modestly, putting on his shirt. "Yeah, a couple of times
a week. I eat healthy food. My girlfriend kills me if she sees me
eating meat or candy."

"Well, I bet she's proud of the way you look," Ila said, regarding
him more wistfully than lustfully. To both of us she added, "I had
such a super figure in college. I ran every morning, I skipped lunch,
but now . . . !" Actually, Ila still has a nice figure but she's said she
can put on five pounds just over a weekend. "Sloan's the same way.
He used to play football in college and now, you should see his
paunch."

"Who's Sloan?" Angel said, getting dressed.

"My—gee, what should I call him? My lover, I guess. My boy-friend? Can you call a fifty-year-old man a boy?" She smiled at An-gel. "I bet you thought Marilyn and I were just sitting at home knitting in our spare time."

"No, I never thought that," he said.

"We're in training to be dirty old ladies," she said. "Right, hon?"

I nodded. Even though I think Ila's right, Angel has a beautiful body, his being the age of my sons is kind of a turn-off. The old oedipal thing, I guess, though I suppose it could work both ways.

Right after that, people started arriving. We'd made two punches, alcoholic and nonalcoholic, because we weren't sure if Griselda drank. It turned out she did, but some of the other women asked for the nonalcoholic. I helped everyone to chicken and passed the salad down the table.

"Ila, you tell that mother of yours this is the best fried chicken I ever ate," Griselda said. She was onto her third piece.

"I would," Ila called down from her end of the table, "only she died five years ago. But she knew. Don't worry."

"It must have been so much work," Lauren said. She was sitting there stiffly like always in a neat little black dress. She always wears her glasses on a chain around her neck. On the collar of her dress was a gold pin of a dachshund with a ruby eye. She has about a hundred little pins in the shape of dachshunds: it's her "trademark."

"What're you going to do now that you're a lady of leisure?" some-one asked Griselda.

She shrugged. "Find some work," she said, and everyone laughed. "I don't have any hobbies, my mother's gone. . . . "

"Yes, I'm like that too," Lauren said. "I've never had hobbies. But then, we're alike, Griselda, we've always had to work, you and I. Not like women who are married where it's just an extra source of income."

I didn't know if that was a dig at me. Several of the other women were married, also, and I know they don't regard working as just being for fun. Anyway, how has Lauren "had" to work? She has enough money to sit idle till eternity if she wants.

"I don't think you're right, Miss Taylor," one of the younger women said. "We have to work too . . . the way prices are now."

"Yes, I suppose that's true," Lauren said vaguely, putting her chicken to one side. She's not exactly anorexic, but very thin. Not an ounce of fat on her anywhere. Ila said once they had lunch together and she weighed everything before eating it on a little scale she carried in a special bag.

"I love working," I found myself saying suddenly. I knew I'd had a little too much of the rum punch. "I don't know what I'd *do* without a job! But it was my husband who wanted me to go back and get it. He believes in women working."

"Aren't you lucky," Lauren said icily, "to have such a supportive husband."

I swallowed. "I think I am," I said. "Definitely."

"He's in career counseling?" she pursued.

I nodded. "It's his own firm. His parents started it."

"How convenient." She smiled at me. "He can always get you another job then . . . if you should ever need one."

A chill went through me. "I'd never get a job through Mo," I said. "I wouldn't want to."

"You'll never need to," Ila said quickly, picking up on the exchange. "With your experience any store would beg to get you." She winked at me as we went into the kitchen, carrying the plates. "That bitch," she whispered.

Angel was lying on the bed, eating a leg of chicken. "Strip, honey," Ila said. "Your big moment hath arrived."

Angel whisked off his clothes. Then he straightened up, looking solemn. "How do I look?"

"Sexy enough to get arrested," Ila said, patting his shoulder. "Don't worry. We've got them all so dopey with Mama's fruit punch they can't see straight." The two of us taped him in and began pushing the serving cart slowly into the dining room. We wheeled it up to Griselda, as everyone was singing "Happy Birthday." Just as we finished, Angel came leaping up through the tissue paper.

"Happy birthday!" he yelled and gave Griselda a big kiss and hug.

She turned bright red but looked really pleased. "Is this my present?" she said. She was almost too shy to look at him.

"Angel Caruso!" one of the older women said. "I never would have recognized you."

"Hidden talent," someone else said.

"He works out at gyms three times a *week*," Ila said. "But he has a girlfriend, so hands off, girls. . . . Angel, honey, go change and come back to have some cake and ice cream with us. Otherwise you won't be safe."

Angel scuttled back to the bedroom while I went into the kitchen to get the real cake. "Was I okay?" he whispered.

"Super," I whispered back. I brought the real cake in and set it in front of Griselda. It was then I noticed Lauren's expression. She looked like a school principal who'd just been hit between the eyes with a spitball. "Would you like some ice cream?" I asked her, "with your cake?"

"No, thank you," she said really coldly.

Everyone else ate like pigs, including Angel, who came back and flirted with everyone in a friendly, good-natured way. At the end of the evening, Griselda got tearful and began patting Angel on the shoulder. "I'll miss you, Angel" she said. "You were always such a sweet, thoughtful young man, saving me a parking space when I came late."

"Hey, I thought you just did that for me," I said.

"Or me," Ila said.

Angel turned red.

"It seems you have many friends, Angel," Lauren said.

He looked abashed. "I guess it's just my personality," he said modestly.

After everyone left, Ila and I cleared up. "I think it was a smash," she said.

I stuffed the paper plates in her big plastic trash can. "I'm not sure how Lauren took it. She looked funny when Angel jumped out of the cake."

"Oh, she always looks funny. . . . God, can you imagine fucking her? I wonder what Double W had to do mentally to get it up with her. Maybe she has a dachshund tattooed on her left boob, do you think?"

"But I think Griselda liked it, don't you?" I pursued nervously.

"She had a wonderful time," Ila said, "and I told her we'd visit her for lunch in a couple of weeks just so she won't feel out of touch."

But when I went home, I still felt bad. Maybe I'm getting paranoid. Everything that happens, like Lauren's expression when she said she wouldn't have more ice cream, I magnify. Probably it has nothing to do with me! But that night I lay awake till past two, tossing and turning, wishing I could be as blunt and carefree-seeming as Ila is. I hope Lauren didn't hear her whisper "that bitch."

Monday afternoon Lauren called me into her office. It'd been a calm morning and I was feeling pretty good, not nervous anymore. "Well," she said, staring at me.

Well what? I just stood there, puzzled, frowning.

"I was really quite staggered," she said, "by that party you gave for Miss Tretler."

Staggered is such a funny word. I didn't know how she meant it. "We just . . . like her a lot," I said.

"I have never in my life seen a woman look so humiliated and horrified as she did when that young man came leaping out of the cake. Never!" She glared at me. "How could you conceive of such a thing? A woman old enough to be your mother! What was in your mind?"

Actually, it was Ila's idea too, but I just stammered, "I think she liked it. She, um, likes Angel."

"You may think what it gives you comfort to think," Lauren went on, "but I can tell you that as we left she confided in me how terribly *terribly* upset she was."

I know Lauren is lying! I know Griselda had a good time. "That wasn't the impression I got," I said, trying to pull myself together.

"I don't understand you, Marilyn," Lauren went on, touching her dachshund pin just lightly. "Sometimes your judgment seems astounding, your *lack* of judgment. Or maybe it's just that Taylor's isn't the best environment for someone of your . . . abilities."

"I've always loved working here," I said.

She said nothing for a moment. "Well, I'm sure that's a tribute to your personality, and I hope it will hold you in good stead wherever you land next. I don't like doing this, I like consistency and continuity in the store, it's a family business for me, but this was absolutely the last straw. Seeing a devoted, kind, elderly woman tormented that way! We've based our business on consideration to others. To see it violated so flagrantly was sad. It made me *very* sad."

"Shall I continue through the week?" I said, swallowing.

"That won't be necessary." She looked at her phone and, as though to oblige her, one of the buttons lit up. She lifted the receiver. "Put him on," she said. And smiled at me, waving me out, as though we'd just been discussing what a beautiful day it was! I stumbled out of the room. I hadn't even had lunch yet. The first thing I thought of was going to Ila, but I knew she had a meeting at one, and what would be the point of bursting into tears in the middle of her working day? How would that help? I just went and got my sweater and dashed off to the parking lot. Angel was sitting on the grass eating a hero sandwich, a can of beer next to him. He waved at me. I tried to smile and wave back. Then I unlocked the car with shaking hands, put my head down on the wheel, and started to cry.

Angel got into the car from the other side. "Hey, hey, what's the matter?" he said. "What happened?" He put his arm around me, letting his hand rest on my shoulder.

I tried to tell him, but I was crying so hard I could hardly talk. Finally I got the gist of it out. "That stupid cunt," he said. "How can she do that?"

"I don't think Griselda was offended, do you?" I said quaveringly. Lauren had gotten me so upset, I couldn't think straight.

"No, she got a bang out of it. She's a good sport. . . . I guess she just hates you, like you said, Miss Taylor, I mean. I had a teacher like that in second grade. She failed me in math just for folding my paper the wrong way! Even when I got all the answers right."

"I really loved working here," I sniffled. "What if I don't get another job?"

Angel kept stroking my bare arm. "You'll get another job. Don't worry. You're terrific."

Right around then I became aware of the erotic underpinning to what was going on, the two of us in the warm car, me leaning against him, weeping, he practically holding me in his arms, stroking me. "We could go somewhere and have a drink," he said. "That'll make you feel better. . . . We could go back to my place. It's not that far from here." He looked at me appealingly.

Oh shit. He's gorgeous, I feel turned on, but I don't think I could live with this one. "I'd better go home and pull myself together," I said. "Thanks for being such a sweetie."

"Listen, I think you're a really nice person," he said, looking at me with his big sincere dark eyes. "I mean that. . . . Maybe tomorrow when you're feeling better, we can have lunch or something."

I kissed him. "Maybe tomorrow I better start looking for another job."

I glanced back at him as I drove off. Damn it, why is weeping on a man's shoulder so comforting? But it would have been too, if it had been Ila's, just not the same way, that provocative, sexy closeness.

Mo and the boys told me the same thing: don't worry, you'll find something. I've been spoiled, having this job so long. I'll have to redo my résumé, try to look pulled together, self-confident. I wish so much this didn't make me feel so rotten. I *have* done a good job! I didn't deserve to be fired! I even called Griselda. I didn't tell her I was fired. I just said I'd been worried how she might have reacted to Angel's jumping out of the cake.

"Isn't he a sweet boy!" she said. "I hope his girlfriend takes good care of him. He's just like my nephew Sammie."

"Did you mind about his being . . . about his not having so—so many clothes on?"

"Why should I mind?" she said. "It's the human body, isn't it? Nothing to be ashamed of in that, especially if you have such a fine one. I wish I could say the same for mine."

Bitch! Cunt! I lay there at night ripping Lauren apart. But what good does that do? I still need a job, I still don't know where I'm going to find one. I just have to try not to get hysterical or, if I feel it, not to show it. I've heard it's harder for women over forty to find new jobs. Well, I look younger, everyone says. Will that help? God, I hope so.

Benjy is making love to me. A moment ago, less even, he came and three moments before that I was floating in some wonderful, magical place, so happy, so close to coming that I deliberately held back. Maybe it was that I started thinking—just a quick thought, like an insect breezing through my brain—that this was the first time we'd fucked since Benjy's vasectomy, that if I came first it might throw him off somehow. But in that split second a whole sea of petty worries crashed down on me. Suddenly I wasn't in a magical realm at all. I was in Ila's apartment, the air conditioner was on the blink, as usual, Benjy was losing his erection, I was terrified I'd never get another job. . . .

"Sweetie," Benjy whispered. A question? A comment?

I opened my eyes and smiled at him wryly. "This isn't my day, I guess."

"We can go on."

I considered. "Maybe later." There's always that moment of loss and sadness when he withdraws. I touched his penis gently. "Seems in working order. He hasn't lost any of his vim or vigor."

Benjy grinned. "I'm relieved. . . . I did have a few manic moments right afterward."

We both looked down at his penis as though it were an object disconnected from his body. "It doesn't *look* any different. . . . Does it feel different?"

He shook his head.

"I wonder if it's like with hysterectomies. I knew one woman who said having one wrecked her sex life, and Ila, who had one, said her sex life is ten times better since."

"Individual variation," Benjy said, looking inexplicably gloomy.

We lay on our backs, looking at the ceiling.

"I got fired," I said. I don't know why, but I'd put off telling him. I was too upset to even say the words for the first week or so.

He didn't say anything. Didn't he hear?

"I just feel so awful," I rushed on. "And really scared, petrified—"

"At least you don't have to worry about paying the rent."

"What do you mean?"

"I just meant, your whole livelihood, your way of life isn't at stake. . . . Or even the way Mo looks at you. You've lost a job. It's a self-contained thing."

I grabbed his shoulder, enraged. "What are you talking about? I feel scared out of my wits, totally demoralized. I feel—"

"Those are just feelings," Benjy said. "It isn't the reality."

I just stared at him, too dumbfounded to speak. He was gazing morosely at the ceiling. "What's wrong? Is it your operation? You said it was fine. . . . Why're you acting this way?"

"It's a—a private family matter."

I can't believe this conversation! "Oh right, you mean, since we just met a couple of hours ago at that bar and hardly know each other—"

"Becky's father went bankrupt, okay? And I *don't* want to talk about it."

A thrill of pleasure, joy even, went through me that was so keen it was almost like a sexual experience, like coming ten minutes after the fact. I hate Becky's money! I hate all it symbolizes for her, her pampered childhood, her big house, the fact that she's never had to work, that she can have baby after baby after baby, knowing each one will have every advantage. I wanted to let out a war whoop of delight and go leaping around the room. Instead I just said, "How can he? I thought it was all invested."

"Some of it. . . . But it seems he took a lot out and reinvested it in some other business that a friend of his owns and the whole thing went poosh. . . . I don't really understand it."

"So, what does it mean? I mean, does it affect you?"

"Of course! God, our whole life-style is based on his money. Four kids, that house. They aren't even in college yet! Becky may have to go back to work. . . ."

"Poor little Becky."

"She's not cut out for that, Marilyn. She's not like you. She's a real homebody. . . . And how can I support her the way she's used to? I'm hanging on by my teeth as it is."

"Well, that's the real world, kid. Everyone faces that at some point or other. She's forty-two. Let her grow up!"

He smiled wryly. "Thanks for being so sympathetic."

"You're so concerned about Becky! Becky, Becky, Becky! *I* just lost my job, and you don't even give a shit."

"Your job—"

"My job is just as important to me as this is to you. And I'm not going to go to pieces because some spoiled overweight housewife has to face life at forty-two. It's about time she did, for God's sake."

"I've let her down in everything," Benjy went on, shielding his eyes, as though from an overly bright light. "What kind of life have I given her? I've betrayed her, I've lied. . . . What kind of marriage is that?"

"You needed me," I reminded him. "She was lousy at sex. You felt desperate when I met you. You said if it wasn't for me, you'd have a breakdown."

"She's *not* lousy, it's just . . . Look, I've betrayed her even there, talking about her, telling you all her most intimate problems. How could I *do* that?"

"Because you love me! Because you wanted to tell someone the truth!"

"Love is just an excuse, a word. . . . "

"Well, I guess I'm different," I said, so wounded I could scarcely speak. "Loving you is the most important thing in my life."

"Maybe that's because you're a woman."

"Benjy, you said it was for you! You said it was the most important thing for *you!*"

"Love, sex. . . . I don't know what it means anymore. I feel totally confused. I just know I've wrecked her life."

"How? She should be delighted you married her. Who would have wanted her? Any other man would've pitched her out years ago. She should thank her lucky stars she has such a guilt-ridden, craven husband."

"Marilyn, that's ugly. . . . And please leave Becky out of this!"

"I didn't bring her in! I don't give a shit about Becky! She's a nonentity. I wouldn't spend one *second* of my life talking about her, thinking about her. I regard her with contempt. . . . And I'm glad her father went bankrupt! I'm overjoyed!"

My whole body was quivering with rage and excitement. Sweat was streaming down my body. Benjy was staring at me as though I was crazy.

"We have to stop seeing each other," he said. "We're tearing each other to pieces. What's the point of this? Once it was love or something, but now—"

"It's still love!" I shouted. "I still love you more than anything."

He tried to speak, stopped. "I just don't know anymore. I don't know what I think or feel."

"You just married her for her money," I said spitefully. "If she hadn't been rich, you never would've gone near her."

Benjy turned white. "That's an unforgivable thing to say."

"It's true! Say it's not true!"

"It's a lie. . . . I loved Becky from the moment I saw her. I still love her, I'll always love her." He had leaped to his feet and was getting dressed. "Look, I never want to see you again. I don't want you to call me, at home or the office, or write. If you call, I'll hang up. If you write, I'll destroy the letters. Do you understand?"

I was petrified. For some reason I could only think of a time when Linus was seven years old and angry with me. He came in and said, "I don't love you anymore. I don't love the way you smell or do things. You skip in stories." Then after a pause he added, "And I'll never love you in the future either." At that time I thought: my God, he's seven and he's already learned that horrible masculine art of total demolition. Where did he find a word like *future?* Now and forever. The end of the world.

Benjy was striding out the back door where his car was parked. I ran after him, naked, feeling the hot wood under my feet as I skidded down the steps. He looked horrified. "Get back inside!" he yelled.

"I won't! I'll call you every day! I'll call your daughters' school! I'll call your parents, I'll tell everyone." I was beating on the side of his car, wanting to make a dent in it. Anyone driving by could have seen me, but I didn't care. "I hate you. I hope you die. I—"

He started the car and began backing down the driveway. I saw his frightened eyes as I stood there in the bright sun, my hair loose. No one was there, just the two of us. It was one in the afternoon. Then the car was gone. I rushed back inside, into Ila's bedroom, and flung myself on the bed.

I kept reseeing that scene at the end, me running down the steps naked, my hair sticking to my neck, Benjy's expression, disgusted, terrified. Right now, right at this second, his car is smashing into a huge truck, the car crumples into a tiny blob of crushed metal. . . . *If you call me, I'll hang up. If you write me, I'll destroy the letters. I never want to see you again.*

Why? Because Becky's father went bankrupt? How can such an irrelevant thing destroy everything, destroy my life? I'm not going to write to him, I'm not going to call him! Why did he assume I would? I have too much pride for that. If he doesn't want to see me, fine, I'll be happy without him, as happy as he'll be without me, happier, maybe. I'll get another job. Another lover even. Men still find me attractive. I don't have to lie here feeling eviscerated just because some weak, craven Jewish husband. . . . Oh, why did I say that? It's true, but so? I'm weak and craven as well, just in another way. How did we get from there to here so quickly, like one of those fires that begins when someone carelessly drops a half-lit match and ends up destroying homes, giant trees, countrysides. If I had come? If that thought hadn't veered into my brain about wanting it to be good for Benjy? No, it was going to happen. I feel I've become like some spy who has to be shot because he knows too many secrets. He's let down his guard with me too often. He wanted that, he needed it, but now I know too much, too many small, petty, hidden things. Without me he can build up the same lying hollow life he had before we met, the same life he claimed was eating him alive. But maybe this time he'll do it better. Maybe the bankruptcy will draw them closer together.

Maybe he'll even confess about me!

I envision the scene. They're at dinner, or no, maybe better in bed. Becky in bed, her reading glasses on, her frowsy flowered nightgown with the ribbon untied. Benjy comes in from the bathroom, looks at her, steels himself. "There's something I have to tell you. . . ." "I know you've been upset lately." "No, it's something else. It's all over now. But there was a woman, she was crazy really, but somehow at that time I felt vulnerable, I . . ." And then I see myself crash through the window, like some avenging angel, screaming, "He's lying! He loved me! Don't believe it!" And Benjy saying, "You see, she's crazy. Don't listen to her." But I have brought tapes, movies, they loom up on the bedroom wall, Benjy and me making love, our bodies dissolving together, his crying, "I love you so much. I can't tell you how much. I wish I could tell you. I wish I knew how."

When Ila came home from work, I was still lying there, naked, half asleep. "Marilyn, what's wrong? What happened?"

I could hardly talk. I just felt terribly thirsty. She brought me a large glass of cold refrigerator water and I drank it all at once. "I want to die," I told her. "He said he'd hang up if I called, he'd destroy my letters. . . . "

Ila got me dressed, bathed my face in cold water. "You've had fights before. . . . Honey, everyone does. Everyone!"

"He said he never wants to see me again! Ever!"

"He felt that way at the moment. Probably right now he's thinking it over, he's sorry for what he said. People say things when they're upset."

"No, he meant it. I know he did. . . . Ila, I said such terrible things! Why? Why did I do that?"

"Honey, please calm down. . . . You'll be fine. Tomorrow we'll go over the want ads together, we'll find you something."

Want ads. Does anyone want me? I think of all those personal sections in newspapers. "I'm forty. My hair looks blond but it's dyed. It's not what it seems. I'm not what I seem. I'm a faithless wife. I have a lover who hates me and two teenage sons, both of whom don't know who I am. I don't know who I am. . . . " A man calls up, "I just read your ad. You sound like exactly what I'm looking for! I love artificial blonds who're going through identity crises. My present girlfriend is in a mental hospital. My wife is making it with my best friend. Let's meet Sunday. I'm bald, overweight, semi-alcoholic, I write poetry in my lunch hours, my boss hates me."

Ila Scotch-taped me together. She brushed my hair, powdered my face. She was Blanche before sisterly rivalries tore us asunder.

"Let's have dinner," she suggested. "Tell Mo I've had a fight with my boyfriend and you want to keep me company."

I called home. Aaron answered. "Hon, is Dad there?"

"Not yet."

"Well, listen, I'm at Ila's. She just had a fight with my boyfriend and I'm keeping her company because she's upset."

"She just had a fight with *your* boyfriend?"

"She just had a fight with *her* boyfriend! I don't have a boyfriend!"

"I know! You just said—"

"She's all upset. . . . Tell Dad I'll be back by ten at the latest."

I put the phone down and Ila and I started to laugh. We went to a nearby Italian restaurant, polished off a bottle of Chianti. Ila regaled me with the most horrible fights she and Sloan had ever had. "Even now," she said, "he says sex with me is the best he's ever had, but I'm too strong for him. In bed he loves that, my passion, my strength. Out of bed he wants a Barbie doll."

"They all do." I love being drunk. I'm going to start being a wino. I'm so stuffed with ravioli I'm bursting out of my dress.

"No." Ila waved a finger at me drunkenly. "They *think* they do. . . . But why do they pick us? Because deep down those Barbie doll types bore them. They want excitement, intensity, drama. . . . "

"Part time," I said, eyeing a man across the room. "They want it Monday, Wednesday, and Friday. The rest of the time they want some slithering slavering blob."

Ila noticed the guy across the room. "Forget men with mustaches. They don't work out."

I told her about Angel. "Maybe I should've. . . . But he's such a baby!"

"You couldn't have lived with yourself."

"Yeah, but why? Men do it all the time, with teenagers, with pre-teenagers. . . . Why are we hung up on all these dopey moral dilemmas?"

She ripped off a hunk of bread. "It was his vasectomy. He was feeling threatened, anxious, afraid he couldn't satisfy you."

"He said no. He said he felt fine. He *was* fine! It was me. . . . "

"He said, he said. . . . They all *say* a million things. What's he going to say? 'I'm scared, I'm afraid you'll reject me, throw me out of bed. . . .'"

I bit my lip. "He's always been a wonderful lover. Nothing could have changed that."

"For you! I'm telling you what was in his head."

I ate the last piece of ravioli. "It was guilt. He's Jewish. He says he can't help it. It's genetic. And he was the good child in his family."

"Those are all excuses. . . . God, they have wall-to-wall excuses! Sloan says it's because his mother was a bitch. Okay, so she was! She actually *was* a bitch! So, *everyone's* mother was a bitch. What does that prove?"

"My mother wasn't a bitch. . . . She's a wonderful person."

"Okay, but that's not the point. The point is—you could invent excuses too. *You're* Jewish. What happened to *your* genes?"

I sighed. "I might as well be celibate. . . . I'll never have sex like that again. I know that."

"Fiddlesticks. . . . A year from now you'll be in bed with someone and you'll think, 'Benjy? Who's he? Oh yeah, that's right, that funny-looking little guy whose father-in-law lost all his dough. Wonder how's he's doing.'"

I tried to imagine that. But would I want that, even—to feel that ten years of my life, caring for someone as much as I've cared for Benjy, could just vanish, without even the formal ceremony of a divorce, as though it had never been?

The waiter approached the table. "The gentleman over there wondered if you would like an after-dinner drink."

"Sure, why not?" Ila said. "I'll have an Amaretto."

"Doesn't that obligate us?" I said nervously, glancing his way again.

"No, don't be silly. We're a fantasy. He's sitting there, making up little stories about us in his head. It's cheaper than going to a movie."

We both drank our Amarettos. Every time I glanced at the man, he was watching us, but gravely, contemplatively. "I wish I had men friends like you," I said, liking the warm sweetness of the liqueur. "I never have."

"It's a lot of work," Ila said. "Who knows if it's worth it? It's like cracking a safe. You press all these little buttons, try this combination, that one, then suddenly—*boing*, after ten years they say one tiny personal thing that a woman would tell you the first five minutes you met her. I have this old friend from my marriage, Lindsey Chesler. He tells me, every time I see him, 'You're my best friend,' and we only talk about politics, the weather, his job. That's his closest human contact!"

"Yeah," I said, feeling horribly sad again. Was I Benjy's closest human contact? He was for me. It wasn't just sex, it was the closeness. But maybe he doesn't need it anymore or maybe he never needed it as much as I did.

On the way out, as we were getting into our coats, the man who'd paid for our Amarettos sprang to his feet. "I hope you enjoyed your drinks," he said.

Close up he looked smaller, less inviting, less debonair. Maybe we did too? "It was a lovely gesture," Ila said, smiling at him.

"I was just curious—are you sisters? You look so much alike, and yet you seem to be enjoying each other's company in a way sisters rarely do."

"No, we're not," I said, basking momentarily in his appreciation of us. What if he had seen me, screaming, naked, six hours earlier, pounding on the car. In the car I said to Ila, "I feel guilty. If he really knew me. . . ."

"And if you really knew him! And if anyone really knew anyone, the human race would grind to a hideous and sudden halt." She smiled at me affectionately. "Ready to face going home?"

I hesitated. I felt so much better, almost normal, but with the pain of Benjy's words still flickering inside me, spitting out little razor-sharp bits of pain. "Let's drive by his house."

"What for?"

"I don't know."

Ila drove there. She'd never seen Benjy and Becky's house. I gave her the directions. We parked down the road a little. The summer evening light was almost gone, but in the dimness the house looked so huge and solid. It seemed like a fortress to me with its turrets and the little tower on the top. Impregnable. No stranger will destroy this home. But it also looked homey, cozy, with lights on in the bay windows. Someone was playing the harpischord—probably their older daughter, who's musical. This is what Becky has created for him: someplace quiet, safe, beautiful, tasteful. In my mind it went up in flames, like the last scene in *Rebecca*.

"Palatial," Ila said, clearly impressed.

I kept staring at the house, its solidity, the symbol of their marriage. What was our symbol? The dozens of random places we'd fucked? "Their daughters have the most beautiful dollhouse," I said, remembering.

We sat in silence.

"What if I could press a button and have the house go up in smoke?" I said. "With Becky in it? Would I?"

"No."

"Why not? Because I'm basically a nice person?" I asked hopefully.

"Because it wouldn't do any good! Because he'd find another Becky. . . . Listen, when I found out Frank was fucking Faith, I did this weird thing. I applied for a job interview at her office under a false name. She interviewed me for a half hour, asking me questions. And I sat there, answering, all the while watching the glass paperweight on her desk. I imagined smashing it down on her head, her slithering to the floor, my escaping scot free. But so what? He'd have found Faith Number Two, and if I'd klonked *her* on the head, he'd have found Faith Number Three! He even said that to me after our divorce. 'I need a Faith.' Not Faith, the particular person. He needed 'a Faith,' a docile, sweet, mindless girlfriend. Just like Benjy needs 'a Becky.'"

I watched the lit windows of their house. "It's just—I thought he needed 'a Marilyn,' too," I said wryly.

A Faith, a Marilyn, a Becky. . . . Do we see men that way too? I don't think I needed "a Benjy." I needed *him* in particular. I don't want a substitute, a version. "He did need you," Ila said.

"And will he miss me?" I said urgently. "Will he think of me? Or will it all just be crushed out of his mind by willpower?"

"He'll think of you. . . . But he'll try not to. He won't finger the memories, he won't torment himself the way you will."

I laughed. "I'm not going to do that. I'm not!"

Ila hugged me. "Good. . . . Just testing you, hon."

At home, Mo was asleep, snoring fitfully. I undressed slowly and got into bed. I felt a little drunk still, and surprisingly, fell right to sleep. But suddenly in the middle of the night I woke up. It was as though I'd had a nightmare, but I hadn't. I just sat straight up in bed, petrified. Mo stirred. He opened his eyes. "What time is it?"

"Three."

"So how was Ila? I heard she had a fight with her boyfriend again."

"Yes, an awful one. That's why I stayed out with her so long."

"I thought they did that every six months or so."

"This was worse. He told her if she ever called him, he'd hang up, and if she tried to write to him, he'd destroy the letters. He said he never wants to see her again."

"She'll find someone else," Mo said sleepily. "She's a good-looking woman."

"She doesn't want anyone else!" I cried. "She only wants him!"

He pulled me close to him. "They'll make it up. They always do. . . ."

I lay there, feeling the warmth of Mo's body, but it was almost five before I fell asleep again.

I went on job interviews. Some went well. During others I was tense, stammered, didn't put my best foot forward. But at some point I realized I would get another job, that if I had the endurance to keep looking, it would happen. And it did. It will mean driving half an hour each way, and the store is a lot bigger than Taylor's, gigantic, in fact, but I liked the woman who interviewed me who'd be my boss. I left her office feeling buoyant, pleased. I wanted so much to call Benjy. Not just as I would have done in the old days, to have him share my pleasure, to hear him say, "Let's meet. We can have some champagne." No, this time I wanted to say to him, "See? My life goes on without you. See how happy I am. You didn't ruin my life. I'm surviving."

If you call me I'll hang up.

I didn't call. Instead, I went home to get the grocery list and do some shopping. Now that I've been without a job, I'm so much more organized. But we still needed a few things, and I thought I would fix a surprise dinner: steaks, a nice salad, strawberry shortcake.

I went to the Express line and began leafing through a magazine as I waited for the woman ahead of me to finish. "No, I have a card," I heard her say. "I'm allowed to write checks for over twenty dollars.

I've been doing that for years. I just forgot it and I don't remember the number by heart. Mrs. Benjamin Fetterman. Yes, that's right. I think it begins with a seven."

I looked up, and as I did, Becky, waiting while the checker trotted off to find the number of her card, caught sight of me. "Hi," we both said simultaneously.

"Dawn's having a sixteenth birthday party," she said, pointing to all the little ice creams and cupcakes. "They're calling it a Regression Party. They're going to play Pin the Tail on the Donkey, Spin the Bottle. . . . Only it's a co-ed sleepover."

"My sons never did that," I said. I was scared I might do something crazy, the way I had with Benjy. What if I start screaming, saying obscene things?

"There's no sex," she said brightly. "It's funny. . . . All they do is drink ginger ale and play Ping-Pong." She smiled in that self-satisfied way I hate so much. "Don't you work? I've never seen you here in the middle of the day."

Why are you here? I'm a good and dutiful husband. Then I must be a good and dutiful wife, huh?

"I was fired," I said.

"Oh, I'm sorry." She looked genuinely sorry. Why? "It's evidently a hard time to find something else."

"I found something else," I said. After a second I found myself saying breathlessly, "The other job was so convenient, so near where I live. But this is just as good, maybe better."

"So many things are blessings in disguise," Becky said.

"Yes." If I press her on the tip of her nose, will a dozen more comforting clichés pop out? Is it that which gives Benjy pleasure?

"My father just went bankrupt," she went on, "and I may have to return to work. You know, I haven't worked since college. But I think it'll be good for me. After all, the twins are ten, Chelsea and Dawn are almost in college. I just hope I can get something. The girls and Benjy have such faith in me. They're sure I'll get something."

"You'll get something," I said. "But it might take a long time and not pay that much in the beginning."

The checker appeared with the number and began putting Becky's packages in a big brown bag. "I need something to get my mind off our child that died. . . . Did you know, we had a child that died a few years ago?"

"Yes, I know," I said. "But wasn't it a miscarriage? Or was it actually a child?"

Becky flushed. "It was a child. She only weighed two pounds. I was in my sixth month."

"I thought that was called a miscarriage." I thought of Ila and the glass paperweight. *If I klonked her on the head, he'd have found Faith Number Three. He needed "a Faith." Just like Benjy needs "a Becky."* When Ila divorced Frank, he married Faith, who evidently looks at him with adoring admiration if he says it may rain on a cloudy day. Is that what all men want?

"If it had ever happened to you," Becky said with a trembling voice, "you'd know that it seems, it *is* real. It *is* a child."

I looked right at her, willing her to know everything. "It never happened to me," I said.

She scurried out of the store.

I watched her enter her car, the same car I'd pounded on, no, not the same, Becky has a Volvo. I am in her mind now. I am playing her the tapes of Benjy and me making love. The images are streaking across her consciousness as she starts the motor of the car. She hears his voice. "Marilyn, I love you, I wish I could tell you how much. . . . "

My bill came to forty dollars and sixty cents.

At home I unloaded the groceries. I called Ila at work and told her the good news. I didn't mention meeting Becky. She was pleased but sounded preoccupied. I called Mo. He was pleased, but sounded preoccupied. Then I went upstairs to take a nap.

At first, opening the door to our bedroom, I thought it was Aaron's body lying on top of Aimee's. A first. I've never seen anyone fucking. It is a shock, especially if it's your teenage son, your baby. But as soon as they sensed my presence, they pulled apart and I saw it wasn't Aaron. It was an unknown boy, blond, young, pulling his cock out of Aimee, who wriggled like a monkey, her face a comic blend of surprise and fear. "Oh, Mrs. Greene. . . . We just—"

"Who is this?" I said, horrified at the whole thing, at it's not being Aaron, at their being in our bedroom.

"I'm Olaf," he said, smiling engagingly. His cock was standing straight out, pointing at me. "We didn't expect you home so early."

"I'm really sorry, Mrs. Greene," Aimee sputtered. "I'm so sorry!"

"Get the fuck out of here," I said, "both of you. Now!"

"But I live here," Aimee said.

"Not anymore."

"Olaf is an old friend," she said. "We're just—"

"We've known each other since childhood," he added. But he began pulling his clothes on.

"I don't give a damn how long you've known each other," I screamed. "Out, out! I never want to see you again."

Aimee was dressing too. "We didn't mean to, we just—"

"It was a case of one thing leading to another," Olaf said. "It wasn't Aimee's fault, Mrs. Greene. It really wasn't. I kind of forced her. I didn't rape her, but I—"

"If you both aren't out of here in five minutes, I'm calling the police," I said, advancing on them menacingly, feeling the thrill of righteous indignation coursing in every vein.

"But we didn't—" Olaf said—"we didn't steal anything. We just . . ."

Aimee rushed into the room she shared with Aaron and stuffed her clothes rapidly into a bag. "You're a bitch," she flung at me. "I've always hated you. I don't know why your husband doesn't leave you. He wants me, I know."

Olaf dragged her by the arm. "Shut up," he said. "Let's go!"

Aimee's squinty little eyes darted at me again. "I know what you're really like!" she said. "I know!"

God almighty. After they'd left, I just sat there, shaking. *I know what you're really like.* What does that mean? A thousand guilty possibilities rushed through my mind. But no, I had the feeling it was an idle threat. I called Mo at the office and told him what happened.

"She's trouble," he said. "I knew that right away."

"She said you want her," I whimpered, not knowing why I brought that up. "Do you? Do you?"

"She's sexy. . . . But do you think I'm crazy? I feel sorry for Aaron, that's all."

"Me too. . . . Well, maybe Valeska will come back on the scene. Why did they use our bedroom? I feel like I ought to air it out, destroy the sheets. . . . "

"I'll come home early," Mo said. "Who the hell is Olaf?"

"Search me. . . . A friend of Aaron's? I hope not."

Aaron took it all much more philosophically than I would have expected. Of course he does that with most things, hides his real reactions, maybe from himself as well. "She's just horny all the time," he said, eating his steak. "She's like a nymphomaniac or something."

"She once made a pass at me," Linus said with a shy kind of boastfulness.

"Oh, she'd fuck an orangutan," Aaron said. "She once told me she used to fuck their family dog. An Airedale. Just to see what it was like."

"Girls are so different these days," I said, feeling absurdly happy to be in "the bosom of my family," Wife and Mother, again. "In my day. . . . "

"Look, she's honest," Aaron said. "She admits what she is. She likes sex."

"I'm glad I told her no," Linus said, his eyes dreamy, myopic. "She wasn't my type anyway."

Aaron looked at Mo. "She thought you were sexy, Dad. She said she used to imagine making it with you. She didn't understand how come you married Mom. She said you could've had anyone. . . . No offense, Mom. She just didn't like you."

"What a sweetie," I said. "And here I fed her, housed her under my roof . . . "

"You're lucky you didn't get VD," Linus said.

"Yeah, well. . . . " Aaron grinned. "Still, it was worth it in a way."

I held up a letter. "Faithful Valeska writing from her family farm. . . . "

Aaron looked dreamy. "With Valeska it's love. She only does it because she loves me. . . . "

"Listen, anyone who makes sweet rolls like that shouldn't be tossed aside lightly," Mo said. All four of us went upstairs and stripped and remade the bed. I'd left everything just as it was for evidence. When we finished, Mo hugged me and gave my ass a loving pat.

"Hey, Dad, no dirty stuff," Aaron warned.

"We're married, remember?" Mo said grinning. "It's allowed."

Tricky Hearts

"*I* want you to read it!" Becky's face was flushed, her voice trembling.

I was finishing my second cup of coffee. A peaceful Saturday morning—the twins playing in their rooms, Chelsea and Dawn both on sleepovers at the homes of friends, peaceful until Becky, searching for a pair of scissors in Dawn's room, unearthed a document which proved to be Dawn's diary of the past year, the year she turned seventeen. "Don't you think she has a right to her privacy?" I said nervously.

"No!" Becky said. "Not about things like this. . . . Oh, Benjy, please, if you don't read it, I'll have to bear the burden of it alone and I can't. Anyway, she left it right out, not locked up. Maybe it's a sign she *wants* us to read it."

"Why don't you just give me a brief summary?"

She came closer. "Why don't you want to read it? Is it just the oedipal thing, that you want to have this image of perfect, sweet little Dawn?"

"No, not really." I doubt, though this is before the fact, that I'm going to be surprised by what I read. That Dawn is not a virgin is a "fact" that I have suspected for over a year now.

Becky placed the purloined book in front of me, on top of the paper. "Please, sweetie. . . . I'm so upset, I don't know what to do. I feel we've failed totally as parents."

I took her hand. "Darling, don't. You're getting more upset than it warrants. Everyone has a stormy adolescence."

"*I* didn't," Becky said plaintively.

Neither did I, actually. "Look at Ginger," I said.

"I know!" Becky said. "*Look* at her!"

"Well, but she's in a terrific law school, getting excellent grades. . . ."

Becky looked pained. "But her social life. . . ! Is that what Dawn will be like, going from man to man, one-night stands, people with *diseases*, married men?" Her voice rose in a crescendo at the thought of these atrocities.

"But now she has a steady boyfriend," I said, trying to sound soothing. "She just needed to sow her wild oats."

Becky's lips were pressed tightly together. "That's all right for men," she said. "Women can't live like that. It isn't right. . . . And this is our daughter!"

I heaved a sigh. "Okay. I'll read it. . . . Do I have to read the whole thing?"

Becky picked up the notebook, holding it with the tips of her fingers as though it might contaminate her. "Read from here, starting on October twelfth." She left me alone.

It was handwritten in purple. Dawn's flamboyant large handwriting was easy to read:

Oct 12th, 1976

I am *so* mad at Perry!!! Nancy says, You have a boyfriend, you're so lucky blah, blah, he's so handsome, so rich. So? He's a disgusting self-centered prick, and seriously I do think the money makes it worse. He's like a spoiled baby about *everything*. If he has one need that isn't fulfilled the second it enters his head, he has a tantrum. Okay, I admit he's handsome and he fucks well, not that I have a vast range of comparison. But does that excuse acting like a child, a *mean rotten* child? All right, here's what happened. You can judge for yourself. I told you how his father's corporation has this great Hall of Fame box at Madison Square Garden, and let him use it for the Jefferson Starship concert? So of course I wanted to go and his parents don't like that kind of music (unlike mine—just kidding) so we set it up for Saturday. All day he's calling me, what am I going to wear. He gets *manic* about my clothes. Maybe he's gay, I don't know. I finally said, "Do you want to come over and select my fucking wardrobe or what?" I had this really pretty blouse I bought at a thrift shop last week and my purple satin slacks and those great sandals with the three-inch spikes that Mom *loathes* (she claims I'll be a cripple for life). I looked sensational, if I do say so myself. Even my skin was acting reasonable. My hair was perfect. Face it, he should consider himself damn lucky that I deign to go near him. I think he does, some of the .ime, actually. Okay!

So, we get to the concert and the box was great. It was way up high, like a private living room almost, and we had it all to ourselves. You could really see well, hear perfectly. They were just starting up when he says, "Suck me off." I said, "What? Are you *crazy?*" So he goes into this thing, that all his life, he's always had this fantasy of having a beautiful girl (that's me, yay!) suck him off at a Starship concert. All his life? When he was five? I said, "Forget it, I want to listen to the music!" He said, "Can't you do two things at once?" I said, "No!" "Well, then just clear out," he says, in this petulant, baby way. I looked at him like he had to be crazy. "Go find someone and do it in the men's room," I said. "Leave me alone." Then he really went berserk. I'd meant, go find a girl, but I guess he thought I meant a boy. "Look, I'm your date, okay?" I said, "and I'm not some exhibitionist." "No one can see," he said. "We'll kneel down. We can do it in the intermission. Then you won't miss any of the music." "No!" "Yes!" "No!" "Yes!" One of those brilliant conversations. So the intermission comes and he looks at me with this pleading expression, like some dog that's about to be gassed at the pound. "I'll do it to you first," he said. "Please?"

I figured if I don't let him do it, he's going to go on about it for the next hour and I won't be able to concentrate on the music. So we crouched down with his coat over us and he caressed me till I practically passed out. If he wasn't so good, believe me, I'd never put up with all this shit. Never!!! But he really has a magic tongue. So then, I did his bidding. While I was doing it, I looked all around at the other boxes wondering what was going on in them. And Perry is kneeling there with his eyes closed, moaning. I felt so totally detached. It was just a weird, bad feeling. Like I'd let him manipulate me again, after saying for the millionth time I wouldn't. I don't know. I just hope this doesn't show I'm going to be some kind of masochist in relation to men. What do you think? It wasn't even like I totally, totally didn't enjoy it. It was that it was his idea, he forced it on me and he always gets his way.

But it was a super concert! Really fantastic. So that part was worth it. And we do kind of love each other in a perverse sort of way. I mean it. Some of the time, I do. For the second half of the concert he kept beaming at me in this infatuated, adoring way. I think that's how he got around his mother all these years. 'Cause if you do what he wants, he acts like a real angel.

Becky passed through the room again, frowning. "Where are you up to?" she asked anxiously.

"I'm finished with the concert."

"What do you think?"

"Well, she has a vivid style," I said wryly, trying to joke.

"Benjy, please! Tell me what you really think!"

I hesitated. "I think she's having a stormy adolescence, that sex isn't, for their generation, what it was for ours, that—"

"But look at Chelsea! *She* isn't like that. I *know* she isn't."

"But people differ, darling. Really. You know that."

Becky sat down, looking ready to cry. "Did you know she wasn't a virgin?"

"I suspected it. . . . Look, she says she loves him. So at least—"

"Love?" Becky's voice rose. "How can you call that love? A boy that would make her do things like that! They could have been arrested! Using his money that way! I never liked Perry, never, even at the beginning. I think we should forbid her to ever see him again."

"How would we explain that?"

She sighed. "I don't know. . . . Just that we don't like him."

"She'll just see him on the sly."

Becky looked at me with her big mournful eyes. "What did we do wrong? It would be different if she came from a broken home, if she'd never gotten any affection . . . "

"It'll pass." I tried for Oriental detachment. But it was true, though I would never have admitted it to Becky, that the image of Dawn, my delicate, beautiful Dawn down on her knees in a box at Madison Square Garden with some guy's hairy cock down her throat—it did cause a strange kind of horror to creep over my soul. Horror mixed, of course, with some excitement. Dawn has always reminded me of Marilyn. Her blond hair, her quick, graceful movements, her taunting rapid (rabid?) wit, that rebellious gleam in her eye. As I was reading, the two of them fused in my mind. Dawn became Marilyn, I became Perry. It was not the box at Madison Square Garden, but Ila's kitchen, Marilyn naked, her back to me, washing strawberries. . . .

I shook my head, trying to clear away that image. Becky, mistaking my gesture, put her hand on my shoulder. "It's good that you don't get so hysterical," she said. "I wish I hadn't read it. But it was just lying there, not locked away or anything. It serves me right."

It has been five months since I've seen Marilyn. Each month I check off the amount of time in my mind, approvingly. I had thought, mistakenly, that the first month would be the hardest. In fact, it was the easiest. Righteous indignation, combined with a feeling I was doing the right thing, got me through that month with only a minimum of pain. What I wanted—this is still true, it just seems a more complex goal than I had anticipated—was to simplify my life, to lead a life that made sense. Yet, ironically, when I met Marilyn, my motive for getting involved with her, to the extent rationality played any part, was also to simplify my life. I thought then that my whole life was a lie. Hating law, hating (in a mixed, ambivalent way) my father, I had yet chosen to be in his profession, to see him every day. I felt I had married too young, had children too quickly. It was as though all day long I was the man they buried while he was still alive. I lay there in my coffin, hearing the footsteps of regular people all around me, wondering how to get out, wondering if I was the only one, if everyone felt the same way.

In the beginning with Marilyn I genuinely felt—though of course there was guilt—that I deserved this, that my "good boy" pose was so deeply and repugnantly false that anything would be an improvement. And of course the joy, the joy of sex, while it lasts in its most intense and ecstatic moments, seems worth anything. For those first few years, no matter what mood I was in, no matter what horrible, stupid, idiotic thing was happening at work, fucking Marilyn was the answer. Magic! Fuck your troubles away! And that seemed a justification. I told myself I would be a better husband and father if I was happy. In some way I think that was true. I was at peace with myself, though obviously at a cost. But maybe everything in life has a cost! Being "innocent" and a good husband had a cost too! If only that weren't true. If only there were some course of behavior that didn't, at some level, cause horrible pain. The pain of guilt versus the pain of deprivation.

Last month I flew out to California to see Kipp. He's had a breakdown, his second in slightly over a decade. He just sat there, his head in his hands, hardly talking, all during my visit.

At the very end I grabbed him, impulsively, maybe wanting through some physical gesture to show how much I cared for him, how much I identified with what he was going through. I thought he might push me aside but instead he let me hold him, almost went limp in my arms. I sat there, tears streaming down my face, half afraid the nurse would come in and say I was being committed too.

Instead, we detached from each other, gently, without a word, and I went down to the hospital coffee shop to have a drink with Kipp's wife, Ariel. She's in a wheelchair, has been for the past ten of the twenty years of their marriage. An automobile accident—Kipp wasn't driving, luckily. Ariel is tall, almost six feet, with a grave, serene, angelic face, hair parted in the middle, a soft, gentle voice. She weaves, which seems singularly appropriate. It's something she took up since the accident and she's gotten really excellent, good enough to have shows, have her work exhibited in museums.

"It's strange," she said. "Here I was the one who had the accident, who has to live with being crippled, and Kipp is the one who goes to pieces. Why? Do you understand it, Benjy?"

I remembered Kipp saying to me once that he was the one English professor on campus—he teaches at Stanford—who didn't screw co-eds. "It wouldn't be fair to Ariel," he said. "I think Kipp was always torn," I said hesitantly. "Maybe your accident brought some things to the surface, but it was there before you met him."

"Yes," she said sadly. "I know. . . . But the pills seemed to work! And now suddenly they don't anymore."

"He'll get better," I said, trying to regain a sense of inner calm. My hands were trembling. "Maybe it's better. He's letting it out. Maybe we should all do that."

"But what good does it do?" she cried. "It makes us all feel so guilty, as though we had failed him! It's selfish! Even about you, Benjy, he said—oh, it doesn't matter. I hate myself for even thinking any of this. If having a girlfriend would've prevented this, I wish he had! I'd have gone out and gotten someone for him." She laughed bitterly.

"I don't think that's it," I said, touching her hand. "I really don't."

"Sex is hard with us," she said wryly. "It is. It's worth it, to me, anyway, but it's . . . Well. And you know what breaks my heart? That in his office he still has this photo of me when we first met, in a bathing suit. I had such super legs!"

I withdrew my hand, after squeezing hers. "He's lucky to have you," I said, feeling how hopelessly inadequate that was.

"Yes," she said, but flatly, her eyes blank with pain. "And I'm lucky to have *him*."

All that weekend I kept thinking back to high school, where I'd first met Kipp—our parents were friends, we didn't go to the same school. He wasn't fat like me, but he was painfully shy, gangling, had been a child prodigy of sorts, wrote poetry at eleven. We talked about girls and sex in the most reverent, blissful way. Would it ever happen to us? Would it ever happen with someone beautiful, someone who wasn't a reject, someone worth having? We agreed that, no matter where we were at the time it happened, even if Kipp's parents had gone to Indonesia (his father was in the Foreign Service) we were to call each other up instantly. And if someone had appeared at that moment and said, "It *will* happen. You *will* meet women just like the ones you've been dreaming of . . . and you'll be just as miserable and tormented as you are right now"—would we have believed that even? Probably not.

Dawn came home from her sleepover at six, just before dinner. I had never thought to question these "sleepovers" before, but now I wondered, watching her pleased little smile as she skipped over, kissing me lightly, where has she really been? Dinner was tense. Becky had decided not to mention anything about the diary. "Did you, um, have a nice time at Ellen's?" she asked, passing the beans.

"Super!" Dawn looked, indeed, beatific, due to what? Seven hours in the sack? Group sex? Drugs?

"How are her parents getting along?" Becky pursued.

"What?"

"Didn't you say they were getting divorced?"

Dawn was munching on a lamb chop bone. "No, that's all passed. He was, like, impotent because she had her breast removed, but he went to see a shrink and now it's all terrific. They're happy as larks."

Becky darted a glance at me and the twins. "And how about Perry?" she said.

"What about him?"

"Aren't you going to see him this weekend? I thought you were sort of 'going together.'"

Dawn's little pink tongue dug into the bone for the marrow. "He's been grounded. His father's mad because he failed trig. . . . Anyhow, he's beginning to bug me a little. I need space!" she said, making a mock dramatic face.

"I think he's sexy," Robin said with her mischievous smile.

Roper made a face as though she were going to throw up. "In what way? He has too much hair!" She leaned over to my plate. "Can I have your bones, Daddy?"

With Roper we hardly need a dog, though we have one, a Sealyham terrier, Margaret. Roper cleans the bones so neatly and precisely that they look like objects found on a beach. I felt Margaret under the table, her chin resting on my shoe, waiting patiently for some forbidden scraps. I looked down at her. She has trained herself not to move, only to lie there, regarding me with passive, gentle, pleading eyes. God, all the eyes of women with which I am surrounded! Becky, Dawn, Chelsea, Roper, Robin, Margaret, our housekeeper. I wish I had the patriarchal temperament, more like my father. Instead, I feel I am something of an impostor, pretending before all these knowing, but also vulnerable female eyes that I know what I'm doing, that I am steering the ship safely on some predetermined course.

When we were just up to dessert, Chelsea came breezing in. She had been at a rehearsal for the high school symphony where she plays the cello. Chelsea is Becky reincarnated—solid, jolly, not sexless but thus far her social life has mainly been a large group of devoted male and female friends. She has a sweet tooth and is always battling her weight. Spying the chocolate cheesecake, her eyes lit up. "Oh God, help. . . . I've been so good all weekend," she said, sliding into her chair. "Do I dare?"

"Have a small piece," I said, cutting her one. Her plumpness is nothing like mine at a similar age. She has Becky's radiant rosy-cheeked healthiness as well, and polished off the cheesecake in a second.

"So, what's new on the home front?" she said, looking at Dawn. "How's Perry?"

"I didn't see him," Dawn said.

"How come?"

"We had a kind of fight."

Chelsea sighed, as she had upon contemplating the cheesecake. "God, he is *so* gorgeous! I think I'd be nervous with someone that good looking."

"Why?" Dawn asked.

"If you had a fight, you'd know he could find someone else in two seconds."

Dawn got up from the table. "I can find someone in two seconds," she said.

Chelsea put her head to one side. "What hideous self-confidence! . . . Were you like that in high school?" she asked, looking from Becky to me.

"Not in the least," I said, watching Dawn go and curl up, with effortless grace, in an armchair.

"I never really had any serious boyfriends till college," Becky said. "Of course, I went to an all-girls high school."

Roper made a face. "Ugh. . . . How could you *stand* it?"

"*I* wouldn't mind," Robin said. "It'd be great. No boys."

"I guess I'll be like you, Mom," Chelsea said contentedly. "I don't think I'll meet anyone, and this is my last year of high school." She identifies with Becky and is close to her.

"Sometimes it's better to wait," Becky said, casting a quick glance at Dawn.

"Why?" Robin asked. "What's good about it?"

"Well," Becky said carefully. "It makes you appreciate what you have, once you have it. Sometimes people who rush into things too soon become . . . sated."

"That's me," Dawn called out languidly. She was leafing through a magazine. "God, am I sated! It's really sick. Too much too soon. . . . And it's all Perry's fault."

"How is it his fault?" Robin said.

"He just has this sick sick mind when it comes to sex," Dawn said. "I don't know. It's exhausting."

"Sick in what *way?*" Roper called out eagerly.

"Oh, I don't know," Dawn said. "All kinds of stuff. I'll tell you in a couple of years."

Roper looked disgusted. "What's the good of that? In a couple of years I'll be *doing* it! I want to know *now!*"

Chelsea began clearing, and she and Becky vanished into the kitchen. I sank down into an armchair opposite Dawn. I stared at her dreamily. She looked up, catching my glance. "Poor little Daddy," she said with a slightly mocking tenderness. "Why do you look so sad?"

I laughed.

She got up and began rumpling my hair, kissing me. "Isn't life what it's cracked up to be?" she said, in that same ironical tone.

"Not always," I admitted.

"Yeah," she said wearily. "I know."

How do the girls see me? Do they, with feminine insight and intuition, see clear through me? Am I just like a pane of glass? Or am I safely hidden in my role as Father of Four? I feel Dawn intuits quite a lot, though we rarely talk other than in this bantering mode. She knelt down next to my armchair, looking up at me, and, inadvertently, I thought of her in the box at Madison Square Garden. How did she look at him? That same mockingly sexy, but vulnerable half smile: do with me what you will?

After dinner Becky began looking in the educational section of the Sunday paper for possible job offers. She would like a job similar to the one she had briefly before we were married, on that *Human Rights* magazine. In fact, it has changed hands and is now more conservative, but she is going down for an interview next week. "It'll be good for me," she said. "I need to know what the real world is like. Daddy has always overprotected me."

True enough. And now poor Daddy has proved as unreliable as I feel myself to be. When we last visited him, he told me that possibly his business misfortunes were due to his not really giving a damn anymore, since his wife died two years ago. "I have nothing to live for," he said. "That's just a fact. . . . Oh, I know, Becky, the girls. But still, at the center there's a horrible hollow. I hope you never have to face that, Benjamin."

When Jane died, he was so despondent and talked so often of suicide that we debated having him come to live with us. Our house is gigantic. I think I could more easily put up with Rolf in my house than either of my own parents any day. But he wouldn't allow it. "I don't want to be a burden, I'm fine," he insisted. The Marshalls are still there. We made them promise to keep an eye on him and Becky made him promise not to take his own life. "Think how *I'd* feel, Daddy," she said. "Please think of that."

"I'm like a wind-up toy," he confessed to me darkly. "Each morning I wind myself up and feel myself wind down. But what for? If there's no human connection, what's the point? I never wanted to outlive Jane. If I'd known the exact day she was going to die, I'd have taken an overdose and died alongside her."

Somehow his talking like this frightens me in a totally different way than it frightens Becky. She is alarmed that her father's love for her isn't strong enough to turn aside these morbid thoughts. I am alarmed at a man being so openly, shamelessly dependent on a woman. Because of that, when he went bankrupt, it was impossible to say a word of reproach or talk at all about my own panic. "I hate myself," he said. "How could I do this?"

Yet curiously I am not positive what Rolf's going bankrupt means. It happened several months ago, yet he is still living in that huge house by the sea and seems to be planning to continue doing so. I had thought bankruptcy meant all one's possessions being taken away, being left with nothing. Evidently, instead, it's some kind of business technicality. Our lives will be affected, but not in the sudden, irreversible way I had anticipated when I first heard the news.

Meanwhile, my own father is not well. He has to have open heart surgery in a month or six weeks. He is being his usual jocular self about the whole thing, joking about death, infirmity, in a way that doesn't quite conceal his terror. My mother is, as would be expected, hysterical. "He's my whole life," she confided to me privately. "What will I do if something serious happens?"

Search me. I toy mentally with the idea of fixing up Becky's father and my mother in case of my father's death. But I fear that what made the two marriages work was that there was one strong person caring for one who was weak. Though Becky's mother was physically ill toward the end of her life, her character was like granite. My mother needs someone who holds forth, whose cloak of irony is impenetrable and total. Rolf would scare her out of her wits with his quoting from Emily Dickinson, his morbid preoccupations with the great beyond. And she would drive him crazy with her fussiness, her eagerness to please, her forty pairs of size three shoes. "He'll be okay," I told her, half believing this. "He'll outlive us all."

"The doctor said he's in wonderful shape, wonderful!" she said, allowing my words to sink in. "And they do these operations all the time nowadays. I'm foolish to be so worried."

"You'll have three more husbands," my father said, putting his arm around her.

"Don't joke about it, Gilbert," she reprimanded him severely. "Please don't!"

At work they have talked for over a year now of a merger with a larger company that produces not only office furniture but household products of all kinds, a European-based chain that has done well in London and Paris. I've spent six months envisioning horrors. If the merger takes place, heads will roll from the top to the bottom. I mentally see my head tumbling with slow precision down, down, down. . . . But no move has been made. The one "blessing in disguise" is that all these anxieties—about my job, my father's im-

minent operation, Rolf's suicidal mood and bankruptcy, my
vasectomy, the discovery of Dawn's vivid sex life—have provided
me with enough excuses to last till I'm eighty when I'm unable (a
more frequent occurrence lately) to make love to Becky.

"Darling, don't worry so," she said one night when, after a few
moments of nuzzling, kissing, caressing I suddenly froze, felt my
libido winging carelessly, heartlessly out the window. "You have so
much on your mind."

Becky is so ready to forgive, to understand. She cradled me in
her arms, kissing me. "We'll be fine," she said. "I'll get a job and
Daddy will pull himself together and your father will be as good as
new. . . ."

"Yes," I said. "I hope so." Becky so much wants men to be as she
imagined them as a child: strong, protective, kind. Why are we all,
to a man, failing her?

"You worry too much. Don't! It's not necessary."

I lay there, not quite sickened with self-hatred, no, just pierced by
the irony of it, that while I was rushing back and forth from Becky to
Marilyn, like a trapeze artist on a bicycle juggling eight oranges at
once—I was fine! Maybe the sheer excitement and insanity of it kept
me aloft. And I "allowed" myself to think of Marilyn when in bed
with Becky. I felt that was only fair, to myself at any rate. But now
any thought of Marilyn is much more likely to freeze me into anxiety
than to be stimulating. My brain forces her aside, but occasionally
she rushes in anyway, not as a stimulant, but as a taunting, witchlike
presence. Oh God! Where is this simple life I had imagined was
lying in wait for me if I gave Marilyn up? Maybe it left for some
distant port long ago. Yet I can't believe this is the final denouement.
It seems too unfair, too spiteful, that I am not even going to be
allowed the horribly mixed pleasures of renunciation! The second
time that evening, to my horror, in the middle of making love to
Becky, I thought of Dawn and managed to rush my way to a furtive
and unsatisfactory climax.

"We could, maybe, see someone," Becky suggested as I lay in a
spent, frazzled heap on her breast.

"Never!" I said. "I won't do it. Look, if I had nameless anxieties that I didn't understand, that would be one thing. But it's all perfectly clear. If I *weren't* a total wreck at this point in my life, there'd be something wrong with me!"

"Yes, well, it's true. . . . No, I meant more for you, really. The male ego thing or whatever. *I* don't mind."

"Maybe you ought to take a lover."

"What do you mean?"

"You're forty-two. . . . Do you not want a sex life? Isn't that important to you?" God, what in the name of anything is wrong with me? I want to stuff a sock in my own mouth.

"Of course it's important," Becky said, "but I know this is just a passing thing. I'm not worried. So if *you're* not worried—"

"I'm not worried at all!" I yelled, my voice cracking under tension like an adolescent's.

"Sex is just part of a whole. . . . What I mean is, it's a way of expressing love, and there are lots of ways. If I felt that you didn't love me, that would be different."

I drew her close to me. "I'll always love you."

"I know," she sighed, but in what seemed a strange, slightly questioning tone. Or was that my imagination?

I lay there, holding her, wondering. Was this the moment to mention Marilyn? Is it really necessary? What for? In hopes Becky will wave some magic wand and remove not only present but past guilt? *Of course I understand, sweetie.* But maybe she's known all along? If so, wouldn't it be just an act of foolish and gratuitous cruelty to rub her nose in it? Wouldn't it force me into more stupid and loathsome lies?

"I'll always love you too," she said. "And the sex thing will pass. I know it will."

I wondered, fleetingly, if I could mention having thought of Dawn? A red herring? But there seems to be enough swimming around as it is. "At least Dawn is—" I began.

"But that isn't what it's all about!" Becky cried. "That's not sex! It's just brutality and showing off! She doesn't know what sex *is!*"

"Well . . ."

"Chelsea will wait till she meets someone she loves," Becky said. "I'm so glad of that."

After Becky fell alseep, I lay in bed a long time, restlessly. Out of the blue a sudden rage at Marilyn took possession of me. I felt her mocking spirit hovering in the bedroom. Her hatred of Becky always seemed so exaggerated and insane to me. I don't hate her husband and never did, not in that vindictive, overwhelming way. I wondered how their sex life has been since our break. I have the horrible feeling it's been fine, wonderful. Maybe she even has a new lover! She must have a new job by now. Of course! She's met someone on the job, maybe even the guy who interviewed her as she sat there, with her legs crossed, licking her lips nervously, looking archly over her shoulder at him as she left the room. *Let's have a drink to celebrate, Miss Greene. . . . Oh, that's Mrs. I'm married. . . . Whatever.*

I leaped out of bed. I want to kill Marilyn! Why? What is this all about? Why, five months after the fact, do I feel such horrible, violent rage? I went downstairs and poured myself a drink. An expensive Scotch Kipp gave us several years ago. I wish, despite his problems, Kipp lived closer to us. I miss the way we used to talk together. I don't talk like that to anyone anymore. You don't, when you make friends after thirty or forty. I thought of those long, absurd, meandering discussions we used to have long into the night. *Call me the minute it happens.* It is one o'clock which means it's only ten o'clock in California where they live. Impulsively I dialed their number. Kipp answered. He's been home from the hospital for six weeks.

"Kipp? It's Benjy."

"Benjy, Christ, how wonderful to hear from you! Where are you?"

"At home." His voice sounded slightly too manic, but better than that awful weighted-down monotone when he was sick. "I just—I just wondered how things were going."

"They seem to be okay. I don't know. . . . Maybe I just need to crash every decade. I hope not. Ariel's been kind of . . . I guess it took a lot out of her."

"She's strong," I reminded him.

"Is she ever! A fucking saint. . . . No, God, how can I say that? Except she is! What can I do? I've married a saint."

"But you're feeling better? Are you teaching again?"

"Next week is the big moment. I don't know. I guess for me the question is: can I do it knowing it's all a total, total farce, that I know nothing, that the kids I'm teaching don't give a shit, that the whole system is rotten, dishonest, that we live in a country which *worships* illiteracy, which *despises* intelligence, sensitivity . . . "

I hesitated. I'd heard a lot of this before. "I was sorry when I visited you," I said, "that I didn't say anything. I didn't know *what* to say!"

"You were good," he said. "I was glad you were there."

"My life is kind of a mess too," I admitted. "I just didn't want to burden you when you were so—"

"How?" he asked eagerly. "How is it a mess?"

"Well, my father's about to be operated on, Becky's father is bankrupt."

"Oh, Christ," Kipp said. "I thought you were having some razzle-dazzle pull-out-all-the-stops affair with some real bitch in your office. Your father! You can't stand him. I thought you once said you'd shoot him if you thought you could get away with it."

I laughed. I always loved this about Kipp, his darting, frantic, terribly accurate way of piercing through whatever crap I dished forth. It also made me horribly nervous. "Actually, there's this woman in my office," I said, lowering my voice.

"Yeah? Yeah?"

"Nothing's happened. It won't. She's married and . . . No, it's just she's been after me, kind of insinuating she wouldn't exactly turn me down."

"So, what's stopping you?"

"Everything! What do you mean, what's stopping me? Becky, my self-image—"

"Benjy, you are so incredibly full of shit! I can't believe it! Your self-image! Fuck that! Will you go out and fuck her the next time you see her or else I'm never speaking to you again. I mean it."

I couldn't help laughing nervously. "I can't! How about family loyalty? How about marital fidelity?"

"You know, it's lucky you live three thousand miles away. . . . Because if you didn't, I'd come over right now and bash your fucking head against the wall. Are you done? Or do you have a little sackful of clichés that you're going to spill out while I sit here, helpless. . . .

Look, I have a crippled wife! You want to switch? You want Ariel? Family loyalty! . . . Is she beautiful?"

"Yes. . . . And she has a wonderful body, beautiful breasts." I felt a stab of pain, rather than erotic arousal, at the memory.

"Benjy, I am serious. When you get off the phone, you are calling that woman and propositioning her instantly or this is the end of a long and wonderful friendship. And think of me while you're going at it, okay? Light a candle for me."

"Listen, why don't you, if you feel it's so important, find someone and—"

"Find someone! There *is* someone! There's a beautiful, haunted, semisuicidal girl in one of my classes with long jet-black hair who doesn't wear a bra, okay? Is that good enough for you? Does that make you happy?"

"It isn't a matter of making me happy," I stammered. "Tell me— tell me more about her."

"Well, she's majoring in witchcraft. She carries this crystal ball in her knapsack. I once tried to lift it and almost doubled over. I could live with her till the end of time and be in a state of total, constant bliss. Listen, she knows ancient Greek! She recites Heraclitus—accurately!" Kipp was a Greek major in college.

"So—do it! Stop giving *me* all the terrific advice."

"I have a crippled wife! I'm crazy! I can't handle that kind of stuff. Not because of all this crap you've been talking about. I just literally can't do it! Listen, do you want to hear one of the most humiliating horrible moments of my entire life? When I got back here, Paloma came to see me, saying she'd heard I was sick, she'd felt so bad, she'd composed an ode in Greek which she wanted to sing for me. So she sits there, singing—she plays the fucking zither! Her hair is hanging down, her voice is like music from the spheres, and I started weeping. I just couldn't stop. I terrified her. I think she's going to drop all my classes!"

"She won't drop your classes. She's probably in love with you."

There was a long pause. "Yeah, she is. She's madly in love with me. And she loves me *because* I'm crazy, because I break down like that. She wants to wrap her long black hair around me and nurse me back to health, sing me plaintive songs. . ." His voice broke. "Oh

God, Benjy, I'm afraid I'm just as sick as I was before. I'm still crazy. Nothing is any different."

"You're not crazy. . . . I feel all the same things."

"Do you, really? You're not just saying it?"

"Everything," I said, seeing Marilyn flying out the door, her blond hair loose, screaming at me. *You're craven. I hate you.*

We sat there, not talking.

"So listen, thanks for calling," Kipp said suddenly in a totally different voice. I heard him say to Ariel who had evidently just entered the room, "Yeah, it's Benjy. . . . Take care. We both send our love."

I hung up and sat there, mesmerized, exhausted. It was only when I turned finally that I saw Becky at the foot of the stairs. "Who was that?" she asked anxiously.

"Kipp. . . . I thought I'd see how he was doing. It's three hours earlier there."

She came padding down the rest of the stairs. "How *is* he doing?"

"Fair." I hesitated. "He's in love with one of his students."

"Oh," Becky said. She stood there in her flowered nightgown. "Does she love him too?"

"Evidently." We stared at each other.

"Have you ever felt that," Becky said softly, fearfully, "for someone other than me?"

"Since we've been married?"

"Yes."

I cleared my throat. "Once, long ago. . . . The twins were just born."

There was another pause.

"I thought perhaps you had once," Becky said, her voice just above a whisper.

"Nothing happened," I rushed on. "It was just. . . . I guess I was just feeling vulnerable. You were so absorbed in the babies."

"I *was* absorbed in the babies. That was *such* a happy time for me!" She looked dreamily nostalgic.

And for me! Ramsey Krosneck's apartment. The giant fig tree in the corner of the living room. Marilyn's tongue licking around my nipples, her slender fingers stroking my cock, her scent, her nails digging into my flesh. *Benjy, my God, darling, don't stop, don't. . . .*

"But it passed?" Becky asked.

"Yes."

"I guess those things always do," she said. "Once the first whatever is gone." She looked wry. "I had such a crush on Loren Boatwright once. He said I had the most beautiful jaw he'd ever seen." Our former dentist who moved to Florida.

I smiled. "You *do* have a beautiful jaw."

"He used to touch me so tenderly. I looked forward, even, to going to his office for root canal work!"

"That's true love," I joked.

"No, it was just an infatuation," said sensible, true Becky. She yawned. "God, it's past two. We'd better get to sleep."

My father is having his operation the day after Thanksgiving. For this reason it will be the first all-family Thanksgiving in years. Ginger is flying in from San Francisco, Stef and Lois with their son, James, from Chicago. On Thanksgiving morning, Becky came down with a virus and a hundred and two fever. "Oh this is terrible," she said, nose stuffed. "How can I go? You mother will think I'm deserting her."

"No, she won't. . . . And it's better. If she were to pick anything up, it would interfere with her round-the-clock obsessing. You don't want to have that on your conscience."

"Benjy, it's a serious operation! You shouldn't joke about it."

The doctor, whom I spoke to when I visited my father in the hospital, said he was confident everything would go fine. "He has a tricky heart, but a sound one. . . . Of course at his age, sometimes unexpected things happen, but I wouldn't worry to excess."

My mother doesn't think she is worrying to excess. She defines "excess" very loosely, however. By mid-morning of Thanksgiving, Chelsea was also feeling lousy. "I don't think I can make it either, Daddy," she said. "I have this terrible headache and I think I might throw up."

That left me, Dawn, and the twins. I looked at Dawn. "How about you, sweets?"

"Bursting with health," she said with a grin. "Raring to go. . . . I'm so glad Aunt Ginger will be there!"

Dawn still adores Ginger, who is a younger Auntie Mame to her, leading, successfully, the life Dawn one day hopes to lead. They correspond. Once Dawn flew out to visit her and together they filed through the replies to the appeal Ginger had placed in the Personals column, hoping to find "Mr. Right" or "Mr. Wrong," as the case might be.

Dawn had made up the twins, who, were they prettier, would have looked like child prostitutes. Instead, they just looked weighed down with globs of blue eye shadow and brilliantly pink cheeks. "Darling, make them take some of it off," Becky begged. "They're ten!"

"They can take it off in the car," I promised, grabbing a box of Kleenex on my way out.

Dawn was wearing a red velour top and tight black slacks, her hair in a Veronica Lakeish dip over one eye. "I want to look vicious," she announced. "It's the new me. Like one of those women who drive men mad with lust and desire and do incredible cruel things. What do you think, Daddy?"

"You look sensational," I said, smiling.

"Do I look like I'd stop at nothing?"

"Definitely."

I drove slowly because it was pouring rain. Dawn regaled the twins with a series of incredibly filthy dirty jokes which she would never have told if Becky was in the car. "I don't *get* it," Robin kept saying while Roper guffawed appreciatively. "What does that *mean?*"

"If you have to ask, you're too young," Roper said.

"I'm the same age as you!"

"Well, your mind is less developed."

"It is not! . . . Daddy, did *you* get that one?"

"I wasn't really listening. . . . I have to concentrate on the driving."

"I bet Grandma's going to be surprised at how we look," Robin said. "Do you think she will, Daddy?"

"Very."

Which proved to be an understatement. When my mother opened the door, she sucked in her breath. "My babies!" she cried in horror.

"We're not babies," Roper snarled.

"It was just an experiment," Robin said. "Dawn helped us."

My mother raised her eyebrows. "I can see what happens when Becky is sick."

Everyone else was already there. Stef and Lois's son, James, came out and shyly said hi. James is fifteen, an only child, ultra-serious. Stef wrote that he is now teaching a course on computers at the private high school he attends. In the car, Dawn pronounced him to be "incredibly uptight and a potential total nerd. . . . Maybe I should deflower him in the closet when Grandma's not looking."

"I didn't know you could deflower boys," I commented.

"Why can't you?" she said.

"Yeah, why can't you?" the twins echoed indignantly.

I saw James look quickly and furtively at Dawn. She gave him one of her mysterious smiles. "So how's it going, James?" she said. "How's your sex life?"

He turned bright red. "I don't have one."

"How come?"

"I don't know."

I grabbed Dawn by the arm. "Come on inside," I said sternly.

Stef had just gotten off the phone with the doctor. We had agreed to call my father later in the afternoon, when everyone was assembled, after we had eaten. "He's evidently doing fine," he said. "Nothing to worry about, Mom."

"I haven't slept for four nights," my mother said. "I just lie there, petrified. I can't think of anything else. I can't eat . . ."

"Mom, he has the constitution of a forty-five-year-old man," Stef reassured her in his bland, almost monotone voice.

"Without him I wouldn't exist," my mother went on. "He's my whole life."

Ginger crushed out her cigarette impatiently. "Mom, come on! What does that mean? You wouldn't exist? You're not a human being except for Daddy? That's crazy!"

"It's love," my mother said angrily.

"I don't call that love," Ginger said. "To have no existence without another person? That's slavery!"

"You've never loved anyone the way I love Gilbert," my mother said, her voice trembling. "You don't know."

"I've loved dozens of men," Ginger flung out, gulping down her third martini.

"You've gone to bed with dozens of men," my mother snapped. "I'm not talking about sex!"

"Well, I thought you and Daddy had done it at least three times," Ginger said, dryly, "or how did we all get here?"

"Ginger, cut it out," Stef said. He turned to my mother. "When will we eat?"

Perhaps because I was right beside her, my mother suddenly flung her arms around me. "Benjy!" she cried.

I could see Ginger's exasperated expression. "Mom, Stef's right. Dad's going to be fine. We can call him now, if that would make you feel better."

"No, let's eat first," my mother murmured. "Everything's ready."

Lois, Stef's wife, is a slim, precise woman with neatly set light brown hair and tortoiseshell-framed glasses She looks very much like James and is a family counselor. "I'm sorry about Becky," she said. We were seated next to each other.

"It's just a virus." I unfolded my napkin.

Stef was looking at Dawn, who was opposite him. "Dawn, you're really getting to be stunning," he said nervously.

Dawn smiled. "What can I say?"

"You must have dozens of boyfriends," he went on.

"Well, I'm sequentially monogamous."

Ginger burst out laughing. "Hey, great! I love it. . . . Who're you sequential with right now, kid?"

Dawn gave her a smile. "I'll tell you later."

"It's interesting how in James's school, the social life is so . . . sedate," Lois said. "No one seems to do very much of anything."

"Not in our school," Dawn said. "We have everything—druggies, sex maniacs. . . . "

My mother glanced at me anxiously. "Isn't it a private school? How can this be?"

"I think Dawn's exaggerating a little," I said.

"Look, Daddy," Dawn said, "face it, private school just means the kids have parents with money. So, they take coke instead of pot. But they're not any more virtuous or anything."

"I thought the drug scene was quieting down," Ginger remarked.

"It is," Dawn said. "Seriously, don't worry, Grandma. It's only a few kids who're really, like, into it in a hard-core way. Most of them just smoke at parties and stuff."

My mother still looked anxious. "It must be so much harder raising children today," she said.

A pause as we all considered our variously troubled and crazed adolescences.

"The turkey is marvelous," Lois said brightly. "You always get it so moist."

My mother beamed. "The butcher saves me one especially. It's from a special farm."

Ginger had just drained her glass. "Stef, I hate to tell you this, what with our blood tie and your being fifteen years older and all, but, kid, you can't mix a martini to save yourself."

Stef looked flustered. He's taller than me or our father, but balding rather than gray. "Have some wine," he said, extending the bottle in her direction.

My mother smiled tensely. "Darling," she shot in Ginger's direction.

"Darling *what?*" Ginger shot back, pouring herself some wine.

"Don't you think you've had enough?"

"Not really. . . . Hey listen, I have wonderful news. First, I have a super job once I graduate. Assistant district attorney for Oakland."

I raised my glass. "Congratulations, Ginge!"

Ginger's face was flushed. She wears her coppery hair in a more lady-like style now that she's a lawyer and dresses more conservatively too, today in a navy dress with a white collar. But there's still a sense of it's being a slight disguise, as though her true self were going to come leaping out. "Even more amazing," she said, "I'm actually getting married. . . . Or at least formally moving in with the man I love."

There was a pause.

"Who is he?" my mother said. "You haven't mentioned anyone."

"Actually, we've known each other for several years," Ginger said, "but he was married. His wife died two years ago, and he has four teenage kids. So we were more friends at first."

"He must be considerably older than you," my mother pursued.

"He's forty-eight," Ginger said. "His name is Earl Wright. I've finally met Mr. Right, how about that?"

"Well, tell us about him," Stef said. "Who is he? What does he do?"

"He's a law professor at UCLA and he's one of the kindest, smartest, gentlest, most terrific men alive on this planet. Plus he holds my undivided attention, which if I do say so myself, is damn hard."

Lois reached over and patted Ginger's hand. "I'm *so* happy for you," she said. "Do you have a picture of him?"

Ginger rummaged around in her purse. "The one of him alone was taken a few years ago, and here's one of us together." She handed the photos to Stef, who was next to her. He looked at them silently and passed them to Lois, who looked at them silently and passed them to me. Earl Wright was a long-faced black man, balding, with grizzled sideburns and sad, penetrating eyes. In the photo with Ginger, though it was taken several years later, he looked younger. They were standing with their arms around each other, Ginger laughing and nuzzling up against him. I passed the photo to Dawn, who was the first to make a comment.

"Hey, he's black," she said.

"So?" said Ginger.

My mother pounced on the photos, brought them up close, and dramatically flung them facedown on the table. "This is positively the last straw," she said.

"In what way?" Ginger asked defiantly.

"Here Gilbert is in the hospital, having a life-threatening operation, and now this! How could you *do* this to me?"

Ginger smiled gently. "I thought you'd be happy, Mom. I thought all these years you'd been lying in bed a nervous wreck because I was screwing all these unsuitable guys."

"Yeah, Grandma, so he's black?" Dawn said, reaching for a turkey leg. "I mean, big deal? Don't be so prejudiced."

"I think what concerns everyone," Lois said smoothly, "is the children that result from marriages like this, the problems they suffer. . . . "

"Well, guess what? We're not having any," Ginger said. "Earl has four and I don't especially want kids. I figure five grandchildren is enough to carry on the much-vaunted Fetterman family line. . . . Everybody happy now?"

"I just can't—" My mother ran from the table in tears.

"What's wrong with Grandma?" Robin asked. She was looking at the photos with Roper.

"It's because he's black," Roper explained patiently.

"Who?"

"Him!" she pointed to the photo.

"Mr. Balner is black," Robin pointed out. "He's our history teacher."

"Yeah," Roper said. "But she's not marrying him."

"Who?"

"Aunt Ginger!"

"Aunt Ginger's *marrying him?*"

Roper sighed and rolled her eyes at all of us. "Don't mind her. She's a little slow on the uptake."

Dawn was polishing off her turkey bone. "I think Grandma's living in another century," she said. She got up and hugged Ginger. "I think he's handsome and nice and you'll live happily ever after."

Stef looked nervously at his watch. "We should call Dad," he said.

"Then he'll have a quadruple heart attack before the operation," James said.

"James, hush!" Lois said. "That's not funny. . . . Look, I think someone should go get Sophie. Should I?"

"I'll go," I said.

I went into my parents' bedroom. My mother was standing near the window, quietly snuffling. "Mom, we're going to call Dad now," I said gently, approaching her.

"She's going to tell him," my mother cried. "He can't be told anything disturbing! It'll kill him!"

"We won't tell him a thing. . . . But, Mom, be fair to Ginger, okay? She loves this man and you haven't met him yet."

"Why does she do this? Look at all the men there are in the world! She does it just to aggravate me. That's all!"

"I think she fell in love with someone and he happened to be black."

"No one 'happens' to be black," my mother screamed. "He was black from the day she met him! Didn't she notice? Doesn't she see properly?"

"What I mean is, she knew him and what started as a friendship grew into love. Not everything is love right from the first moment."

"But look at you and Stef," my mother said. "You've married nice, sweet, bright girls, you've never given us a moment's worry or anxiety."

I sighed, amazed at my mother's selective amnesia, her ability to block out the years I was disastrously overweight, the years Stef was boinging back and forth from rabbi to psychiatrist to rabbi, the subdued uproar when I decided I wanted to switch from law. "Ginger's an independent person," I said. "She doesn't do anything to hurt you. She wants to feel you love her and accept her as she is."

But my mother brushed all that aside. She just hugged me. "I'm so glad you're here, Benjy. . . . You're such a comfort to me through all this. You're such a wonderful man! Becky is very *very* lucky." She beamed at me, moist-eyed.

We were standing before a large mirror which hangs opposite my parents' bed. I glanced at myself, gray-haired, not quite plump. The Good Child rides again. Is there no way on earth I can free myself from this? Or is it that I don't want to, don't have the courage? I led my mother to the living room.

We divided up. I took the kitchen phone with Ginger, my mother went with Stef and Lois to the bedroom. Stef dialed. My father answered right away.

"Well, Dad, we're all thinking of you," he said heartily. "How're you feeling?"

"I've felt better," my father said, "but basically as well as can be expected. Listening to a bit of Brahms never hurt anyone."

"The radio's working all right?"

"Perfectly." We had gone and installed a hi-fi in his room and brought a carton of his favorite books.

"Gilbert?" my mother's tremulous voice came on. "I miss you!"

"I miss you, dear. . . . Did the dinner go all right?"

"Yes, beautifully," she quavered. "But I had no appetite."

"We'll be around to see you tomorrow," I said. "Becky's home with a virus."

"Oh, sorry to hear that," my father said. "And Ginger? Is she there?"

I gave Ginger the phone. "Hi, Daddy! . . . Yeah, I'm terrific. I was just telling everyone about a wonderful job offer I have for when I graduate. . . . Sure, I deserve it. They're lucky to get me. And I have some more super news, but I'll save it for when you're better. . . . No if. You'll be fine."

There was more chit-chat and then we hung up. Stef and my mother and Lois returned to the dining room. "I hope we didn't tire him," my mother said.

"He'll be fine," Stef said for about the hundredth time that day. "He sounded just like normal."

"Did you think so?" my mother said. "I thought his voice sounded a little weak."

"I didn't think so," Stef said. "Did you, Benjy?"

"Well, he must be sedated a little."

My mother sighed. "This is the price you pay for loving someone," she said dramatically.

Ginger looked at me and half raised her eyebrows. "Hey, Mom, how about a game of Scrabble? It'll take your mind off things."

"Can I play?" said Dawn.

"Can I?" said James.

"Oh, you'll beat us," Ginger said, "but okay."

Lois followed them in to join the game. Stef and I were left alone. We went into my father's study. Stef closed the door. He lay down on the couch. I sat in an armchair.

"Oh God," he sighed, closing his eyes.

"Oh God what?" It was amusing in a way to have him reclining as a patient, me in the "doctor's" chair. I wonder if it's because Stef is a shrink that I have such a suspicion about psychiatry. When Stef was a rabbi, he drove everyone crazy talking about God and the Jews. Then he switched to Freud, and did the same with all his theories about the human psyche. Yet I always had the feeling his belief in both systems was equally shaky.

"I haven't been sleeping well for months," he said. "I wake up in the middle of the night and I just lie there for hours."

I thought of the other night, calling Kipp. "Kipp had a breakdown again. . . . He was in the hospital for three weeks, now he's home."

"Yes, well he always had suicidal manic-depressive tendencies, as I recall," he said in his professionally unctuous voice.

"It's gotten worse since Ariel's accident," I went on. "She's the one who's actually disabled, but he's the one who can't handle it."

"It's often that way," Stef said. "And of course everyone seizes on whatever excuses life tosses their way."

I never know if Stef would annoy me as much if he weren't my brother. "Do you?" I asked.

"Do I what?"

"Seize whatever excuses life tosses your way?"

"Sure, all the time."

I looked over at him. His eyes were still closed. "Are you and Lois happy?"

Stef laughed. "Of course we're happy. . . . Do we look *unhappy?*"

"No, I mean, one can't usually tell."

"We're as happy as anyone is in the modern world," he said. "We share common interests, we adore James, we fuck from time to time and it's not an excruciatingly painful experience. . . . "

I winced. "And that's all one can expect?"

He propped himself up to look at me. "What did you expect?"

"Ecstasy? Divine insight? Joy?"

I'd thought Stef would shoot back an ironical reply, but he just smiled sadly. "Well. . . . " he said, sinking back.

"Why do you have insomnia?" I pursued. "What do you lie there worrying about?"

He laughed. "I'm in love," he said, trying to mock his own words.

"Wonderful. . . . Who's the lucky girl?"

"Sabrina Abrahms."

I thought a second. The name sounded extremely familiar, but I couldn't remember from where. Then it came to me. Sabrina Abrahms was a girl from Stef's high school class. I couldn't remember if they actually went out together or if she just came over and studied with him. She had been small, delicate, dark-haired. "The one who wrote poetry?" I said.

"The one who wrote poetry."

"I thought she vanished from the face of the earth eons ago."

"She vanished and reappeared. . . . No, it was curious. James kept telling us about this teacher, Ms. Abrahms, and how fantastic she was. I thought the usual schoolboy crush and thought nothing of it. But I was pleased because he's always been so into computers and suddenly he was reading poetry, wanting to go to plays with me. So one day I went to his school for a conference and there was Sabrina! Totally unchanged! It was amazing. I just stood there, feeling in some kind of time warp. She said she felt the same thing."

"And?"

"And we sat and talked about James, I said how grateful I was to her, and she said how delighted she was to have him as a student, and at the end of twenty minutes we were madly in love with each other."

"Madly and chastely?" I asked wryly.

"For a few weeks. . . . The usual: can I? should I? dare I?"

"But I gather you could and did?"

"Right." Suddenly he lowered his voice to a whisper. "Lois knows nothing. Don't . . ."

I closed my eyes. I didn't know whether to feel a perverse pleasure in the news or what. Instead I just felt a horrible debilitating sadness. Was it my father's illness, the rain, the memories of Marilyn, the feeling something was horribly wrong with the way I was living?

"Did you ever read *The Good Soldier* by Ford Madox Ford?" Stef asked.

"No."

"There's a wonderful quote, 'But the real fierceness of desire, the real heat of a passion long continuing and withering up the soul of a man, is the craving for identity with the woman that he loves. He desires to see with the same eyes, to touch with the same sense of touch, to hear with the same ears, to lose his identity, to be enveloped, to be supported. For, whatever may be said of the relations of the sexes, there is no man who loves a woman that does not desire to come to her for the renewal of his courage, for the cutting asunder of his difficulties. And that will be the mainspring of his desire for her. We are all so afraid, we are all so alone, we all so need from the outside, the assurance of our own worthiness to exist.'"

My brother has a fantastic memory. He can also recite "To be or not to be," and you'd think he was reading from the back of a cornflakes box. But perhaps because his flat, monotonous voice repeated the words so without emphases, they struck me all the more. When he came to that line, "We are all so afraid, we are all so alone," I felt like a thin blade had been drawn clean through me. I couldn't speak.

"Sabrina said that passage surprised her. She thought only women wanted to be enveloped and supported." He glanced over at me. "Are you okay?"

My heart was beating too fast. "I don't know," I said. "I feel funny. . . . Could you open a window?"

He leaped to his feet, opened the window, and then came over to where I sat. "Was it the quote? What is it, Benjy?"

Usually, when I get attacks like this, I'm afraid I'm about to have a heart attack. This time I felt maybe I was having a nervous breakdown. The room seemed to be spinning around and around, as though we were in a giant cave with those words bouncing and echoing off all the walls: *a passion long continuing and withering up the soul of a man . . . to see with the same eyes, to touch with the same sense of touch . . . we all so need from the outside, the assurance of our own worthiness to exist . . .*

Stef was kneeling beside me, a combination of concerned brother and psychiatrist in residence. "Tell me what's going on," he said urgently. "Is it an anxiety attack? Do you want some Valium?"

"I don't think I'm worthy to exist," I finally said.

"No one is," Stef said.

"No, that's not true," I said. "It's me. I've made such a mess of things, Stef. You don't know."

"Tell me."

But I didn't want to tell him. I didn't want to reduce Marilyn and me to some little episode like Stef and Sabrina Abrahms, some trivial little "confession." Even now, when he was being and acting so nice, I felt a surge of hatred for Stef for never stepping out of that doctor, older brother, unctuous role.

"It must be Dad's operation," he mused. "You're afraid. . . . I feel that too. It shows we're mortal."

"I *know* we're mortal!"

"No, but it's the reality of it. . . . And the fact that if he goes, we're the fathers in that final oedipal sense. We take on his identity."

"I don't care if he dies or not," I said. "It doesn't matter to me."

"That's what I mean," Stef said. "You've always denied it. You've always tried to pretend you don't care about him. Yet you went into his firm, you almost destroyed your career—"

"It has nothing to do with him!" I shouted.

"Well, what does it have to do with?"

"Sabrina Abrahms!"

He stared at me, bewildered, clearly beginning to be afraid I was going over the edge.

At that moment Ginger opened the door. Seeing the two of us, me in the chair, Stef kneeling beside me, she looked startled.

"Hey, what's going on here?"

"Close the door! Close the door!" Stef whispered urgently.

Ginger closed the door. She came over and looked at me. "Hey, Benjy, what's up? Are you okay?"

I mumbled, "No, yes, I don't know. . . . "

"What were you two talking about?"

"Sabrina Abrahms," I said, lifting my head to look up at her.

"Who's she?"

"She was a girl in his class in high school," I said, "who had a crush on him."

"Why are you talking about *her?*"

"Stef's having an affair with her," I said.

"With Sabrina Abrahms? I don't get it."

"She's James's English teacher," I supplied.

"Does Lois know?" Ginger said.

"Are you crazy?" Stef said. "Of course not!"

Ginger put her head to one side. "So, what's with *you,* kid?" she said, looking at me. "Why do *you* care if he's fucking Sabrina Abrahms?"

"I don't."

They both looked at me.

"He's having some kind of anxiety attack," Stef explained.

"It's not that." I took a deep breath. "For ten years I've been having a love affair with a woman named Marilyn Greene. She's married, she has two sons, and I . . . love her."

"Does Becky know?" they asked in chorus.

"No!"

Ginger looked at me. "Ten *years!* Holy moley, you ought to be in *Ripley's Believe It or Not!* God, I've never lasted more than nine months!"

"How did you manage it?" Stef wanted to know. "How can you live that way? How did you keep Becky from knowing?"

I laughed. "I don't know! I don't know!"

Ginger smiled. "God, I can't believe this! Look at the two of you! Well, I can tell you one thing, you have absolutely made my day, to say nothing of my year, my life, even."

"Why?" Stef asked.

"Because for thirty-three years I have gone around saying to myself: here I have these two perfect goody-goody big brothers who have never done anything wrong, got perfect grades at school, were toilet-trained at birth, only fucked darling little all-A students from Vassar or Mount Holyoke—"

"Lois went to Sarah Lawrence," Stef put in.

"Okay, same difference. . . . Anyway, what I'm getting to is it turns out, to my infinite delight, to be a total sham! It's all a front, right? Here you both are doing seedy, furtive things that Mom and Daddy know nothing about. . . . Or do they?"

"Please!" Stef said. "Mom and Dad know?"

"Well, you've made me feel absolutely super. . . . Think if I went in now and told Mom the whole thing! Can you imagine her expression?" She chortled.

"Ginge, I'll kill you if you tell Mom," Stef threatened.

Ginger kissed him and then kissed me. "Relax, relax. I was just joking. I'm not telling anyone. This will be our little secret. The three screwed-up Fetterman siblings."

"I don't think I *am* screwed up," Stef said stiffly. "I really don't.

. . . I fell in love with someone I loved at sixteen. If anything, I think that shows a certain consistency."

"How about you, Benjy?" Ginger said.

"I'm totally screwed up," I said. "No consistency. None of it makes any sense."

But it was strange. Was it finally, after all these years, telling someone, was it the absence of Becky and my father, the two super-ego figures of my unconscious life, was it Ginger's horsing around or Stef's pomposity—whatever it was I felt a buoyant, almost insane feeling of pure elation and happiness. If I were a helium balloon, I would have sailed up and boinged against the ceiling.

"I think," Ginger said, "that if we stay in here any longer, our absence will become, as they say, conspicuous."

"Lois and I should probably be going back to the hotel," Stef said, looking at his watch.

They looked at me, waiting. "I think I'll stay here a minute," I said. "Tell the others I'll be back soon."

They left me alone. I looked around the room. *We are all so afraid, we are all so alone.* . . . I walked to the window. My parents' apartment is on the fourteenth floor of the Eldorado on Ninetieth and Central Park West. You can see a sweep of Central Park, misty now from the rain which had stopped. I've always loved New York at twilight, the streetlights going on, the traffic spiraling slowly. From a distance or a great height there is no dirt or violence. It's a perfect, self-contained world.

And then suddenly, from nowhere, a curtain seemed to rise and I remembered my whole final argument with Marilyn, every word, every expression. It simply appeared from nowhere, like the view lying in front of me. How strange to think that perhaps everything we've ever felt or thought or done, that seems to have vanished, is simply hiding somewhere in the deep recesses of the brain.

I went over to the phone and dialed her number. She answered the phone. "Marilyn?" I said softly, trying to keep my voice from shaking. "It's me."

There was a pause. Silence. Had she heard me? Had she hung up?

"I, I've been thinking about you a lot, wondering how you were. . . . . Are you there? Are you alone? Can you talk?"

Again there was a long silence, then a choked whisper, "I'm alone."

"Listen, I don't know. I know I said a lot of things that . . . I felt, I truly did feel we would both be happier apart. But it just didn't work! I love you. I need to see you."

There was another silence. I could hear her breathing heavily, as though trying to catch her breath. "I can't . . . talk," she gasped.

"Are you alone?"

"Yes." Like a hiss.

"Tell me, please, what is it?"

"I can't," Marilyn wailed.

Then I knew she was crying, not so much because I heard her sobs but because of the texture of her voice. "Darling, please don't."

"Oh Benjy, I just . . . "

"Don't cry. We had a quarrel. Lovers always do. It's over. It'll never happen again."

"I can't bear it," she said, her voice still strained and breathless. "I couldn't go through it again! It was such torture! I tried every day not to think of you, to hate you. . . . "

"It was the same for me," I said. "I tried . . ."

"It was horrible!" she said. "You don't *know* how horrible it was!"

"I do. . . . I missed you terribly every second, every single second."

"It's been six months," Marilyn said. "It seems like longer, almost. Like years."

"Yeah. . . . Did you get a job?"

She laughed. For the first time her voice sounded almost normal. "Yeah, I got a job. At Bonwit's. Are you proud of me?"

"Very proud. I love you. I wish you were here. I wish we could—"

"Where are you?"

"At my parents'. My father's having open heart surgery tomorrow. Becky's home with a virus. It's—" Suddenly the door opened. It was Robin.

"Daddy, when are we going to—" she began.

"Get out of here!" I yelled. "Out! Right away!"

She fled, terrified. I felt a momentary regret for the severity of my voice. "That was Robin," I explained softly.

"The reason I'm alone," Marilyn said, "is Linus is in the hospital. He had to have his appendix out. They're all over there, visiting him. I was just—resting."

"Do you still love me?" I asked, nervously.

"Horribly. . . . Even when I hated you, even when I lay there plotting how to murder you in a million grisly ways, I loved you."

I lifted the paperweight on my father's desk, and turned it slowly back and forth, deliriously happy. "I'm so sorry for those things I said. I guess I felt if I didn't make it final enough, I would break down."

"I said some pretty awful things too," Marilyn said. "I mean, like, I know you didn't marry Becky for her money."

"Well . . . "

"I wanted to hurt you. . . . I wanted to strike you to the heart."

I laughed, imagining her face, her expression.

"Why do we do that to each other?" she asked urgently. "Do you understand it?"

"The closeness, it explodes. . . . "

"*Did* I hurt you?"

"Yes, very much."

"Good," Marilyn said. "I wanted to. Oh, I wanted to so much! . . . But did you really suffer? I can't believe men really suffer."

"Darling, I'm lying here in a pool of blood. Watch out or it'll start seeping through the phone. Five minutes ago Ginger and Stef were ready to have me committed. I started going berserk."

"You did sound a little funny."

"Right now I feel better than I ever have in my life. . . . Listen, let's meet now, tonight! Do you want to?"

"Benjy, it's Thanksgiving. They're coming home in a second. How can I?"

"I want you so much. . . . 'There isn't a particle of you that I don't know, remember and want.'"

"What a sweet thing to say!"

"It's a quote," I admitted. "*Private Lives*, Noel Coward."

"Oh Benjy, you're so smart! You're always quoting things!"

"You're just as smart as I am."

She hesitated. "Do you really think so?"

"Yes."

"Listen, tonight's impossible. I can't. There's no way."

"Tomorrow?"

"Tomorrow, sure. I'll have to change a million things around, but . . . Oh God, I've violated all my . . . I've planned this phone call in my head so many times. How vicious I'd be, how cold, how contemptuous, how I'd make you crawl. . . . What's wrong with me?"

"We need each other," I said. "It's one of those things. And maybe everyone's life is like this. I really wonder. Only we don't know. We just see the surface."

"That's what Ila says. Not that everyone's is screwed up in the same way, but no one's life is what it seems."

"My brother's screwing a woman he was in love with at sixteen, his son's English teacher."

"My sister's in love with a man who's eleven years younger than she is."

"Really?"

"Yeah. . . . He makes ancient instruments, lutes and harpsichords. They adore each other! She looks around ten years younger."

"Terrific. . . . Ginger's marrying a black law professor and my mother's hysterical. She just announced it over Thanksgiving dinner."

Marilyn laughed. "It sounds like it was quite a day for you, sweetie."

"It *was* quite a day." A wonderful day, a perfect day.

"I've got to hang up. They'll be back any second. I'm kissing you in my mind everywhere. Do you feel it?"

"Umm. . . ."

"'There isn't a particle of you that I don't know, remember and want.' I love that! That's a wonderful quote."

"It's true," I said.

"It's true for me too," Marilyn said softly. "Every particle."

"See you tomorrow. Sleep tight. I love you."

I placed the phone back in the receiver. I felt the same buoyant excitement, maybe more so, but glazed over with some kind of exhaustion. The happy ending is when the man and woman get married and live happily, faithfully ever after. Isn't it? I walked into the next room.

"Stef and Lois had to leave," my mother said. "Are you all right, dear? Ginger said you suddenly got a terrible headache."

"It's okay now," I said.

"I feel so much better too," my mother said. "I think I was a little hysterical before. After all, if Ginger has found the right man and he'll make her settle down, what difference does it make what color he is? . . . And Gilbert will be fine. I was standing there and it just came to me that he would be fine and that I didn't have to worry."

I hugged her. "Good." Then I noticed that Robin was hunched over in the corner, looking awful. I remembered yelling at her. I knelt down beside her. "I'm sorry, sweetie," I said softly. "I'm sorry I yelled at you."

Suddenly she began to sob. "You sounded so mad! I got so scared!"

"Darling." She is so small, weighs scarcely seventy-five pounds. I drew her close, stroking her fine hair. "I didn't mean it. I love you. Will you forgive me?"

Robin sniffed. She stopped sobbing. "Okay," she said. "I forgive you. . . . But don't *ever* do that again!"

"I won't," I promised. "Never."

PART THREE

◆

1981

Periods of Remission

*T*urning fifty-five really got to me. I don't know why. I sailed past fifty with scarcely a thought. Usually it's the entrance into a new decade that grabs you. Of course, it's also what's happening in your life at the time. But fifty-five—Jesus! Halfway to sixty! I've barely gotten used to thinking of myself as middle-aged and now old age isn't that far away. The other day Marilyn asked me if I thought she should keep on dyeing her hair. Her sister, Blanche, who's now living in bliss with this guy who makes ancient instruments, has let her hair go gray and looks ten years younger. First, if Blanche does look younger, it's because she's happy, probably for the first time in her life. And Blanche never looked that great at any time. I said, "Hon, listen, I married you as a blond. Why change course? Unless there's some special reason."

"No," she said. "I just wonder sometimes how I'd look the 'real way.'"

Marilyn's theory is that women dye their hair, not for themselves, but to make their husbands feel young. There may be something in that. I look at Marilyn and, apart from her being ten years younger than me, the fact that she's still in good shape and youthful looking does help in maintaining some inner illusion that time is not passing as horribly rapidly as I know deep down it is.

Fifty-five. It's not just that I'm fifty-five. It's that if I'm fifty-five, my mother is almost eighty, my sister is almost sixty, to say nothing of the kids both being old enough to vote. I'm trying to think why turning fifty didn't strike me that much. No, it was more fifty-two, fifty-three that did it. First I got tic douloureux, that same nasty business that felled my father. But, unlike him, I'm not letting it wreck me. I take the drugs. I go for acupuncture sometimes. There are periods of remission when I'm fine. But when the pain is there, it's a killer. Don't ever get it, if you can avoid it. It's also a disease where you don't have a lot of company. It's pretty rare, incurable, chronic. Well, everyone has something, right? I say to myself if I've got this, God'll figure: leave the guy alone and save cancer and heart disease for the other suckers.

Recently I was sitting in the acupuncturist's office—it's way downtown, in the Village—when I saw a young woman eyeing me across the room. That happens, but no longer with great frequency, so I looked back, just curious, absolutely no intention of carrying it anywhere. For one thing, when you're about to go in for acupuncture, you're not in a very sexy mood. Basically I think these guys are onto something. But at other times I wonder if they're not just a bunch of little sadists who like sticking needles in people.

She was thin, nice legs, a black dress, sunglasses, short hair. Suddenly she smiled at me. "Remember me?"

I hesitated. "Not exactly."

"I used to go out with Aaron." She took her sunglasses off. "Amy?"

"Aimee . . . Your wife really got mad at me once. She—"

"Oh yeah, right." It came back to me. She looked a little older, more sophisticated, but not very different.

"Did you ever go around the world?"

I laughed. "Nope. . . . I still think about it from time to time."

"I'll go with you. . . . I told you I would."

"Don't you have a job?"

"I'm kind of between jobs. . . . Actually, I thought of contacting you. But now I think I'm onto something."

She told me she was an assistant in an art gallery in SoHo, that she'd had a boyfriend who used to show his work there. "I live right around here," she said. "Paul's in Japan now and he's letting me use his loft. We're not really together anymore, but we're still friends."

She was having acupuncture for her right leg. "I had this weird accident. A car hit me and I went flying up in the air and landed on the hood. I had to have physiotherapy for months. Now I'm pretty much back to normal, but I still get pains. . . . How about you?"

The advantage and disadvantage to being over fifty is the same: life stops surprising you. You're ready for the punches, you don't squeal "What? No!" so often, but you lose your capacity for surprise and delight just a little. Maybe you don't lose it altogether, but it dims. You know the next step down the road, and knowing it before you get there changes the way you go into it, changes even your desire to take the next step. I sat there, listening to Aimee, watching her animated bright face, sexy, avaricious eyes, and wondered if it would be worth it. Not because of Aaron; he wouldn't even remember her name now. When you get down to it, there are two problems with casual sex: disease and emotional involvement. The latter I think I can handle but I don't relish bringing home some exotic variety of herpes.

Aimee's appointment was before mine, but when I got out, she was still there. "You might like Paul's work," she said. "Do you ever buy modern art? He's terrifically talented. I don't mean that because he used to be my lover. He was a lousy lover, but I think he's a wonderful artist."

All during the acupuncture I'd been batting it back and forth in my mind. I knew it wasn't just me she wanted, I was some kind of symbol for her. But so? Evidently my hesitation communicated itself. "If you don't have time now, let me give you my number."

"It's not a matter of time."

She grinned. "What's it a matter of? Your wife?"

I shook my head.

"I'm clean. . . . Is that what you're worried about? I know you think I'm some kind of promiscuous slut, or that's what your wife thinks, but it's not true. I bet I haven't had any more lovers than you have."

How does she know how many I've had? I smiled. "How many is that?"

"I just have the feeling you fooled around a bit. . . . You said you didn't marry till you were thirty. But listen, no hard feelings if I'm just not your type. I am a little weird, no doubt of it."

"In what way?"

Her eyes twinkled. "Well, if you're too chicken to even come up and see Paul's paintings, you'll never know."

A challenge. There is no doubt that even at my age that sudden deeply buried desire for a final adventure, a final piece of total idiocy flickers up to the surface with alarming speed. Still, I hesitated. Aimee came over and put her hand on my arm. "We could have had a good time, going around the world. I wasn't joking about that."

"I know you weren't."

Okay, I did it. I told myself I knew what I was getting into, that I wasn't destroying the romantic illusions of an innocent young thing. Most girls that age could crumple and the guilt would be horrendous. But Aimee seemed tough. It was good, that first afternoon and even several after that. She had a lithe, snakelike little body, always that taunting gleam in her eye, and that feeling of being touched by the hands of someone new, who doesn't know your body, is deadly. It is exciting, no matter how many warning signals you send out to dim it, to keep it in control.

"I always used to think of you when I fucked Aaron," she confessed. "He was such a baby, sweet, but a baby."

"Why me?"

"My shrink says it's all oedipal. See, I hated my mother, and she was just like your wife. She hates me just because I exist, has from the second I was born. She didn't want me. She'd been married eight years and she was afraid I'd wreck her figure or something. Only she was scared of abortion. She actually arranged to give me up for adoption, but then at the last minute, my father made her reconsider, at least take a look at me, and I guess I was so adorable, she broke down. . . . But it was for him. He was desperate for a kid. He knew this was his last chance. And then when I was ten, he died."

"I don't think Marilyn hated you," I said. When she lay flat on her back, her hip bones jutted up, the tuft of dark pubic hair looked unusually luxuriant, crinkly.

"Yeah, she did. . . . I pick up on that, because of my mother. Oh sure, I can be a little paranoid, but some women just hate me. Maybe they see me as a sexual rival, or they're scared of me. I think your wife was a little scared of me."

"Afraid you'd steal me away?"

"Something. Maybe she had a lover or something. All I know is she was so happy that day she found me and Olaf together. She was so happy to have an excuse to pitch me out! You should have seen her face! I thought she'd kill me." She reflected on it with some satisfaction.

"What makes you think she had a lover?"

"Something. . . . Some phone call I overheard. I walked in the room and she knew I'd overheard or was scared I had. You can just tell, the way a woman's voice sounds. . . . Hey listen, you think she's straight? Maybe she is. I'm just giving you my impressions." She kissed me lightly, lingeringly, on my throat. "Maybe she knew you wanted me. Maybe that was it. You did, didn't you?"

I laughed. "Well. . . ."

"I'm a great mind reader. But it was mean to Aaron. I shouldn't have told him I thought you were sexy. It really upset him. I guess he wanted to think of you as way past all that, just some old farty guy who just thought of making money."

Probably that's how Aaron still thinks of me.

"What's he up to now? Does he have a girl?"

I told her about Aaron's girlfriend. He graduated from college six months ago and got a job doing copywriting for an advertising agency. When he'd been there about a month, he met Sonya. She's thirty-four, twelve years older than he is, with a ten-year-old son from her second marriage. She's dark, verging on plump, Mongolian high cheekbones and sensuous lips. I gather her husband pays her enough dough so she doesn't have to work. She dabbles, takes ballet classes, is learning bookbinding. She's like someone out of an earlier generation—no desire for "independence" or a career, adores her kid, adores Aaron. The funny thing is, Aaron and the little boy, Sean, are best friends. The former husband lives in Spain and doesn't see the kid all that often. Aaron must be some funny cross between a stepfather and an older brother. When we go over there for dinner—they live together at her spacious six-room West Side apartment—the two of them play Monopoly together while Sonya watches them indulgently.

"Weird," Aimee commented. "God, I could never like anyone

twelve years younger than me. Of course, I'm just twenty-six. He'd only be fourteen. . . . Still, I feel like I want to learn, not to teach."

I let my hand run down her body. "What do you want to learn?"

"Oh, I don't mean specific things, but I just like the fact that, with someone like you, say, you're not in it just for the symbolic thing: wondering if you can get a girl my age. I hate that thing of being a symbol!"

I wondered later that day, after I'd left her, if that was true. Maybe everyone is always partly a symbol, of something remembered and good, or a way of rewriting a past experience that soured. I know in some way Aimee is connected to that period in my life five years ago—Fetterman's wife coming to see me, the offer to sell the business which I turned down, taking Linus to a call girl. Maybe that was partly it—the boys both finally becoming sexual adults, that remaining difference between us vanishing.

But it ended badly with Aimee. It's like looking at a road map. You see the dangers, the rocky ridges, whatever, but you think: There's a way around them. I let her talk me into taking her to L.A. when I had to go there one week. We stayed at the Chateau Marmont.

I guess I half knew she was on drugs some of the time, but it never seemed extreme. I'm not a puritan. Drugs just don't happen to do it for me, I'd take alcohol any day, but ever since the kids went through being teenagers, I've gotten slightly paranoid on the subject. Very, very few people can take drugs without overdoing it. I don't know why that's so, but it's been true in every case I've seen. We got out there and I'd be gone all day, working. I'd come back and either Aimee'd still be in bed, sleeping, at five in the afternoon, or not there, returning with some vague excuse, looking spaced out, or she'd be sitting by the pool playing cards with someone. I guess there's a part of me that likes to play the savior with women. It wasn't just fucking her. I felt she was a bright, good kid who'd had a rough childhood, and who half wanted to pull herself together. Maybe she saw that in me and played into it, pretended to want to settle down herself. But out there she let the other side come out. Either she'd want to fuck every two hours or she'd just pass out and lie there, looking half dead. I felt disgusted and one night I told her to pull herself together or clear out. She went berserk.

"Listen, what are you, my mother? I'm twenty-six years old! I don't do anything I can't handle. I'm on a vacation! I'm out here to have fun."

"Is it fun to sleep all day?"

"Yeah, sometimes. . . . Depends on who's around."

"What does that mean?"

"It means you're gone all day and I do what I feel like to keep myself amused, okay? I'm just not into masturbating, is that so strange? I ran into someone I used to know. . . ."

"I don't want to get some disease," I grabbed her, furious.

"What's wrong with you? You're more paranoid than my mother! I ought to fix you up with her, you'd make a great pair. Look, I like sex. I don't feel like just doing it once a night and going to sleep! I'm sorry, but we all have needs. . . ."

"Get out of here, okay?"

Then she tried turning it around, how wonderful I was, how she wanted to live up to my "high ideals" about her, but couldn't, how it was the same with her father. He wanted her to make something of herself and she was always disappointing him. She started sobbing, begging me to let her stay. Luckily, by then we had only two more days. For that time she was as good as gold, but not there. Mentally she'd checked out. She sat belted into her seat on the airplane ride home staring straight ahead with blank glassy eyes. There was something pathetic and infuriating about her at the same time. She turned to me in the middle of dinner and said, "There have been lovely things about this trip. I guess I'm not worthy of you. Men always end up hating me."

I kissed her forehead gently. "I don't hate you."

But by then I'd seen enough to not to want to hang in for Act Two and Three. It's sad how even adventures like this, where you think your wants are minimal and simple, never turn out simply. No regrets, though. She was clean, probably due to some divine protection.

Maybe even at seventy you're still waiting for that one final delirious adventure. You remember the feeling of being tossed high in the air, the exhilaration of it. You forget the thunk as you hit the ground.

The one nice thing that's happened in the last couple of years is my sister's remarriage. After thirty-five years of marriage, Ward finally came to her and said he wanted a divorce. There was no other woman, he just wanted out. Kevin McDonnell's wife had died of cancer a year earlier, and he asked Harriet to marry him, but she'd felt she couldn't "do that" to Ward. When he told her he wanted a divorce, she said she started sobbing with joy, sobbing so hard he got alarmed. He told her she'd been a wonderful wife, that it wasn't her fault, that they'd always be friends, and meanwhile Harriet sat there feeling like a total hypocrite because till then she'd just been hoping that he might die some quick, painless death.

So now she and Saints Preserve Us are married. They're the happiest couple I know. Figure it out. Here's this guy, Kevin, a hard-drinking red-faced guy, like a taller, beefier Spencer Tracy. When he's around, it's like she married five guys. Ward was always so totally silent. Kevin booms everything out, like he was talking through a megaphone. He just seems to take up a lot of room. He used to play football for Oklahoma State and he watches the games on TV with an avidity that's almost comical. "Will you look at that pass," he'll say to me, grabbing my arm. "I can't believe that. He is *really* something."

I know and care nothing about football. Maybe once or twice a year, if I have nothing better to do, I watch a game. Okay, some of them are good, but who cares, really? Kevin McDonnell, beer can in hand, watches like his life literally depended on the outcome. Solid, warm, single-minded. He looks at Harriet, who is not, by any standard you could *ever* apply, anything near a knockout, like she was a cross between the Virgin Mary and Bo Derek. He calls her "Princess"! Harriet confessed that the night they were married, he actually carried her up a flight of stairs. "I've been waiting to do this for fifteen years," he said, "and, by God, nothing's going to stop me."

"I was really worried, Mo," Harriet confessed. "He has a bad back, and it's twenty steps, plus the landing." She didn't add that she must weigh in at one thirty-five, at least.

Well, he made it up the steps. Not only that, but Harriet says every Sunday morning, after making her pancakes (or is it before?) he insists on making love to her three times, minimum. He says that all those years of going to church made him need a special ritual on Sunday morning. "He says making love to me he feels closer to God," Harriet confessed, blushing.

Whenever she talks about him, she blushes. At night, when they watch TV, he tells her to put a blanket over her legs so he can't see them. Otherwise, he says, he'll go wild with desire and have to put it to her right in the middle of his favorite TV show. Harriet does have nice legs, but, let's face it, she's fifty-nine years old. Still, everything is in the eye of the beholder, right?

"I'd feel so guilty," Harriet said, "being this happy, if it weren't for all those years that we suffered so, when Maureen was alive. I think, maybe, we deserve this. I think God appreciates how much we suffered."

"Sure he does," I said. Somehow, while Kevin is now a Jew, Harriet is sounding more like a Catholic to me every day. Or maybe they're meeting in some vague middle ground of their own creation. One night, when he'd had a few too many, Kevin gave me his theory of how the Jews and the Catholics are related. It seems—don't ask me to repeat the evidence for this because it didn't even make sense at the time—that we all originated in some little tribe somewhere and fanned out. "It's in the genes," he insisted. "We're both dark, brooding, intense people." It turns out that Kevin's father was Jewish and his mother was Catholic. They married at the age of sixteen and thirteen respectively, had a dozen kids who were raised as Catholics. His father even took his mother's name, less out of liberated feeling than because he felt it was a protection against anti-Semitism in the business he was in in Boston. "My mother took one of us to Mass every Sunday, but my father never knew," Kevin said.

"Where did he think you were going?" I asked.

"I don't know. . . . But he never knew. It would have killed him. Just before he died, when he was having terrible pain from cancer, he told me he was afraid God was punishing him for marrying a Catholic girl." The intricacy with which people hide the truth from themselves if it's something they don't want to know!

When I got back from L.A., Marilyn said Sonya had called and wanted us to come over for dinner to celebrate Aaron's twenty-third birthday with them. "Do you want to?"

"Sure," I said.

Marilyn has trouble with Aaron's living with an "older woman." I don't know if it's that she feels a rivalry or what. In the car on the way over, she said, "It's not the age difference. I just don't understand the way she lives."

"She married a rich guy. She's living off him. What else is new?"

"But how can she do that, in America, in nineteen-eighty-one? How can she have any pride?"

"Probably it's a drop in the bucket for him. She got a good lawyer. She's raising their kid."

"It's strange your being so indulgent about it," she went on. "Usually you say you don't believe in alimony. *I* don't."

"You mean, if we ever split, you'd just walk away with a wave and a smile?"

"Definitely."

Sure. If you ask me, Marilyn would get the best lawyer she could lay her hands on and I'd be lucky to get out alive. "Anyway, the point is, she's good for Aaron. Who cares how she lives or why."

"Do you think she's really good for him?"

"Yeah, it's just what he needs. . . . *I* did that at his age."

"Did what?"

"I had a thing with an older woman. You need it when you're a kid, wet behind the ears. In Europe it's commonplace."

"What if they get married?"

"They won't get married."

"How do you know? I think he adores her. . . . Who *was* that woman, anyway?"

"Who?"

"The one. . . . When you were his age?"

"Summer stock. The director's wife. He was making it with someone in the cast. She was lonely, at loose ends. A sweet, screwed-up lady. . . ." I thought of Aimee, sitting on the toilet seat, her face cupped in her hands, staring at me balefully.

"Sounds like you had quite a few of those," Marilyn said smiling. "What was it? Didn't you like anyone normal till you met me?"

I laughed. "The knight in white armor thing. They wanted to be rescued, I wanted to rescue them. . . ."

"So why didn't it work? It sounds perfect."

"Nothing's perfect." I hesitated. "Everything's half what it seems. They half wanted to be rescued and half didn't. And you don't realize till you're knee-deep into it, that it's a full-time job. You don't just do it once. You take it on for life."

Marilyn was silent. "I don't think all women want to be rescued."

"Maybe not."

"Do you think it's that I'm jealous?" she asked a moment later with sudden urgency. "She's almost my age! Well, eleven years younger. Maybe it shows I didn't mother him enough."

"Or maybe you did such a good job, he wants to keep it going as long as possible."

She kissed me. "Thanks, sweetie."

I don't know if it's the exotic cooking she does or some perfume she wears, but Sonya always smells like an Indian curry: apples, cloves. She has beautiful eyelids, very heavy and white and always just slightly closed, like she was dreaming of something wonderful and far away. I envision her as a woman who never thinks of dieting, her fleshiness is part of her charm. Even her fingers are rounded and white, like a baby's. She kissed both of us and then stepped back to look at me. "No tan?" she said.

"I just work when I go to L.A.," I admitted.

"No play?"

I just smiled.

"My husband always had to go out there on business," she said. "I hated it. No sense of culture. And now, you know, it's ironical, he lives in Europe, which I would have loved."

Aaron and Sean were sitting on the floor, watching TV. It's really strange—the little boy actually looks like him, the same dark, slightly tilted eyes, the same cut of hair. He seems to accept the situation without any self-consciousness. Maybe he's gotten used to a stream of lovers moving through. If they break up, he's the one who will suffer, I imagine, who will miss Aaron the most. "Hi, Sean," Marilyn said.

I watched her, thinking: this is how it'll be when we're grandparents. A final step in accepting that youth is over.

"Hi, Mom, hi, Dad," Aaron called.

"Tell them the good news," Sonya called from the kitchen.

"Oh, it's not. . . . At work they just decided to use a campaign slogan I made up. It's dumb."

Aaron has decided he wants to be a writer, that having a job which doesn't use his brain is ideal because it "frees" him mentally to think great thoughts and also frees him to have unqualified contempt for the people he works with.

"Will it be on TV?" Sean asked.

"Maybe," Aaron said.

"He wrote a story," Sean said, excited, "just for me."

Aaron looked embarrassed. "It's just the stuff they publish for kids his age is so inane. Anyone could do better."

Dinner was some kind of Hungarian goulash, but not the kind that gives you indigestion at first bite. Noodles, beans, a good wine. I looked at Sonya, helping everyone to seconds, hovering over Aaron and her son in that indulgent way. It was a little like seeing my mother brought back to life in another size and shape.

"It's our anniversary too," Sonya said, ruffling Aaron's hair. "We've been together nine months."

"That doesn't count," Sean said, his mouth full. "You have to wait for a year to count it."

"Everything counts," I said.

"How long have *you* been married?" she asked. "Aaron wasn't sure."

"Almost twenty-five years," Marilyn said.

She looked pretty, slightly flushed from the wine. And yet, seeing her next to Sonya, I noticed more than I usually do, how her skin had fine lines around the eyes, some of the sparkle dimmed. You don't see it or notice it when you live with a person, day in, day out. A version of one's own mortality, seeing one's wife age.

"I was a baby when I got married," Marilyn said. "Just twenty! No one does that anymore."

Sonya smiled. She has a faint downiness on her upper lip, not unattractive. "I was a baby too. . . . Just eighteen. Paul was my first boyfriend. My parents were very strict. I never even had dates! He was ten years older than me. He seemed so wise, so cosmopolitan. Now I think he was more scared than me."

"Just like us," Marilyn said. "Mo's ten years older than me."

Sonya looked at me. "How old are you?"

I hesitated. "Fifty-five."

"Incredible. You look so much younger."

I saw Marilyn staring at her with slightly narrowed eyes.

"I don't feel fifty-five," I admitted.

"What's your secret?" Sonya asked, her eyes softly luminous.

"Yeah, Dad," Aaron said sarcastically. "What's your secret?"

"He's young at heart," Marilyn said dryly.

Evidently their tones failed to get through to Sonya or she chose to not mention it. "It's all how you feel inside," she said. "Inside I'm still eighteen. That's why Aaron and I are so good together."

"I don't agree," Marilyn said.

Everyone looked at her.

She half smiled. "I guess I do feel forty-five . . . whatever that is."

I thought of Aimee again, lying asleep when I returned one day, naked on her stomach, her hands stretched out over the pillow, like a limp rag doll. "Do you want to fuck?" Without even opening her eyes. What if it hadn't been me? Or wouldn't she have cared especially?

"I think you should both be proud," Sonya said, bringing forth the "birthday cake," a dobos torte. "Twenty-five years is a long time."

"Seems like a minute," I said, smiling at Marilyn, who still had that sad expression, her mouth set.

But Marilyn was looking at Sonya. "It seems like a long time to *me.*"

"Hey, Mom," Aaron said. "Stop being so morose."

"I'm *not* morose," Marilyn snapped. "I'm realistic."

"I still think you should be proud," Sonya pursued. "You have each other, wonderful children. You've worked for it, you've earned it."

There was a pause.

"This is marvelous cake," Marilyn said, taking a bite.

It was. I accepted a second helping.

"You see, with me, I never know how long things will last," Sonya said. "No matter how much I love someone, right from the beginning I think: This won't last. If I have a poet, I want a businessman. If I have an architect, I want a farmer. I have so many sides to my nature."

"Not me," Aaron said, grinning. "I'm a simple guy."

"Men are simple," Sonya said, ladling whipped cream into her coffee. "They have simple needs. I admire that so much!" She looked at Marilyn. "Don't you think?"

Marilyn looked flustered. "I don't know what I think," she stammered. "I'm not sure."

"What was sad with my parents," Sonya went on, "was they were married almost as long as you two, till I was married myself and then—boom! And it was such a shock to me. They'd always seemed so happy. It turned out it wasn't true. It was all a sham, it was for my sake."

"Maybe it wasn't a sham," Marilyn said. "Maybe they half believed in it, while it lasted. Once something ends, people are so bitter, and that's not the real truth either."

I wondered if she was thinking of the time of her life when she went through that business with Fetterman. It seems eons ago. In fact, I saw him a couple of weeks ago at the train station and he looked like hell. Talk about people not aging well! He looks my age, easily. Whenever I see him, I feel—contempt's too strong maybe, maybe some anger. I can't really describe what it is, but it's like a visceral reaction. He's so cringing, just his expression. His posture is worse than Linus's. Actually, I was sitting in the train, at Grand Central, when he came walking down the aisle, looking for a seat. His eyes caught mine, flew away, looked back. I knew he didn't want to sit next to me, but there was a seat empty on the aisle and as he passed by, I half waved.

He eased into the seat. He looked bushed, gray under the eyes, skin pale, suit jacket crumpled. "One of those days," he said.

"I know what you mean. . . . How's the furniture business?"

"Fine, really. . . . It's just our company has made some stupid moves. It's kind of hideous right now. People're being fired right and left. . . ."

I wondered how secure his own job was. Maybe I just can't be objective, but I can't imagine him being that competent at anything. "Well, the economy in general isn't in such wonderful shape."

"True." He took his jacket off. "My wife's gone back to work. Usually we drive in together, but today she was home sick."

Becky. Big worried eyes. What did he do with the photo? Is it still there? Does he take it out and gaze at it mournfully for old times' sake? "What does she do?"

"What?"

"Your wife. . . . You said she was working."

"Oh right. She, uh . . . it's a magazine she worked for years ago. They've changed hands quite a bit. Of course she had to start at the bottom, but I'm sure she'll be given more responsibility as time goes on." He took out a handkerchief and wiped his brow. "Is it very hot in here? I feel slightly strange."

"It is a little hot." I looked at him, getting a perverse kind of pleasure in the way he looked, his nervousness. "My wife has always worked. She dropped out of college to marry me, but then she went back and now she's doing fine, has her own business."

"Oh." He hesitated. "What sort of business?"

"She and a friend started a store for women who wear large sizes. Fat women, basically. I guess there must be a lot of them. Their sales tripled last year."

"That's very impressive." He cleared his throat. "You have two sons, I believe?"

"Yes. Linus is at Princeton. Aaron's working at an advertising agency in the city."

"I have four girls." He smiled wryly. "It's a big responsibility."

"I can imagine."

"I think boys might've been easier. With girls you worry about everything—what professions they'll enter, who they'll marry. The whole sexual thing is so much more . . . confusing."

"In what way?"

"Well, things are so different than when we were that age, so much more open—which basically I think is good. Perhaps they won't suffer all the confusions we did, but still they're also deprived of certain rules which maybe were . . . helpful. Or at least were there!" He was starting to talk more rapidly. "What I mean is, with daughters, you want them to end up with men who'll take care of them, who'll have some of that old-fashioned desire to protect them, respect them, not just guys who're out for a quick roll in the hay."

"I thought girls were pretty tough these days," I said. "Tougher than the guys, even."

He shook his head. "No, absolutely not. And they'll never be. I think it's just not physiologically possible. My second daughter has had quite a few . . . experiences, but still she gets very emotionally involved, she gets hurt. I find it very painful to watch." He tried to smile. "But she just keeps hurling herself into the ring."

I smiled back. "I guess she must be enjoying *some* of it, then."

"I hope so. . . . Maybe it's oedipal. Maybe I don't *want* to think she's enjoying it. Well! . . . But I had the feeling boys would be easier. Aren't they?"

"I guess. I don't worry about it very much." He has a kind of nervous energy which began getting to me, like he couldn't stop talking, even if he wanted to.

"I love having daughters," he said. "I don't mean to give the impression that . . . And probably I would have been lousy with sons, that whole competitive thing which I had with my father. I would hate to be living with someone who felt about me the way I felt about him. But I do think somehow girls, women are more. . . . They do seem to have a kind of, well, purity or sweetness or whatever."

I laughed. "Whatever! Maybe some do. I've run into a few that weren't all *that* sweet."

"But even the ones that aren't, in some way. . . . Well, it's an illusion probably. But then one needs illusions, don't you think? *I* do."

"No, I don't think I do," I said. "Not especially. I prefer seeing things as they are."

He seemed taken aback by that. "Well, that sounds healthy," he said. "A healthy way to approach life."

"What's the point of believing in things that aren't true?" I said. "I don't get that."

"No, you're right, you're right," he said rapidly. "I admire that attitude. I've always. . . . No, you're quite right."

"You've always what?"

"I'm not sure what I meant to say." He was silent. Then, after a few moments he said, "Your business is doing well, you said?"

"Extremely. . . . Someone offered me several million for it a few years back. But I turned it down." It felt good, being able to say that.

"It must be nice to turn down a sum like that."

"Yeah, it was nice. . . . It was my parents' business. I built it up from nothing. But if I sold it, I figure I wouldn't know what to do with myself. I'm not the type with hobbies, all that. I work, I have my family, that's it."

I wasn't sure he'd heard me. He was just sitting there, staring straight ahead. "I could be fired this month," he said suddenly. "I'm near the top, but they're restructuring everything."

Despite myself, a glimmer of pleasure flickered through me. "Sorry to hear that."

"I hope it's paranoia. . . . It's a place where *everyone* is paranoid, even the people doing the firing. Everyone hates and mistrusts everyone else. So it's hard to judge anything after a while."

I've always found it strange, when men talk that openly about failure, even the chance of failure. I've never understood it. I've never felt I was a failure, but if I did, I wouldn't talk about it to anyone, certainly not to some guy I met on a train whom I hardly knew except for the fact that I'd fucked his wife a couple of times a decade or so ago. Was that what Marilyn liked about him? It made him seem more "vulnerable" and all that crap? I know for a fact women do find that appealing, in some men, at some times. But one thing I do know—she would have ended up killing this guy, if they had ever lived together. I mean, he doesn't look in wonderful shape anyway. Was he a great lover? Sorry, I can't believe it. Look at him! Maybe he just gazed at her mournfully and she had orgasms long distance.

"It's our wedding anniversary tonight," he said, in a different tone of voice. "I hope Becky's feeling better." He smiled. "We've been married twenty-five years."

"So've we."

"You and—"

"Me and Marilyn, my wife."

"Oh right. . . . So, you must have married around when we did. Nineteen-fifty-six?"

I nodded. A great head for figures.

"By today's standards I think that's pretty good," he said, still in that trying-to-be-cheerful way. "Not that many couples reach that point."

"True."

"Of course, luck plays a large role. What does one know at twenty about anything?"

"I was thirty."

"Even at thirty. But, that's true, thirty *is* different. . . . Anyway, I feel. . . . I'm glad for our children. So many of their friends seem to come from broken homes."

"Yeah?"

"Don't yours? And I think basically just as I had the example of my parents, who're still together, they can look back at us and perhaps it will give them a foundation for whatever choices *they* make. That's what I hope."

God, is he running for office? And when the fuck will we get there? If I'd known he was such a talker, I wouldn't have waved at him.

"My children are one of the few things about which I have no regrets," he said.

I smiled at him. "It's good to have a few things like that."

When we got to the station, there was his wife, looking fairly healthy, in a denim skirt, blouse, and sandals. She came over and kissed him, then turned to me. "Oh, hi, Mr. Greene. . . . Did you come out together?"

I nodded.

"Can we give you a lift?" Becky said. "Or do you have a car?"

Actually I'd been planning to take a cab. I looked around. There were none waiting.

"Or is your wife meeting you?"

"No, no. She works late Tuesdays. . . . Sure, that would be fine." I followed them down to the parking lot.

"Sweetie, I'm feeling so much better," Becky said to her husband.

"My fever's totally down. I guess it *was* one of those twenty-four-hour things." To me she said, "It's our anniversary tonight. We're going to try that new restaurant. Ciro's? Some friends said it was really good."

"We haven't tried it yet."

We reached the car. Becky got into the driver's seat. Fetterman said, "Maybe I'll stretch out in back. Okay? I'm feeling a little beat."

She looked alarmed. "Are you getting sick? Are you okay?"

"I'm fine. . . . Just one of those days."

To me she said, "The place he works at is just the most terrible place! So disorganized! And they were just taken over by the most vicious, incompetent men! They don't know what they're doing."

"Most places are like that," I said.

"Really? I guess I'm terribly lucky. The people in my office are so friendly and bright. I feel like they're real friends. They let me take work home."

"Sweetie, they're working you to death for peanuts," Fetterman called out from the back seat.

"They're *not* working me to death," Becky said crisply. To me, she said, "Of course I had to start at the bottom because I hadn't worked in so many years. That's only fair. But gradually that's changing. . . . The point is, how else can one learn?"

"True." I began feeling mildly claustrophobic. I wished I hadn't accepted her offer of driving me back.

"You know, I think the store your wife opened is such a wonderful idea!" Becky said. "I have a friend who's a really beautiful woman, but a bit heavy. That's just the way she's built! There's nothing she can do about it, and her husband adores her, men think she's terrific. . . . But for years the only clothes she could find were these mousy little gray and black dresses and she loves color. Red! Purple! . . . So I think it was so smart of your wife to realize there was a real need for that."

"Yeah, it's doing well," I said.

"She must be terribly good at business."

"Well, she's learning. . . . She was like you, started at the bottom."

"That's encouraging." She turned to look back at her husband, who was lying with his eyes closed. "Did you hear that, dear? Mr. Greene's wife started at the bottom, just like me."

He made an indistinguishable grunt.

"I think everything is a matter of how you feel about yourself, don't you?" she went on, turning back to me. "If you think you're good, other people will think it too. And I think I *am* good—at what I do, I mean. Not at millions of things."

"Yeah, that's important," I said.

"I feel our daughters are slightly spoiled," she said, pressing on her horn. "They expect everything to just happen. Perfect jobs, perfect men! I tell them: 'That's not the world. Everything you get you work for. Nothing just happens.' But their generation has such elevated expectations. . . . Are your sons in college still?"

"One is, one's with an advertising agency. He wants to be a writer, though."

"Oh, so does our second daughter, Dawn. They should get together. Of course, I should warn you, she's terrible with men. She runs through ten a month." She laughed dryly.

"Actually, Aaron has a girlfriend at the moment." I described the situation briefly.

"Goodness! How interesting! Did you hear that, Benjy?"

"What?" he mumbled.

"The Greenes' son is living with a woman who's ten years *older* than he is. . . . Well, that's very modern, isn't it? And she, I suppose, doesn't mind? Must even like it."

"She seems to be crazy about him."

"Actually, I'm two years older than Benjy. Which was quite unusual at the time we got married. I felt I was robbing the cradle." She laughed.

We were in front of our house. Becky stopped the car. She looked back at her husband. "Sweetie, are you seriously all right?"

He sat up, groggily. "I'll get in the front seat."

Just as he was getting out of the car, Marilyn came out. Seeing the three of us, she stopped, hesitated, and then came forward. "The Fettermans gave me a lift," I said.

I watched her look from me to him. No visible reaction. "Our car is being fixed," she said.

Becky had gotten out of the car and was standing beside her husband. "I was just telling your husband how wonderful I think your store is. . . . I have a friend who goes there all the time."

"The first year was tricky," Marilyn said, "but now it does seem to be going well."

"There must be a lot of fat women," Fetterman said.

Marilyn smiled. "Well, enough to keep us in business."

There was a pause.

"We're going to Ciro's tonight," Becky said. "Do you know it?"

"I've heard of it. We haven't actually been there."

"It's our anniversary. Our twenty-fifth."

Marilyn looked quickly from him to her. "Congratulations."

"Come in for a glass of champagne," I said. "How about it?"

They looked uncertain. "I don't think we have time," Fetterman said.

"We don't have to be at the restaurant till nine," Becky said. "That was the only reservation I could get."

"Listen, you stay right here. I'll bring it out. . . . Just a glass." We had a bottle in the refrigerator from a few weeks back that I never took out. I grabbed it and four glasses, put them on a tray, and brought everything out front. The bottle opened neatly, just fizzing over a little.

"This is very sweet of you, Mr. Greene," Becky said.

"Mo. . . ." I raised my glass. "So, here's how."

"To marriage," Becky said softly, clicking her glass against her husband's, then mine, then Marilyn's.

"To love," Fetterman said. After a second he added, "We wouldn't have marriage without love."

"No, that's true," Becky said. "We wouldn't. . . . Did we mention our older daughter is getting married, Chelsea?"

"I didn't know that," Marilyn said. "Congratulations again."

"She's marrying a fellow student," Fetterman said.

"Do you like him?" Marilyn asked.

Fetterman laughed. He looked at his wife. "Do we like him? I guess we do. . . . Naturally he's not worthy of her, but. . . ."

"Oh, I think he's worthy of her," Becky said. "In what way isn't he?" To us she added, "He comes from a very fine Jewish family in Missouri."

"I didn't know there *were* Jews in Missouri," Marilyn said.

"They just happened to settle there," Becky said. "And they love it."

"Good," I said, refilling everyone's glass. "To Jews in Missouri!"

"Honey, come on," Marilyn said. I knew she thought I was drinking too much. "Will it be a big wedding?" she asked Becky.

"Not gigantic," Becky said. "Perhaps two hundred. . . . The sad thing is they only have a week for a honeymoon! They both have job offers that start the month they get married. I think that's terrible. Everyone should have a long honeymoon."

"They'll take a long one later," Fetterman said.

"It's not the same," she countered. "I wanted them to go some place wonderful, Spain or Italy, the way we did. But, the main thing is, they're in love, and that's all that counts, really."

"To honeymoons!" I said. I *was* getting a little sloshed, but I felt terrific.

Marilyn sighed. "On our honeymoon we went to Las Vegas and Mo won a thousand dollars. He has a system."

"Gambling makes me so nervous," Becky said. "I could never. . . . Even watching it."

"Me too," Marilyn said with sudden vehemence. "It's a sickness, really. People get totally carried away. They just can't stop!"

"I'm not like that," I said. "I know exactly when to stop. . . . Anyway, that's true of everything. You just have to know when to stop, before it becomes an addiction."

Becky cleared her throat. "Well, this was so kind of you both. . . . I hope we can offer you a drink when you—"

"We had our anniversary already," Marilyn said. "Two months ago."

"Oh. . . . Well, the next one then."

"To the next one," I said.

They got into their car and drove off. I waved at them, but when I turned, I saw I was alone on the lawn. Marilyn had gone inside.

She was in the kitchen. I could tell, from the set of her mouth, that she was angry. I waved the bottle at her. "Come on, sweets, don't be a party pooper," I said. "Have another glass. . . . Where did we get this stuff anyway? It's fantastic." I put my arms around her from behind, kissing her neck. "Umm, tastes good. Can I have a bite?"

Marilyn turned around. "Mo, how could you *do* that?"

"What'd I do?"

"Inviting them to have a drink like that. We hardly know them!"

"So? Look, she gave me a ride home. I was just being neighborly, a good neighbor."

"She's such a bovine busybody!" Marilyn hissed.

"A bovine busybody. . . . Hey, I like that." I filled the two glasses and gave her one. "To bovine busybodies . . . and their bedraggled, boozy husbands."

"I wouldn't talk about boozy husbands if I were you."

"You're too tough on poor old Becky. She's a good kid. Listen, if there weren't any fat ladies in the world, you'd go out of business!"

"Oh, she's not fat like the women who come to my store. Mo, you should see some of them! You know, it's amazing. Like, today, this woman came in with her husband. She must have weighed two hundred pounds. And she kept trying on dresses and coming out and saying to him, 'How does this look?' and he'd say, 'Wonderful.'"

"Well trained."

"No, he meant it! You could tell. In the end she bought *six* ninety-dollar dresses! He clearly just adored her. And he was just a regular, thin, nice-looking guy. So, what I mean is, maybe it doesn't matter—all of that, what people weigh or what they look like. I just don't know. . . . Would you love me if I weighed two hundred pounds?"

I considered. "Maybe."

She finished her glass of champagne. "Don't worry. I'm not about to do it, but it does give one pause."

"God, he's really a basket case, isn't he?" I said, throwing away the bottle."

"Who?"

"Mr. Becky."

"His name is Benjamin."

"Whatever. . . . She may be bovine, but he looks like a truck ran over him."

"In what way?" Marilyn asked nervously.

"His skin, his eyes. He just looked at the end of the road to me."

There was a long pause.

"I didn't notice," Marilyn said.

I went over and put my arms around her again, squeezing her breasts. "Hey, let's postpone dinner, okay? I have spring fever."

"I'm a wreck," Marilyn said. "I haven't even had a chance to wash up."

"You look gorgeous," I slipped my hands around her, cupping her rear end. "Come on. . . . You can just lie there and think about your profits tripling."

"I wish that were still a turn-on," Marilyn said, relenting. "Oh well, what the heck. I guess I'm a little high too."

Three years ago Marilyn had a partial mastectomy; she had to have one breast removed. Much hysteria, anxiety which I felt maybe not as keenly as she did. But for months afterward there was suddenly a new, shy, prudish Marilyn who wanted to fuck in the dark, undressed in the bathroom. "I feel deformed," she'd say. "I hate seeing you look at me." The fact is, it affected me a hell of a lot more than I let on. You reach out automatically and there's this empty space. There's something eerie about it. The only way I could get around it mentally was to pretend they were both still there. I did that by caressing the one on her right side and then moving around to other parts, finally returning to the same breast. It was like you've always gone somewhere by a certain route, they tear down the highway, so you get used to going another way. By now it's routine and I don't think Marilyn ever noticed; I give myself credit for that.

We did it with Marilyn on top. For some reason, if she's tired, she says it's easier that way. Any way is fine with me as long as she's there and giving signs of life. It's funny. I guess when you get it on at fifty or sixty, you feel a kind of pride, in yourself, in the two of you. There you are, still able to work up a little steam, an aura of lust. Maybe even poor old Fetterman will make it with his wife tonight for old times' sake. I hope so.

"It's funny," Marilyn said. "Blanche says they do it four times sometimes on weekends. Of course Reid's in his thirties."

"Jealous?"

"No!" She leaned against me, warm, drowsy-eyed. "I'm glad for her sake, though."

"Does he have tattoos all over or just on his arm?"

"I never asked."

"I once did it with a lady who had a tattoo on her rear end. A tulip. Kind of cute."

"When was this? In your flaming youth?"

"When else?"

She shrugged.

"Ladies with tattoos would scare the wits out of me now."

"I'll bet."

"I'd be hiding under the bed." I stroked her breast lightly.

"Well, I can tell you one thing, if I had a tattoo, I'd do something more original than a tulip!" Marilyn said. She tried to sit up. "Oh boy, I think it's take-out Chinese food tonight."

I worry about my mother. She's seventy-seven now, Emil's seventy-nine. Maybe the two of them will go tottering along for another decade, but it's hard to visit Boston without hearing of another physical blow that's hit one or the other of them. He's been pretty deaf for years now. My mother still can get through to him. Maybe he lip-reads her more easily. *Her* problem is with her eyes. Six months ago one of them went, just like that. She was sitting in the doctor's office and lost total sight in her left eye. The doctor claimed it was not uncommon and rarely happened in both eyes. But for my mother, for whom reading is one of the main points of living, it was scary. It took her months to learn to use the one that's left, but now she says she has the hang of it.

"You wake up in the morning and you think, 'What's going to give out today?'" she said.

I was in Boston for the weekend for the first time in several months. Actually, I hadn't even had time to see her the last time I was there. "I know what you mean," I said jokingly.

"You!" she said scornfully. "Look at you! You're a spring chicken."

"Not exactly."

She nudged Emil, who was reading. "Doesn't Mo look well? Be honest."

Emil winked. "A killer."

My mother frowned. "A killer? What does that mean? Mo, you're a handsome man and you're aging well."

"Like a good cheese?" I said.

"As long as you don't smell like one," Emil put in.

"Well, I feel it," I said. "I'm not what I once was."

"Who is?" My mother shoved another slice of pie at me. I refused, pleading fear of excess girth.

"What wonderful willpower! You get that from your father. He could eat one bite and then stop."

"How about me?" Emil said. "I have willpower too."

My mother patted his hand. "Of course you do." To me she asked, "And how's Marilyn? Still busy busy busy?"

Ironically, now that my mother's "retired" after a lifetime of working, she's begun criticizing Marilyn for working too hard and "neglecting" me. "You don't have to tell me," she'll say. "I can tell just by looking at you."

"Mom, the kids are grown. You always said Marilyn ought to be out working."

"She's never home! She never answers my calls, never writes."

"Getting a business off the ground is tricky. You ought to know that."

My mother leaned forward. "But, Mo, you forget. Your father and I did it together. Hand in glove. We left for work together, we worked together all day, we came home together. It was all for you and Harriet. We wanted you to have everything."

"I couldn't live like that," I admitted. "I like it the way it is."

"Well, I hope Marilyn appreciates it. . . . She never could have done it without you, the way you encouraged her, supported her."

"She could have done it without me."

"Why're you so modest all of a sudden? Look, it's water under the bridge, but when you married Marilyn, I took one look at her and I thought: with all the girls in the world at his disposal, he picks a blondie with no college degree." To Emil she said, "He could have had anyone! He could have married the Duchess of Windsor!"

"I think I'd take Marilyn over the Duchess of Windsor."

"The same with Harriet," my mother went on. "She could have had anyone. So, first she picks someone who never opens his mouth and second she picks someone who never stops talking."

"Harriet's happy," I said. "And Kevin's a good guy."

"A good guy. . . . Sure, he's a good guy. But did we need a Catholic in the family that desperately, with all the Jewish widowers running around at their wits' end?"

"Are there that many Jewish widowers at their wits' end? I didn't know."

"Mo, listen to me. I don't want you to repeat this to Harriet, but he drinks too much! He puts away *three* Scotches one after the other."

"She knows, Mom."

"Does she? I can't tell with Harriet."

"She's known him for fifteen years."

"No, you're right. She's almost sixty. If she can't make her own mistakes now, when will she be old enough. Right?"

"Right," said Emil. "She loves him, Leah. Stop worrying."

"He pinches her behind right when I'm in the room!"

I laughed. "Anyway, he's half Jewish. His father was a Jew."

My mother's eyes narrowed. "I don't believe that story. Do you? There's something fishy there. Twelve kids raised as Catholics and the father never knew? Come on."

"People sometimes look the other way."

"What does that mean?" my mother said. "Look the other way? You look, you see. I don't understand how anyone looks the other way unless they're blind."

I finally got her off the topic of Harriet, only by taking out some new photos of Linus and his girlfriend he'd sent a month earlier. My mother pored over them. "Is this the same one?"

"The very same."

"She looks different. . . . Was she always so short?"

Linus's girlfriend, Petra, is barely five feet tall, a foot shorter than he is. She's a physics major too. They're both planning to go on and get their doctorates. He's doing his senior thesis on "Fog." My mother has never met Aaron's lover. I don't want to stretch her forbearance beyond its capacities. But Linus and Petra are a quiet, intense pair, more like friends to the outside eye, always studying.

"He's still so thin!" my mother said.

"It's the way he's built."

My mother sighed. "He's a genius. . . . Even smarter than you, Mo. I hate to say it, but it's true."

"I know it's true."

"You were more . . . artistic, clever." She looked dreamy, as she always does when thinking back on the wonderful career I passed up as an actor. Emil, for the past five years, has been trying to teach my mother Russian so she could read Shakespeare in it. He claims Shakespeare is better in Russian than in English. Privately my mother has confessed she thinks he's crazy. "How can it be better in Russian? Is Pushkin better in English?"

At the end of the evening, as I was leaving, she said, "Well, the main thing is you're all well, as well as can be expected."

I had planned to meet Bibi for lunch the next day, had written her about it, but by eleven I realized I couldn't make it. I don't have any phone numbers for her, but I decided to call Tufts, where she teaches, and see if I could leave a message. "I wondered if I could speak to Noorbibi Dahr?" I said after being put through to the sociology department.

"Who?"

"Noorbibi or Bibi Dahr? She's on the faculty."

"Sorry, you must have the wrong place."

"Is this the sociology department?"

"Yes."

"You don't have anyone named Noorbibi Dahr on your staff?"

"Nope."

"Look, who are you? Are you a student?"

"I'm an instructor. Bill Thorndyke. Who're you?"

"I'm a friend of Ms. Dahr's. . . . Look, is there a woman on the faculty, about five foot nine with black hair? She wears it parted in the middle, she's married to an Indian man who's an engineer, has two kids. . . ."

"You mean Sasha?"

"What?"

"Sasha Weinberg."

I hesitated. "I don't know."

"Well, she's the only person in the department like that. Should I get her?"

"Would you? Thanks a lot."

Noorbibi's voice came on the phone a moment later. "Yes? Who is this?"

"It's me," I said. "He didn't seem to know who you were. Or something."

She laughed. "Well, it's a long story. . . . I'll tell you at lunch."

"I can't make it for lunch. That's why I'm calling."

"Dinner?"

We arranged to meet at the same place at eight, which I knew would give me time to finish up anything else that came up during the day. Sasha Weinberg? Who was Sasha Weinberg? Bibi's friend, the one I always wrote to. I forgot about it till I sat down at the table with her. She smiled and handed me a book. "I'd been meaning to give you a copy anyway."

I took it. *Patterns and Deviations in the Erotic Life of American Men,* by Sasha Weinberg. . . . I frowned, puzzled.

"That's me," she said. "I wrote it. It's an autographed copy."

"Congratulations." I turned it over and saw her photo, a small one, on the inside back jacket. "Why'd you use a pseudonym?"

"It's not a pseudonym. It's my name."

I set down my drink. "Wait a sec. . . . Then who's Noorbibi Dahr?"

"An invention. Well, half an invention."

Bits and pieces of things began colliding in my brain. "Let me order another drink first, okay?"

"I'll have one too." She smiled. "Okay, where do I begin? . . . The true part is: I'm married to an Indian engineer whose name is Ravi

Dahr. I have two children whose photos you've seen and I teach sociology at Tufts."

"Okay, should I guess the rest?"

"Sure."

I thought. "When you stopped seeing men, you wanted to make a fresh start so you changed your name?"

"Wrong." She held up two fingers. "Two more guesses."

"You were afraid it would be harder to get a job if they knew you were Indian?"

She shook her head.

I laughed. "God, let me think. . . . You're only half Indian? One of your parents was American?"

Noorbibi, Sasha, was smiling. "You're getting warm."

"Listen, put me out of my misery. I'm not good at games."

"Will you be angry?"

"How can I tell ahead of time?"

"That's one reason I've never told you. Once you tell one lie, you don't know where to stop. It's like you're on a treadmill." She took a deep breath. "Remember the summer we met?"

"Sure I remember."

"You told someone you liked the looks of Indian women. They showed you a photo."

"Yeah?"

"Well, I was out there for the summer. Okay: first big confession. I'm not Indian at all! I was born and raised in Great Neck. Both my parents are Jewish. The only reason I looked Indian to you was my hair and skin, the saris."

"But why did you do it? Weren't you really a call girl either?"

"I'd had what I guess you would call a 'stormy adolescence.' I left home at sixteen, dropped out of college, traveled in the East—India, Japan. Followed a guru around for eighteen months. The whole 'sixties thing. Became a vegetarian, lost a lot of weight, reexamined my 'spiritual values.' That was when I met Ravi. I got a job as a secretary in Calcutta and he was a student. To him I was a real exotic, the first Jewish girl he'd ever met, the first American. All those things that in America were 'big deal, so what' to him were exciting, amazing, wonderful. . . . And we fell in love."

"I'm glad *he's* real anyway."

"Oh, Ravi's real, all right. . . . Anyhow, he went to his parents and said he wanted to marry me and they had a fit. They're upper middle class English-educated Indians. I must have struck them as a scruffy, on-the-make little slut, which I half was then. They said they'd disown him, the whole thing. Then, when they saw that might alienate him forever and he might elope with me on the spot, they made him promise to wait for five years, to finish his education. They were sure after five years' separation, we'd both find other people."

"So, you went back to the States?"

"I went back, finished college. I guess somehow I'd gotten most of the rebelling out of my system. I got my degree in two years and then I went out to L.A. for the summer to visit a friend, Gay. A would-be actress, not a call girl, really. She just did it occasionally to make a little extra money, but she knew the scene. I wasn't a virgin by any means. I'd done a lot of reckless, dumb things with men. Basically I was 'beyond' all that, but I knew I wanted to get my doctorate in sociology and I decided to do some 'field research.' To see what men were really like when they were with women they paid, if there was a difference, what it was. Gay weeded them out for me, nothing hairy, just guys like you who wanted a little adventure, something different."

I shook my head. "A Jewish girl from Great Neck! My mother would die!"

"*Your* mother would die? How about mine?"

"Don't tell me your father's a doctor?"

Sasha smiled. "A dentist."

I was a little bombed, still trying to piece it together. "But that was it? Just for the summer? So why'd you pretend with me that you—I mean, why keep it going?"

"I liked you." She looked embarrassed. "Okay, second big confession! I sort of fell in love with you, actually. I don't exactly know why. I knew I was going to marry Ravi. I never had any doubt about that. It was, like, set in my mind. . . . But somehow, I don't know, we got along. . . ."

I touched her hand. "I know."

"Maybe it was one of those I wanted my cake and wanted to eat it too? I didn't want to get seriously involved with anyone but I couldn't see being celibate for five years. I never found a really good way to handle it, actually. And maybe if you'd lived in Boston, it wouldn't have worked. . . . But the fact that you just came in occasionally. It was there, but I knew it would never get out of hand. I knew *you'd* never let it." She hesitated. "I hated you at times for that."

I was taken aback. "I'm sorry. . . . If I'd known—"

"If you'd known, you wouldn't have seen me! . . . No, and it was fine. I could have been an actress except it's such a crazy, unstable life. But I liked fooling you. I liked the whole thing with the saris. . . . Though at times I thought you saw through it. You really never did?"

I remembered Linus saying, "I'm sorry, Dad, but she's not Indian." "I didn't. . . . I wondered what you did about men, that was all."

"Not much. . . . I saw a few. No one at the college. I kept that part of my life separate. Oh, and Ravi was doing the same. It was what we'd agreed on. We never discussed it, even now, but he had girls too. . . . In fact, I think he had another American girlfriend. Some woman showed up once and seemed horrified he was married."

"Why did you take my money?"

"I really thought you wouldn't do it unless it was within that context. Was I wrong? I felt like you . . . didn't want to get that involved."

"Maybe." I stared at her. The dusky skin, thick eyebrows, gold earrings, heavy coarse hair. A Jewish girl from Great Neck?

She was staring at me. "I really was half in love with you. . . . And it was weird, knowing if you liked me at all, it was because for you I was someone that didn't exist! I used to even imagine going to New York, meeting your wife. I imagined that you had problems together, that that was why you saw me, that you'd leave her. . . ."

"And?"

"And nothing. It was a fantasy. Do—do you have problems with her? You never seemed to want to talk about her."

"No problems. . . . We just had our twenty-fifth anniversary."

She hesitated. "Do you have a picture of her?"

I took out my wallet. I had one from a couple of years ago, of both of us. Linus took it. We were standing in the yard, Marilyn leaning against me a little.

Sasha examined it closely. "God, she's so different from what I imagined! She's pretty!"

"What did you imagine?"

"I don't know, kind of that classic overbearing Jewish housewife type, a little heavy. . . . you know."

"Never in a million years!"

"Is she Jewish, even? She doesn't look it."

"Yeah, from Sloatsburg. A real exotic, just like you."

"What does she do? Does she work?"

"She started a store with a friend a couple of years ago. They specialize in clothes for fat ladies. It's doing very well."

Sasha gave the photo back to me. "It's so strange. For years I guess I half justified seeing you, thinking she was this. . . . Well, just someone like my mother, I guess, hated sex, that you were too Jewish and straight and all that to really fool around. I thought I was doing a good deed."

"You were."

She frowned. "But here she—she's beautiful and nice and. . . . She doesn't know about me, does she?"

"No."

"I'm glad. I'd feel awful. . . . Anyway, it isn't like we really had an affair. It was more just. . . ." She trailed off.

I looked down at her book. "Am I in here?"

"No. I would've felt funny. It's all a combination of people, anyway." She cleared her throat. "This is funny, but for years I always wanted you to meet my kids. Will you? Ravi's away for the weekend."

"Who will you say I am?"

"A professor who came to lecture at the college. I've had people over before like that."

After dinner we took a cab to her apartment. We kept looking at each other. "You're really not mad?" Sasha said.

"I don't know," I admitted. Suddenly I exploded. "Why do women always do this kind of thing?"

"What kind of thing?" she said, alarmed.

"Inventing things, fooling around with reality! What's the point? To make us feel like idiots?"

"That wasn't my motive. . . . Would you have seen me if you'd known who I really was?"

I shrugged.

"That was why. . . . Really, Mo. But you're right."

"What if this thing hadn't come up yesterday? Would you *ever* have told me?"

"I always kept being about to. Can't you understand what it's like? Each time I told myself I would. But then . . . I didn't. Please understand."

Sasha's apartment was the lower half of a brownstone. When she let herself in, the baby-sitter leaped up from the couch. "Hi, Mrs. Dahr."

"Hi, Julie. . . . Everything okay?"

"They went right in. . . . I'm not sure they're asleep, though."

"That's okay." She paid her. "This is Professor Greene. He gave a lecture at the university this afternoon."

The baby-sitter accepted the information impassively, pocketed her money, and left. Sasha led me down the hall to a room with a bunk bed and toys scattered around. The child on the bottom, the boy, seemed to be asleep. There was a night light on and the bathroom door was open. A head popped up on the upper bunk. "Mommy?"

"Hi, honey. How come you're still up?"

"I had a long nap. . . . Who's that?"

"A friend of mine, Professor Greene. . . . Want to come down and meet him?"

The little girl, Mimi, scrambled down the bunk bed in a second. She looked around seven, big black eyes, curly dark hair, long pink nightgown. She followed us into the living room. "I didn't have any dinner," she announced.

"How come?" Sasha asked.

"I wasn't hungry. But I'm hungry now."

We went into the kitchen and Sasha brought out milk and some slices of cold turkey. "Are you a grandfather?" the little girl asked me.

"Not yet."

"Why not?"

"Neither of my sons is married."

"Why not?"

"They haven't met anyone they want to marry yet."

"Why not?"

Sasha laughed. "This could go on all night. . . . Sweetie, not everyone is a grandfather, ever."

The little girl smiled mischievously at Sasha. "You'll never be one because you're a lady. Right? But you'll be a grand*mother.*"

"Not necessarily. . . . Not unless you or Josh have a baby."

"I'll have a baby," she said. "Sometime." She was wolfing down the slices of turkey. "I was practically starving to death!"

"Mo, do you want anything?" Sasha asked. "Coffee, maybe?"

"Sure." I sat on one of the stools next to Mimi. "You look very much like your mother."

"Everyone says that."

"It's a compliment."

Mimi jumped off the stool. She lifted her nightgown up high. "I have new underpants. See?"

They were white with purple hearts. I smiled. "They're pretty."

"Hon, come on," Sasha said.

Mimi let the nightgown fall. "I got eight different kinds." She approached the stool where I was sitting. I lifted her up onto my lap. She didn't protest, just sat there thoughtfully, looking at me. "Why do you have such funny eyebrows?"

Sasha protested. "He doesn't."

"Yes, he does. Look at them! . . . They're a different color from his hair."

"That's true of many people."

Mimi touched my eyebrows lightly. "I like them. . . . Mine are too bushy."

"You have beautiful eyebrows," I told her, flirting back a little.

She thought a moment. "I have beautiful hair."

"Yes, that's beautiful too."

"And I have beautiful eyes, Daddy says."

Her eyes were the same shape as Sasha's, large with long thick eyelashes. "He's right."

"I have beautiful clothes," she went on. "And beautiful earrings."

"No false modesty in this family," Sasha said.

"But I have ugly ears," she said plaintively. She showed me her ears, hidden behind the mass of thick hair. "See?"

"They look fine to me," I said. "What's ugly about them?"

"Too big."

"Mine are big too," I said.

Mimi touched my ears. "They are big," she conceded, "but all of you is big."

Sasha lifted her off my lap. "Sweetie, it's late. . . . Go back in, okay?"

"I'm still not tired!"

"Just lie there and think interesting things."

Mimi smiled at me, a lingering over-the-shoulder smile. "Nice meeting you."

"It was nice meeting you."

After she'd left we had our coffee in the living room. "What a flirt!" Sasha said.

"I wonder where she gets it," I said wryly.

She laughed. "I don't think I'm a flirt. I know that sounds funny, but I always thought I was pretty straightforward with men. . . . I wasn't a tease, anyway."

I thought of her in the apartment she lived in before she got married, the sari unwinding, sliding to the floor, that pungent, musky smell.

"Ravi and I are happy," Sasha said. "I didn't used to think I could be. I thought I'd feel claustrophobic with just one man, but, I don't know. I guess the urge becomes less strong. Or maybe I got it out of my system."

"I did," I said.

"Once somebody actually did come to lecture at our department and I felt. . . . It wasn't love at first sight. More, like at first sight. We talked till two. But he lived in Australia, luckily."

I told her about Aimee. "It was a mistake, in retrospect."

"Wouldn't your son be terribly upset, if he knew?"

"He'll never know. . . . No, that's not what I mean. I felt like maybe I'd crossed some barrier. You lose the curiosity. It doesn't seem worth the risks."

"Right." Her face, as she gazed at me, was thoughtful, melancholy. She sighed. "I'm glad you met Mimi. Did you like her?"

"I want a granddaughter like that someday."

Sasha leaned over and kissed me. "You'll get one."

Leaps and Turns

"Watch me!" Benjy called.

"I am." I was standing on the edge of the rink, clinging to the rail. Actually it makes me nervous to watch him, especially when he does those fancy leaps and jumps in the air and has to land on one foot. He just took up ice skating about two years ago, the first sport he's ever been good at, he says. He takes lessons twice a week with a Polish lady who told me she was "staggered" at how quickly he'd improved. Despite that, last year he fell and broke his leg. I admire it in a way, trying something totally new at forty-five, really pouring yourself into it. Benjy is funny that way, unpredictable, lazy and disorganized about some things and then, when he decides he wants something, going after it with a passion.

Whew, he made it. He smiled at me and then began doing more easy, graceful turns. I feel like we could be in junior high, the guy showing off for his admiring girlfriend. If only I was a better ice skater! I meet Benjy here every Sunday morning because it's a time I have set aside—Mo knows I ice skate but has no desire to come along, same with Becky as far as Benjy is concerned. It's a small rink and they set aside Sundays for private groups. Now, though it's April and getting warmer, they can still keep the surface cold enough.

Partly it's that I've never been good at any sports, but worst of all at winter sports because I hate the cold. I never understood doing anything when it's cold and you could be indoors. All that ever sounded appealing about skiing was huddling in front of the fire afterward drinking hot rum drinks. And you don't have to go skiing to do that. But for Benjy's sake I've tried and I really am better. When we skate together, we're not exactly like a couple in an ice show, gliding in perfect synchrony. But at least it isn't like the first few times when I would lurch from one side to the other, practically dragging Benjy down with me. "It's funny," he would say. "You *look* like you'd be so graceful." What can you say to that?

While Benjy has his lesson, I sit and read usually. Afterward we have hot chocolate at a small indoor café connected to the rink.

"I don't really understand why you sat next to him on the train," I said.

"I couldn't avoid it. He was there, he saw me. . . . I thought not to sit next to him would have looked odd. Why? Did he say anything about it?"

"Not especially." I scooped up the whipped cream. "Why did you offer him a ride home?"

"It was Becky's idea. She likes him."

I smiled. "Maybe we should fix them up."

"I can't figure him out," Benjy said. "The way he came rushing out with the champagne. I mean, you don't even know us that well officially as a couple."

"He's given to expansive gestures at times. I like that in him."

"He was certainly putting it away."

"Yeah, I don't know. . . . He doesn't have a drinking problem, if that's what you're trying to say. It just makes him horny."

Benjy just looked at me.

"Why are you looking at me that way? Look, you do it with Becky!"

"Do I?"

"That's what I was given to understand. . . . That's nice about Chelsea. Becky must be pleased."

"She is, up to a point. It's funny. Now that Dawn is in this women's lib phase and won't wear dresses, claims marriage is a form of prostitution, I think in some weird covert way it excites Becky. All the things she would never allow herself to think, even, spouting forth."

"Maybe she'll be influenced. You'll have to learn to cook."

"No, it won't affect our actual lives," he said quickly.

I laughed. "Never can tell."

"Look, a feminist girlfriend is all I can take. If I had to deal with it at home too . . ."

"What would happen? You'd crumble? . . . Am I a girlfriend? That sounds so blithe for fifteen years of—"

"Of?"

"Loving."

He took my hand and kissed it. "God, I'm exhausted. I don't know what's wrong. I used to be able to do this and not feel it at all."

"You said you'd go for a checkup."

"I will."

I worry about Benjy, though I try not to be obsessive about it. He does look terribly tired and I've noticed that he talks about feeling exhausted all the time now. I remembered how Mo said he thought he looked bad. It's so hard to judge someone's looks if you've seen them every week almost for so long. I think if Benjy hadn't mentioned feeling worn out, maybe I wouldn't have noticed it. When we make love, it doesn't seem any different. Maybe there's not the intensity and excitement of ten years ago, but I think that is just our getting older.

"When will the wedding be?" I asked.

"Early fall."

"And you like him?"

He smiled. "I don't think he's worthy of her. Maybe there's no way a father can think anyone is worthy of his daughters. But he's not a schmuck. He's a first child, outgoing like Chelsea. It's a friendship marriage. I think that's okay."

"Linus is like that with Petra. . . . Some people don't want the volatile thing."

"Dawn does. . . . But she won't settle down for a while now."

"You think the thing of being gay is just a phase?"

"I imagine."

I shrugged. I've never totally understood why people are gay. I'd understand if they found stereotyped sex roles oppressive and wanted to escape that, but the few gay couples I've known just seem to set up patterns that are just as rigid, sometimes even more so—one macho person, one retiring one. So why bother?

Blanche and Reid are staying with us for a few days, but they decided to go off for a drive. Reid makes ancient instruments: dulcimers, lutes, harpsichords. He used to have a tenured teaching job and gave it up in order to live the way he wanted. He loves boats, sails a lot, writes an occasional poem, and, if an order comes in for an instrument, works on it intensively for several months. Blanche said at first it was hard for her to get used to being with a man whose yearly income, by choice, is so much lower than her own. But now she says he's the only man she knows who's living the life he wants to and doesn't give a damn about social status or material possessions.

For me the main thing is she's so happy now. It's hard to even imagine all those years with Dwight and the years after they broke up when she was so tense and angry and I felt guilty even being in the room with her. Now I feel jealous almost that, without even looking especially, she met someone with whom she has a kind of rapport I don't have at all with Mo. I think they have a terrific sex life—maybe that's all "rapport" boils down to in the end.

"Next time we'll come with you," Reid said. "I like ice skating."

"You go," Blanche said. "I can barely keep on my feet."

"I've gotten a little better," I said, "but not much."

"I admire you," she said. "Well, I run. That's enough."

It's funny that Blanche, though she's let her hair go gray and frizzy, looks younger than she used to. She lost weight, her body is lean and compact. I've never told her about Benjy. I think maybe now I could, now that she's happy and has become so much less judgmental. But I don't want to. I looked over at Reid, who was sitting on the kitchen chair, whittling a small table out of wood. As a hobby he makes dollhouse furniture. It's almost too good for children, really delicate reproductions of Shaker furniture. He made some pieces for Blanche's daughter, but Blanche says Marianne's not interested in dollhouses. She's going to save it for her grandchildren.

"Aaron called," Blanche said. "He said they might come over later. . . . He sounded happy. Is it still going well?"

"As far as we can tell."

"I think it might be perfect for Aaron," Blanche said. "Someone settled like that, who knows what she wants. Jim is having such a hard time, finding a girl who'll stay put for more than a second. They've all turned into such promiscuous little run-arounds."

"Well, not all," I said. "I think he'll leave her, eventually, don't you? For someone more his own age?"

"No, why should he?"

I hesitated. It's true Reid is ten years younger than Blanche, but at their age the difference doesn't seem so great.

"If it weren't for all the bullshit society heaves at us, I think all women would pick younger men," Blanche said vehemently. "It makes so much more sense. Women stay young so much longer, we grow sexually. I look at some of my friends and their husbands are old, gray, falling apart. It's so depressing!"

I thought of Benjy and how tired he looked. But it's sort of useless to think of these things in the abstract. You fall in love with someone and you figure out a way to justify it. But Blanche still likes to theorize about things. "What if he wanted to have children?" I couldn't help saying. "She's in her late thirties."

"So, she'll have one or they'll adopt. . . . Or maybe he doesn't want one. I wonder if men really want children. *We* want them so they say—fine, go ahead, have them. But if it were up to them? Look at Dwight! He sees the kids twice a year, he hardly knows who they are."

"Not all men are like that."

"Pretty much."

"I think Aaron really likes Sonya's son."

"So, there you have it. A built-in family." She stood up and went over to Reid's chair. "God, the patience! Look at the legs on it!"

Reid went on whittling. He doesn't talk much more than Dwight, but his silence is somehow comfortable, as though he just doesn't find words that necessary or important. When Blanche runs on about something, he listens thoughtfully, but I never can tell if he's agreeing, disagreeing, doesn't care.

Blanche rubbed his shoulder affectionately. "Let's take a walk," she said suddenly to me.

"I feel so zonked from the skating."

"We'll just walk . . . slowly."

It was a windy, brisk day, the sky very blue. Blanche smiled at me affectionately. "I just meant before, don't worry about Aaron. Everyone finds someone special at some point in his life. It just takes some longer. Look at me! Till I was forty I really didn't give a damn about men. I married Dwight to have kids. It would've been cheaper and more sensible to have artificial insemination. . . . Remember when we went to the movies as kids, in junior high, and you'd come out squealing, 'Oh, he's so gorgeous, he's so sexy . . .' and for the next week you'd be sighing and moaning and I'd think, 'What's it all about?' I never knew if you were just pretending, if everyone was just pretending, or if there was some deep dark secret I was excluded from."

A boy rode by on a bicycle and almost hit us, then went zooming on. "That was how *I* felt until . . ."

Blanche looked at me. "Till what?"

"It just takes a while," I said evasively.

"To what?" Blanche pursued. "Has sex gotten better with you and Mo? Or worse? Or the same?"

"Both," I stammered. "There've been bad periods, or not bad, but times when. . . . I guess I feel uncomfortable talking about it."

She laughed. "I used to feel uncomfortable. . . . In the old days you used to keep bringing it up, remember? Had I ever done this or felt that? It drove me crazy! Remember?"

"No," I said. "When was that? When we were kids?"

"Even later. . . . And I thought, 'God, is she *doing* all those things or does she just have a great imagination?'" She looked at me askance. "I used to wonder if you were faithful to Mo. You were always such a flirt."

"Well, that was just—" I began.

"It's just the way you are," Blanche conveniently finished for me. "It doesn't mean anything. I know that now. . . . Anyway, you don't even do it anymore."

"Don't I?"

"No, not really. I told Reid, before he met you, 'I have this kind of kooky little sister who really makes eyes at everyone and if you start doing it back with her, even for fun, I'll kill you.' So he met you and later he said, 'What'd you mean? She's not at all like that.'"

I wonder if I have changed. I think Blanche is right, but for so long it hasn't been necessary or maybe your vanity blurs into other things. When I had my breast removed, a lot of that flared up suddenly, like a terrible pain. What if that was all there was to me, a good body, and without it everything would vanish? I used to cringe when Benjy even touched me. It didn't bother me so much with Mo. There's always something basically perfunctory about our love-making, anyway. Mo never touches me anymore on my side where the breast was removed, whereas Benjy caresses that part just as long and tenderly, and the funny thing is I feel just as aroused when he touches me on that side. Or maybe I'm just so grateful for his tenderness that that itself turns me on.

"Having the operation changed the way I think about all that," I said.

"You mean, men? Or being mortal? Or what?"

"I realized I wasn't just a pair of boobs. . . . I'm not sure what I mean. Mainly, maybe, once you stop being afraid you're going to die, you're so relieved that just losing a breast seems minor by comparison."

Blanche pointed to herself. "I don't even have anything to lose! I could have them both taken off and Reid wouldn't even notice."

I put my arm around her. "He'd notice."

Blanche smiled. "Yeah, he would. . . . He likes my body. It's strange."

Sisters. I'm aware of how odd a scene like this would have seemed to me ten years ago, Blanche and I walking casually with our arms around each other, relaxed, affectionate. Jeanette has a sister she calls every day; Ila says if she never saw her sister again, that would be fine. I think with Blanche it's that time has blurred the distinctions between us, made what used to seem important less so. I have a career now; she doesn't care so much about hers. She's discovered sex. I no longer think of it as so important. I sometimes even think or wonder anyway if Benjy and I could meet without ever going to bed together.

I thought of that when Mo and I went to Boston together for the weekend. We were all having dinner at Harriet's house with her, Kevin, Leah and Emil. I was helping her in the kitchen. She's a terrible cook—everything is either horribly overdone or underdone. I never realized there was an art to cooking till I ate at Harriet's.

"This is our anniversary," Harriet said.

"I thought you were married in July."

She blushed. "Of when we met."

"That's right—you knew each other for a long time, didn't you?" I'm not sure how much she knows I know and Harriet is so prickly, I try to be careful.

She was adding margarine to the carrots, stirring it around. "We were lovers," she said suddenly, turning a still darker red.

"All along?" I decided acting surprised was better than admitting I knew already.

"Oh no, not all along. You see, we were both married."

"I know."

She looked up at me, her eyes blazing. "I think it's hard to understand if you haven't been in that situation, but the guilt is so terrible that in the end you can't live with yourself. You become so filled with self-hatred that it's not worth it."

I murmured something incoherent. "But you saw each other, anyway?"

"Yes, but it was terrible." Harriet was breathing rapidly. "Being together and not being able to do anything about it. You see, neither of us had very sexual marriages so. . . . But we were both married to good people."

"Good in what way?" I said, more sharply than I intended.

She looked puzzled. "Well, just in that . . . they hadn't ever done anything bad."

"Oh." I looked at her. Unlike Blanche, she looks her age, slightly heavy, her hair neatly styled. "And you don't have any regrets—about the years in between?"

"What kind of regrets?"

"You could have been lovers all along! You could have been happy all along!"

"No!" Harriet cried. "We couldn't have, don't you see? That was the problem. There was no way for us to be happy."

"But only because you set it up like that," I said, as excited as she was, wishing I could let it drop. "And if you loved each other, then you were living a lie anyway. What difference would it have made if you had consummated it?"

"All the difference," Harriet said sharply.

There was a pause.

She visibly pulled herself together. "Marilyn, I'm sorry. I guess I still feel upset about it, even now. . . . And it's what I said. I truly think if you haven't been in a similar situation, you can't imagine what it's like."

"A friend of mine was in the same situation," I stammered, "and she continued seeing the man and sleeping with him for fifteen years! In fact, they still do it and they're still both married . . . to 'good people.'"

I had thought she might flare up again, but she just said in her mild but firm Harriet-like way, "Well, if they can live with themselves, that's all that counts."

Later I looked over at Kevin. He's such a burly, beefy kind of man. I tried to imagine him and Harriet sitting together, looking at each other longingly, for fifteen years, like lovers in a Renaissance poem. *If they can live with themselves.* Sometimes I have the feeling that Benjy is there, at moments like this. He's in my head, I start describing what's happening to him even while it's happening.

After dinner we went to a movie. As we were getting our tickets, I noticed a woman staring at Mo. She was with someone, a man, but he was facing the other way, reading the review printed on the billboard. Finally, she came over to us. "Hi," she said, tapping Mo's shoulder. "How'd you like it?"

"We haven't seen it yet," Mo said. He introduced her to all of us. "This is Sasha Weinberg. My wife, Marilyn, my sister, Harriet, and her husband, Kevin, my mother, Leah, and her husband, Emil."

Sasha looked at me the longest. She smiled. "I'm so glad to meet you," she said. "Mo's talked about you so often."

Who the hell was she? Had he ever mentioned her? I couldn't

remember. "I'm glad to meet you too," I said, in case he had and I'd just forgotten.

She waved to the man she was with and he came over. He turned out to be her husband. "Very disappointing," he said.

"I liked it," Sasha said. "The beginning is a little slow."

"I think we better go in and get seats," Mo said. "It was nice to run into you."

As we entered the theater, I hissed, "Who was she?"

"Someone I knew in college. Sasha Weinberg. I've mentioned her, haven't I?"

"I don't think so," I said. "A girlfriend or what?"

"Just a friend." He smiled.

"I remember her," Leah said. "A very nice girl. . . . Who's that man she was with?"

"Her husband," Mo said.

"He looks like some kind of Indian."

"He is."

"Why'd she marry an Indian?" Leah said.

"I guess she fell in love with him," Mo said.

"I thought he was nice looking," Harriet said.

"She wasn't bad either," Kevin said, winking.

"If she lost ten pounds," I couldn't resist putting in. "Are you sure she's not an old girlfriend?"

"I swear," Mo said. "She's not my type."

"I thought you had catholic tastes."

"She's too exotic."

"Exotic? She just looked like a Jewish girl. What's so exotic about her?"

"The eyes," Kevin said.

Men! God, if you put eye makeup on a donkey, they'd call it exotic.

I liked the movie, but in the middle of it I fell asleep. I haven't been sleeping that well lately. I dreamed something about the woman, Sasha, but in the dream she looked like Aaron's Sonya also. They were both in our store, trying on clothes, and I was advising them on what to get. But when I went into the dressing room, one of

them was sitting there without any clothes on, just staring at herself
in the mirror. She only had one breast, like me. Suddenly she got
hysterical and said she was afraid she was dying. She was weeping,
pleading with me. . . . After that it all got blurry and then Mo was
shaking me. I blinked.

I shook my head, trying to pull myself together. "I'm sorry. . . . I
just—was it any good?"

We were staying at a hotel, the same one Mo always stays at when
he's in Boston. "You never mentioned anyone named Sasha Weinberg," I said as we were getting undressed.

"You just don't remember."

"What does she do?"

"Teaches sociology at Tufts." He started brushing his teeth.

"Well, I can tell you one thing, you went to bed with her once, at
least."

"How can you tell that?"

"The way she was looking at you."

He smiled. "Sorry to disappoint you. It was always strictly pla-
tonic. She used to like to tell me her problems. He lived in India.
They were engaged a long time."

"I think you're lying."

He spat out into the sink. "Okay, I was. . . . Actually, she used to
be a call girl in L.A. and I made it with her a couple of times out
there."

"*She* was a call girl?"

"Just for the summer."

"What summer?"

"Nineteen-sixty-one."

I looked at him. "We were married then."

"Right."

I got into the hotel bed. "Was that something you did often?"

"Occasionally, not all that often."

"What for?"

"Variety, whatever. . . ."

I knew I didn't have any right to feel jealous or even angry, but I
did. "You're lucky you didn't pick up any diseases."

"Yeah, I'm a lucky guy." Mo turned off the light and got into bed next to me.

We lay there in silence a few minutes.

"But you never became that attached to any of them?" I asked.

"No."

"You just saw them once and that was it?"

"I saw Sasha more than once. . . . She claims she was in love with me."

"When did she claim that?"

"Years later." He put his hand on my shoulder, caressing it. "Jealous?"

"Yes!" It came out more vehemently than I'd intended.

"Good," Mo said, letting his hand slide down my body.

In the middle of the night I got up to go to the bathroom. I wondered about those women Mo used to see, or maybe still does see. Was it that easy for him, never to become involved, no matter how exciting or good it was? I envy him for being able to be that detached, I hate him for that. Getting back into bed, I saw that he was half awake.

"I bet you did it with Liana too," I said.

"Who?"

"That woman who lived next door to us, the swimmer. You did it with her."

"Never."

"I know you did!" I cried. I felt suddenly excited and furious, as though she were right in the room with us.

"Sorry, I never laid a hand on her."

"Well, you wanted to."

"Sure, that's a different story." He yawned. "It was all so long ago."

"Why did you lie about Sasha? How can I tell when you're lying?"

"That was so long ago, Marilyn," he said again.

"That you can't remember?" My heart was beating too rapidly.

"It doesn't matter anymore. . . . What's the difference what either of us may have done when we were that young? Everyone does some crazy, dumb things."

What either of us have done. Crazy dumb things. I wished in a way the thing with Benjy was something that was over, that I could confess too and then feel wonderful, lighthearted, peaceful. If he had never called after our quarrel, by now maybe he would be just a vague memory. I remember getting out of bed that afternoon to answer the phone, hearing his voice and feeling the room spin around and around. For months I'd waited, hoping he'd call. But by then I'd stopped hoping. I'd even stopped thinking about him very much. I remember Blanche telling me how once their pediatrician told her one of her children had some very rare incurable disease. She went around thinking that was true for two whole days, then he called and said he'd gotten her child's chart mixed up with another child's. She said from then on every time she heard his voice, she started to shake, because he'd sounded the same both times, both the time he called to tell her the terrible news and the time he called to tell her it was a mistake.

"How did he do it?"

"He jumped out of a window." Benjy's voice was shaking. "Mar, he was my best friend."

"I know." Benjy's talked about Kipp so much over the years that I felt a strange kind of pang, though I'd never met him and don't think he ever knew I existed. "Will you fly out for the funeral?"

"Tomorrow. . . . We'll be back at the end of the week. God, why didn't he try and get in touch with me earlier?"

"Maybe it was beyond that. Maybe there wasn't anything to say."

"But he'd gotten better before! He should have known it was a mood."

"He's the one whose wife is in a wheelchair?"

"Yeah, God, poor Ariel. . . . But she's strong. I think she'll be okay." His voice sounded so flat and hopeless I didn't know what to say.

"Call me as soon as you get back," I said. "Don't—"

"Don't what?" he said sharply.

"Nothing."

It's hard for me to know how to judge Benjy's friendship with Kipp. Men seem so different with friends. Once he told me they never write to each other and often go a whole year without seeing each other or speaking on the phone. To me that could only happen if the friendship had gone dead. Otherwise I'd want that constant contact. I remember how once, before she was married, Jeanette had a job in Paris. Neither of us are much good at writing, and calling was so expensive. It was a horrible frustration. Once I called her impulsively and we talked for fifteen minutes. I was scared even to look at the phone bill.

But maybe, because it's a friendship that goes back so far, almost to childhood, and because Benjy doesn't have that many other friends, it means more to him than I realized. I know he and Becky give lots of dinner parties and he has colleagues at work that he's friendly with, but not with that kind of closeness. Maybe I'm jealous. I want to think of him being close to me and not to anyone else. I've always felt that about Becky and now even though he's no longer alive, Kipp suddenly seems like a rival, someone who possessed a part of Benjy that I didn't have.

We met Saturday at Ila's apartment. She still goes into the city to see Sloan, when they're in one of their "on" periods. It's still the most convenient place for us to meet, roughly halfway between where each of us lives. We went into the bedroom and undressed. Then Benjy lay there, naked, staring into space.

"I couldn't get over his wife," Benjy said.

"In what way?"

"She was so cool, so self-possessed. . . . Everyone else was screaming and going to pieces, and she just—I don't know."

I don't know the woman, but I felt angry on her behalf anyway. "Benjy, look, how do you think she coped all those years, being crippled, being married to someone who kept breaking down like that? It must have been a nightmare for her. . . . He probably needed a strong person like that."

"Yeah, right, he did," Benjy said in a monotone. "Strong women, wobbly men—the story of our age."

I hate it when he does that self-involved kind of generalizing. Am

I that strong? Is he that weak? I put my head on his shoulder. *"I'm not that strong,"* I said.

"Sure you are," he said. "Look at you! You started your own business, raised a family, you look after me. . . ."

I laughed. "I don't 'look after' you!"

"You tend to all my perverse and peculiar emotional and sexual needs."

"What's so perverse about them?"

"I think Dawn has the right idea," he said. "If I were a woman, I'd be gay."

That has to be one of the most peculiar remarks I've ever heard. *If I were a woman, I'd be gay?* "What does that *mean?*"

"I don't know." He put his hands over his face. "I just miss him! I miss him so much."

I touched him lightly. "I'm sorry, sweetie. Really."

"Did I tell you he called the night he did it? I was lying in bed, it was around three in the morning and I heard the phone ringing. The first time I was asleep and just as I woke up, it stopped. Then about five minutes later it started again. I was sure it was some crank call. We get them sometimes. I lay there and suddenly jumped out of bed and when I got there, the phone was dead."

"How could you have known? It could've been just a crank call. . . . Maybe it was."

"No, it was him. I know it. His calling twice. It even occurred to me, just for one second, but then I—" He broke off and began to sob.

I gathered him up in my arms. "Darling, don't. . . . Even if it *was* him, what could you have said? What could you have done? You'd talked to him before."

"Yeah, maybe it's an illusion, I could have saved him, just some piece of egomania? We were friends since we were thirteen. I'll never have that kind of closeness with anyone else. He was the only person who really knew me."

I recoiled. "What about me?"

"Men and women don't know each other. They can't."

"Why not? What do you mean?"

"Sex destroys it."

"That's horrible! It's not true. . . . I love you just as much as Kipp did."

"You love me, you hate me, whatever. . . . But you don't see me as I am."

"I do! How can you say that?"

"You don't know anything about me, really."

I felt so hurt I could hardly speak. "I do! I know *everything* about you!"

"You see me as I fit or don't fit into your life, not as an objective—"

"No one knows anyone 'objectively.' That doesn't make sense. . . . Look, I have friends too. I have Ila, Jeanette. But they aren't more important than you are. I still need you."

"They can't fuck you, that's all."

I felt so angry I wanted to hit him. But it seemed unfair when he was so upset. "That's *not* why I see you. . . . I love you as a *person.* I see you and understand you as much as Kipp ever did."

"He was right about us, about all of this. 'If it's bad why bother, and if it's good, it destroys your marriage.'"

"How has it destroyed your marriage? You have a wife who adores you! You've told me that a million times."

"Yeah, right. I have a wife who adores me," he said wearily.

"Your daughters love you, *I* love you. . . . If that isn't enough, there's something wrong."

"It isn't a whole!" he cried. "It doesn't fit together."

"Nothing does!" I cried. "That's just the way life is."

"I want it to fit together."

"It can't. . . . Don't be a baby, Benjy." I started kissing him. I really felt like biting him, not just playfully. I felt like seeing blood come spurting out, but instead I just kissed him all over, delicate, light, ironical kisses. He just lay there, like he was dead, and then in the middle suddenly he came to life and grabbed me. We made love but there was something desperate and ugly about it. When we were done, I started to cry.

Benjy didn't comfort me or caress me the way he usually does.

"Look, that's all I have in me for today, okay? I'm at the end of my rope. I don't feel understanding or kind or considerate. I don't feel like a human being."

I didn't say anything.

"Maybe he's better off," Benjy said. "Why am I feeling sorry for him?"

"Right, we'd all be better off dead," I said. "God, I hate it when you're like this! It's so dishonest. I hate it! I hate Kipp. Just because he's dead you're idealizing him beyond recognition. *I* love you, Becky loves you, your kids. . . . If all that isn't enough, you're just a selfish, spoiled, egomaniac."

Benjy laughed. "Thanks."

He went in to shower. Often I shower with him and it's fun, playful, soaping each other, washing each other's hair, but this time I stayed in bed the whole time. He came out looking clean and chastened. "I'll sit out back," he said.

I took a long hot shower, as hot as I could stand it, and somehow that helped. When I got out, the bathroom was so filled with steam, I couldn't see, but I felt better. After I got dressed, I went outside and found Benjy reading in Ila's backyard.

"Is Jeanette married?" he said. He had fixed two glasses of iced tea with ice in them.

"Yeah. . . . Her husband's a writer—playwright. He doesn't earn a lot."

"So how do they live?"

"She's always worked."

I wondered why he was asking. Maybe he just wanted to get off on a detached topic, if there was one. "I had a wonderful shower," I said. I felt like the anger had drained out of me.

"Me too." He smiled and held out his hand.

We didn't try to talk or "resolve" anything. We just sat there for a while in the garden, holding hands, drinking our iced tea. In a way, I wished we hadn't made love, at least not that way.

All week I kept thinking of our argument. We shouldn't have met so soon after he got back probably. Benjy claims I don't know him. But I think I know him enough to know that when he gets into a down cycle like that, he just lets himself spin down, like someone deliberately taking his feet off the brakes. I think I've always tried so hard to control my feelings when I'm feeling down that I half admire Benjy for letting go that way and at other times feel angry at the self-indulgence of it. If you think about anything long enough, it becomes depressing, just like saying a word over and over till it loses its meaning. But also, I think he's wrong. Maybe in the beginning sex does what he said, disguises things, blurs them, but after fifteen years? What is there about Benjy that Kipp knew and I don't? So Kipp knew him when he was fat and felt an outcast! So Jeanette knew *me* when my hair was light brown and I was a virgin! Does that mean she's closer to some "inner truth" about my personality?

Ila and I hardly have time to talk during the day, especially Saturdays, when the store is busy. But I drove her home after work and told her about Kipp and the argument I'd had with Benjy.

"Oh, men need those illusions," she said. "Let them have them."

"Which ones?"

"All that male bonding crap. . . . The fact is, when they're together they sit around asking each other who they'll vote for and whether the price of gas has gone up, but they think there's something mysterious, deep, and real about it."

"But maybe it's not like that. We don't know."

"Hon, I had three older brothers and half the time they didn't know I was there. I sat around listening to all their talk, about women, about sports, about hunting . . . and I don't think one meaningful, honest word was spoken."

"Well . . ." Maybe because I never had a brother or men friends and my father was so silent, what men are like when women aren't around has always been mysterious to me. "But how about the thing that if you're having sex with someone you don't see them clearly? Do you think that's true?"

"No. . . . Sloan shows me sides of himself he wouldn't show to another man if a gun was put to his head. Not sexual things. I think the sexual closeness is the only thing that makes most of them really let down their guard." She crushed out her cigarette. "Your mistake was picking a fight when he was feeling down. Just let him babble on if it makes him feel better."

"Maybe I should've." But that seems demeaning to Benjy, not taking what he says seriously enough to even argue about it.

"When Sloan gets what I call his 'monthlies,' I just have to sit there and listen to gloom and doom nonstop for twenty-four hours, about his career, the modern world, civilization. I could recite it all to you backward in my sleep! . . . It's probably hormonal, who knows. Me, I just want to pay my bills, have a few good times in bed, read an occasional super thriller, and feel the business is going okay."

I kissed her. "Me too. . . . Does that show we have petty minds?"

"Probably. . . . See you Monday, hon." She got out of the car and walked into her house.

At home I did some scurrying around, getting dinner ready. Aaron and Sonya were coming over, and though I know I don't need to go all out for them, she's such a terrific cook, usually I try to fix something a little special. At six Mo came down. He'd been napping upstairs. "They're not coming," he said.

"How come?"

"It sounded like they had a fight. . . . Aaron said he might drop over alone later."

I was taken aback. "What did he say?"

He yawned. "I can't remember. I was sleeping when he called. He'll tell us when he's here."

"Did he sound upset?"

"Mar, relax. . . . He's a big boy now. He can take care of his own life."

I wish I really believed that. I know Mo thinks Linus is the "vulnerable" one and Aaron is too defensive and sarcastic, but I think Linus has a kind of detached, calm, complete-unto-himself quality which removes him from things. I worry more about Aaron. But Mo's right. He's in his twenties now, not a kid.

Still, all through dinner I felt preoccupied and wished I had been there when Aaron called. Usually I can tell just from the sound of his voice how serious something is. We finished supper, Mo settled down to watch something on TV, and I started cleaning up the kitchen when the doorbell rang.

Aaron was alone. I hugged him. "You missed a good dinner."

"Yeah, well. . . . Where's Dad?"

"In the den, watching TV. Should I get him?"

"Let him finish watching." He followed me into the kitchen. "Any coffee left over?"

I poured him some. "I made something gourmet-ish because Sonya always fixes such terrific meals."

"Well, you can go back to hamburgers," he said. "We're not seeing each other anymore." He looked ready to cry.

"I'm so sorry, hon. She—"

"She's a bitch."

"In what way? We always liked her." Only half true, but still.

"She sees other guys. . . . Well, one really. Someone from before she was married. She's been seeing him all along!"

"When?"

"Afternoons, when I wasn't there. . . . Some old guy, forty-eight or something. She says he's a 'father figure' for her. Only he's fucking her so I guess it's not exactly. . . . Look, who cares?"

"I think she loved you," I said hesitantly. "You can't fake that."

He shrugged. "I don't know."

"She did, Aaron."

His eyes were blazing. "Mom, listen, I don't care, okay? It's over! I'm never going to see her again."

"What about Sean? He always seemed so fond of you."

His face softened. "Yeah, well, I don't know. . . . I can't see him without seeing her so. . . . At least if she'd told me! I told her whenever I saw someone, girls from college, whatever. Once I even slept with one of them and I told her and all she said was, 'I understand,' and I thought: wow, isn't she bighearted?" He laughed bitterly.

"I guess she must have felt mixed."

"I guess."

The phone rang. I answered it. Sonya's voice said, "Mrs. Greene?"

"Yes?"

"I wondered if Aaron was there."

"Uh, sure." I put my hand over the phone. "It's her."

He leaped up. "Tell her to jump off a bridge." He walked out of the room.

"He. . . . Maybe you'd better call him later," I said.

"I guess he's really angry," Sonya said in her soft, caressing voice. "I'm so sorry. I care for him so much, still. I didn't want to hurt him."

"I think he is hurt."

"I really thought my relationship with George was over," she went on. "I wasn't being deceitful. . . . Or maybe it was more I thought I could keep them separate."

My mouth felt dry. "He felt you should have been more honest. He says he told *you* whenever *he* saw someone else."

Her voice got lower. "Yes, I should've. . . . He's so young! I really didn't . . . I do love him, but he's right. Give him my love, anyway."

"Okay." I tried to feel angry at her, for Aaron's sake, and couldn't. I just stood there, knowing how she felt, and wishing I'd been more sympathetic on the phone.

Mo and Aaron were watching the end of a movie. A commercial was on for life insurance. "She said—" I began.

Aaron put his hand up. "I don't *care* what she said! She's just a stupid, lying bitch!"

"That's not true!" I said sharply. "She cares for you a lot. The other man was someone she's known for a long time."

Aaron turned on me. "Mom, look, will you stay out of it? You don't know anything about it. . . . She lied to me around nine dozen times, about lots of things, not just him."

"That doesn't mean she didn't love you."

Mo turned off the TV. "Christ, how can I concentrate with the two of you going on like this? Aaron, look it's water under the bridge. She took you, you've learned a lesson. On to the next!"

"That's a horrible way to put it!" I said. "She didn't 'take' him. In what way? She fell in *love* with him!" To Aaron I said, "She probably realized eventually you'd find someone your own age. She was trying to protect herself."

"Bullshit," Mo said.

"Yeah, Mom, I don't get it," Aaron said. "Why're you defending her? You don't know a damn thing about her."

"I'm just saying she wasn't a bitch. Not all women are bitches."

"I didn't say *all* women were bitches. I said *she* was. . . . What do you call someone who lies to you and fucks other guys behind your back?"

"I—I don't know," I stammered.

Aaron laughed. "Okay, I'll use another word. She's a whore, okay? How's that?"

I sat down. "It sounds so ugly," I said helplessly.

His voice rose. "But how about what she did? That wasn't ugly? I mean, here I was, meeting girls at work, really nice, pretty, smart girls, and telling all of them right off I wasn't available . . . and she's making it with this guy who's practically Dad's age!"

"She has good taste," Mo said dryly. "A lot of women like older men."

Aaron jumped up. "Well, the two of you are a big comfort," he said. "Thanks a lot."

I ran after him. "Honey, stay. . . . We were just . . ."

"Listen, I'm tired. I have to go home. I'll speak to you." He was out the door before I could stop him.

Mo was still in the den, leaning back in his reclining chair, his eyes closed. "Why am I so sleepy?" he said. "I had that nap."

"I feel so bad," I said. "He seems so hurt."

"He'll recover. . . . Look, there are a million women like that in the world. So, he'll wise up a little. He'll get a tougher skin."

"I think she loves him."

"Maybe."

Mo is always like this with the boys, so detached and cynical, almost. Benjy is probably too much the opposite with his daughters, worrying, always concerned, but I wish Mo had some of that. I don't want Aaron and Linus to become cynical about women, expecting the worst, putting them down automatically. "Well, I guess he'll be better off in the long run with someone his own age," I said.

"Sure," Mo said. "Want to bet he'll be in the sack with someone by the end of the week? He's good-looking. He won't even remember her by the end of the month."

"I think he takes things more seriously than that."

Mo shrugged.

"I *want* him to take things more seriously," I said. "Not just hop from girl to girl without even—"

"He's a kid. That's what youth is for, hopping from girl to girl. When he's thirty, he can find someone good and settle down."

"Look at Linus. . . . He isn't doing that."

"Li is different. He's a funny person. I don't think sex is all that important to him."

I don't know if it's because he's my son, but I hate thinking of Aaron being the way Mo was at that age, just seducing girl after girl and then moving on. I don't think he *is* like that.

"At least we don't have daughters," Mo said. "I hate to even think what *that* would be like."

"Why would that be so bad?" I said. "I wish we *did* have one. I would have loved to have a daughter."

He shook his head. "Ten times more trouble. They get pregnant, they can get raped, you don't have a moment's peace, worrying what kind of mess they're involved with."

"Well, I hope we have granddaughters anyway."

Mo smiled. "Don't get your hopes up. I don't think it's going to happen tomorrow."

"Maybe not tomorrow, but eventually."

I always imagined it would be Aaron who married first. He was the first to be interested in girls. Linus always seemed so vague, dreamy, out of it. But when he and Petra stopped over a few weeks later and Ila had dinner with us, I heard him saying to her, "My wife and I've both applied to MIT for grad school."

I came rushing into the living room, not sure I'd heard him right. "Are you married?"

Linus blushed. "Yeah, well. . . . We figured why not."

I looked at Ila. We both laughed. "When? You never mentioned it!"

"A couple of weeks ago. . . . I'm sorry, Mom. I *was* going to mention it, but I figured we'd be seeing you so soon."

"Do your parents know?" I asked Petra, who was sitting cross-legged on the floor in jeans and a sweatshirt drinking beer.

"Yeah, I told them last week. They were pretty good about it.

I think they were relieved, even. I was always such an oddball, I think they were afraid I'd never get married." She laughed good-naturedly.

I felt a pang of disappointment that there had been no wedding, no party. "We could have a party for you if you like," I suggested hopefully.

"No, that's okay," Linus said. "I mean, it's no big deal, basically. We were living together anyway. It just seemed easier."

"You're a mother-in-law!" Ila said, hugging me.

"God, right." I bent down and kissed Petra. "I'm really happy."

Ila said, "We ought to have some champagne. . . . Should I run out and get some?"

"We don't drink it," Linus said apologetically. "But if *you* want some . . ."

Petra raised her beer can. "I'm fine with this."

I went into the kitchen and poured some white wine for Ila and myself. We clinked glasses. I touched my glass to Petra's and Linus's beer cans. "Happy marriage," I said.

"I figure we probably will," Petra said. "Mom and Dad have been together since they were sixteen and you and Mr. Greene have been married a long time too, haven't you?"

"Twenty-five years."

"My grandparents just had their sixtieth." She munched on a handful of peanuts from a bowl next to her. "I sort of thought it might feel different, but it doesn't so far."

I swallowed. "Do you ever think of . . . kids?"

"Hey Mom, slow down," Linus said. "We just got married last month."

I turned red. "I just meant in general, not right away."

"Grandmother fever," Ila said. She looked gracious and lovely in her white suit.

"Yeah, I'd like a kid," Petra said. "How about you, Li?"

"Sure, but not this very second."

Petra jumped up and hugged him from behind. She practically only comes up to his waist. "I have to be careful because I come from one of those families where they just look at each other and bingo! But I'm on the pill so . . ."

I kept thinking of Benjy's family, of Becky planning the big wedding for Chelsea, inviting all their friends. Probably they'll have it at her father's mansion in the country, bridesmaids, everything. I finished my wine. "You're both so calm and sensible about it," I told them. "The night I got engaged, I went *crazy* I was so excited! I couldn't think of anything else for a week."

"Our generation was crazy," Ila said. "I slept with some guy a few times and when he wouldn't marry me, I really thought of killing myself! I thought life was over. And I was twenty, twenty-one."

I think Ila's right, but I wonder if there wasn't more excitement to it for us just because of those illusions. I remembered myself in the white dress I'd picked after trying on dozens, my cheeks flaming, feeling so excited seeing Mo standing beside me that I thought I might faint. Even our honeymoon was just the way I'd envisioned and wanted it. We did have champagne in our room, making love did seem special (though maybe it helped that we'd done it before).

"My sister got married in this huge, big-deal wedding," Petra said, "and a year later she had it annulled. My parents had such a fit! They practically wanted her to stay married to this guy, who was really crazy, just to justify spending a load on the wedding."

"Same with me," Ila said. "My parents were poor, really poor, and they blew half their savings on a big wedding. When I came to them and told them Frank and I were getting divorced, it was 'How can you do this to us?' I said, 'Look, you did it for *you*. You have the album, the photos. I can't live the rest of my life for you.'"

"That's what my sister said," Petra agreed. "She said, 'It's *my* life.' But Mom and Dad almost died. They said the next time around, even if she marries the King of Spain, they won't spend a cent for the wedding or even go to it."

"You and Dad aren't like that," Linus said to me. "You don't care about all that, do you?"

I knew he was saying it approvingly so all I could say was, "No, we just wanted you to do it however you wanted."

Petra was beaming at me. "That's so great, that you're so liberal and all. I mean, like, with my parents, all three of my sisters and me weren't virgins when we got married, but if you even mention that to my mother, she starts running around in little circles and screaming. She won't even discuss it! It's so primitive."

"I think we've got the same mother," Ila said. "You'd think it would be the fathers."

My mother thought I was a virgin too. But I never would have thought of trying to tell her the truth, even about having done it with Mo before the wedding. I told them quickly about Aaron since he was coming over later. Petra and Linus had met Sonya once.

"Well, he'll meet someone else," Linus said gently. He's very sweet about Aaron, as though Aaron were the younger of the two of them.

"She didn't *look* thirty-eight," Petra said. "But it was weird her having that kid who was ten."

"I think Sean'll really miss him," I said. "Aaron was like a step-father and a brother rolled into one."

"But she was too old," Petra said. "I mean, eventually, he'd have met someone his own age, don't you think?"

"Yeah, I do," I said.

"It's European," Ila said, sipping her wine. "Over there they're big on that, the woman being older and initiating the man."

"I saw a movie about that once," I said. *"Devil in the Flesh."* God, fifteen years ago! Can it have been that long? I was wearing my leopard dress. We'd made love three times and that was all I could think of during the movie, even though I was sitting next to Benjy's father. I was sure he could tell, the minute he looked at me. And Benjy getting so hysterical. *This is the worst thing that's ever happened to me.*

"I never did it," Ila said. "Every man I've ever liked was about my own age, maybe five years older at most. You'd end up mothering them all the time. Men are such babies anyway!"

Petra nuzzled up against Linus. "Baby," she whispered affectionately.

Linus looked embarrassed. "I think that's a stereotype," he said stiffly.

Petra smiled. "I'm the older woman. I'm eight months older than him."

Linus squeezed her. "And she never lets me forget it."

They seemed so relaxed and good together that I couldn't feel too regretful about the wedding. I told Mo as soon as he walked in the door. He looked startled. "So, we're in-laws," I said gaily. The wine had made me cheerful. I felt good.

"Jesus. . . . I should've stopped off for champagne."

"They don't drink it."

Mo gave Linus and Petra each bear hugs. "You really surprised us," he said. "We thought kids like you just lived together for years."

"Maybe it's my Ohio upbringing," Petra said. "I have this, like, conventional streak."

"I like being married," Linus admitted. "I like saying 'My wife. . . .'"

"There was this girl," Petra said, "in our class and every time I was sick, she'd sit next to Li in class, ask to borrow his notes. So the day after we were married, I came in and asked her if I could borrow her pencil. She saw my wedding ring and almost died." She laughed.

"Well, she didn't really—" Linus began, abashed.

"Yes, she did!" Petra insisted. "God, that college is just full of these horny, rapacious girls. You can't imagine."

Mo smiled. "Sounds like fun. . . . It wasn't like that in my day."

I touched his hand. "Poor sweetie. . . . What did you have to do, get down on bended knee and swear undying love just to get kissed?"

"Practically. . . . You couldn't get through a first date without being grilled about what you thought about marriage."

"*I* never did that," I said, teasing him.

"Didn't you?"

"No. . . . I didn't even *want* to get married. Jeanette and I were going to go around the world and meet men who looked like Cary Grant."

"That's right," Mo said. "You were cool. It was cute. . . . Remember the night you cut your hair?"

I turned bright red, maybe because Linus and Petra were there. "Well. . . ."

"She was a knock-out," Mo said. "Absolutely."

"I think Mom's still very beautiful," Linus said, so gravely and sweetly that I had to bite my lips to keep from crying.

"I'll be fifty in a few years," I said mournfully.

I wonder what it would be like if I could be my same age, forty-five, and look the way I did at thirty. Would it make any difference? Is there anything I want that I could get with looks? Not that I can think of.

Aaron arrived just as we were sitting down to eat. I'd just made a pot roast, not thinking it would be anything more than a family dinner. It's Linus's favorite. "Sorry I'm late," Aaron said, taking his seat. "Hi Li, hi Petra."

"They're married," I said, doling out carrots and onions.

Aaron laughed. "No kidding! You really did it?"

Linus shrugged. "Just a civil ceremony. It only took a couple of minutes."

Aaron looked good-naturedly puzzled. "What does this make me? An uncle?"

"You can't be an uncle until they have kids," Ila said.

"You're a brother-in-law," Petra said. "You're my brother-in-law."

He jumped up and kissed her. "Congratulations."

Linus said, "I always thought you'd get married first somehow. . . . Maybe because you did everything else first."

Aaron reached for a roll. "I'm not in any hurry."

"He's like me," Mo said. "He wants to play the field awhile."

A conflicted, pained expression crossed Aaron's face and then disappeared. "I met a nice girl at work," he said. "I mean, I knew her already, but. . . . I would've brought her except, well . . ."

"I'm sorry about Sonya," Petra said suddenly.

He kept on eating. "It's fine. We're still friends."

"Are you?" I asked, surprised.

"Yeah. . . . I went over and saw Sean today. I guess she wants someone who can really take care of her, pay the bills, all that stuff."

"An old-fashioned girl," Mo said ironically.

"She was a good cook," I said.

"Too much paprika," Mo said. "Yeah, but she was good."

Aaron smiled. "I gained eight pounds. . . . I've started running again, to get it off."

"You look fine, honey," I said.

I felt so proud of both of them. Maybe it was just being a little high, but when I think back to when they were teenagers, the stormy scenes, Mo's being sure Aaron was smoking pot, my getting hysterical the time Mo took Linus to that call girl in Boston, Aaron getting such terrible scores on his SATs—it all seems so far away. Here they are, grown-ups almost. I thought how if I'd married Benjy, this scene would never have taken place. Or if it had, it wouldn't have been the same. How could Benjy have cared, really, about either of my sons, when he had four girls of his own? He might've been good and tried to be fair, but I wonder if you can really feel anything that deep for anyone's kids but your own. I don't think I could.

I glanced over at Ila. She's told me that knowing our family so well is almost like having one of her own. She had a hysterectomy while she was married, probably an unnecessary one, and her husband never wanted to adopt. She seems fine about it, not devoured by regrets, but she once told me Aaron was the kind of son she wished she'd had, if she'd had one. She said he even looks a little like her ex-husband.

Over dessert, Aaron said playfully to Petra, "So, when're you going to make me an uncle?"

"Bite your tongue," Petra said. "We're getting our doctorates. We've got more to think about than making you an uncle."

"I want to be an uncle," Aaron said, pretending to pout. "I always felt like Sean's uncle."

"Get married yourself," Linus said. "Have your own kids."

Aaron wrinkled his nose. "Having your own is trickier. . . . Anyhow, I don't even have a girl yet."

"Do you want one?" Petra said. "We could fix you up with a million girls, if you want."

"Who?" Linus asked.

"Liza, Annabel, Carrie. . . ."

"They're not his type," Linus said. "Anyway, that never works. I just went on one blind date and it was a disaster."

"I'll find someone eventually," Aaron said.

"Eventually is the right idea," Mo said. "Look before you leap."

"Don't worry, Dad," Aaron said dryly.

The three of them went into the den to watch something on TV. Ila said she had to be going. "You have super kids," she told us.

After she'd left, I said. "I'm sorry she didn't have any of her own."

"She seems more of a career woman type," Mo said. He never likes discussing might-have-beens.

"Are you pleased?" I asked. "About Li and Petra?"

"She's a nice kid. They seem a little young, but—"

"She's almost the same age I was when I did it," I reminded him.

"Yeah, you were a child bride, weren't you?" he said, smiling. "God, I feel beat. Maybe I'll just turn in right now."

He looks so gray! Mo's hair stayed dark till he was almost fifty, but in the last few years it's changed rapidly. Whereas Benjy looks almost the way he did when I met him, the thick gray-white hair, the soft dark eyes. Mo went upstairs to get ready for bed. It was only nine-thirty. I didn't feel sleepy. It's hard for me to fall asleep before eleven. I fiddled around in the kitchen for a while, wishing I'd asked Ila to stay longer.

Aaron came out of the den. "Gotta go." He kissed me. "Great meal, Mom. Speak to you."

Linus and Petra were lying on the floor. She was resting her head in his lap. They were watching a science special, both intent on the screen. I came in and sat in the big chair, envying their closeness, their youngness, their being in the same field, seeming so affectionate, starting off as friends as well as lovers. Have Mo and I ever been friends? I don't think so. Yet I know we have what anyone would consider a happy marriage.

I helped them unfold the sleep couch and put on the sheets. Petra took a small box of birth control pills out of her bag and swallowed one with a glass of juice she'd gotten from the kitchen. "I used to have a diaphragm," she said, "but it broke down on me. . . . I mean, I got pregnant, even with it in. So after that—"

"When was that?" She looks so young to have been pregnant.

"Last year. . . . Li said why not have it, but I wasn't ready. I mean, I know he'll be a great father and all, but I wouldn't want to start off that way."

"I have an IUD and I got pregnant with it in too," I said. "Or maybe it fell out. They were never sure."

"Before they were born?"

"No, three years ago."

She looked surprised. I probably seem so old to her to be getting pregnant. But I'm still getting my period. Luckily, maybe, I never found out about being pregnant until it was over. I thought it might be early menopause because my period was so late. Then, when it came, I was bleeding so heavily, big clumps of blood, that I got a little scared. And suddenly a huge lump fell out. I took it to the gynecologist and he said in his dry, ironical way, "Yes, this appears to be nature's way of perpetuating the species."

I came home, afterward, and felt strange and sad for a week afterward. It could have been Benjy's, I guess, but that wasn't why I felt sad, though I suppose deep down part of me would've liked to have a child with him. I remember once—it seems so crazy now—I even thought I'd do it, get pregnant on purpose, without telling him. Just have sex with him when I thought I was fertile, but raise it with Mo. I had it all planned in my head, how I would never tell either of them, how it would be my "secret." And then I realized how dumb and impossible that would be, how torn and weird I'd feel raising a kid with Benjy's face, eyes, movements.

"Did you think of having it?" Petra asked, tossing out the pillows.

"No." I told her how it happened. "I'd have been in my sixties when it was ready for college. Mo would've been in his seventies. I always felt sorry for kids like that, with such old parents. My best friend from high school, Jeanette, her parents were old and she hated it. They looked like grandparents."

Linus was in his pajamas. He looked thin and gawky, his glasses off. "So, sleep well, Mom," he said.

"You too, both of you."

I went upstairs quietly. Mo usually falls asleep the second he hits the pillow. I've always envied that. No, it was true, I didn't have any regrets three years ago when it happened, but I did feel a certain sadness when I realized that I wouldn't get pregnant again. When I was a teenager and for years later, I hated getting my period so much, the cramps, the smell, everything. And now, knowing it'll just be for a couple more years, I almost like it. I don't want it to stop.

Benjy could have had five kids if Becky hadn't miscarried that time. Was it going to be a boy? I can't remember. I think she had amniocentesis. No, another girl, I think. "I'm fated to have girls," he said. I started daydreaming about the baby I'd almost had, showing it to Benjy. It was a boy and he looked surprised, delighted. The only thing Becky hadn't been able to do for him. We looked through the Name Your Baby book together. After his father? But his father's still alive.

In his sleep, Mo rolled over and put his arms around me. "Are you sleeping?" I whispered.

He murmured something I couldn't understand.

Father of the Bride

"*D*o you want me to go with you?" Kelly asked.

"No, I can handle it . . . unless you're going to be anywhere near there after lunch."

"No problem. How's three? Bring the drawings, okay?"

In the last two months the firm I work for has split asunder. Two of the biggies went off to merge with a much larger outfit. Some of us were asked to join them; I was one of them. I declined, partly because I feel more comfortable in a smaller firm. What remains is a slightly younger group, a motley assemblage. Our first meetings were a combination of nervous exhilaration and pure panic. We decided to consolidate, stick to what we'd already been doing, office furniture, and maybe expand into interior decorating just a little. If we keep it small, we'll have control, was the idea. Kelly Merrill has only been with the firm for a year. She's single, energetic, full of ideas. She claimed she was glad to see the others go, that they were "sexist as well as overbearing and obnoxious."

I feel mixed. Before, I was one of several vice-presidents around my age. Now suddenly I have a kind of spurious authority born of being one of the oldest and the one who's been with the firm for the longest time. None of them even knows about my shaky credentials, how I started out as a lawyer. They mainly know me through the limited success I've had with certain designs, among them a chair shaped like a baseball glove. I designed it originally for a businessman with back trouble. It caught on for kids' rooms and we now produce it in vinyl, leather, all colors. Marilyn and I fucked in it a few times at the office on weekends. Whenever I see it, I remember that. A warm day, our skin sticking to the leather, the two of us in a round, panting ball. Maybe it's been used for that purpose by others, who knows.

I can't say that the field would have been different if I'd remained a lawyer. But every half decade or so I've had some kind of minor inspiration which, combined with some luck, has pushed my career further along. Once it was a modular wall system which we were importing from Europe. I discovered because we had it at home that the parts holding it together were impossible to get in the U.S. If it broke down, the whole thing was useless or had to be partially dismantled. I tinkered around and ultimately came up with a version where we could use American-made parts. A few years later there were half a dozen companies producing variations on the same product, but because we came up with it first, we had a head start which worked very much to our advantage.

From the obsequious attitudes of some of the younger employees, I realize I am that dreaded object, a "boss," someone with authority and power. I don't revel in it and it often makes me queasy to witness the amount of gratuitous cruelty on the part of many who do. I have a colleague who comes in all aglow after firing someone, literally rubbing his hands together and exclaiming, "There'll be blood all over the floor!" I don't have the killer instinct or whatever it is that drives so many men my age to work around the clock. But I guess I'm enough of a plodder, with enough wit and imagination that I don't have to sit around worrying about having to relocate to Oklahoma City either. A major relief.

A movie star, a moderately famous one, based in New York, currently in a Broadway play, commissioned us to redo part of her gigantic penthouse on Riverside Drive. Married three times, she's adopted or acquired through one means or another, a veritable horde of children, six or seven, maybe even eight. Gemma Carucci. She's American born and bred, but I think her father, a well-known director, was Italian. I was taken aback when she opened the door.

She was taller than I expected, almost my height. In films, she's a funny combination of an earth mother and a waif. Very white skin, frizzy, angelic, dark red hair that stands out in all directions, streaming almost to her waist, a soft, uncertain voice. "Mr. Fetterman?"

"Yes." I walked past her into the brilliantly sun-filled living room. Some preteenaged kids were lying on the floor, playing a board game. Somewhere else in the apartment someone was practicing the piano.

"It's so kind of you to come here. I hope I haven't put you to any trouble."

"Not at all."

I followed her through the apartment as she described what she wanted done, what the problems were. "When we took the apartment, we never thought we'd be here so long. The children were almost babies then. But now that it looks like a permanent arrangement, we have to have real working space for all of them."

"I have four of my own," I said, "so I know what it's like. Of course, we live in a house so it's somewhat easier."

"What do you have? Boys? Girls?" She looked genuinely interested.

"All girls."

She smiled. There was just a trace of fine wrinkles around her eyes—maybe it was that her skin was so delicate you could almost see through it. Extraordinary eyes—pale blue, limpid. "I had all boys, but I'm raising three of my sister's. She died in a car crash five years ago, and her husband wasn't able to cope. . . . And then my boyfriend has one of his own that he shares with his wife. Complications!"

Kelly had said Gemma's boyfriend Nicky was in his twenties, a rock musician. There was no sign of him around the apartment. "You don't look old enough to have so many," I said, feeling awkward. You had the feeling she'd heard every compliment and come-on line that had ever been invented. I'm not at ease with women this beautiful at the best of times, even when they're not movie stars.

"Oh, I'm old enough," she said. "I'm thirty-nine."

"Well, you look much younger."

"It's probably living with Nicky," she said with a smile. "He keeps me young. He has so much energy. This morning he was up at five. He runs four times around the reservoir!"

Running made me think of Kipp. He used to run every morning when we were in college. He died four months ago. Yet I still find I think about him all the time. It's almost an obsession. Curious when for years, while he was alive, I would often not think of him for months. We were both so bad at writing letters, and just picking up the phone and calling him, for no reason, seemed peculiar. Yet, whenever we would talk, no matter how much time had elapsed, we could pick up instantly, as though we'd been in touch every day. What was so valuable to me in Kipp, which I doubt I'll ever find in anyone again, was that he saw through me totally. He had a kind of merciless regard for the truth, not a vicious thing, but, maybe from having known me so long, he could tear past every rationalization I could invent, every idiotic excuse. And yet I felt he loved me. It wasn't like some shrink peeling away the layers just so you could lie there, bare, screaming at your own stupidity. Maybe that was what did him in finally, that he didn't allow himself, either, any excuses.

I keep circling and circling around the fact of his death, wanting to find a reason, a way of seeing it that would make it inevitable. I don't want to think that if only I'd answered the phone that night, he'd still be here. And then I think of so many people I've known, half the people at work, who seem as crazy as Kipp ever was and yet are still functioning. His marriage? But I always felt he needed Ariel, though he had ambivalent feelings about her resourcefulness. I remember that student he told me about, the zither player with the crystal ball. What if he'd broken down, had an affair with her. . . . But he couldn't have. And, as I know as well as anyone on the face of the earth, that creates as many problems as it solves.

I want him back to talk to or maybe all I want is the knowledge that he's there, that I *could* talk to him if I wanted. It's strange that, in all these years, I never actually told him about Marilyn. Why? He was totally noncensorious. No one would have understood better. I just couldn't. Maybe, though I knew it was a lie, I wanted to preserve that feeling he always had that *my* life made sense, that his was messy and fragmented but mine was some kind of whole. Oh Christ, vanity, cowardice, deceit, spiraling outward like waves, never ending.

The designs were spread out on the table. Gemma was looking through them. She has a loveliness which filled the room, almost like a perfume. I don't think I'm reacting to her sexually, but only in that, in any real sense, she's beyond the pale. Has she done it with hundreds of men? Does she love this young kid she's living with? "I'm not quite sure I understand how this will fit into the space," she said, looking up. "Could you explain?"

I took her back to the three rooms in question and was explaining where everything would go, when the bell rang. It was Kelly. Normally, I think of Kelly as a knockout, but suddenly she looked pretty ordinary with her freckles and angular features, boyishly short red hair. "I was just taking Ms. Carucci through the plans."

"Oh, let me explain something," Kelly said. The two of them went to the back of the house again. I went to the window and looked down. We were on the twentieth floor, a penthouse overlooking Riverside Park. The Hudson below, a large boat moving slowly downstream. A view as dramatic as the one from my parents' apartment in the Eldorado. Why is my father alive at eighty-one and Kipp dead? Where is the justice in that? A flicker of rage went through me. I began feeling strange, almost faint, and sat down abruptly, my head in my hands.

When I went for a checkup a year ago, the doctor said my blood pressure was way out of control and put me on some pills. Maybe it's the pills, adjusting to them, but I still feel lousy. Those moments of sudden weakness, like my knees are going to buckle. Once in a meeting I actually thought I was going to faint and it scared me. He gave me all the usual bullshit. Avoid stress. Tell me how, doctor. And the very next day I had that stupid fight with Marilyn. I try so hard, with Marilyn, with the kids, at work, to keep it all in, but it's hard. These hideous black moods rise up and overwhelm me; I don't seem to have the energy to fight them. Becky, as always, is understanding. Midlife crisis, Kipp's death, the firm reorganizing. God, I've been having a midlife crisis since I was born! When is it going to end?

"Can I offer you both a drink? Tea? Coffee?" Gemma and Kelly were back, both looking pleased.

Kelly asked for Scotch. I decided to stick to tea.

"Do you work together often, as a team?" Gemma asked, setting down our drinks.

We explained about the reorganization.

"Benjy's an old pro," Kelly said. "I've just started. . . . I thought I wanted to be an illustrator, do *New Yorker* covers. But I don't think I have the gift."

"I used to want to paint," Gemma said, stirring her tea. "But my father said: absolutely not unless you're a genius. It's odd because with acting, directing, he said it was all a con game, but about some things, like art, he was *so* severe! And we all listened to him."

"I know!" Kelly said. "Why do fathers *do* that? And why are we so malleable? Do you do it, Benjy, with your kids?"

"Not at all," I said. "Whatever they want to do is fine with me."

"What *do* they want to do?" Gemma asked. "Or are they too young to be thinking about it?"

There was something really entrancing in the way she asked questions, even though you knew it was a learned, much practiced manner. As though her life depended on the answer . . . and those lovely eyes. "My oldest daughter is getting her M.B.A. And the second, Dawn, wants to write. She's written some wonderful poems but—well, it's not a very practical way to earn a living."

"Maybe she'll be famous," Gemma suggested. "Maybe she'll be a famous poet like Dylan Thomas."

"I, well. . . . I'd like her to settle down a little. She—"

"Does she have a boyfriend?" Kelly asked. "Isn't she the beautiful one?" Dawn had come to the office once.

"She's had several." I hesitated. "Right now she's in love with another woman. My wife's very upset about it."

"Oh, that's a stage," Gemma said carelessly, brushing back her hair. "Everybody goes through that. Men are such a bother, you think—I'll try women. But that's just as complicated."

Kelly laughed. "Wow, you sound so blithe about it. I had a crush on a woman teacher in college and I wanted to kill myself, I felt so ashamed."

"Have you ever loved a man?" Gemma asked me.

I was startled. "Loved as . . . in what way?"

"In any way."

They were both staring at me. For some reason my heart started beating too rapidly. I felt the presence of Kipp, his reactions to the two of them. He would pick Kelly. Gemma would terrify him. "I've had close friends, but it's never been a sexual thing . . . as far as I know."

"Nicky has a friend from his childhood," Gemma said, "and they're still so close. He's just a shoemaker—he lives in Holland where Nicky grew up—and they still have this extraordinary bond."

"I'd be jealous of that," Kelly said. After a second she added, "I'm a very jealous person."

We went over the plans again and departed at four-thirty. Outside it was gray, mild, misty.

"What'd you think?" Kelly said, the minute we were outside.

"Of what?"

"Her, the apartment, everything!"

"She's really lovely." I couldn't go beyond that.

"But would you really want to fuck her, if you had the chance? There's something sort of cold about her."

I laughed. "I'm not going to have the chance."

"Come on, Fetterman, use your imagination! If you did . . . "

"I can't," I stammered. "She is very beautiful. Perhaps not my type, exactly."

Kelly looked at me with fond exasperation. "Oh God, you married men! You're like my brother. He won't even look at anyone other than his wife. It's perverse! Bo Derek could twine herself around him, naked, and he'd go on reading the paper."

"I'm not that bad."

"How long have you been married?"

"Twenty-five years."

She whistled. "God, and you've been faithful all that time? You deserve a medal."

"My wife is a wonderful person."

"Yeah, but still. . . . No, seriously, it's sweet. I admire it. I re-member when I first came to the office, the first time I met you, I had a totally different impression. You struck me as the type who might have girlfriends. But then I realized I was totally wrong. I heard you talking to your wife on the phone and I could tell you'd never strayed and never would. . . . I'm glad. I hated working with Bernstein and Wallaby and all those guys, the ones that come on to you as a reflex. Sickos!'"

The curious thing is that I feel she's right. I am the faithful type. Monogamy never seemed a horrible burden to me in principle, as it does to so many men, and maybe a good many women as well. And even now I feel as though all I've done is create a hideous new life-style: double monogamy. It's as though I'm married to two women, both of whom I love, care for, feel responsible for. If I flirt with someone at a party, I feel guilty about both Becky and Marilyn. If either of them has troubles at her job or is upset about anything, I want to solve the problem, I want to help. All it's meant is that in fifteen years I've never had one moment of feeling really true to either of them. Marilyn hates Becky. Becky, if she really knew the full extent of my relationship with Marilyn, would surely hate her. I wonder, did this just "happen to happen"? Or did I, in some strange, unerring way, create a life based on the central ambivalence of my character?

"Anyway, I think it'll work out fine," Kelly said, "and I think she did like you." She gave me a kiss. "See you tomorrow."

In fact, if I were free, I would more readily go to bed with Kelly than with Gemma Carucci. I like Kelly's openness, her breezy down-to-earth humor, the salty stories she tells me about her boy-friend, a potter who works as a technician in a cancer research labo-ratory. For years Marilyn has had a manic distrust of any secretary I have hired. Even when she meets them and they're married or thor-oughly unattractive, she's still sure that deep down I am lusting after them. Actually, though I'm sure there could be exceptions, I've never felt attracted to any secretary I've hired. I don't think I want someone to look up to me with that slightly awed admiration based on a totally false conception of my character. I'd prefer someone closer to my level like Kelly. She "admires" me a little, but it's an admiration well tempered with common sense.

Driving home, I thought how calm Gemma Carucci seemed about

Dawn's homosexual connection, how "blithe," as Kelly said. I don't know exactly how I feel about it. Not as Becky does—I don't have any firm sense that the heterosexual life is the only true path to sanity or happiness. When Dawn was going through her promiscuous phase, I felt anxious and also often jealous of the boys and men in her life. Sometimes I concealed it under fatherly concern—sometimes I was genuinely alarmed. Once, when she took an overdose of sleeping pills because some man she'd been seeing proved suddenly unfaithful, I was so upset, I almost went to pieces. I remember her sobbing on the bed, hysterical, blurting out bits and pieces of the relationship. I felt like killing him, killing all men who would ever go near her with anything other than the purest intentions. I don't feel that kind of intensity or jealousy about Ava, who seems like a calm, introverted person, nowhere as physically attractive as Dawn, already a published poet, much more sure of herself intellectually. It's Becky who takes it as a sign that we have done something wrong, that our marriage has not been glowingly perfect enough to entice Dawn into forming a similar union.

I am glad, for Becky, that Chelsea, at least, gives signs of being ready and eager to lead the life Becky feels makes sense. Her fiancé, Mitchell, is a stoic, hearty young man. When they're together, they look alike, like brother and sister. He's the kind of person you forget ten minutes after you've talked to him. But then I think of Rolf Gibson, the awkwardness of our relationship, my trying so hard to please him, to live up to whatever standards he was using to evaluate me, never being sure if he thought I was worthy of Becky. I still feel unsure, even though he died two years ago.

At home the twins were assembled for dinner. Robin, who's become a dedicated ballet dancer, goes into the city every day for her classes. Sometimes I pick her up and drive her back with me. She's delicately built, quiet, a lot of physical energy. Roper has been trapped by Becky into enrolling in an all-day tennis program at a camp nearby. Whether due to rebelling against the twinship or just natural sloth, Roper has as little physical discipline as I do. In fact, at fifteen, she reminds me scarily of myself at that age. She's overweight, not to the extent I was, but enough so that she'll clearly have an impossible time socially for years to come. Her hair is always falling in her face. When I see her reach for a second helping of potatoes or pie, that all-too-familiar lust for gobbling gleaming secretively in her eyes, I want to apologize to her for passing on whatever Fetterman genes have brought her to this impasse. But perhaps in her future lies a summer of awakening, a discovery of a body underneath the protection of all that fat, a Becky in male form who will protect and care for her, maybe even a Marilyn in male form who will ignite her sexually.

"I hate working," Dawn announced, sliding into her seat. She has a job at a local bookstore, mainly because its hours, noon to seven, coincide with her own. It's a small bookstore which specializes in women's books and has a large poetry section.

"I thought you said it was so slow," Becky said, "that you didn't have anything to do."

"I *want* something to do!" Dawn said. "It's the pits, just sitting there all day, waiting. You can't really concentrate on reading."

"You could write a poem," Robin suggested.

"Yeah, I try to, but I seem to be in some kind of dry period." Dawn glanced at me. "How's life, Benjamin?" She calls me that affectionately now that, as she puts it, we are both adults.

"Fair to middling." I told all of them about Gemma Carucci and her apartment.

"She is *so* beautiful," Roper said. "We saw her in that movie. Remember, Rob? The one about the circus?"

"She didn't act that well," Robin said.

"If you look like that, you don't have to." Roper gazed gloomily out the window. "Even when she was soaking wet, she looked beautiful."

"Well, was she?" Becky asked.

"Not my type," I said, smiling.

Dawn smiled. "What *is* your type, Benjamin? I didn't know you had one."

I turned red. "What I mean is, she seemed slightly cold, detached. So many men must have approached her—"

" . . . begging for her favors," Dawn said, rolling her eyes. "I wonder if she's ever made it with a woman."

"I gather she has," I said.

"I got a letter from Chelsea today," Becky intervened. She hates it when Dawn discusses her "sexual predilections" in front of the twins. "She says Mitchell's parents are really excited about the wedding. They offered to lend them their island for a honeymoon."

Mitchell's parents own an island in Maine where they take summer vacations. "I thought they didn't have time for a honeymoon," Roper said.

"Oh, they'll take a little time," Becky said.

"How much time did you and Daddy take?"

Becky beamed. "We had six weeks in Europe. It was wonderful. But, of course, I wasn't working, not in the serious way Chelsea will be."

"Serious?" Dawn said sarcastically.

"Yes. I think Chelsea's career is very important to her, don't you, dear?" Becky looked at me for protection.

"Of course," I said, "though it can't be compared to writing poetry." I often feel caught between the two of them these days, trying to placate both sides.

"It's just making money!" Dawn exploded. "God, that's all Mitchell ever *talks* about. His investments and his portfolio. I bet he dreams about huge dollar bills floating down on him out of the sky."

"I think he's cute," Roper said. "He looks sort of like Dustin Hoffman."

Robin stared at her. "In what way?"

Roper shrugged. "I don't know. Just his smile or something." She reached for another slice of carrot cake.

"Sweetie, why don't you stick to just one?" Becky said. "Don't you think one is enough?"

"I only had a half," Roper said disconsolately. "I'm still hungry. They really kill us at this place. We spent four *hours* hitting backhands today!"

"Are you getting any better?" Robin asked.

"Yeah, world class. . . . Will you play with me on Saturday, Daddy? You said you would."

"Sure, if you'll be merciful." My tennis game was never better than mediocre, but the doctor said I needed exercise, was overly sedentary.

Roper laughed. "This guy, the pro, he said I was a killer at the net. He said, 'Either you're a total idiot or completely fearless.'"

After dinner I went into the living room and tried to read, gave it up, and lay down on the couch. Becky and the twins had vanished. Dawn came drifting in, dressed as she had been at dinner in short shorts and a faded T-shirt, barefoot. She held a piece of paper. "I just wrote a poem. . . . Do you want to read it?"

"Could I a little later?" I opened my eyes. "I feel kind of bushed."

"Poor thing." She knelt down beside the couch. "Should I give you a back rub?"

I hesitated. "Sure." Dawn gives wonderful back rubs, her long delicate fingers more caressing than probing. I feel guilty about how enjoyable it is. "Are you working too hard?" she asked almost in a whisper.

"It's not that." My eyes were closed. I wanted just to lie there forever.

"What is it then?"

There's a part of me that would like to tell Dawn everything, things I've never told, all about Marilyn, all my confusions about my life, but I know I can't. It would be a kind of incest, that kind of confessing.

"Just life in general," I murmured evasively.

"So many girls," she said softly.

"What?"

"All of us, Mom. . . ."

I half smiled. "It's not a bad lot."

"You look tired," she said. "Maybe you should take some time off."

"I can't. . . . That feels so good, right there."

She smiled with pleasure. "Maybe I should get a job in a massage parlor."

I let that one drift by. No, just for me. Now that Dawn is gay, at least temporarily, I am the only man in her life. I imagine her saying, "No one lived up to Daddy."

"You miss Kipp a lot, don't you?" Dawn said suddenly, continuing to rub my back.

"Yes."

"I never knew him that well, but he always seemed . . . well, like a very intense person. He'd stare at me with those strange eyes. It was scary almost. Why do you think he did it?"

"I don't know. . . . He always had problems. But so many people do."

"I wonder sometimes why everyone doesn't kill themselves," Dawn said. "Don't you?"

I half sat up, startled. "No. . . . You don't still think about it?" I was horrified. I assumed that mood had just been connected with the man she'd been seeing at the time.

Dawn sat back on her heels. "I think about it. But I won't do it. It's just sometimes I feel like nothing makes sense. I get up, I go to work, I write poems. . . . But it doesn't all fit together."

I wanted to say something fatherly, comforting, urbane. "No, it doesn't," was all I could manage.

She smiled tenderly. "Do you feel better now, from the back rub?"

"I do."

The father of four daughters. That sounds so formal. And they're all young women now, not girls. They could all have children. If we lived in another society or another part of this society, I could have been a grandfather ten times over. Marilyn says she can't wait to be a grandmother. I can wait. I'm not ready to move on to the next stage. How can I still think of myself as a mixed-up kid when I have a grandchild asking me to tell him stories of my bygone youth? "What was it like when you were young, Grandpa?"

On Saturday, I allowed Roper to drag me out for tennis. We never joined the local club, but there are public courts where there's never a long wait. "Don't hit it to my backhand," she said. "Okay?"

"I don't know if I have that much control, but I'll try."

Actually, once I was out, it felt good, moving around a little, working up a sweat. Roper's game is wildly erratic. She'd hit a few good ones, then a bunch that were several feet back of the baseline. I tried calling encouraging remarks, "Nice one. . . . Good swing."

Then, out of the corner of my eye, I spied Marilyn with a young man, walking onto the back set of courts. I've had this fantasy so often that for a moment I couldn't believe it was actually happening, that I was finally catching her with another man. She knows I never play tennis. It would be a perfect place for her to meet someone. He looked, though I couldn't see too well, a lot younger than she. All those remarks. *Devil in the Flesh. They can fuck six times in one night.* Marilyn is supposedly the jealous one; I never thought I was. But I felt such a pang of fury that it was like a physical blow. I stood there hanging onto the fence, immobilized.

Roper came to the net. "Are you okay, Daddy?" she called.

"Sure."

I tried to continue playing, but I felt like I was flying apart at the seams. Marilyn's back was to me, and whoever she was playing was too far away for me to see his features. I had a terrible pain in my side, and it seemed impossible to breathe normally. But for Roper's sake I kept on, almost wincing each time I hit the ball.

"Why don't we stop?" she said, looking at her digital watch. "We've played almost an hour. I'm kind of bushed."

"If you like." I pretended to be reluctant.

She dropped the balls back in the can. "You look really funny."

"I'm a little out of shape." I tried breathing deeply through my mouth. The sky seemed to be tilted on an angle.

"Let's sit down a little." She brushed her bangs back off her face.

There was a set of green benches directly opposite where Marilyn was playing. I looked at them, torn. "We can go over there," I said decisively. We walked side by side. I knew I was going to make a terrible scene. I felt a weird kind of excitement, as though I were a child in an R-rated movie. Maybe I'd attack him. Maybe I'd just rant and rave.

We reached the bench and sat down. Just as we did, Marilyn, retrieving a ball, caught sight of us. She hesitated just a second, then waved. I waved back, my hand trembling. Then she walked over, opened the gate, and came to where we were sitting. "I didn't know you played tennis," she said.

"I go to a tennis camp," Roper said.

"I used to play." I looked at her icily. She was in a white tennis dress with green trim at the neck.

"We could have played doubles," Marilyn said cheerfully. "Aaron's really good. I'm awful." She beckoned to him. "Hon, come on over. These are some friends of mine." To Roper she said, "I'm Marilyn Greene. This is my son, Aaron."

Oh Christ. Am I going crazy or do my eyes just need a checkup? As Aaron came closer, I realized how absurd the whole fantasy had been. But I haven't seen him in years. He's an adult now, serious, handsome. He shook my hand.

"They're just finishing," Marilyn said. "Otherwise, I thought we could challenge them in doubles."

"Would you like to?" He looked from me to Roper.

"Maybe a quick set?" Roper said eagerly. Everyone was looking at me.

I glanced at Marilyn. She was smiling. "It's up to you," she said. "We can do men against women, how about that?"

"Yeah, let's do that," Roper said, jumping up.

Apart from feeling like a jackass, my wind was returning. I only prayed that, of the motley four, I would not be obviously and intrusively the worst. "Only one set," I repeated. "That's all I have in me."

"We *heard* you, Daddy," Roper said with some of Becky's impatience.

I felt glad it was Roper with me, if it had to be anyone in the family. Her hearty, good-natured personality would not pick up on anything. Aaron played seriously and quite well, but he was less good than he looked, double-faulted constantly, and, for some reason, never went to the net. Everyone stayed at the baseline. Roper walloped backhands over the fence and cried out, "Oh no, not again," each time. Marilyn was not too bad, though every time she looked at me, she got nervous. We stopped at five–five.

"We could do sudden death," Roper said.

"Let's just stop," Marilyn said. "I'm tired too."

"Maybe we'll rally a little," Aaron said, looking at Roper. "Want to?"

Her excitement was palpable. "Sure. Do you really want to?"

Marilyn collapsed beside me on the bench. "I thought he was your lover," I whispered.

She kissed me. "You're such an idiot."

I glanced nervously at the court. "Watch out . . . I don't want—"

She moved an inch away so that our bodies barely touched. "I'm glad you're getting exercise. You could be good if you did it more often."

"You're not so bad yourself, kid. . . . Except you kept giggling every time I served at you."

"I wasn't giggling!" She sat dreamily, her hair moist, a smell of sweat and cologne coming from her skin. "You really thought I was two-timing you? You really think someone Aaron's age would look at me twice?"

"I couldn't see him that well."

"You, in actual fact, *could* get someone that age, if you wanted."

"In actual *fact*, I doubt it."

"Well, I'm just telling you, you could. . . . God, you looked so strange before, I was really worried."

"Just jealous rage . . . plus being out of shape."

Marilyn beamed. "Jealous rage sounds terrific. Was that it really?"

"I came over, intending to challenge him to a duel."

Marilyn looked at Aaron, who had just hit a beautiful forehand drive. "Isn't he wonderful? I feel so proud of him."

"He's a nice-looking boy," I admitted. "I think Roper has a giant crush on him."

"She should lose a little weight," Marilyn said, observing her. "Not much. Just five or ten pounds. She's sweet, otherwise."

We sat in silence, watching our progeny play. If we had ever married, this whole scene would be different. Probably our kids would have hated each other. To Aaron, I would be the despised stepfather who stole his mother away. Roper would resent Marilyn, find fault with her. Tears, fights. I'm glad we never seriously contemplated that. No, Marilyn did, in the beginning, talked about it nonstop, in fact. If we had married, by now we might be divorced. Could a relationship like ours have survived the daily grind? I looked at her.

She looked back questioningly. "I love you," I whispered, as though in penance for my thoughts.

Her eyes softened. "Me too."

Such a peaceful, lovely moment, the spring air, our children getting along. I saw, off to one side, a couple emerging from the woods, hand in hand, so obviously in love they seemed to emanate rays of youthful ardor from fifty feet away. Marilyn saw them too, and smiled at me, a smile that substituted for a touch. This is all there is. I know that, and I must try and accept it. Just moments, some wonderful, some planned, some unplanned, but not linked together, not making any final sense. Don't try to fit it into a box, a pattern.

As the young couple passed closer to us, it was clear the woman was pregnant. He helped her carefully along, gazing at her with adoration. "Maybe *we* should have had a child," Marilyn said wistfully, watching them.

"How?"

"Just . . . I could have gotten pregnant, made sure it was yours, and just raised it. You could have known it was yours."

"But Mo would have assumed it was his?"

"Yeah."

It sounded ghastly to me. I know I would have gone crazy, having a child of my own raised by another man, making the complications of our lives actually visible. "I don't think we needed that," I said.

Marilyn sighed. "No, you're right. . . . But sometimes one wants, well, you know the way marriage has so many symbols, houses, kids, insurance policies? One wants a symbol, a proof that what we have exists."

"For who?"

"No, you're right. . . . "

"*We* know. . . . That's enough."

At that moment Aaron and Roper came bounding off the court, both looking exhilarated but streaming with sweat. "That was fun!" she exclaimed enthusiastically.

"You've really improved a lot, sweetie," I told her.

The four of us walked to the parking lot. "Thanks," Marilyn said. "Let's do it again sometime."

As soon as we were in the car, Roper turned to me. "Do you think we could do it again? Do you think she meant it?"

"Well—"

"Boy, he is so handsome! He looks like a movie star, practically. . . . Do you think he liked me?"

I hesitated. "He's in his twenties, Rope, out of college."

"So? I'm fifteen. Millions of couples are like that." She sank down in her seat. "I wish I'd been better! I wish my backhand wasn't so awful."

"He wasn't all that terrific."

"Do you know that lady? Could you ask her if we could play again next week?"

"I know her, but . . . " I stopped. "I think her son lives in the city. He probably doesn't come out here every weekend."

"But could you just ask?" she said, exasperated. "Would it *kill* you to just ask?"

I couldn't help smiling at her vehemence. "I'll ask. Only Rope . . . "

"Yeah?"

"Would you mind not mentioning to Mom that we met them? She doesn't like Mrs. Greene that much."

Roper looked at me in surprise. "How come?"

"They once had a fight about something."

"I thought she seemed nice," Roper said. "I was glad she wasn't that good a player. At least it didn't make me the worst."

But at lunch, in response to "How'd it go?" from Robin, Roper burst out with, "God, you should have *seen* the guy we played with! He was, seriously, the most handsome man I've ever seen! God!"

"Who was he?" Robin asked. "I thought you just played with Daddy."

Roper turned bright red. "Oh yeah, right. . . . Well, he was just there with his—with some woman, so we played a set of doubles."

"Anyone we know?" Becky asked casually, passing the egg salad to me.

"No, I think everyone we know plays at the club."

I thought I got past that smoothly enough, but after lunch Roper cornered me in my study and said, "Daddy, listen, do you think maybe you could get his picture for me? You said you, like, knew his mother."

"Absolutely not!" I yelled. "He's twenty-three years old! I think he's living with someone. I don't want you making an idiot of yourself. Cut it out!"

She dissolved. "Okay. I just thought I'd ask." She slunk out of the room and I felt awful for losing my temper that way. Though, in point of fact, I don't think there's a chance in the world that Marilyn's son would have the slightest interest in Roper. Not just her age, but her looks, her personality.

When I saw Marilyn the following week, she said, "Well, he's kind of playing the field since Sonya pitched him out. It seems like there's a new one every week. Mo says it's good, that at his age that's normal, healthy." She looked at me as though for confirmation. We were having a drink in Ila's garden. I was due home in half an hour. Sex had been good, not sensational. But right afterward I'd fallen into a deep sleep and had woken up feeling amazingly peaceful and cleansed, ready to forgive the world and myself all our sins. For six months after Marilyn's mastectomy, making love with her was really painful for me. It wasn't so much the limits of erotic stimulation. It was that the sight of her naked made me think of death, of the fact that both of us are crumbling. It seemed like every other day I'd hear about a woman who'd had a similar operation which seemed to go all right and then suddenly, out of the blue, a recurrence, a sudden decline. Even though I've fantasized at times over the years at how much simpler my life might be without Marilyn, when I thought of losing her, I panicked. There's some need there that, at this point, goes beyond sex or needing the ego boost of having a girlfriend, whatever propelled me into this originally. But now that almost two years have passed since her operation and she seems fine, those thoughts have receded. There are still occasional days when it's so good, I go home feeling unspeakably guilty, a turn-on in its own way, no doubt. But mostly it's like it was today—something I need and want, but not, ironically, all that different from doing it with Becky.

"At his age I was married," I said wryly. "What do *I* know?"

Marilyn touched my cheek. "Poor thing. . . . Do you regret that horribly? Do you wish you'd done it differently, fooled around a lot and then settled down?"

"Well yeah, twenty was certainly too young. . . . But I'm not sure it matters all that much. How about you?"

"I should have waited. But no one did then. Well, Jeanette did, but she never had that manic thing about wanting to get married. It's funny. Her parents were happy together, did everything together, and she thought it was claustrophobic. Not me. . . . The night Mo proposed, I couldn't sleep all night I was so excited."

It was hard to imagine that, a twenty-year-old Marilyn, lying awake, blissfully planning a marriage with a man who ran a career counseling firm and went to CCNY. "How did he propose, formally?"

"I can't remember. . . . No, it wasn't that formal. We were already 'doing it.' It just seemed the natural next step. But I was a little surprised. I thought maybe Mo was the perennial bachelor type, always moving on. And I must have seemed like such a baby to him, really wet behind the ears."

"He probably liked that."

"True." She sighed. "God, I'm so glad you didn't know me then! I was awful!"

"You wouldn't have looked at *me*."

"I would have struck you as a witless goofy kid with teased hair. I remember I went out a little with this really intellectual guy. He was the editor of the school literary magazine and he was talking about some literary critic, David Daiches, I think it was, and I thought he meant Daitch's Dairy. It was so humiliating! He looked at me like: who *is* this dimwit?"

"He sounds like an ass. . . . I would have been struck dumb at the sight of you. I wouldn't have opened my mouth."

"Really?" She looked touched. "Well, I would have seen through to your true self too, no matter what you looked like."

I think we know we are, if not lying, then reshaping reality to suit the moment but, sitting in this sun-dappled garden, that seems forgivable in both of us.

Preparations for the wedding are proceeding apace. Chelsea came in for the weekend and she and Becky bought a wedding dress in the city. It's not a really formal gown, just a long, white, cotton, lace-trimmed dress with a full skirt. Chelsea does, indeed, look radiant with health and happiness, maybe just her age, a sense of well-being.

"I want to get married in a dress just like that," Robin said as Chelsea modeled the dress.

"What was your wedding dress like, Aunt Ginger?" Roper asked.

Ginger and her husband, Earl, were staying with us for the weekend. They've been married four years and by now my mother has simmered down about it. My father took the whole thing calmly. He told me privately he was more taken aback that Ginger would pick someone so much older than herself than that Earl Wright is black. But Ginger is settled herself these days, calmer, working hard. She seems truly to have sowed her wild oats.

"Oh, I just wore a dress I already had," Ginger said. "It was blue, I think. I didn't want to go through a whole rigamarole."

Chelsea moved around the room, still posing. "Mitchell's mother doesn't think this is *enough* of a rigamarole. She got married at some huge hotel with eight hundred guests."

"Sick," was Dawn's dyspeptic comment.

"She says it was the happiest day of her life."

Dawn crossed her eyes and uncrossed them. "If Ava and I ever decide to get married, we will just do it and not involve anyone."

Becky glanced at her nervously. "Benjy, can you come inside a second?"

When we were in the bedroom, she said, "I told you to speak to her about that!"

"What?" It hadn't been a good day. I'd woken up feeling dizzy and had a headache.

"I don't want Chelsea's wedding spoiled by Dawn, by her making ugly and inappropriate remarks. You have to speak to her!"

"Leave me alone!" I snapped. "I don't give a damn about any of that."

Becky flushed. "You have no concern for Chelsea? For her happiness?"

"Of course I do, but let's leave Dawn out of it. She has a perfect right to her own life, to make her own mistakes, if they are mistakes. . . . Who's this Mitchell? What's so wonderful about *him?* I'd rather have Ava as a son-in-law any day."

"That's shockingly cynical," Becky said.

"Sorry."

"I thought you'd be so pleased. . . . Sometimes I wonder if you care about anyone other than yourself."

I was silent. I couldn't, for the life of me, feel anything but impatience and rage. I just wanted to get out of the house, away from all the talk of weddings, marriages, dresses.

"Do you wish she *wasn't* getting married?" Becky said, her voice rising. "Do you think no one should get married? Should *we* never have gotten married?"

I sat there staring out the window. "I don't know."

She was staring at me impatiently, waiting for an answer. "You know, sometimes, Benjy, I think all this is pure self-indulgence, these moods. We're happy! We're as happy as anyone ever is, and to want more is just . . . fanciful!"

"It's just I have a bad headache," I said inadequately.

"Maybe it's those pills," she said. "You said you were going to talk to the doctor about it. Have you?"

"Not yet."

"It's a drug, and drugs affect your system. You used to say you thought Kipp had been affected—"

"This is completely different!" I said impatiently. "It's for my blood pressure! He was being given incredibly high doses of drugs which they really know nothing about. Those doctors use people as guinea pigs."

"I think Kipp had the best treatment available," Becky said stiffly. "He—"

"Please don't talk about him," I said, closing my eyes.

"I'll talk about him all I want," Becky said, breathing heavily. "Why shouldn't I? And why are you only concerned about poor Kipp? How about poor Ariel? How about his wife?"

"He's dead, not her."

"But how about that terrible student of his who carried on so at the funeral! Think of how Ariel must feel! I know he was sick and therefore not responsible for his actions, but—"

"She was just a student who loved him. She wasn't his mistress."

"Ariel says she was."

"She wasn't. . . . Kipp wasn't that kind of person."

Becky gave me a long withering glance and left the room.

I think I'll go into a monastery. Maybe that's the answer for the second half of one's life. Solitude, musing on what has been, no sex, no confusion, no weddings. I thought of that glance Becky gave me. Maybe that's what she thinks of me, a moody baby, worthy mainly of contempt, unreliable, a liar. She's out in the world now, meeting other men. What a delicious irony if Becky, at forty-seven, were to take a lover. Some heavy-set white-haired man who collects Oriental bronzes and used to be in the Foreign Service.

At work on Monday Kelly strode briskly into my office with, "My sister's getting married! She—"

I put my hand over her mouth. "Not a word about weddings! Not a word."

She laughed and then looked at me, puzzled. "What's wrong?"

"Too many people are getting married, falling in love, doing absurd, irresponsible things. I don't want to hear about it."

"Fetterman, you're crazy, do you know that?"

"In point of fact, I'm the one sane human being left on this planet."

She shook her head. "Good," she said firmly. "Okay, I want to talk to a sane person. Let's have a drink after work."

"Terrific." I looked forward to it all day, pleased she was looking so appealing in a short red dress, dangling earrings. When we finally got out of the office, it was past five, and I was back to my usual exhausted state of mild distemper.

"Where should we go?" Kelly asked, looking down the street.

I mentioned a nearby hotel with a bar that's usually fairly quiet. I sometimes go there with clients. I'm not in the habit of having drinks, however casually, with attractive young women who work for the firm. Partly it's that I'm usually zonked at the end of the day and it's a forty-minute drive home. But more, I don't see myself as capable of casual flirtation. If Kelly hadn't proposed it, I wouldn't have suggested it. Still, as we walked down the street, I felt a certain elevation of spirits, even excitement.

We took a table toward the back and ordered our drinks. Kelly, leaning forward, said, "So, what's so bad about weddings? *I* want to get married. Is that so crazy?"

"How old are you?"

"Twenty-nine."

"That's different. . . . I was thinking of kids who rush into it when they're too young to know what they're doing."

"The way you did?"

"The way I did, the way my daughter's doing."

Kelly lit a cigarette. "But what's the alternative? What else *is* there? So you live together, you try that? But what else *is* there?"

I was taken aback by her ferocity. "Seeing a variety of people—"

"That's all shit," she interrupted. "Anyway, I've *done* that. So, great, you do it, overcome your inhibitions or whatever, go to singles bars, fuck strangers. Why is that so wonderful?"

The drink was working. I felt as though we were floating in space. "I don't know," I stammered. "I never did that."

Kelly laughed. "You're just a bloody innocent," she said. "You're married with four kids and you're giving *me* advice and *you* got married at twenty. Sure, so to you it sounds like a wonderful thing, but you don't know. Fetterman, I'm telling you, you don't *know*."

"I know," I said. "I know I don't know."

She ordered another drink and, after some hesitation, so did I. "No, really, it's what's sweet about you, that you're not lunging at every piece of ass in the office. I bet if I tried to seduce you, you wouldn't even wobble."

I laughed. "I might wobble."

"No, you wouldn't. Because you'd know it would be dumb. It would just be sex. Okay, so I'm cute, I'm sexy . . . but you wouldn't get all that much out of it. Believe me."

"Is this a proposition?"

"I don't know."

"I have a mistress," I said. "I've been seeing her for fifteen years.

The only reason I wouldn't ever do it with you is because of her."

I was as amazed to hear those words come out of my mouth as Kelly obviously was. "You're kidding! I don't believe it."

"Yup. . . . So it's all a sham. I'm just like those guys you despise."

"No, you're not," Kelly said solemnly. "You're not. . . . Who is she?"

"She's my age, lives in the same area I do, married, two sons out of college. . . ." Whatever I say, however I put it, doesn't describe it. Maybe that's why I've never told anyone, other than Ginger and Stef.

"Fifteen years?" Her eyes were bright, liquid. "Why didn't you both run off and get married?"

"Inertia, cowardice. . . . We just didn't."

Kelly gulped down her drink. "Oh, I hate that! That's so unromantic! You meet someone you're crazy about, she's crazy about you, and then—nothing? How awful!"

I sighed. "I just don't know how different it would have been in the end if we had done it. We both have kids, all those complications."

"Yeah, but you would have had love! You would have had romantic passion!"

"I love my wife. . . . What's wrong with romantic passion once a week?"

She made a face. "Ugh. . . . This is a bad story, Fetterman. You said you were the one sane person left on this planet. You're letting me down."

"I know," I said sadly.

"Once a week! Is that how often you see her?"

"Basically. . . . Oh, there've been hiatuses when we quarreled, but in the end one of us always broke down."

"And no one knew? Your wife or her husband?"

I half laughed. "I don't know. . . . Maybe they both half know."

Kelly looked solemn. "I really don't like this story," she said, looking depressed. "I mean, you loved your wife when you married her, didn't you?"

I nodded. "I still love her."

"And that's what it all comes to? Cheating? Once a week? That's worse than *my* life. That's worse than singles bars!"

"I'm sorry."

Kelly was high. her voice quavered a little, her earrings swung back and forth. "See, when I marry, I want it to be forever. And if John ever strays, I'll kill him! I want black or white, not all these mucky halftones."

"You're twenty-nine," I said. I was drunk myself. My moods sailed up, crashed down from moment to moment, but not in an unpleasant way. Her anger came across as a kind of flirtation, whether intended or not.

"God, is that condescending! So, I'm twenty-nine! So what? Does that mean I know any less about life than you? I probably know more."

"True." I watched her earrings, her delicate pink earlobes. "I don't really know a damn thing. . . . Look, Kelly, I didn't mean to tell you a gloomy story. It just came out. I'm sorry. Marry your boyfriend. You'll be happy, you'll be different."

She stared at me. "No, I won't. . . . I have the feeling he'll be like you. You've convinced me."

"My life is just my life. Don't draw any far-flung conclusions from it."

She looked as though she were about to cry. "But do you, like, feel it's been worth it, in some way? Even once a week? You don't regret it, wish you never had, or wish anything?"

"That's too big a question, and I'm too drunk to answer it."

"Me too."

We got up and wove our way out into the beautiful late summer evening. Kelly, in the soft half-light, looked lovely, young, intense. "I'm glad you told me all this," she said solemnly. "Because in some ways I guess I've had a crush on you, and now I see it was all an illusion. You're not what you seem, or not what I fantasized you to be."

I smiled. "No," I said and bent forward to kiss her tenderly on the lips. The kiss escalated without any conscious intention on my part. Her lips opened just slightly, her hand reached up to touch the back of my neck. We broke off, startled. I felt sexually aroused, confused, dizzy.

"Well I don't know what to say about *this!*" Kelly said, with a comic look of alarm.

"You're beautiful."

"But what do you want to *do?* . . . This is a moment for action, Fetterman, for clear thinking."

"I'm incapable of that even at the best of times."

She moved closer to me so her nose almost touched my cheek. "Do you want to come home with me?" she whispered.

"Yes." I became, with marvelous ease, two people. One was driving home, looking out for the traffic, wondering what Becky had fixed for dinner. The other was in a cab speeding downtown, kissing Kelly rapturously, hungrily, stroking her delicate neck. I thought of a movie I'd seen where a couple made love in a cab. I'm too old for that. No need, anyway.

She lived in the Village, a four-floor walk-up. Each flight seemed twice as long as the one before, as though I were in some fairy tale where climbing the steps was part of some grueling ordeal I had to undergo before the princess would deign to give me her favors. "Only one more!" Kelly said cheerfully, just ahead of me.

As we reached the top landing, I thought I might topple backward, roll down all four flights, helplessly. Bright spots of light were zigzagging in front of me. I saw her outlined in the doorway of her apartment. "Are you okay?" she called.

I was too out of breath to speak. I staggered into the apartment and closed the door behind me, then stood, my hand on the doorknob, trying to catch my breath. It was a one-room apartment, a big plant in the corner, a couch with large bright pillows. Kelly turned, and with one gesture, pulled off her dress, as though it were a T-shirt. Underneath she was wearing underpants, no bra. She kicked off her shoes. She was skinny, long-legged, her breasts so small the nipples seemed unusually prominent, like soft noses. I froze.

Barefoot, she walked over to where I stood. "What's wrong?"

"Kelly, listen, forgive me. . . . I can't do this. I just can't."

"What happened? In the cab you seemed so—"

"I just can't. . . . Will you forgive me?"

"Of course I'll forgive you." She put her arms around me in a hug that was meant to be more comforting than erotic and I hugged her back and then, to my horror, collapsed, weeping into her arms. She led me to the couch. "I'm so sorry," she said. "Don't. . . . I don't mind. It was me. I was stupid. I'm always like that."

"It's not that. . . . I'm a wreck. My daughter's about to get married, I have a mistress. Why am I here?"

Kelly kept holding me in the same maternal way. "You're here because I made a pass at you, and I was so irresistible, you couldn't refuse."

"You *are* irresistible."

"I'm so irresistible, I scare everyone off! I shouldn't have taken my dress off like that. You must think I'm a floozy, that I bring men up here all the time. Would you believe you're the first man who's ever been here except John and my brother?"

"I do." I felt gradually more self-possessed, though drained.

"I'll make you some tea and then drive you home." She put on a white terry cloth robe and bustled around in the kitchen. "John says I'm the kid sister type. He went with this really voluptuous Spanish girl in college who smelled of garlic and did all these crazy things in bed. He says I'm as wholesome as Mom's apple pie. Jesus!"

"If I had another life, I'd marry you in a second," I said. The tea was hot and good.

She smiled. "You got me worried, the way you looked after you'd climbed all those steps."

"How can you do that every day? You must be in wonderful shape."

"Yeah, I am basically. But I always forget that it is kind of a long haul. Was it that, the steps? Or my taking off my dress? Tell me."

"I'm not good at casual things," I said. "If we could have done it once, enjoyed it, and still seen each other every day, fine. But I'm not like that."

"Me neither. . . . Boy, isn't it great, my hitting on a person with common sense! You're right—imagine every day at the office. You would have been lurking furtively in corners every time you saw me.

Remember that Cheever story where he sleeps with her and then fires her and she's kind of crazy and he thinks she's going to kill him, only she doesn't? It was on TV."

"I didn't see it. . . . But I wouldn't have fired you. And you're not crazy. I think those are different people he's writing about."

Kelly got into jeans and a shirt and we took a cab back to where my car was parked. I called Becky and invented some excuse for my lateness. She's so absorbed in the wedding these days, I'm not sure she noticed or cared. "I can drive," I said once we got there.

"You're sure? You're absolutely sure?"

"Absolutely."

She kissed me affectionately. "Look, forget all that junk I said before. I'm twenty-nine, I'm a snot-nosed kid. What do I know?"

"Take care. . . . And thanks."

I drove home very slowly. I didn't feel quite normal, but the concentration on driving was good, relaxing, easier than talking to Kelly for forty-five minutes would have been. Saved. But by what? And from what? I remembered moments: open-mouthed kissing in the cab, delicious, delirious, almost. Then the unending climb up the steps to the apartment. There must have been a hundred steps, two hundred! Her sudden nakedness, her lovely nipples. But whatever the reason for my sudden change of heart, I felt enormously relieved. And maybe women are used to that these days, men collapsing weeping into their arms. John Wayne is dead and probably, off screen, never existed. And, as Ginger would say, "Who the fuck *needs* that?"

It was the day of the wedding. A perfect, cool, bright September morning. When I entered the kitchen, Becky was already out of bed, dressed, on the phone. When she hung up, she saw me, still in pajamas. "Benjy, it's ten. Please hurry! I want everything to go well today. Be good, okay?"

"I'm always good."

"Be—" The phone rang and I poured myself some coffee.

By eleven I was in my gray suit, looking, I thought, wary, moderately attractive, puffy cheeked. I hope I don't look to others the way

I look to myself, that my eyes don't have that anxious, inquiring expression all the time. Father of the bride. I will wrap myself in that stance: good-natured, sentimental, self-possessed.

Mitchell's parents, the Emerys, were staying at a local hotel. Mrs. Emery was tall, heavy, resplendent in a vivid orange dress, like a boat sailing forth. Her husband was small, a compulsive talker, a maker of puns. The advantage to both of them was that they needed hardly any response. She was delighted with herself, the world, and her son's wedding. Nothing short of a joint nervous breakdown on the part of Chelsea and Mitchell would mar that. He had been making the same little quips and jokes for years and probably did it in his sleep. They had an older son, unmarried, who looked like the mother, and a younger daughter, about the age of Robin and Roper.

"I hope the house at the island will be good at this time of year," Mrs. Emery said. We were gathering at our house, prior to departing for the church. "We rarely use it this late in the year."

"You mean the weather?" I asked.

"It can get chilly. . . . The heating is mainly suited for summer. Do you go away summers?"

"My wife's parents had a house that we used sometimes, but otherwise, no." I noticed Dawn at my elbow. She was dressed in slacks and a shirt, elegant, but not what Becky had wanted. "Have you met my daughter Dawn?"

Mrs. Emery smiled. "The poet?"

Dawn half nodded sardonically.

"My husband used to write poetry when we first got married. Some of them were quite good. He had a schedule. Every Saturday morning he wrote a poem. But I think at some point he stopped. . . . It's hard to combine it with earning a living. But, of course, for girls it's different. Your husband can support you and you don't have to worry about all that."

"I don't have a husband," Dawn said.

"Well, but you will," Mrs. Emery assured her. "It took me till I was almost thirty to find Hilton. There were other men. I mean I had other offers, but I was choosy. I knew what I wanted and I was willing to wait."

"What did you want?" Dawn asked, baiting her.

She looked taken aback. "Well a man of culture, of course, some-one from a similar background, someone who loved travel, the arts. I didn't want one of those hopeless young men who's always 'finding himself,' who keeps changing professions. My sister married one of those and she's had no *end* of trouble."

"Sounds like you, Benjamin," Dawn said, nuzzling me affectionately.

I gave her a wry look. "Thanks, sweetie."

"Do you have any special beau?" Mrs. Emery inquired.

"I'm off men at the moment," Dawn said, "but I guess that could change."

Mrs. Emery pressed her hand. "Oh it will, my dear. Don't worry. We all go through dry periods." She looked around. "Are those the twins? Mitchell tells me it's so unusual to have met a girl who comes from such a big, happy family. All his other girlfriends, not that there were very many, came from broken homes."

"Mom and Dad are too crazy to live with anyone else," Dawn said. She gave me an affectionate poke. "Especially him. He'd drive any-one but Mom up the wall in no time flat."

Mrs. Emery was saved from having to answer that by Becky ap-proaching us with a worried face. "Robin's nose is bleeding!" she said. "Benjy, come quickly. I don't know what to do!"

Robin was lying down in her bedroom, a towel over her face, while Roper looked at her with concern. "I think it's stopped," she said as I came in. She put the towel down. It was streaked with blood.

"Can she go to the wedding?" Roper said.

"Sure."

"What if it starts bleeding again?"

"It won't." They were both in pale pink dresses, Robin looking ethereal and graceful, Roper chunky and messy. I went downstairs with the two of them and spied my parents who had just arrived.

My father looks more fragile since his operation, but still holds himself very erect and speaks precisely. My mother, who had a mas-tectomy the same year as Marilyn, seems smaller, her eyes watchful, her hands tremble sometimes. This is the first wedding of any of their grandchildren. "Where is the bride?" my father asked.

"You can't see her till later, Grandpa," Roper said. "It's bad luck."

"I thought that was just for the bridegroom," my mother said. "You look fine, Benjy. Are you ready to be a father-in-law?"

My father patted my back. "Of course he's ready."

Becky was swooping back and forth, introducing people, looking harried but attractive, like an actress playing a favorite role. I realized she actually enjoyed all of this, not just the fact of Chelsea being married, but the ceremony, the gathering of friends and relatives. I would just as soon they'd eloped.

Ginger's husband approached me. "Buck up," he said. "I've been through it three times. It gets easier."

"Does it?" I hadn't remembered he had that many children. Ginger says she enjoys having a ready-made family, most of whom have accepted her and are fond of her. She claims that's as close as she ever wants to come to raising children.

"My son's the only one left who hasn't succumbed," he said in his gravelly voice. "Of course, he's not that eager, being a man."

I've never known what to say to remarks like that. "He wants to wait till—"

"He's enjoying his freedom," Earl said. "He said to me, 'Why'd you remarry so fast? You could've had a great time.' What kind of great time? I found Ginger, the Lord blessed me twice. I don't need more than that. Do you know what I mean?"

"Yes, Ginger's wonderful," I agreed.

"She is a unique and extraordinary person," he went on. "*You* know that. And she loves you very much."

I had the feeling he'd had a few drinks, he was staring at me so intently with his dark somber eyes. "I love *her*."

"Brother and sister. That's the closest bond after husband and wife and father and mother. Blood kin. I'd give my life for mine without even thinking about it."

Not me. Not for Stef, certainly. My life? No, sorry. I saw Stef and Lois off in the corner. "I'm glad Ginger found you," I said. "I wasn't sure if she'd ever find someone she could live with permanently."

"Oh, I'm easy to live with," Earl Wright said. "I'm as easy as they come. Too easy, my first wife used to say. 'You just take things lying down,' she said. 'It's Oriental,' I told her. You see things from the vast distance of time and who cares if this, if that. . . . Am I right?"

"You're right." I looked around nervously, wanting to get away.

He clapped me on the back. "Don't be nervous. It gets easier. Remember that. By the time little Roper there is doing it, you'll be an old pro."

An image of Roper, her hair hanging into her eyes, standing before a minister or rabbi, appeared before my eyes and then floated away. "I see my brother," I said. "I'd better see how he's doing."

When I reached Stef, he was alone. Lois had disappeared somewhere. He always looks balder than I remember, older. "I should have done this first," he said.

"Done what?"

"Been the first to marry off a child. Seniority and all."

"I started younger." How absurd, though presumably he is being jocular, that he actually feels jealous of something so minor.

"Why isn't it a Jewish ceremony?" he confronted me.

"Because neither of them is Jewish. Mitchell's folks are Episcopal, I think, and Chelsea—well, kids are the religion of their mother, technically."

"Folks! Since when do you use words like *folks?* And that's absurd, Benjy! Don't you have any influence? You should have told Becky it mattered to you. She would have listened."

"It doesn't matter to me," I said, getting angry myself. "I don't give a damn about how they get married. I'm an atheist. The Jewish religion seems as ridiculous to me as any other."

He pointed a finger at me. "But they would have put you in a concentration camp, even if you'd told them that a hundred times."

Give my *life* for him! I'm glad I haven't killed him by now. "Look, who's going into a concentration camp? My daughter's getting married, okay? Give me a break."

"You're still so rebellious," Stef said, shaking his head gravely. "Even at—how old are you? Forty-four?"

"Forty-five. . . . I thought you'd given up on all that years ago. I thought that was why you pitched the whole rabbi thing."

Stef stiffened. "I didn't 'pitch the whole rabbi thing,'" he said. "I simply felt I could make a more meaningful contribution through psychiatry, help more people. But going to temple, feeling myself to be a Jew is a central force in my life."

"Great," I said. "Okay, great. . . . Different strokes for different folks."

For a moment he looked too dismayed at my flippancy to reply. "Mom and Dad are deeply hurt," he said. "I hope you don't talk like this in front of them."

"About what?"

"About this ceremony, about your total, flagrant lack of regard for Jewish values. They feel they've failed as parents."

"Who doesn't?" I said.

"I don't," Stef said. "James is a very fine and remarkable human being and I feel proud to be allowed to call myself his father."

I remembered how Ginger used to say she couldn't get through any family get-together without at least three viciously strong martinis. I think she's right. "So, how's it going with Sabrina?" I said to turn the tables.

Stef looked as though I'd just pulled out a police badge and was about to arrest him. "It's over," he said, tight-lipped.

I stood there looking at him. He looked like he was about to cry. "I'm sorry," I said.

He looked around nervously, saw that Lois was out of sight, and muttered, "Lois found out."

"And the shit hit the fan?" I don't think there's anyone I am as awful with as I am with Stef. Blood kin, thicker than water, definitely. Only I think I prefer water.

"She's gone back into therapy. She feels she failed me. I tried to tell her it had nothing to do with her. It was a reexamination of my past. If anything, it's made me love Lois more. We've never been closer."

"All's well that ends well, then?" I suggested.

"Yes," he said, as though this had been a brilliant insight. "I feel that's true. It was something I had to go through. I know more about myself and my needs." He looked deep into my eyes. "Sabrina was a very disturbed woman, very intense. . . . I suppose I saw that, but I deliberately didn't focus on it."

Because she fucked so well? Was it wonderful, ecstatic? I tried to imagine Stef feeling something close to ecstasy, and gave up. "And you?" he said, but at that moment Becky veered up beside us.

"Chelsea wants to see you a minute, sweetie," she said. "Oh hi, Stef. Are you okay?" I moved past them and up the stairs to our bedroom where Chelsea was dressing for the wedding. She was in her long white dress, her hair piled up in a more elaborate, formal style than she usually wears. Chelsea has beautiful skin, like Becky. Her cheeks were glowing. She looked like a milkmaid out of Thomas Hardy, not a conscientious young woman about to embark on a career in finance. "How do I look, Daddy?"

"Beautiful." I kissed her. The other three girls were in the room, Roper and Robin lying on our large double bed, Dawn sitting, cross-legged, in the rocking chair, reading.

"I'm scared suddenly," Chelsea said. "I don't know why. I shouldn't be, should I?"

"No, there's nothing to be scared of. Mitchell is a fine person, you love each other—"

"You don't think we're too young? You used to say people should wait till they're thirty."

"No, why wait? If you've met the right person."

"Mr. Right," Dawn said flatly, without looking up.

Chelsea looked at her, dismayed. "She thinks it's all a farce."

"No," I said, looking sternly at Dawn.

Dawn looked up at me challengingly. "Yeah, I do, Daddy. I think it's all a bloody farce. I think nine-tenths of married people hate each other's guts and would kill each other if they could get away with it."

"Daddy doesn't hate Mommy," Robin said indignantly.

I felt ready to throttle Dawn and stared at her warningly. "Of course I don't," I said firmly.

"And Mommy loves Daddy," Roper said.

"They've been married twenty-five years," Chelsea said. "I don't see why you're so cynical. Look at them!"

Dawn looked right at me and then smiled. "Yeah, well. . . . "

I felt certain that she instinctively knew everything, knew all about Marilyn, but would never say anything. "Everyone's marriage is different," I said. "We were very young when we did it, but what I

mean is, we were more naive too, less knowledgeable about ourselves, about the world." I sounded convincing to myself and managed not to look directly at Dawn, who I'm sure was regarding me
with her condescending half-smile.

Robin got up and hugged Chelsea. "I think you're doing the right
thing," she said. "I think Mitchell's so nice. I hope I'll meet someone just like him some day."

Chelsea hugged her back. "You will, sweetie."

Roper, still lying on the bed, looked at the two of them affectionately embracing. "So they'll get married and Dawn and me'll be
famous or something."

"You'll find someone too," Chelsea said to her.

"Who?"

"Someone who'll love you just as you are. Mitchell knows all my
faults, every single one, and he says he doesn't care."

"You don't *have* that many faults," Roper said gloomily.

Chelsea laughed. "Sure I do. Tons! I'm plodding and unim-
aginative, I have heavy thighs and pouchy cheeks and my bottom
teeth are still crooked, even though I had braces on for three *years.*"

"Really?" Roper slung herself off the bed and examined Chelsea's
lower teeth. "Yeah, they are. Look, Daddy."

"You have lovely teeth," I said.

"Men don't want perfection," Chelsea said. "They want us to be
like them, flawed, not goddesses."

"That's my problem," Dawn said. "I'm perfect. I scare them all
off." She looked at her watch. "How much longer? I'm getting
ravenous."

"You should have had breakfast," Roper said. "Should I get you
some ginger ale and peanuts?"

"I'll go," I said, and went downstairs again. Had there been a
crisis and had I solved it? In the kitchen my mother was standing
near the window, looking out with a melancholy expression. I
thought of Stef's remark that they minded the ceremony's not being
Jewish.

"Oh Benjy," she said, turning. "I've been looking for you. Where
were you?"

"Chelsea had a few butterflies," I said. "But she's okay now."

"She seems like such a baby," my mother said sadly. "I can re-member the night she was born. How can she be getting married already?"

I shrugged.

"Remember how in high school I used to nag you so about asking girls out? I was really afraid you'd never do it, never find anyone. . . . And here you are with four grown girls! It's unbelievable."

My father walked in, looking tired. "What's unbelievable?"

"Sit down, dear," my mother said, pulling out a chair for him. To me she added, "All this noise bothers him. It makes him weak."

"Nonsense," my father said, "I'm as right as a trivet." But he sat down.

"I think Ginger looks so tired," my mother said. "She's been working so hard. That's all she does nowadays, work."

"Well, she did enough flitting around in the old days," my father said. "Life is work. Why shouldn't she work?"

"Life *isn't* just work," my mother said indignantly. "It's love and pleasure, relaxation."

"She has Earl," I pointed out.

My mother was silent a minute. "I do think they're happy," she said in a half-questioning voice, "even if he is, even if they both, even . . ."

My father reached out and took her hand. "They're happy," he fi ished for her. "Almost as happy as us."

My mother beamed. I thought back to that day in the movies. *I did something like that once.* And Stef, looking so miserable: *It's over.* I thought of kissing Kelly in the cab, that whoosh of unex-pected excitement, dry leaves catching fire. I opened the refrig-erator and took out some ginger ale for Dawn.

Becky came into the kitchen. "I think we should start assem-bling," she said.

"Dawn was hungry," I explained, holding out the glass.

"Oh, did you speak to Chelsea?" Becky asked. "She seemed ner-vous suddenly."

"She's okay," I said, "Everyone's nervous just before they do it."

"I wasn't," Becky said, "not for a second. I knew I was doing the right thing." She said that, looking me right in the eye, my parents watching, with such breathtaking lack of irony or bitterness that I was floored. I kissed her on the tip of her nose.

"Connubial bliss," Ginger said, watching from the doorway. "Mitchell wants to know if he should start herding everyone into cars."

I realized I hadn't seen Mitchell all morning. I went into the living room and found him with his parents. "I shouldn't tell you this," I said, "but she looks gorgeous."

"She always does. . . . Is it time? I think we're supposed to be there at twelve-thirty."

"Let's get going, then." For some reason my heart was beating rapidly, as though with excitement or fear. Did I take my pill this morning? I couldn't remember and went into the bathroom and swallowed one with the ginger ale just to be on the safe side. I thought I looked pale and a little peculiar, but maybe that's how I always look. I straightened my tie and stood up straight.

"We'll take the girls," Becky said. "Ginger said she and Earl can take your parents, and Mitchell will take Stef and Lois and his parents." She was like a general, mobilizing her troops, excited, her color high, her voice a little hoarse.

We waited until everyone had departed, then went upstairs to collect the girls. Dawn trailed to the door, her book still in her hand. Becky yanked the book away and tossed it on the bed. "Not during the ceremony," she said.

"It's Adrienne Rich," Dawn said, smiling. She took my arm. "How's it going, Benjamin?"

"Shaky," I confided softly. "I feel a little strange."

"Me too."

She sat next to me in the front and Chelsea sat next to her, the twins and Becky in the back. We were all silent, immersed in our individual thoughts. I felt Dawn's slender body beside me. My delicate darling. I was glad it wasn't her leaving me first.

At the church everyone was already assembled. Becky opened the door and we all peered in. "Full house," I said.

They had chosen Purcell for the wedding march. I was going to

walk down the aisle with Chelsea. We had rehearsed it twice in the
past week. We waited and then, at our cue, Chelsea squeezed my
hand. "Wish me luck, Daddy."

I squeezed her hand back.

Chelsea isn't tall, but she walks with beautiful posture, head high,
almost regal. I felt strange, feeling her arm linked with mine. The
walk down the aisle seemed very long, almost ominously long, and I
had the same feeling I'd had climbing the stairs to Kelly's apartment.
I saw us walking, walking forever. Becky, the girls, the minister
seemed tiny, blurred figures. Suddenly I got frightened. There's
something wrong with me. A sharp pain flickered up and zigzagged
through my body. Oh shit, let me collapse when it's over, not in the
middle. Please, God.

We made it down the aisle. The minister gave his oration, mer-
cifully brief. It seemed very hot in the church, stifling. I felt sweat
dripping down my forehead, trickling into my collar. I'm not living
the right way, something is wrong. And then suddenly I knew what I
was going to do. I would leave Becky and marry Marilyn. It seemed
so simple. The girls were grown. I had done my duty, been a good
father, a good husband. Becky was financially taken care of, she had
a job, her father had left her a trust fund. She would, surely, find
someone as good as me, better, to take care of her. I glanced at her
grave profile, feeling purified rather than guilty at my decision. Who
knows how long I'll live. I want a simple, sane life, one that makes
sense. I thought of Marilyn, moments from the past fleeting across
my consciousness, her beauty, our joy together. It would work! I
would make it work!

Chelsea and Mitchell were kissing. He reached out for her and
held her by the elbows, prolonging the kiss just slightly so that it
became, if not passionate, more than a perfunctory peck. Afterward
they both stood, dazed, staring into each other's eyes. I watched
them, entranced, moved.

Then, as I turned, a sudden violent spasm grabbed me. For a
second I thought it was a person and turned around to see who it
was, but as I did, a horrible, terrifying pain engulfed everything, all
my senses. I can't see, hear. Oh my God. I had the feeling I'd
fainted, there was something cold under my head, but the pain was

so extreme I couldn't speak or even give out a cry. I heard Becky calling, "Get an ambulance, please! Get *someone!*"

Her voice was like an arrow, piercing me. Then I felt her hand on my arm. "Benjy, are you conscious? Can you hear me? Please say something."

I tried to open my eyes to tell her, and then someone must have sunk a needle into my arm because the church, Becky, everyone at the wedding, the world vanished.

PART FOUR

◆

1981-84

My Wife, the Zombie

hree years ago, a September afternoon, a Tuesday, I came
home from work a little early—I can't remember why—and before
dozing off in the armchair, waiting for Marilyn to come home, I
glanced through the paper. I rarely read it thoroughly in the morning and, by evening, I figure, why not wait for the TV news, but this
time I began leafing through, not even reading, just glancing at the
headlines. On the obit page my eye hit on:

Benjamin Fetterman, a designer of furniture for Lapidus Home
Design, collapsed and died of a heart attack today, at the wedding
of his eldest daughter, Mrs. Chelsea Emery. He was forty-five
years old.

Mr. Fetterman was born in New York City, attended the Little
Red School House and Elisabeth Irwin High School, and was graduated from Amherst College in 1956. He received a law degree
from Columbia in 1959 and practiced law from 1960 to 1966 with
the firm Fetterman, Barclay, Guzman and Linzer. His father,
Gilbert Fetterman, is a lawyer and well-known Judaic scholar.

He is survived by his wife, Becky; four daughters, Chelsea,
Dawn, Roper, and Robin; a brother, Dr. Stefan Fetterman, a psychiatrist residing in Chicago; a sister, Ginger Fetterman, a lawyer
in San Francisco; and his parents, Gilbert and Sophie Fetterman of
New York City.

What did I feel? Okay, a flicker of delight, joy is too strong maybe.
I sat there, thinking of that time six months earlier when I'd met him

on the train, how bad he'd looked, like his days were numbered. Yet guys can look like that for decades. As I recalled, he always looked older than he actually was. I remembered his wife driving me home, Marilyn coming out onto the lawn. I tried, as though it were a movie I could replay backward slowly, to resee the expression on Marilyn's face as the three of us appeared, but I don't remember anything much. Maybe a little nervousness, but nothing extreme. Look, even if they did it a couple of times a decade or more ago, Marilyn's the type that would still be nervous. She isn't that casual about things like that.

I reread the obit a couple of times, but it really wasn't much, just a few lines. It wasn't like he was a famous guy, well known for anything. He fucked my wife a few times, they're not going to put him on the front page for that. I'm not going to bear grudges, especially when he's not around anymore. I tossed the paper on the floor and dozed off to sleep. A little while after that Aaron showed up. I'd forgotten he was coming for dinner. He disappeared upstairs and, about half an hour later, in breezed Marilyn, carrying a big bag of groceries.

I went into the kitchen, carrying the paper. I'd folded it over precisely to that page. "So, have a good day?"

"Yeah, I'm really bushed though. . . . Is Aaron here?"

"He came a while ago. I think he's upstairs in his room." I put some packages of frozen vegetables in the freezer. When I turned around, Marilyn was sitting in one of the kitchen chairs. I handed the paper to her. My heart was beating rapidly. "Seen the paper yet?"

I guess that's about as close as I'll ever come to killing someone. That's what it felt like, anyhow. Take aim, fire! I know Marilyn doesn't look at the paper till evening either, if at all. She looked down, saw it, and then looked up at me. I don't know how to describe her expression: hatred, fear, some kind of wariness like maybe it was a joke I was pulling. I just shrugged.

Then, about one second later, she doubled over and started screaming. Jesus, what a sound! It was like someone being sawed in two, a horrible wailing, over and over. I think she must have tuned out. I'm sure she didn't see me or hear me, she just kept shrieking over and over. Aaron came bounding down the steps.

"What's going on?" he said, looking at me angrily, like it was my fault. "What's wrong?"

"A friend of hers died," I said.

"Hey, Mom, come on, stop, take it easy." Whereas she had brushed me off, wouldn't let me come near her, she accepted it when Aaron put his arms around her. "Come on, it's okay. We're here. We'll take care of you." He held her like a lover, murmuring soft, kindly endearments. Marilyn put her arms around him and hung on tight. I walked out of the room, disgusted.

He took her upstairs. They were gone a fairly long time. Then Aaron came down, alone. "She's resting," he said. "I gave her a couple of Valium." He hesitated. "She seems pretty upset. . . . Who was it who died?"

"Someone." I looked up at him. Actually, I was glad he'd been there when it happened. I got spooked hearing that sound.

"Look, I think maybe I'd better hang around here tonight," Aaron said. "I don't want to leave her like that. I'll go to work from here, or maybe I'll stay home, if she's still really bad."

"Suit yourself. . . . How about dinner?"

"I'll find something. . . . Did you eat yet?"

I shook my head.

We went into the kitchen and got together some stuff for an omelet. "God, I got really scared," Aaron said, "when I heard her screaming like that. I thought maybe somebody'd broken in."

"She can get kind of emotional at times." I finished off the omelet.

"Not like that. . . . I wonder if it has to do with her operation."

"That was two years ago."

"Yeah, but I read that sometimes people don't react at the time. They repress it or whatever and then some little thing, which doesn't seem connected, sets them off. . . . Do you think that's it?"

"You're the psychologist."

"Don't you even care?" He glared at me. "Christ, if it was my wife, I'd be really worried."

"Wait till you have a wife, okay?"

"What's *that* supposed to mean?"

I left the room. I was glad he was there, but I didn't especially feel like talking about it. And I guess I felt annoyed at the way Marilyn shoved me aside and fell into Aaron's arms like he was her savior.

When I went upstairs later she was sound asleep, lying flat on her back, breathing evenly. When I woke up the next morning, she was still in that position, but her eyes were open. "I'm not going to work this morning," she said.

"Okay, suit yourself."

I know I'm not good in situations like this. I hate people who go to pieces over things. God, I've had nine million things where I could've checked out, but I didn't. You get a blow, you take it, it hurts, and then you straighten up and get on with it.

But that's not what happened with Marilyn. For six months practically she checked out. My wife, the zombie. Harriet said I should put her in a hospital. "It sounds like a nervous breakdown," she said astutely.

"She'll get over it. . . . What can a place like that do for anyone? They're loonie bins."

"No, Mo, that's not true. . . . They have many modern advances, new drugs."

"She's getting better. Maybe she was working too hard."

"Of course! I told you that. Ever since she started the business. And the way she went right back after her operation, not taking any time off. Remember how I said I thought you should go away for a while, just to relax?"

"She didn't want to."

"I think she's always trying to prove to you she can do it, the way Mom did, but she's a different person. . . . And maybe you never showed her you thought she was doing a good job."

"Maybe." No one in the family knows about Fetterman. Everyone had his own theory and who knows, maybe everyone was right. For a while I worried because sometimes I'd get home and Marilyn wouldn't be there. She'd wander in around seven or eight, looking dazed. Once, in the middle of the night, I woke up and found she wasn't there. I got up and went downstairs. She was in the den, the TV on, but sleeping, one arm hanging over the edge of the couch.

I think she was into Valium a lot, maybe something more, I'm not sure. At times like these your family can be a big nuisance, but one thing I have to say: Aaron was a big help. He even moved back home for a couple of months. He was like a little house husband, just like you see on TV. He'd do the grocery shopping, set something going for dinner. I've always had Aaron down as a really tight-assed, self-absorbed kid, but in this situation I couldn't have gotten through it without him. Oh, I'd have gotten through it, but it would've been hell. I'm not going to remember it as the best year of my life, but with Aaron there to help it was manageable.

Once I came home from a business trip and the two of them were having dinner in the kitchen. They'd opened a bottle of wine and put a fair amount of it away. Marilyn looked rosy and flushed. I heard her laughing, but the minute I appeared she clammed up, they both looked guilty almost, and for the rest of the evening there was total silence. Can you figure that out? At times they made me feel, both of them, as though I were the villain, as though *I'd* caused the trouble. But still, let's face it, for whatever reason, Aaron did things with her and for her that I didn't have the heart to. He'd take her on outings on the weekend, for drives.

"You've just got to be patient," he said to me one evening when, in the midst of nothing, Marilyn suddenly ran sobbing up the stairs.

"How am I *not* patient? What am I supposed to do?"

"She's been through a lot. . . . She needs to feel you really love her."

I guess I could've blown Marilyn's cover by telling him about what had happened, but I didn't want to. Part of me was tempted, but I didn't really think it was any of his business. The only thing that irritated me was the pleasure he obviously got criticizing me. What does a kid of twenty-three know about women? His batting average isn't so hot.

The other person who helped a lot was Marilyn's friend Ila. I've always liked Ila, though I'm not sure she's exactly my type as a woman. A little too hard-boiled: I've seen it all, what do you have to show me. But she could have just taken over the business and pitched Marilyn out. Instead, she came to me the same week it happened. "Listen, I don't care when Marilyn goes back to work," she said. "I just want her to take care of herself. Don't push her back till she's ready. I can handle things on my own."

"It may be a while," I said, wanting her to know where things stood.

"Mo, listen, Marilyn's not just a business partner, she's my best friend. She's been through a lot. I know what that's like. All I care about is getting her through it." She stared right at me. "Any time you need me to come over, I mean any time, day or night, you just call, okay? You have my number."

Everyone said that: Marilyn's been through a lot. A lot of what? I don't know. Maybe I underestimated the effect of the mastectomy. Okay, so in the beginning it bothered me a little and maybe I let that show, but I got used to it. You've been married twenty-five years, you're not swinging from the chandeliers anyway. I figured we both knew we'd had our chances at walking away and we didn't.

One thing I know. If Marilyn had really wanted Fetterman, she'd have gone after him and gotten him. Marilyn isn't aggressive about everything, but if she wants something badly, she goes for it. I figure deep down she knew he was kind of a schlumpy little guy who she would have gotten sick of before the honeymoon was over.

He died in September. By January she was getting better, enough so Aaron moved back to his own apartment. I'd been glad he was there, like I said, but I was glad to have him gone too. I don't need a half hour's amateur psychologizing from my own son every other day. He still called a lot, just to check in, but I think he figured by then, Marilyn was going to make it.

One evening, around that time, she came home after I did. Seeing me in the living room, she looked startled. "What time is it?"

"Past seven." I didn't start dinner because I figured maybe tending to some minimal household tasks might give her something to do. "Where've you been?"

"Oh, I was over at Ila's."

"Wasn't she at work?"

"Yeah, I just . . . sometimes I go over there."

"What for?"

Marilyn looked guilty. "I just like being there. She has a nice house."

"What do you do?"

"Nothing special. . . . Just read or watch TV."

"You could do that here."

"I know." Suddenly she looked angry. "I like being there! Why do you care? Why does it matter?"

"Hey, Marilyn, it doesn't matter. I was just curious. Does Ila know you go there?"

Marilyn nodded. "But actually, I decided on the way home, I'm not going to go there so much anymore. There's no point."

What could I say to that?

"I'm going to try going back to work."

I hesitated. "Good. . . . I think it'll be good for you."

Marilyn looked drained. "Right, it'll be good for me," she repeated flatly.

After that for the next year or so I guess you could say things were back to normal. Or that they seemed back to normal. Marilyn went to work, made dinner, we went to the movies, saw the kids. But it wasn't the same Marilyn. Even when we fucked, it was like someone else was lying there, a definitely eerie feeling. Everyone else assumed things were fine. My mother chortled that Marilyn was taking on too much again, neglecting me. Harriet questioned if Marilyn wasn't a Valium junkie. She'd caught her swallowing two or three at some family dinner.

"Look, Hari, what she does to get through the day is her own business, okay? Kevin drinks, Mom kvetches. . . . Everyone has his thing."

Harriet looked upset, as she always does if I criticize her. "I was just afraid she might get addicted."

I shrugged. "Right now she needs it. When she doesn't need it, she'll stop."

Another thing: she stopped dyeing her hair. At first I didn't notice it. Maybe I was more focused on how she was acting than how she looked, but around Christmas I looked up and there was Marilyn, not a blond anymore. Her hair was growing in half gray, half brown. Even after she started fixing it in the same style, it looked completely different, more sedate, middle-aged. A month or so later Aaron's girlfriend, Carol, came over and was looking at a photo album of the family with Marilyn. "Oh, who's that?" I heard her say. "Your sister?"

"No, that's me," Marilyn said. "I used to be a blond."

Carol looked startled. "Really? That's you? Gosh, you look so different."

"I started dyeing it when I was sixteen," Marilyn said, looking at the photos with her. "But then I figured it was time to look natural."

"I think natural is prettier," Carol said. "It suits your face more. It looks sort of harsh that way you used to wear it."

"Those were my glamorous days," Marilyn said sardonically.

"You're still glamorous, Mom," Aaron said.

She laughed bitterly. Or anyway it sounded bitter to me.

Of all the things that helped Marilyn get better, the best was Carol. She was a secretary at the advertising firm Aaron worked at, not his usual type, quiet, pretty in an understated way, soft-spoken. She'd only gone to a junior college and I think Aaron must have seemed like Einstein to her. If he said mixing red and blue made purple, her eyes would widen with awe. But she was, is, a sweet kid. She comes from Illinois, one of four children. I guess in a quiet way she had her eye on him for a long time, but during the time he was living with us, he didn't date much. "I thought that was so nice, the way he looked after you when you weren't feeling well," she said to Marilyn one night when the two of them were over. "He's such a thoughtful person."

Usually, when girls like that liked Aaron, he ran for cover so fast you didn't see his tracks. But this time he just stood there and let her snare him. Maybe it was Linus's being married, not wanting to be outdone by a younger brother. The night they came over and announced they were getting married was the first night Marilyn acted really excited and happy about something in almost a year. She hugged Carol and then Aaron and then me. "I've just been praying you'd do it," she said. "But I didn't want to say anything."

Carol blushed. "I've been praying he'd propose."

Aaron looked sheepish, but pleased.

"So, when's the wedding?" I asked.

"We thought maybe June," Carol said, "but just something small. I hate those big formal things."

"With dancing?" Marilyn said eagerly. "Dancing is fun at a wedding."

Carol smiled shyly. "I don't dance that well."

Marilyn looked like she'd just won the lottery. "This is so exciting," she said. "I'm so happy. . . . When did you decide?"

"Oh, I think I knew right away," Carol admitted, "but I wasn't sure about Aaron, if maybe he had someone steady tucked away because he never paid attention to anyone at the office. When I told them, they said, 'Him?' They thought he was a permanent bachelor type."

"I've had enough of that," Aaron said. "Eventually you want to settle down."

Eventually! The kid's right out of college. Look, maybe times have changed. In my day it was so hard to escape being snared by a girl, that you got a kind of kick out of it. Nowadays, now that sex is ready and available, maybe the fun-and-games part of it is diminished. "I didn't reach that point till I was thirty."

"What did you do till then?" Carol asked.

"Played the field."

"You didn't fall in love with anyone?"

"Oh sure—in, out, all the time."

"I couldn't do that," she said. "In high school my boyfriend said he wanted his freedom and I cried for a year. My mom kept saying I was silly, just eighteen and there were tons more out there, but you get attached to someone, you know? And it's hard to keep starting over."

"I know," Marilyn said. "I was never good at casual things either. I only did it with two guys before I met Mo, and, I don't know—it just wasn't my thing."

I looked at her in amazement. "You did it with two men before me?"

Suddenly Marilyn turned bright red and giggled. "Yeah. . . . I never told you because I thought you had this hang-up about needing to marry a virgin."

"Me?"

"Yeah, you."

"Never. . . . Who were they?"

Marilyn smiled. "One was a basketball player, and the other was my cousin, Andrew."

Aaron looked shocked. "You did it with *Andrew?*"

I whistled. "How old were you?"

"Sixteen, no seventeen." She looked pleased. "So even I had a sordid past, of sorts."

"Well, I did it with two guys before Aaron," Carol admitted. "I don't think that's so bad. I was in love with both of them."

"Nowadays everything's different," Marilyn said. "In my era it was a very big deal. You were supposedly used goods, or something."

"I once did it with a girl who was a virgin," Aaron said. "And it was murder. She was screaming through the whole thing. I don't get why that's supposed to be such a turn-on."

I was glad to see Marilyn back to her old self, more nearly. From then on, whenever I wanted to tease her, I'd say, "Cousin Andrew?" and she'd turn bright red. "Never tell his wife, okay?" she said. "We promised never to tell whoever we married."

No wonder she seemed to take to sex so easily! I remembered thinking—well, just a relaxed, sexy girl who enjoys it. I didn't look for deep-seated reasons. "It wasn't like I lied," Marilyn said. "You just never asked me."

"True." The less you ask, the less you'll find out that you don't want to know.

Anyway, like I said, Carol became the high point of Marilyn's life. I couldn't exactly figure it out. I'd thought Marilyn would prefer Petra, who's more the way she'd wanted to be, very serious about her work, a feminist, wanting to put off having children till she's established in her career. Maybe it was that Carol liked it when Marilyn made a big fuss over her, took her shopping, gave her tips on what furniture to buy. "She's like a little lost soul," Marilyn said. Evidently Carol's mother had died when she was seven and she'd only had brothers so she'd never had anyone to do all that women's stuff with except an occasional friend. It turned out that she was pregnant when they got married, only about a month, and, as both of them said, they would have gotten married anyway, had decided to before they found out.

That thrilled Marilyn even more, the prospect of being a grand-mother. Every weekend she went into the city and took Carol around to places to buy baby furniture, baby clothes. The business with Ila was doing well, and Marilyn claimed she got a bang out of being able to help them "get started." It seemed to me a big mis-take, having kids the first year they were married, but no one was asking my opinion so I didn't offer it. One night Aaron showed up at our place alone. The baby was due in two months: It seemed he and Carol had had a fight.

"I think maybe I made a mistake," he said. "I don't even know if we have anything in common. She never reads the newspaper. She doesn't know where Lebanon is, she—"

Marilyn nearly went up in smoke. "So? Neither do I. So what? Aaron, you listen to me, you are so lucky to have a girl like Carol being willing to marry you. How many girls are there like that these days? She loves children, she's really looking forward to being a mother."

"Yeah, but that's just because she doesn't know what else to do with herself," Aaron said.

"She's twenty. What do you want from her? Later she'll find something, but for now she'll be a wonderful mother."

"But how about me?"

"What do you mean, how about you?"

"I need attention too."

Marilyn turned to me. "Why are men such babies? 'I need atten-tion too.' You get enough attention. Don't be like that. You desert her and I'm never speaking to you again, do you understand?"

"Mom, relax, I'm not deserting her." He shrugged. "Maybe I just need to get laid. She's so gigantic. . . ."

Marilyn grabbed him. "Sex is not that important," she said. "It's important, but it's not . . . You have someone wonderful. Don't go trying to mess everything up. Do you love her?"

"Sure I love her," Aaron said, slightly cowed by the vehemence of Marilyn's attack.

"So, that's all that counts," Marilyn said. "She won't be pregnant forever."

"I'm not so sure," Aaron said.

The baby, Mary, was born late, two weeks late. We got tired of sitting around waiting so that night we went out to a movie. The minute we walked in the door, the phone started ringing. It was Aaron. I realized that from Marilyn's shrieking, "She had it? Already? How could she have it already? We just got back from the movies." To me she called, "It's a girl. They're both fine." Then, turning back, "So, tell us all about it. Was it an easy labor?"

Half an hour later, when Marilyn had eked out every detail, she came into the living room. "They're calling her Mary. Isn't that sweet? Such a plain name. I didn't know anyone called babies Mary anymore. I thought everyone was Samantha or Amanda." Then she came over and with actual tears in her eyes, hugged me and said, "I'm so happy, Mo. . . . I'm so happy it's a girl."

To me it didn't make much difference, whether it was a girl or a boy. But it was true, we raised two boys, maybe a girl would be a nice change. "I'm happy too," I said.

"I mean, of course whatever they had would've been fine, but deep down I was hoping for a girl. I didn't want to jinx it by saying anything. . . . He said we can drive in in the morning. I'm not going to sleep all night, I know it."

The baby was a funny-looking little thing, bald, tiny. Carol lay slumped back against the pillows, looking exhausted but triumphant. "It happened so fast," she said. "I didn't have a chance to do my breathing exercises or anything. And she was a breach so they had to give me gas."

"That's why she's so perfect looking," Marilyn said. "Isn't she beautiful, Mo? Look at her ears!"

She looked almost like a grandmother, sitting there, her hair grayish, beaming contentedly at the baby. But I don't agree that Carol is like Marilyn was at that age. Marilyn said that when we drove in, that Carol reminded her of herself. Marilyn had more spark, more fire. This one is a bit limp, timorous.

"*You* hold her," Marilyn said, holding the baby out to me.

What could I say? I haven't held a baby for years. I took her carefully and tried to remember how you were supposed to do it. "We've been thinking about being grandparents for years," Marilyn said.

"You know what they say: you're more relaxed with grandchildren than you were with your own. You don't make so many mistakes."

"Did you make mistakes?" Carol asked. "You seem so relaxed."

"Millions," Marilyn assured her. "Especially with Linus."

"Someday," Carol said, "I want to be like you, have a job, once they're older."

"Oh, you will," Marilyn said. "I started at the absolute bottom, but I inched my way up."

The grandchild changed our life. Every weekend we went into the city to see her, bringing roast beef, baked ham, eggplant casseroles. "It isn't fair," Marilyn said, "to make her do all that cooking. Becky says she brings a roast ham every time she visits Chelsea."

"Who's Becky?"

"Oh, she's. . . . Remember, she drove you home once that day and you opened champagne?"

"Since when are you friendly with her?"

"I met her outside the Grand Union. She was getting petitions for a nuclear freeze thing. I told her I'd help." She hesitated. "She's a nice person."

One night Marilyn had a meeting of the women in the nuclear-freeze group in our home; Becky Fetterman was among them. "Do you want to join us?" she asked as I tried to sidle out of the room.

"Politics isn't my thing," I said.

"But this is larger than that," she said. "This is a matter of the survival of the human race."

"You think it deserves to survive, huh?"

I went into the den and watched something on TV. I thought of Benjy Fetterman. Now that it doesn't matter anymore, I know as a fact that he and Marilyn were lovers, maybe for longer than I suspected at the time. She just isn't, somehow, the same person anymore, since his death. You could put that down to middle age, whatever. Marilyn might've decided to let her hair go gray anyway. She might have gotten just as excited about having a granddaughter. But something's gone, some spark dimmed. Still, you can't win them all, right? He's dead, I'm alive. What else counts?

The Real World

*T*he other evening we were at a party and some woman I didn't
know very well was telling me about her sister. "She just went completely crazy," she said. "I don't just mean neurotic, like everyone. I
mean totally off the wall. I don't know if she's ever going to be normal again."

I never knew what any of that meant: going crazy. Now I do. I
think that first year after Benjy's death I was crazy. I think this is
what craziness means. You can't bear the real world so you create
one of your own. But deep down you know it's not real, which is why
it doesn't really work. It's like a play where you write all the lines,
act all the parts, direct it, but there's no audience except yourself.
The woman at the party talked to me as though I was like her, someone to whom craziness would seem something very far removed,
incomprehensible almost. I didn't know her well enough to say how
much I could identify with her sister. I've never told anyone, even
Ila, what that year was like. I guess I'm ashamed, or maybe it's that
it's so private I don't want anyone to know. If people ask, I say, "I
was depressed." I let them fill in the blanks, that it was a delayed
reaction to my mastectomy, change-of-life crisis. People need to find
a "reason" and then they're happy. I didn't want to live without
Benjy, and I didn't have the guts to die. That was the reason.

There's a lot about that year that I don't remember. It must be
some kind of selective amnesia. I can't remember Aaron's moving

back home with us. I remember his being there a lot, but I don't remember details. Whole days, weeks, months drifted by without my knowing what I was doing or where the time went. It seems like a year that never was, floating out in space, not like all the other years when things happened in a sequence.

The beginning of the craziness was going to Ila's. The first time the idea struck me it was midafternoon, a time Benjy and I sometimes met there. I half knew it was a game, but I decided to pretend it was a year earlier and that I'd arranged to meet Benjy there. I showered, got all dressed up, nicely, for the first time in ages, put on perfume. While I was doing it, a voice inside me kept saying: he's not going to be there. But then I decided it was a test. If I pretended hard enough, he would be. I entered the house, opening the door slowly, and walked into the bedroom. Guess what? He wasn't there. I knew, knew absolutely he couldn't be there but I still looked in every room, even opened closets. I called out "Benjy?" But when I heard my voice, I got scared and started to cry.

Maybe it was worse because I didn't go to the funeral. I didn't feel I could, because of Becky. If you actually see someone in a coffin, dead, it's probably harder to pretend. I tried to think: if I didn't see him dead, maybe it didn't really happen. After that I kept going to Ila's almost every day. It was as though, in some way, Benjy *was* there. I felt his presence, I imagined him into life again. Sometimes I'd take all my clothes off and get under the covers, I'd masturbate and then fall asleep, feeling a little groggy from the Valium. Once, just as I woke up, I really forgot he was dead. I opened my eyes and in that split second before I was really awake, I thought he was in the bathroom, showering. I stared at the bathroom door and thought: in one second he'll come out. I lay there, scared, staring at the door. *Please come out.* He didn't.

I thought a lot about death, partly just the unfairness for Benjy, to live such a short life when even his parents were still alive. But I also thought a lot about wanting to die myself. I think if I'd been a person who believed in an afterlife, I might've killed myself just to have that illusion I was "joining" him. But I don't. Benjy's just gone. He doesn't exist anymore. I'll never see him again, talk to him, make love with him, touch him, scream at him, hear his voice on the phone. Whenever I think back to the fights we had, they seem so stupid. Why do people do that, especially if they love each other? Why do they waste things that way? But probably, if he were alive, we'd fight again. It was part of loving each other.

Once I took a whole bunch of pills that I'd saved and mixed them with a whole bunch Ila had in her medicine cabinet. I brought all of them into her kitchen. Mine were yellow, hers were red. I spread them all out on the table, first in rows, then in patterns. I just sat there, with a glass of orange juice next to me, looking at the pills, thinking ahead in my mind to taking them, vanishing. Death, spread out on the table. But I didn't. I guess I'm too much of a coward. Or maybe it's that there's more to me than what I felt for Benjy, important as that was. All I know is, I spent an hour rearranging the pills in different shapes and patterns and ended up putting them back into their little bottles.

Another part of the game I used to play was to fix two glasses of iced tea and bring them out into Ila's garden, when the weather was nice. I'd sit there, in the chair I always sat in, and look at the chair Benjy usually sat in. I'd imagine he was there. I talked to him in my mind. Maybe I even talked to him aloud, I don't know. Once Ila came back and found me out there. She saw the two glasses of iced tea, but she didn't say anything. She just sat down and started drinking from the second glass, as though I'd fixed it for her. Ila was so good, through all of this. She never gave me any pep talks or forbade me to come to her house. She'd just talk about routine things, the business, events that had happened at the store. She'd pretend I was the same Marilyn I'd been, and sometimes I'd reply. Sometimes I just sat there, staring at her, unable even to take part in what she was saying. I guess she must have known what I was doing, going there so often, even though I wasn't always there when she came back.

After Aaron got engaged, Carol told me one afternoon that her mother had committed suicide. She said when it happened she was so little they didn't tell her the truth. They said her mother died in an accident, and it wasn't till Carol was in college that someone let the truth slip. She said ever since she found out, she thinks about it all the time. And that she promised herself, when she got pregnant, that no matter what happened in her life, no matter what bad luck or tragedies, she wouldn't let herself do that. "You don't ever get over it, ever," she said. "I think about her every day."

I told Carol that I'd gone through a time of being depressed and she said she knew, that Aaron had mentioned it. "Was it anything special?" she asked.

I knew I couldn't tell her, though I'm so fond of Carol, almost as though she were my daughter, but then I wouldn't tell my daughter either, if I had one. "Someone I was close to died, a good friend."

She told me how that had happened to her in high school. A friend got cancer and died a month after it was diagnosed, from pneumonia brought on by the chemotherapy. "Maybe it was the shock of having it happen so fast," she said, "but for a year almost I couldn't believe it. I'd start dialing her number by mistake or once, when I was in a drugstore around the time it was her birthday, I actually started picking out a card and then I got so scared, I ran straight out of the store."

Some time in that first year I did another peculiar thing. I called Benjy's father. I called him from Ila's apartment. He answered the phone in a soft hesitant voice.

"Mr. Fetterman, this is Marilyn Greene. I was a friend of your son, Benjy's. . . . We met once at the movies many years ago."

There was a long pause. After all, he was over eighty and we'd met once, almost twenty years ago. But he said, "Yes, yes, I remember."

"I was going to be in the city next week and I wondered if you'd like to have tea with me."

"I'd love that," he said. We arranged to meet at a coffee shop near where they lived.

I'd let myself go to seed in those months after Benjy's death, just dressing automatically in the morning, not bothering about what I wore. But that week I went to the beauty shop and had my hair done. I'd decided to let it go gray, but I had it cut and set and it looked pretty. I looked at myself in the mirror for the first time in months, curious that I was still there, my face, my eyes. To meet Benjy's father I wore a suit that Benjy always liked. It's a deep blue wool, and with it I wore a blouse he once gave me for my birthday, white silk with a ruffled collar. I told Mo I bought it for myself. I thought I looked elegant and ladylike, the way Benjy said his father liked women to look. I didn't really know why I was doing it or what I was going to say.

Benjy looked more like his mother than his father. I never met her, but I'd seen photos. He had her slight build and her big dark eyes. But still there was something about his father that sent a pang through me, some resemblance that it was hard to pinpoint. I know all the mixed feelings Benjy had about his father, but to me he just seemed like a very sweet, gentle, thoughtful person. He asked if I still worked for the firm, if I was still in shipping. He'd remembered that lie from twenty years earlier.

"I started my own store with a friend," I told him. "We specialize in clothes for heavy-set women."

"You don't look like that would be your problem," he said, smiling.

"No, but my partner, Ila, felt there was a need for it." I described how I'd worked in different department stores. I never said I'd lied about being in shipping. "Do you still give lectures?" I asked him.

"Very rarely," he said. "It's extremely tiring, just standing for that long, using your voice. Sometimes I speak to smaller groups, but not more than twice or three times a year. My wife thinks I should give it up altogether."

"I never met her," I said suddenly.

He looked startled.

"Benjy spoke of her often, but I never. . . . We were lovers," I said it almost as a question, as though I were asking his permission for it to be true."

"Yes, I know," he said.

"How did you know?" I couldn't imagine that Benjy had told him.

He smiled, but sadly. "I knew my son a little bit," he said. "I saw the expression on his face when he looked at you."

"He was so ashamed that we met you. He thought you'd have contempt for him."

"I'm not that censorious a person," Mr. Fetterman said. "But

Benjamin always thought of me that way, tried so hard to impress me. I don't have any rigid idea of how people should live."

"He thought perhaps you might have once loved someone other than your wife."

He shrugged. "So many years ago! Goodness." He broke off.

I sat there, staring at him. "I miss him so much!" I blurted out, trying not to cry. "I can't stand it."

He took my hand. "My dear," he said, "we all do. . . . To outlive your own child, that's the worst punishment God can inflict."

"Yes." I sat there unable to say anything more, wondering if I'd only been selfish in calling him. And part of me wanted to say to Benjy: You see, he knew it was love, not just sex, he knew.

After we finished our tea, he insisted on paying and walked me to the bus stop. "I'm glad that you came in," he said. "Thank you."

I watched him out the window. He looked so frail, leaning on his cane, his hair wispy and white. Why couldn't Benjy have lived that long? What was the point in his dying?

Then, one day, I saw Becky outside the Grand Union. She was getting signatures for a nuclear freeze petition. I saw her and stopped, wanting to turn and run in the opposite direction. I remembered that conversation Benjy and I had, watching Aaron and Roper play tennis, where I said I wished I'd had a child with him, had some symbol that our relationship existed. He said, "We know. Isn't that enough?" There was Becky, looking so much the same, plump, graying, that fixed, cheerful smile on her face, and I thought: what good did all those symbols do her? She has the house, the children, but so what? She doesn't have him, any more than I do. I think I went over for something like the same reason I went in to see Benjy's father. I wanted to be with someone who'd known Benjy and loved him. Even without saying anything, I wanted to be with someone who felt the same pain.

Becky was sitting next to another woman whom I didn't know, a thin-faced woman with reddish hair and glasses, who began explaining to me what the petition was about and why I should sign it. I looked at her, trying to listen, and none of it made any sense. I couldn't hear anything. It was as though the words flew out at me and then vanished, before they could cohere into sentences. I felt petrified, the way you do as a child when you don't know the answers on an exam. But I took up the pen and signed my name. The pen seemed slippery, my handwriting came out all crooked and strange, almost illegible. "I have to do it over," I stammered, taken aback at the way it looked.

Becky reached out and took my hand. "It's fine." Then she looked directly at me. "I'm so glad you signed," she said. "This was a cause that was very important to Benjy."

Why did she say that? I stood, staring at her, feeling my knees buckle. I held onto the table. "Are you all right?" asked the other woman.

"I think she's feeling faint," Becky said, and stepped forward to slide a chair under me just as everything started going black.

Becky and the other woman were extremely nice to me. They went into the supermarket and got some ginger ale. The other woman had some little packets, dipped in astringent, in her purse; she put one on my forehead. "I'm so sorry," I said finally, once I was feeling better. "I'm getting over an illness. This is my first day out."

"My whole family has had that," the woman said. "It's going around. You have to be very careful not to overdo. Can you make it home all right?"

I nodded and thanked both of them.

A few weeks later Becky called and asked if I wanted to help them seal envelopes and send out notices for a march that was being held in Washington in a few months. I went over to her house, and spent the evening with a group of four or five women. None of them were women I knew. Most of them reminded me a little of Becky, very earnest and sincere and intelligent. I didn't talk much. I felt strange, sitting in Benjy's living room. In the middle of the evening I went upstairs to the bathroom, and when I was done, I glanced into Benjy and Becky's bedroom, which was right nearby; the door was open. There was still a double bed in the middle of the room, and on the bureau, a photo of Benjy and Becky on their wedding day. He looked so young and funny-looking and awkward. Becky looked like his big sister. She's not really taller than him, but she looked so pleased with herself, so beaming and bright-eyed, and he looked so nervous and ill at ease with that Benjy-like half smile. There were more photos, mostly of their children at different ages.

When I went downstairs, they were talking about being grand-mothers. Evidently Becky had just told them that her oldest daugh-ter was pregnant.

"I envy you so much!" one of the women said to Becky. "My daughter just broke up with her boyfriend, a darling boy, who adored her. I felt so upset. He used to come over in the afternoon and talk to me while I did the ironing. I became really fond of him. She said, 'Look Mom, don't get so attached to them because I'm not going to be like you. I'm going to try a whole lot of people before I settle down. And I'm not getting married till I'm thirty, at *least*.'"

"Mine said if she hadn't met a man by the time she was thirty-five, she'd just have a child on her own," another woman said. "I guess that's better than nothing."

"How about you?" the first woman asked me.

"My daughter-in-law's pregnant," I said. "I don't have any daugh-ters."

"Oh, with sons it's a whole other ball game," the second woman said. "You never get to see the babies!"

"I like my daughter-in-law a lot," I said. "I think I will get to see her, or him, whatever it is. I'm hoping for a girl."

"Girls are wonderful," Becky said heartily. "I think everyone should have girls."

"You should know," someone said.

Then everyone began talking about which were easier—girls or boys. When I drove home, I thought how odd it was that the evening had been fine. Even when I'd stood there, looking at the wedding photo, I hadn't felt any of the terrible rage that I'd expected to feel. It was a year after his death, but still I was surprised. I'd thought my hatred for Becky would last forever.

And so, Becky and I became friends. Not friends the way I'm friends with Ila and Jeanette, where we're as close as if we were married, maybe more so. But I wonder if I'd ever have had that kind of friendship with Becky. I remembered way back, even before the thing with Benjy started, I'd think whenever I ran into Becky at our kids' school: should I be friends with her? She was always friendly, she seemed a little at loose ends, a little lonely, but we never quite clicked. I don't even know how much being friends with her now is connected to Benjy, wanting, in some way, to prolong the contact with him. At first it would send a chill through me every time she referred to him. She didn't always call him by name. She'd say, "My husband always felt we should sell the house, it's so big," or "I think husbands rarely like going to the ballet. Mine was no exception."

But then it became Benjy. "Benjy was glad I went back to work. He never had any problem with that," or "I think Benjy would be pleased at how well Chelsea's marriage is turning out. He didn't think Mitchell was worthy of her." In a weird way it reminded me of a time in high school when I had a crush on a boy that another girl was going out with. I didn't especially like the girl, but I used to sit with her every day at lunch just to hear her talk about him; every time she said his name—"Scott"—I got a thrill. I wondered if something like that was true for Becky, whether she knew we had something in common that she would never have with any other woman. We started playing tennis together in a group, two other women and the two of us. Sometimes I'd play on Becky's side, sometimes I'd play with Nancy, or we'd do a round robin. None of us was very good, but I think I was better than Becky, maybe just more fool-hardy. I'd run to the net and attempt overhead smashes, thinking I was Billie Jean King. They usually went out. Becky always stayed safely on the baseline, blooping shots back. Her only good shot was a lob which arced high in the air and took so long to come down that you often missed it out of sheer exasperation.

The other women in the group, Nancy and Marion, were married, but Marion had once been widowed like Becky. They were always urging her to go out and attempting to fix her up with this man or that one whom they knew from work. "I don't think I'm ready yet," Becky would say. "It's been a year. That doesn't seem like long enough."

"You're never ready," Marion advised her. "You have to push yourself."

Becky was looking off to one side. "It would seem like such a betrayal of Benjy."

"Why?" Marion said. "He's not here. And, believe me, hon, if it'd happened to you, he'd have found someone else."

"You don't know that," Nancy said. "My father never did, after my mother died."

"Yeah, but he was seventy. . . . Men always find someone."

I'll marry you if Becky dies. Is that what you wanted me to say?

"What I had was so good," Becky said, "I don't think I'm going to find that again."

"You'll find something else," Marion retorted. "Grant isn't like Howie, but he's a good guy. What's the fun of getting into bed alone for forty years?"

Becky laughed. "I'm not going to live to ninety!"

"You might." Marion looked at me. "Don't you think she should at least give it a try?"

"Sure," I said, "if she can find someone."

"Who would want me?" Becky said with comical plaintiveness. "Look at my hips!"

"Men like hips," Nancy said. "They want mature, well-rounded women, something solid."

"Eat a little less," Marion said. "I'll lend you my diet book. It's terrific."

All through the conversation I saw Benjy in my mind's eye looking down on the scene with his wry smile. What would he think?

Somehow I didn't think Becky would ever remarry. She seemed so settled into middle age, such a homebody, so wrapped up in her kids and grandchildren. But then, about a year later, she started dating a man she met through the nuclear freeze organization. He was a widower, Harvey Bell, a tall, gaunt-looking man with sunken cheeks and piercing eyes, a very soft voice. Becky said he reminded her of her father.

"Isn't it awful how that always gets you?" Marion said. "With men it's the opposite. They meet someone who reminds them of their mother, and they run for the hills. But a woman meets someone like her father and she's a goner."

"He's been widowed for ten years," Becky said.

"He'll never remarry," Nancy said. "That kind doesn't."

"I'm not sure I want to either," Becky said. "That's what appeals to me in him. He likes to let things proceed slowly."

One day I was helping Becky hand out leaflets when Harvey Bell came by to pick her up. They looked like Jack Sprat and his wife. He must have been six feet four with not an ounce of fat on him, as different looking from Benjy in physical type as you could find. He seemed shy and a little awkward, didn't talk much, but I had the feeling he cared for Becky. There was a tender expression in his eyes as he looked at her. "This is my friend Marilyn Greene," Becky said, and he ducked his head and murmured something unintelligible under his breath.

The next time I saw Becky she said they had become lovers, and that he was considering moving into her house for the summer "just to see how it goes." He had a small apartment in the city and a summer house in Maine.

"How old are his kids?" Nancy wanted to know.

"Oh, grown," Becky said. "His daughter's married and his son lives in Seattle. . . . I wonder if it's a good idea to have him actually move into the house."

"Why not?" Marion asked. "You're all settled there."

"Yes, but wouldn't it be a betrayal of Benjy, living in the very same house?"

Nancy sighed. "Becky, listen to me. Benjy loved you! He'd be delighted to know you've met someone. He'd want you to be happy."

Becky looked uncertain. "Benjy was such a devoted father, and Harvey doesn't seem to care about his in the same way at all."

"He's a different person," Marion assured her. "He has other virtues."

I wanted to let out a howl. Here she was married to a man who was the most wonderful, passionate lover in the world and all she could say was he was such a devoted father! Or maybe she never saw that side of him—that's what I'd like to think. I got a kind of perverse pleasure out of Becky's new romance. You see, I said to Benjy, *she's* already unfaithful, not me. Benjy always acted so jealous if I talked about any man I'd met at work. He seemed to think of me as someone who was ready to nip off at a moment's notice with whoever came along. He never realized that that time we met in the supermarket and went on that picnic and I leaned over and kissed him was one of the few impulsive things I've ever done. And here, his solid, devoted little Becky who he thought would worship his memory forever was already in bed with someone else.

In the beginning I thought of that, the way when your dog dies, they say: buy a new dog. Your lover dies, find a new lover. But even allowing for the fact that it would be harder for me now, a one-breasted, graying, almost fifty-year-old lady, I don't think I'd want to. There've been a few men who've given me interested glances, a few lunches, glasses of wine, mournful stories. And some of them seem like nice men, to the extent it's been possible to judge. But the urge is gone. It's like the way I felt when I got pregnant and then miscarried, that time when the boys were grown. For a second I was devastated, only remembering the good parts of raising them, conveniently forgetting the bad. But then I thought: I did that. I'm glad I did, no regrets, but it's a part of my life that's over.

Whenever I see a romantic movie, a scene where two people turn to each other and cling, I think of Benjy. I'll always connect him with all those words: passion, romance, love. Even though, when I look back on it, I wonder exactly why our relationship lasted so long. We were such different people, we came from such different backgrounds. There were always so many more reasons we could have parted than stayed together. Part of it was Benjy's sense of loyalty, but it wasn't just that. I wonder at times if we would have gone on forever, if, even at seventy or eighty we would have been hobbling off to other people's apartments or trying to figure ways to sneak off together. It might've been so much easier now, with all our kids grown and away, with Becky working. I remember how once we thought of taking a real vacation together, for several weeks, to Europe or the Caribbean. We got maps, we went to a travel agent, but in the end we chickened out. It seemed too risky, too nerve-racking. Neither of us had the bravado for it.

I feel like Mary has taken Benjy's place in my heart, if anyone has. I love Carol, she's wonderful, but I feel so glad she had a little girl and so glad that she's willing to let me look after her, take her places. I know daughters-in-law aren't always like that. I get a kick out of how Carol looks to me for advice, about babies, marriage, men, as though I were some kind of expert. When she was pregnant, I used to take her to department stores and wait with her while she tried things on. One day, after we'd bought a whole bunch of things, we went out to have a drink and she suddenly started to cry. She said she was afraid she wouldn't be a good mother, that she'd trapped Aaron into marrying her, that she'd gotten pregnant half on purpose because she was afraid otherwise he might change his mind.

"He wouldn't have," I said. "He's not like that. Aaron's very steadfast."

"I knew right from the moment I saw him, I wanted to marry him," she said, sniffing. "Isn't that crazy? I didn't even know him. It was just like: *boing!* Did you ever feel that?"

"Once," I said. "A long time ago."

"See, what I worry about," she said, "is that that's not a good foundation for marriage, for something that's supposed to go on forever. What happens when the boing goes away?"

"It doesn't have to."

"I hate the way I look now," she said. "I can see Aaron looking at other women, wanting them. It makes me feel so bad." She still looked red-eyed and somber. "Did your husband ever, I mean when you were pregnant or whenever. . . ."

"Sure," I said. "I'm pretty sure he did."

"And you weren't devastated? I mean, you didn't want to kill him? You didn't feel it meant you were awful and nothing?"

"I felt bad sometimes," I admitted. "But none of them were very big deals."

"He didn't love them, you mean," Carol said.

"Right. . . . Just an itch. And usually when he was traveling."

She sipped her tea. "That's a good attitude to have," she said. "I mean, I still hope it never happens, but you can see he loves you, so maybe it shows men are like that. Do you think that's what it shows?"

I smiled. "I'm not sure what it shows, hon."

One weekend Jeanette flew in from California on business and I brought Mary to her hotel room. She was nine months old then, a perfect baby age, fat and pink with chubby hands and feet. It was the first time I'd seen Jeanette since Benjy's death, since I'd let my hair go gray, though we still talk on the phone every few months. She looked at me in disbelief. "I can't get over it," she said.

"Over what?" I had the baby on my lap and was jouncing her up and down.

"Look at you! Grandma Greene! You look like you ought to be selling deep-dish apple pies on TV."

"Maybe I will. . . . Isn't she a sweetie, though? Give me your unvarnished opinion."

"What can I say? A baby is a baby is a baby. She has no visible defects."

"Look at her hair! Look at her skin!" I rubbed my finger against Mary's velvety cheek.

"You know something?" Jeanette said, narrowing her eyes. "I like your hair that way. Maybe we both made a hideous mistake. Maybe you were never meant to be a blond. It didn't really go with your personality." Jeanette's hair is still black and curly.

"I developed a personality to go with it," I smiled. "You know, at first I let it go gray just out of laziness or self-hatred. I wanted to get fat and ugly and bury myself alive. But now I like it."

"Not trying to sell yourself on street corners anymore, huh?"

"Them days are gone forever." Tears came to my eyes. "I still miss him, though."

Jeanette leaned over and hugged me. "Well, you had a good run."

"Yeah, we did. . . . I wish so much you'd met him. It seems so strange, both of you so important in my life. He used to say he felt like he knew you."

"I felt like I knew him. Oh, Val, you know in the beginning, I have to admit not just in the beginning, I hated him. I thought he was just wrecking your life, driving you crazy. Especially when you had that horrible fight. . . . But in the last five years or so, I saw he was something you needed."

"We needed each other," I said, shifting the baby to my other knee.

"I never had that," Jeanette said. "Rich and I have a good marriage, no major problems or none we haven't handled, but I guess for me it's been other things—work, friends, the kids. I've liked some men, I like sex. . . . But no one I want to dive out the window after."

We played with the baby for a while. Once she fell asleep, we ordered drinks from room service and had a good long talk, as though it was the old days.

When Mary was two, Carol decided to teach her to ice skate. It seems Carol was a really good ice skater herself once. I began going with her and Aaron and the baby on Sunday mornings, just the way I used to with Benjy. I asked Mo if he didn't feel like learning, but he said he wasn't up to it. Carol was sensational. She really slimmed down after Mary's birth and wore one of those short skirts and tights. She flew across the ice, just the way you're supposed to. When I saw her and Aaron trying to skate together, it reminded me of the way Benjy and I used to look. Aaron was hanging onto her, looking like he was about to collapse.

I've never been all that good at skating, but as I did it, it kind of came back to me. It was the same kind of crowd that used to gather at the place Benjy and I went to. The tiny kids who go whizzing around, the good skaters in the center, practicing their turns, the teenage boys who zoom back and forth like demons, an occasional family dividing up into pairs. Mary got the hang of it right away. She clutched my hand, but she moved her skates in even lines, beaming up at me with a look of dazzled triumph.

Looking in the center of the rink where the good skaters were, searching for Carol, I noticed a woman who must have been in her seventies. She had curly white hair, a cheerful Bess Truman kind of face, but she was wearing a micro mini in shocking pink, so short it barely covered her behind. She had terrific legs, in skin-colored tights, Betty Grable legs, and she skated back and forth looking so pleased with herself that I couldn't take my eyes off her.

"Look at her," I said, when Aaron came skating up next to me. "Look at that lady. She must be seventy at least."

"That's what you'll be like at that age, Mom," he said.

How can I not love him?